Please renew or return items by the date shown on your receipt

www.hertsdirect.org/libraries

Renewals and enquiries: 0300 123 4049

Textphone for hearing or speech impaired 0300 123 4041

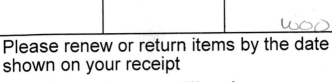

D1355193

467 514 86 4

Also by Douglas Reeman

Path of
the Storm

Douglas Reeman

ARROW

First published by Arrow in 1967

17 19 20 18 16

Copyright © Douglas Reeman 1966

Douglas Reeman has asserted his right under the Copyright,
Designs and Patents Act 1988 to be identified as the author of
this work

First published in the United Kingdom in 1966 by Hutchinson

Arrow Books
The Random House Group Limited
20 Vauxhall Bridge Road, London SW1V 2SA

Addresses for companies within The Random House Group Limited
can be found at: www.randomhouse.co.uk/offices.htm

The Random House Group Limited Reg. No. 954009

www.randomhouse.co.uk

A CIP catalogue record for this book
is available from the British Library

ISBN 9780099591566

The Random House Group Limited supports The Forest Stewardship
Council® (FSC®), the leading international forest-certification organisation.
Our books carrying the FSC label are printed on FSC®-certified paper.
FSC is the only forest-certification scheme supported by the leading
environmental organisations, including Greenpeace. Our
paper procurement policy can be found at
www.randomhouse.co.uk/environment

MIX
Paper from
responsible sources
FSC® C016897

Printed and bound in Great Britain by
Clays Ltd, St Ives plc

For Cherry Kearton,
my good friend

'In the path of the storm
all men are fearless'
Old Chinese saying

Contents

Contents

1

Reprieve

The British Crown Colony of Hong Kong seemed crushed beneath the glare and relentless heat of the midday sun. Even for high summer it was unusually hot, the humid air almost wet to the touch, so that the colourful crowds jamming the waterfronts scarcely moved, but jostled in buzzing and aimless confusion.

But it was Sunday, and as usual the crowded harbour and anchorage was alive with craft of every description, from fussing paddle-wheeled tugs to timeless stern-sculled lighters. Tall, ribbed-sailed junks barely moved through the throng, their ragged reflections poised on the flat blue water like bats, whilst here and there smart navy launches and gigs of pale grey and gleaming brass scudded on small, fine bow-waves as their perspiring coxswains strove to make sense out of the harbour regulations.

The lush green heights of Victoria Peak were lost in a shimmering heat-haze which mercifully hid the jumbled misery of squatters' shacks and refugee hovels which were beginning to invade what was once an area reserved solely for the rich, whose villas still managed to maintain a kind of lordly reserve in the world's most overcrowded city.

The British naval dockyard, however, was quiet by any standards. Sunday was Sunday in any language, and apart from a few gloomy watchkeepers, the sleek destroyers and tall cruisers were deserted, as if the heat had winkled out every living thing from the high bridges and grim gun-turrets.

Hong Kong was still the most popular liberty port in the world, and daily the sailors of the American Seventh Fleet and men of the local British squadrons surged ashore in search of amusement. The Americans found particular pleasure in taking a taxi to the colony's border and recording the surly-faced

Communist guards on the other side of the wire.

For months at a time the men of the U.S. Seventh Fleet patrolled the Formosa Strait, watched over the countless shipping movements, and kept the seas open from Japan to as far south as Australia. Every mile of the Red Chinese mainland presented some hidden menace, a fault of navigation or error of seamanship could spark off an international incident, which again could escalate to open conflict. Every man knew this, yet newcomers to Hong Kong gathered their Japanese 'Leicas' and hurried to this strange, defenceless-looking frontier between East and West to record for all time the actual face of the enemy.

At this very moment a giant aircraft carrier lay like a grey cliff in the centre of the anchorage. The fourth largest ship in the world, she represented merely by her presence the sleepless power of the Seventh Fleet. Other warships browsed at their moorings nearby, but the tourist steamers and bobbing harbour craft were only interested in the carrier, and, even in the blazing heat, hands were busy with uptrained cameras the puffing craft swam in the carrier's great shadow, and devoured every item of interest. The bright, toylike planes, wings folded, which just peeped over the edge of the flight deck, the maze of radio antennae and busy radar scanners, even the size of the ship alone, was enough for the tourists, and every Chinese guide thanked the heavens for her visit.

It was hardly surprising, therefore, that few observed the one warship moored on the fringe of the anchorage, aboard which, Sunday or not, there was a sign of life and activity.

The submarine chaser U.S.S. *Hibiscus* was twenty-three years old, and in spite of her new coats of gleaming grey paint and freshly burnished brasswork, a closer inspection quickly laid bare the lie presented by the three months' refit which had been completed only the previous day, when shyly and unsurely she had been coaxed from a deep dry-dock and warped to her present mooring beneath the towering cranes of the loading jetty. Since her keel had touched the water for the first time in Portland, Oregon, she had lost count of the miles she had steamed, forgotten the dozen captains who had conned her through the bleak Atlantic in 1942, or dodged that crazed *kamikaze* in the Pacific. The captain who had rammed another chaser on the last day of the war with Japan, or the one who had been court-martialled for running the ship aground in the Korean war. *Hibiscus* had seen them all come and go, like the men who had looked after her, and the work they had done together. Normandy, Korea, Viet Nam, each leaving some scar or dent on her one hundred and seventy-three feet, every mark like part of the navy record itself. As she grew older her jobs grew less vital, and like this particular day she got used to being on the fringe of things. Target towing, carrying food and blankets for earthquake victims, instructing eager ensigns in the mysteries of navigation, or merely suffering months of mothballed retirement, *Hibiscus* had little left to experience. Only one crisis after another in the struggle for world mastery had retained the necessity of keeping 'just one more ship', but even the mounting tension with Red China had seemed insufficient to prevent her last journey under the flag which now hung limp and unmoving in the unwavering sun.

She was a graceful little ship, flush-decked, sleek and uncluttered by the top-heavy mess of radar and antennae which bruised the outlines of her newer and more powerful counterparts. There was a small, open-topped bridge behind which a raked mast and squat single stack made up the bulk of her superstructure. She was narrow-beamed, barely twenty-three feet at her widest part, which was not the fantail, where the assembled crew were packed in a tight, sweating circle of white starched caps and upturned squinting faces, as each man craned to listen to the voice of the new, and supposedly the last, captain under the American flag.

Lieutenant-Commander Mark Gunnar stood on the top of a life-raft, stared gravely above the heads of the waiting men and looked along the full length of his new command. The brief ceremony of taking over the ship was completed against the background of sounds from the harbour, the clank of a winch, the mournful hoot of the Star Ferry steamer, even the far-off roar from the Happy Valley Racecourse. The stilted words, the carefully phrased paper which gave him command, control of this small, tired ship, six officers and some sixty men. The sea of upturned, anonymous faces, blank and meaningless. In time, in a very short time, the people would emerge from these faces, the weak and the strong, the ambitious and the incompetent. All in good time.

Gunnar stood quite still, the effort of appearing relaxed making his back ache, so that he was conscious of the sun's glare across his slim shoulders, the painful throbbing behind his quiet grey eyes. He could feel the sweat beneath the rim

13

of his cap, and his short fair hair moist against his forehead. A few moments longer, and then he would go to his quarters. The quiet, dark room below the bridge, where he would find peace, even for a short while, to think and plan. All the quick-fire elation he had tried to retain since his arrival in Hong Kong had faded, even the gentle stirring of the little ship beneath his feet as a tug surged pantingly abeam failed to disperse the ache of disappointment which had met him within minutes of landing at Hong Kong airport.

After all those months in hospital. The patient agony of surgery to his back, the meaningless promises of the doctors and the silence from the appointments office. The long, slow-healing process on his shattered mind, and the final feeling of weakness, mingled with delirious excitement, he had felt on the day of his discharge.

He often thought back to those days, the months before the hospital. Viet Nam—the very name was like a knife turning in his insides, yet he seemed unable to leave alone the terrifying memories. In that wretched country, as one of the many U.S. advisers, Gunnar had thought of returning to the States for many reasons. Now, all he wanted to do was cut free of the land and return to the sea.

His new-found buoyancy had stayed with him on the long, well-organised flight to Hong Kong, had lasted until his trip to the flagship, the giant carrier out there surrounded by gaping tourists.

Gunnar was to get a command well enough. The *Hibiscus*. A small, clapped-out submarine chaser which had been refitted so many times that hardly anything of the original ship remained. She had been overhauled for the past three months in a British dockyard with the sole intention of handing her over complete, a going concern, to the Republic of China Navy on Taiwan. No doubt Chiang Kai-shek's naval arm had already selected officers and men for the very ship Gunnar was being offered as his own.

Captain Anderson, the admiral's chief of staff, had handed Gunnar the thick wad of orders and one large sealed envelope. He was a big man, and had sat comfortably on the edge of his desk, swinging one fat leg, and staring at the envelope as it lay in Gunnar's motionless fingers.

'The handover to the Nationalists has been delayed.' Anderson tried to make it sound interesting. 'Not exactly indefinitely, but long enough for you to get the feel of things again.'

Gunnar had felt the spacious room closing in on him. Get the feel of things again? Trite, meaningless words. What the hell did this captain know about it?

What could Anderson understand about the constant nightmare, the recurring dream of pain, and desperate fear? The Viet Cong had not the luck to capture many Americans alive. When they did they made the most of it. Gunnar could still not bear to have anyone stand behind him. In the jungle headquarters of the Communist guerrillas he had steeled himself not to look at the shadow of the man whose turn it was to go behind him, to strip away his raw skin with a bamboo blade. It went on and on, so that he had listened to his own screams like someone on the outside of himself. Even after his escape, and his return to supposed sanity, he still heard those screams.

But once aboard the flagship he began to see through the façade of friendliness and compassion. The admiration was false. It *had* to be. They were not even jealous of the medal awarded to him by the President. Jealous perhaps of the navy's reputation, but not of him. Even this final jolt, the awaited-for command, was like a slap in the mouth.

Anderson had continued evenly: 'You're only twenty-nine, Gunnar. In a while or so something better will come along. But after your past experiences you'll want to get back into the swing of things as easily as possible, eh?'

Only twenty-nine, but with an unspoken slur against his name. It would have been better to be court-martialled. Better to have died.

'I had hoped for something a little better, sir.' Gunnar's youthful features hardened slightly. His racing thoughts were playing havoc with his carefully preserved calm.

Captain Anderson had folded his arms and regarded him thoughtfully. 'The Seventh Fleet is stretched to the limit. We've not got ships to throw about any more. Experienced officers are worth gold bars, and your sort of experience is at an absolute premium.' He dropped his eyes. 'However, there *are* certain factors. You have been very ill after your treatment from the Reds. Before that you were some months away from the sea. *Hibiscus* will be a sort of "coming home" for you. You've got your orders there, they'll explain what is wanted by the admiral. Make a good job of it, and I guess you'll not suffer.'

'And if I botch it? I suppose they'll say I'm running true to form!' Two spots of colour glowed suddenly on Gunnar's

15

pale cheeks. It had burst out before he could check himself. Well, what the hell. 'I know what they're saying about me——'

Anderson interrupted sharply: 'I didn't hear a word of that. Things are different in the navy today. It's more like a big business concern with directives being issued by a Board who only care about results in some major plan that we on the spot cannot envisage. They don't care if a man here and there gets hurt. Fighting to keep the peace is our business. But the *sort* of peace is very much their affair!' His voice had softened a little. 'Get to the ship, Gunnar. It's a command for you, and I would say a fair offer under present circumstances.' He grinned comfortably. 'You've no enemies aboard here.'

Gunnar had found himself on his feet. Already the fast-moving events seemed to have left him behind. 'Can I see the admiral, sir?'

'Negative.' Anderson's voice was showing signs of impatience. 'He's too busy, and in any case he instructed me to do the honours.'

Gunnar had walked in a semi-daze to the smart launch which was waiting at the main gangway to whisk him across the harbour to his ship. This ship. Once he had looked back at the giant carrier, and wondered what the admiral had really said.

His searching mind came back to the present with a sharp wrench, and he had to re-focus his eyes on the faces around him. He cleared his throat. 'So this is the picture. This ship will stay in commission until further orders. Men due for other appointments and long leave have been replaced by others among you, so there will be no additional work per man. We will leave Hong Kong at dusk and get the feel of being a ship's company again.'

He dropped his eyes to the broad shoulders of Lieutenant Robert Maddox, the executive officer, who was standing immediately below him. A giant of a man, but at twenty-six was showing signs of running to overweight. Gunnar had told him the bones of his orders, but was unable to fathom the exec's inner reactions. Apart from that they had hardly spoken. The twenty-four hours Gunnar had been aboard had been a whirlwind of activity, from gathering stores, topping up the fuel tanks to their maximum of sixty tons, to reloading ammunition to the magazines.

It was odd to realise that Maddox too was almost new to the ship. He had come from a shore appointment on the navy

16

staff in Japan. He had been exec only while *Hibiscus* had been in dry-dock, when her crew had either disported themselves in Hong Kong's nightlife, or prepared to leave the ship for the last time after it had been handed over to the Nationalists.

Gunnar glanced quickly at the other officers. Regan, the first lieutenant and gunnery officer, a trim, hawk-faced man with very dark eyebrows which joined above his beaked nose. Kroner, lieutenant (jg), the communications officer, handsome and empty-faced, like a naval officer in a recruitment advertisement. Malinski, the engineer, who had been in the ship on and off for six years. A typical engine-room product. Tough, sallow, with the deceptively sleepy appearance worn by his kind when suddenly forced to mix with the upper deck. A frail, willowy lieutenant (jg) named Inglis made up the wardroom, except for the doctor. Captain Anderson had made this point very clear. *Hibiscus* would be detached from the main fleet operations, and a doctor might be essential. So Bruce Connell, whose piercing blue eyes had watched Gunnar almost unwinkingly since he had started to speak, had joined the ship.

Gunnar cleared his throat again. 'I know that some of you were expecting to go to newer and bigger ships, were perhaps hoping to see a bit of shore-time.' He set his mouth in a smile, but sensed the latent hostility in the faces and the quick exchange of glances. 'Well, in this man's navy every day can bring a surprise. The job in hand is the one that counts. The one we have to concentrate our efforts on.'

In spite of his every effort Gunnar was unable to work up any enthusiasm, even his own words seemed to mock him. *The job in hand!* What a joke! By a roundabout course he was to take the *Hibiscus* south-west and then north-east to the isolated island group of Payenhau, about one hundred miles south of Taiwan, Chiang Kai-shek's stronghold. They couldn't have sent him further from the scene of operations if they had posted him to Niagara Falls! Payenhau was off the shipping routes, pretty barren and seemingly useless but for one thing which had just been noticed by the brains in Washington. The tiny group lay between Taiwan to the north and the uncertain hotch-potch of newly hatched nations, Malaysia, Indonesia and the Philippines, to the south. A small chink in the protective ring around the Communist mainland. Its very isolation was one good point, but the fact that its sheltered anchorage was extremely well protected and deep decided

17

the next course of events. *Hibiscus* would, without fuss or drawing attention to herself, carry out a survey of the anchorage, check the island for security and then report back her findings. Then, if all went well, Gunnar was ordered to prepare permanent moorings for one vessel, one of the navy's cream, a Polaris submarine.

The planners thought that it would be a nice quiet place for a single submarine to rest up during a tour of duty, without actually being taken off operational control. There the crew could find a small break in the monotony of canned movies and stale air, could stretch their legs and sniff at the grass, if there was any. Small maintenance jobs could be carried out in the sheltered safety of the anchorage, and perhaps in time bigger things would be laid on.

The other important point was that the arrangement would be with the full blessing of the Nationalist government in Taiwan. The Chinese would be in it, and not just onlookers. It was their island, and not just another American base. Short of actually supplying the Chinese with nuclear submarines for their own use—and this was generally decided to be nothing more than laying the keel of World War III—it was thought to be far better to make them feel they were entirely involved in the full naval operations of the China Seas. Like a constant barricade, the terrifying power of the Seventh Fleet guarded the Formosa Strait, and was in constant readiness for a major conflict, but the Red power for subversion and inner destruction had to be fought by the people themselves. American help was always generous, but it was more than often wasted. It started as a bonus for the underprivileged peoples of South East Asia, and then became part of their lives. From that moment they came to rely on American help, and when at any time it was withdrawn, it left behind not gratitude but bitterness and even open revolt.

Gunnar's orders made the *Hibiscus*'s task sound almost important if not actually vital. But, try as he might, Gunnar could see no further than the personal slur this assignment implied.

Suddenly he could find no more words, no further explanations. He nodded to the big lieutenant. 'Very well, Mister Maddox. Dismiss the hands.'

Lieutenant Maddox turned about and saluted, his tanned, athlete's face uncomfortable. 'Oh, Captain, the matter of liberty!' He looked vaguely over the port rail towards the

18

town. 'A last look for some of them, sir?'

Gunnar felt a surge of unreasonable anger in his throat. They had not even been listening to his words! All they thought about was getting ashore again, women and cheap drink!

'No liberty!' His grey eyes had hardened. 'We sail as planned. Tell the O.O.D. to stay at the brow and ensure that no one goes ashore for any reason!'

Maddox nodded glumly. 'Very well, sir.'

Gunnar stepped from the raft and swayed. He realised that he had been standing too long in the blazing sun, and his shirt was already black with sweat. Damn them, he thought vaguely. But they're not going to mess things up for me, the ship, or anything else!

Maddox stepped to his side, his voice quiet. 'Are you okay, sir?'

Gunnar turned, the anger checked just in time. 'Thank you, yes. I'd like to see you and the engineer officer in half an hour.'

With quickening steps Gunnar hurried down the narrow side deck which he knew he would soon know like his own skin, and within minutes had thrown himself full length on his bunk in the semi-darkness of his small cabin. It was no use. He would have to exercise more self-control. They would be looking for weakness, watching him at each testing moment. He lay back and closed his eyes. Perhaps it would be better once they were at sea. Deep in his heart he knew that was not so. He not only had to prove himself to the ship and to the admiral, he had to believe in his own judgement and ability. Nothing could change the past. But only the immediate future could help ease the inner pain of it.

* * *

Lieutenant Robert Maddox watched the seamen breaking away and hurrying below to the doubtful coolness of the overhead fans, and then removed his cap. Thoughtfully he ran his fingers through his thick, rebellious hair and stared at the blinding glitter across the crowded harbour. Now the actual moment had arrived he was more than apprehensive. Inwardly he cursed himself for his lack of foresight. After all, he had done staff work in Japan, he should have known the mind of top brass well enough to foresee a change of sailing orders for the *Hibiscus*.

19

For three months Maddox had lived a life of comparative bliss as executive officer of the dry-docked ship. Half the crew had been discharged, and the remainder were either billeted ashore or merely dropping aboard from time to time to attend to small jobs outside the province of the dockyard workers. The officers lived in hotels, and but for the O.O.D. hardly ever put in an appearance. Even the O.O.D. usually managed to detail one of the chiefs for his job while he joined his friends in some bar or other. It was an ideal existence for the officers, a suitable ending to a fairly uneventful commission. Maddox, as a high-and-dry exec, enjoyed the luxury of granting the other officers' fancies and requests. It was unlikely that they would ever meet again in another ship, so what the hell? The previous captain had been flown home to the States to be discharged. He was old for his rank and had been too often passed over for advancement to be given a new appointment. Unable to see the end of his last ship, or even greet the man sent to relieve him, he had passed from their lives with hardly a word, except to the engineer officer, who still refused to say what had passed between them.

Now there was Gunnar, as young and fresh as the previous captain had been jaded and bitter. With the complication of new orders, and the sudden influx of spare men to replace the discharged ones, it should have been fine to receive a captain like Gunnar. Impassive, competent-looking, with decorations to prove his worth, he should have been the man for any job.

Maddox decided that his own sense of guilt was more than half to blame for his inner uncertainty. If only he had kept a tighter rein on things during the refit, not allowed the other officers to gang up and take advantage of him. Before it had not mattered. Soon, within hours of this moment, the ship would be alive again, at sea, a moving factor which contained and controlled them all. And *he* was exec, expected to enforce discipline over the men who had done as they liked under his control in the past, and expected to present the little, dated ship to the new captain as a going concern. It was all very worrying.

Maddox was unconcerned about his own ability as an officer. What he lacked in open ambition he made up for with dogged determination and stubbornness a mile wide. As a lieutenant (jg) he had served his time with the Sixth Fleet in the Mediterranean, where every officer, high or low, was expected to perform ten duties at one. His tough and cheerful accept-

20

ance of tasks, his ability to handle even the most reluctant seaman plus the fact that he had captained the water-polo team which beat the British at Malta, had brought him to the area of recognition. Upon promotion to lieutenant he had been appointed to the communications staff in Japan.

Japan. Just to think of it made Maddox's wide mouth water. The life dreamed of by every unmarried officer. And a man of Maddox's simple earthy requirements had found all the enjoyment he needed. Office hours, not too much work, and a new world to be found every night. And there was Mary. She was a navy nurse, and should therefore have known better, Maddox told himself repeatedly. They had had a whirlwind affair which lasted six months. When she had told him that she was pregnant Maddox had been shocked, and immediately protective. Three hours later he managed to convince himself that it was not completely his fault. The following day he was certain that *he* had been wronged. Sitting at his desk at headquarters he had been idly leafing through a sheaf of despatches concerning ship movements when he had spied the one referring to the old *Hibiscus*. Two swift telephone calls, and a brief interview with the flag lieutenant had done the rest. Within three days Maddox was winging over the East China Sea en route for Hong Kong and his first post as exec.

His nagging feelings of guilt and uncertainty were soon lost in the excitement and noisy gaiety of Hong Kong. A fine-boned Eurasian secretary had finished the job for him, and only that morning he had left her crying quietly in his hotel room. And Mary? She had probably already been flown State-side and been cared for by the system.

Maddox had anticipated a quick return to Japan after *Hibiscus* had been handed over to the Nationalists at Taiwan, but overnight everything had changed again. The new captain for instance. He had started off friendly enough, yet Maddox, who was not entirely insensitive, felt that Gunnar was finding every hour of contact with his exec a tremendous effort. That first meeting in Gunnar's cabin, he had watched his almost boyish features harden with surprising swiftness at the slightest mention of the past. When Maddox had spoken indifferently about Payenhau and the job *Hibiscus* had been given, Gunnar had burst out, 'We'll make a good job of it whatever they give us!' Then he had looked almost embarrassed and said: 'Sorry. I'm a bit tired.' He had stood just below the overhead light, his short fair hair giving his pale features a touch of Scan-

21

dinavian coolness, yet the quick movements of his hands making a lie of his outward calm.

Maddox walked to the rail and stared down at the scum and flotsam which bobbed trapped alongside. He would have to watch Regan, the first lieutenant, he thought grimly. Next to the departed captain, and Maddox's predecessor who had been promoted to command a destroyer, Regan was the senior officer remaining from the original wardroom. He was a hard man with little conversation. But he retained the knack of short bitter attacks on anything and anybody who crossed his path. He took a malicious delight in riding the two junior lieutenants, Kroner and Inglis, and was not slow to taunt Maddox when he had explained that the actual task allotted *Hibiscus* was a secret prior to sailing.

Regan had grinned, showing his big teeth like an evil rabbit. 'Why all the secrecy then? It's a load of unnecessary crap to make the new skipper feel a bit more important than he really is!'

When Maddox had failed to answer he had added: 'One more damned has-been, I guess! Who else would be given this rust-bucket?' He had laughed his short, barking laugh. The sure sign of a man lacking real humour.

Maddox had made his first effort at that point to assert his authority. 'You know you shouldn't speak about the captain like that in front of me!'

Regan's grin had widened. 'Oh Jesus! Surely you're not crawling to *him*!'

Kroner, the communications officer, who was a bit scared of Regan's cruel wit, had laughed weakly.

Maddox had let his heavy limbs relax slightly. Open conflict was unwanted, but it was something he understood very well. 'Talk like that again in my presence, Alan, and I'll log you!' He had felt a grin spreading in spite of his faster breathing. 'Then I'll smash your goddamed teeth down your throat, okay?'

They had not spoken since.

He glanced up at the stack, from which he could just make out the shimmering haze of gas. It would soon be time. Just a few tugging wires kept the ship tied to the other world of temptation and personal ambition. Once free, their destinies would be bound together, and under the hand of Mark Gunnar.

Half an hour before the captain had mustered the crew to

'read himself in', Maddox had asked jokingly: 'What sort of people do they have in Payenhau anyway, sir? I've been looking at the manuals and the place seems a bit bleak.'

Gunnar had torn himself from some inner thoughts with obvious effort and looked at him for several seconds. 'It's a Chinese penal settlement.'

Now Maddox wondered if the captain had suspected him of asking a trick question. He had heard it said that Gunnar had been a prisoner of the Reds in Viet Nam. Maddox shook his head and sighed aloud. In this heart, and with a dozen sailing preparations to complete, it was possible to attach stupid significance to anything.

Chief Tasker, the chief gunner's mate, clumped to his side and stood watching the exec with dull, embittered eyes. He was a dour man, tall and gaunt like a skeleton, yet so efficient that he could usually foresee any accident on deck, be it with gear or a matter of seamanship, before it had happened. He had been in the ship a long time, and refused one transfer after another. Like the engineer officer, he never explained his reasons. In fact Tasker rarely explained anything. He disliked officers, yet sought no companionship from the enlisted men.

Maddox eyed him warily. 'Well?'

'About this liberty.' Tasker's small jaw jutted stubbornly. 'Some of my party want to slip across and buy some gear before we sail.'

Maddox sighed. 'You heard the captain, Chief!'

Tasker grunted. 'I'll tell them *you* said they can't go, sir.' His dull eyes seemed to gleam momentarily with some small pleasure. 'They'll like that!'

'They can go to hell as far as I care!' Maddox was tired. Weary from three months of sexual pleasures, and now dragged down with the burden of duty. 'And so can you, Chief!'

Tasker touched his cap. 'Thank you, sir.' He strode away, his heels digging at the steel decks with each long-legged step.

Deep in thought, Maddox walked slowly to the brow where Lieutenant Inglis, pistol on hip, stood gloomily staring at the water.

'Okay, Peter?' Maddox joined him at the rail.

Inglis shrugged. 'O.O.D. is grim at any time.'

Maddox stretched his massive arms. 'I'm going to shower and change. I'll be below if you want me.' He suddenly remembered that he could no longer call his room his own.

23

Accommodation was tight at any time. The additional body of the doctor, Connell, had been quartered with him in the upper bunk.

I wonder why they want a doctor? he thought uneasily. Various visions of one pox or another flitted through his weary mind, but he could find no satisfaction. Nor could he with the captain's explanation. He suspected that Gunnar was a bit puzzled too.

He forced a grin. What the hell was the use of moaning all the time? There had to be a break somewhere!

He slapped the young lieutenant's shoulders. 'See you in hell!'

After all, he told himself as he stood noisily twisting beneath the cold shower, a change was everything. In any case, even on Payenhau there might be one more girl who wanted to share her problems.

The thought gave him immediate comfort, and he began to sing.

*   *   *

Before the sun had time to touch the glittering horizon line the nightlife of Hong Kong had swung into first gear. Every house, shopfront and moored merchant ship, seemingly every window in the smooth-fronted skyscrapers, sparkled in a million lights of as many hues and shades. It was as if each of the thousands of searching, restless souls was out and about in search of final salvation, and the sounds of pumping music mingled with the slow grinding growl of traffic even reached the darkly shadowed hull of the *Hibiscus*.

The fading light along the dockside gave the ship a kind of beauty, and as the navigation lights opened their red and green eyes on either side of the bridge it was indeed like a reawakening.

The brow had been dragged ashore, and only a few lines now held the slender hull to the squeaking pontoons.

On the bridge the duty officers moved quietly and purposefully in the cramped space, the only lights coming from the ready-use chart table and from the gyro repeater. Voice-pipes squeaked and stuttered, their voices connecting the bridge with every part of the ship, while telephones buzzed, were answered and then discarded as the ship went through the final motions of getting under way, with the indifferent thoroughness of a

24

ballistic rocket about to be fired from its pad.

Mark Gunnar plucked at the collar pins of his shirt and glanced briefly along the shadowed jetty. A warm evening breeze pushed impatiently at the hull and chilled the skin at his throat. He could see the mooring wires tautening and slackening with each moist breath of wind as the hull was pushed jerkily away from the land.

All the reports had been completed. Lieutenant George Malinski had sounded quietly competent from the bowels of the engine room, and Gunnar had had a brief picture of the composed little man standing loosely on his catwalk, whilst around him the dials and repeaters clicked and purred into life, and the engines waited like great shining beasts to be unleashed. He was a good man, Gunnar thought. He would have liked him up here on the bridge.

He could sense Lieutenant Inglis at the rear of the compass platform by the telephone talker, his frail figure outlined against the black rectangle of the charthouse door.

Maddox was half lying over the port wing, his big body jerking as he called down instructions to some of the side party.

That would be Lieutenant Regan in the eyes of the ship, his face in dark shadow as he stood beside his fo'c'slemen watching the bridge.

Aft on the fantail Kroner could be heard shouting in his high-pitched voice at some anonymous seaman who had failed to release enough wire to allow the impatient dockworkers sufficient slack to free the shore end of it when the order was called.

All ready. All waiting.

Gunnar knew too that a fat tug was hovering somewhere out in the harbour, just in case anything went wrong. He had seen its navigation lights momentarily reflected against the shining sides of an anchored British cruiser, and he guessed it was waiting to rush to his aid if he misjudged his manœuvres. Well, it was a British harbour. They could afford to be worried.

'All lines singled up, Captain!' Maddox's voice sounded thick.

'Very well. Stand by all engines.' Gunnar found that his throat was dry.

The telegraphs jangled noisily, and almost at once the deck and bridge fittings began to vibrate with steady persistence.

The wheelhouse was directly below the bridge, and all wheel orders were passed down a brass voice-pipe. Gunnar got another small picture in his mind of the helmsman leaning forward against the well-worn spokes, his ear cocked to the bell-mouthed pipe, his telegraphsmen beside him, their faces aglow in the compass light. It was always a tense moment.

There was a faint step on the deck, and Gunnar looked round to see the shape of Connell, the doctor. He was wearing a pea jacket, his eyes dark in his face as he looked uncertainly at the captain. 'Is it okay if I stay up here?' He had a soft, gentle voice, but Gunnar did not wish to start up a conversation at this moment. Not with him.

Doctors, doctors. Gunnar nodded briefly at Connell and walked to the port wing. He could remember so clearly the bloodied fingers of that doctor in Viet Nam. Stitch, stitch, stitch! God . . . he ground his teeth together to control his tumbling thoughts.

He peered down at the fo'c'sle. The white hats of the sailors floated like moths along the dark steel, and he could see Chief Tasker testing a mooring wire with his foot.

'Let go aft!' Gunnar had spoken almost unconsciously. He heard the talker repeating his order and the brief splash from the fantail as the wires were slipped and then whipped aboard.

'All gone aft, sir.'

'Good. Slack away bow lines!' Gunnar gripped the cool steel with all his might as his order was relayed and the figures on the fo'c'sle moved with such painful slowness.

Caught by the offshore breeze and freed by her aft lines the *Hibiscus*'s stern began to swing away from the jetty. Very slowly, and then gathering momentum, her three hundred and eighty tons opened up a widening angle of black water.

Gunnar heard Regan shout hoarsely, 'Watch those fenders!' Men scampered to lower the big rope fenders between the jetty and the overhanging bow as it swung slowly above the stonework. He added: 'Dabruzzi, you're as much use as a snowball in hell, you useless bastard! Now *jump* to it!'

Gunnar closed his ears to all of them. He peered through his binoculars towards the stern and the harbour beyond. It was now or never

'Let go bow lines!'

He mentally counted the seconds. 'All engines back one-third!'

With sudden gaiety the twin screws beat the water into a

26

madly dancing froth below the low counter, and very gently the ship began to move astern.

Like a pale grey shadow the ship glided back between the big cruiser and a pair of moored destroyers. Here and there a figure waved or saluted. Gunnar noticed vaguely that there were women in long gowns and officers in mess dress on the quarterdeck of the British cruiser, and several paused at the rail to watch the small submarine chaser back past.

Gunnar found that his glasses hovered on the small, colourful group, and he felt the surge of old bitterness as he remembered Janet and her pale arms and red mouth.

Maddox said quietly, 'The carrier's getting close, Captain.'

Gunnar felt the sweat like ice on his neck. Christ, the carrier! He had lost himself in his thoughts for those vital seconds.

'All engines stop!' the throbbing faded and the ship rocked gently on her wash. Gunnar moved quickly to the forepart of the bridge and stood high on the gratings. Astern, the towering side of the carrier seemed to mock him. What a godalmighty start that would have been. Slap into the flagship!

Gunnar found that he was grinning stupidly to himself. 'All ahead one-third!' Sharpness edged his voice as if to cover his discomfort.

The ship began to move forward for the first time. 'Right standard rudder!'

A white crescent of foam marked the ship's course as it swung clear of the cranes and the dark tangle of dockyard buildings.

Gunnar's voice was stiff and controlled as he passed one helm order after another, and he checked each impulse to watch the departing shore as it glided into the dusk.

Past the cheerful glow of the Yacht Club and the unlit bulk of the Supreme Court building, and with quickening power into the first wide stretch of water. A bobbing police boat without lights curtsied in their wake as its occupants waited patiently to search the next junk or coaster suspected of carrying refugees or opium, and two cormorants rose flapping soundlessly from a weed-encrusted buoy as *Hibiscus* dug her stem into the growing power of the open sea. Past Green Island with the lights of Kennedy Town beyond, and then southwest into West Lamma Channel.

Gunnar said flatly, 'Bring her left to one-nine-zero.' He wondered if somewhere over there on the great sprawling mass of dark and pinpointed lights the ship's absence had already been

27

reported, her course followed and mapped. They probably knew his destination as well as he did, he thought bitterly.

He half turned to Inglis. 'Take the con. Bring her on to the new course as soon as you pass the outer buoy.'

Gunnar heard the young lieutenant stammer his assent and knew that he was confused by the sudden order. In a more friendly tone he added: 'I'll be here. But you might as well get the feel of her inshore.'

He stepped from the gratings and walked to the starboard wing, deliberately turning his back on the lights of Hong Kong, the lights of the land.

The first deep-water roller moved lazily out of the gloom and passed hissing beneath the ship's keel. With the contempt of an old sailor *Hibiscus* lifted her raked bow and then cocked her stern with disdain as the water broke in twin white breakers along either beam.

Gunnar said, 'Check the wires, Mister Maddox, and dismiss the hands.' As the big exec turned to climb down the ladder Gunnar added, 'And thanks!'

Maddox stared at him with surprise. 'A pleasure, Captain.'

Gunnar leaned against the steel and stared hard at the water. His hands were still shaking, and he was glad that it was dark in the bridge's private world.

But it was too late now. They were committed. Him most of all.

The ship's low hull blended with the sea as the darkness crept down to meet her, so that soon only her bright, unmatched eyes were visible to those who still watched from the shore.

Within half an hour even they had been swallowed up, and the two cormorants returned to the buoy, and the night.

2

Memories

The public address squeaked and then purred into life. 'Now hear this! General drills will recommence at 1400!' Some of the men around the bulletin board between decks swore and

28

shook their fists at the speaker. Others, still clasping coffee mugs and knives and forks, merely swore obscenely.

Pirelli, a tall, darkly tanned seaman, groaned. 'Jesus Christ! It's like bein' back in a battle-wagon!'

Grout, one of the *Hibiscus*'s sonarmen, blinked his small eyes at the board and then pushed after the others towards their mess. 'Hell yes! It's bad enough goin' on some crappy survey assignment without all this drill stuff!'

In the main crew space the low deckhead held down' the mingled aroma of the midday meal coupled for good measure with that of fresh paint and insecticide. Most of the crew off watch were already straddled around the hard-topped mess tables, their feet automatically braced, although the ship was completely steady. On either side of the eating and complaining men the ports were open on to a bright blue sky. Each port was divided in two by the dazzling horizon line which shone like a continuous diamond necklace above a pattern of deeper blue.

Pirelli slumped in his seat and sniffed loudly. A gunner by trade, he was a tough, professional seaman, and he was already feeling sick of the influx of new faces around his particular table. Of the ten men who sat hunched over their greasy plates, only he and his friend Grout were of the original crew. He peered darkly at the man directly opposite him. A good-looking Italian boy of about twenty with black, restless eyes and a soft, rather petulant mouth.

Pirelli said slowly, 'Excuse the chow, it's not up to your usual standards.'

Several men laughed, but Bella, the one addressed, only stared down at his plate with obvious nausea. Bella's thoughts were elsewhere. Like many of the other new crew members, he had been switched from another ship at the last moment to complete the correct numbers. He was in fact from the carrier which *Hibiscus* had so nearly rammed. Throughout the fleet, many officers had rubbed their hands at the prospect so suddenly dropped in their laps to get rid of deadbeats, troublemakers and men like Bella, who simply were better off out of their environment.

Bella moved his fork broodingly around the pile of beans and bacon which lay soggily on the plate. He came of a poor longshoreman's family in San Francisco, the youngest of eight kids. In the crisp, busy life of the navy it was hard to remember his third-floor apartment, and the fact that his father hardly ever spoke in any language but that of the old country. Bella had tried to forget them all, if only so that he should not despise them with their labour rallies, interspersed with bouts of religion and drunkenness. The trouble with his father's sort was that they did not want to lose their old identity. They hated change. They would never dream of leaving America, yet they never seemed to become part of it.

Pirelli tapped the table, two bright beans running from one corner of his mouth. 'I'm talkin' to you, Wop!'

Bella jerked from his brooding, his eyes suddenly alive with fury. On top of everything else the old 'thing' had happened. He stood up. '*Wop* your goddamned self!'

Knives and forks clattered into stillness, and many expectant eyes turned towards the slim, wild-eyed boy. This was more like it. After two days at sea under the new skipper most of the crew were ready for anything. Drills and exercises every day in spite of the blazing heat which pinned the ship down to the lazy sea like a crippled dragonfly.

Pirelli grinned lazily. As his big mouth twisted sideways the tightening skin of his right cheek revealed a deep white scar. He was a fighter, and knew all the signs. Under other circumstances he would have ignored Bella's quick return, for, like most professional lower-deck brawlers, Pirelli was no bully. However . . . He stood up, almost a head taller than the other man.

'Me? A *Wop*?' He roared with laughter, revealing his strong if uneven teeth. 'If anything I come from Ireland originally!' He looked round the mess space. ' 'Course that was a long time ago!' He became serious. 'But these here Eyetalians are different. Now when I was in the Sixth Fleet we went ashore in Messina, and there were all these little greaseballs, stuffin' themselves with yellow worms!' He rolled his eyes. 'Horrible it was!'

It was then that Bella hit him. Although classed as a seaman, Bella was rated yeoman because of his obvious sharpness and eagerness to learn. Hours of work over books and publications in one of the carrier's offices had robbed his slight frame of most of its muscle, and with dismay he saw Pirelli's grin return even as the shock ran up his arm.

The big gunner dabbed the red patch at the corner of his mouth and then lashed out. Bella's legs trapped him against the mess stool, and with a sob he cannoned backwards on to the deck. His head thumped the unyielding metal and a thou-

30

sand stars danced across the grinning faces which swam above him. With a choking gasp Bella staggered to his feet and lunged to the attack, his arms flailing. A fallen dish of beans skidded under his shoe, and this only added to his wretched fury which had been brought to a head by Pirelli's casual insult.

All the agony of the last weeks roared through his brain, the girl's tear-stained face, and the grim features of the carrier's captain when he had told him for the last time that no permission was forthcoming for Bella to marry a Chinese girl. They were both under age; time would heal; opportunities would occur . . . all the unfeeling, senseless phrases surged across his mind as he reeled blindly against someone who stood between him and the now silent Pirelli. With one final effort Bella punched forward, but a grip of steel encircled his wrist and the blow halted in midair.

Bella went limp and stared up into the bleak, hollow-cheeked face of Chief Tasker, who had been in the process of conducting one of his prowling inspections of the crew's quarters.

There was complete silence.

Tasker released the boy's wrist from his hard, cold hand and stepped back to stare at him. 'Well, speak up!' His thin mouth opened and shut like a rifle-bolt.

Bella hung his head. It was all happening. What was the point of trying to do anything?

Pirelli said lazily: 'Hell, Chief, we was only sparrin'. I was just showin' the lad how I took a Lascar in the Primrose bar at Gib!' He rolled his eyes. '*Honest*, Chief!'

Tasker grunted. 'I know what I saw!' He blinked rapidly, so that his hooded eyes made him look like death itself. 'Just watch it in future, Bella! Otherwise it'll be "mast" for you, got it? I don't like troublemakers in my ship!'

He turned on his heel and clattered up the steel ladder.

The tension eased, and Pirelli patted his bench. 'Come and squat, you mad bastard!'

Grout saw the boy's miserable reluctance. 'That's an order, lad!' He grinned across at Pirelli as the young seaman slid on to the seat. 'Welcome to the club!'

Pirelli peered sideways at his new companion. 'Okay, Bella? What's yer name?'

'Mike.' One word, small and still wary.

'Well, Mike, on this scow you've got to hit something.' He bellowed again. 'It might as well be me!'

Bella's mouth crinkled into a slow smile, but if Pirelli had

31

seen the dull light in his eyes he would not have been so confident of his conquest.

* * *

In the wardroom, too, the midday meal was progressing through its final course. Slattery, the white-coated senior steward, watched his two messboys like a mistrustful eagle as the ice-cream and tinned peaches were ladled into the waiting dishes. The open ports, crisp tablecloth and well-worn silver gave the wardroom an almost holiday atmosphere. Even the Seventh Fleet crest above the mahogany sideboard, with its much quoted motto, 'Ready Power for Peace', gleamed with new paint, and the dazzling reflections from the passing bow-wave helped to hide the cracked leather on some of the chairs and the numerous dents and scratches on the scanty furniture. The room was spacious compared with the rest of the ship, and ran the full width of the vessel. The port side contained the dining table, around which the off-duty officers sat in silent contemplation of their peaches, and the starboard side comprised the space allotted easy chairs, bulletin board, sideboard and pistol rack. Piles of *Esquire* magazines, weeks-old newspapers, unfinished airmail letters completed the normal small ship litter.

Gunnar sat at the head of the table, his hands hidden beneath the cloth. Occasionally he glanced around at the others, taking mental notes, withdrawing reservations, installing others.

Maddox was at the opposite end, his strong face set in a frown of concentration as he spooned in his second serving of ice-cream. Gunnar noticed the way Maddox's unruly hair always managed to stay in the same state of disorder yet seemed set that way. He had a kind of animal toughness about him, Gunnar thought, one minute relaxed, the next alert and semi-belligerent, like a gundog.

On Gunnar's left sat Kroner, the communications officer, and Malinski, whose sallow face still showed one small streak of oil as if to defy the closeness of his open-air colleagues. Kroner had bored them through most of the meal with a long dissertation on registered publications and the weaknesses of *Hibiscus*'s sonar equipment. Both topics were dull enough, but from Kroner's languid lips they were sheer misery.

Eventually Connell, the doctor, who sat on Gunnar's right,

32

had remarked, 'Seems a lot for a jg to know?' It was a small, seemingly innocent remark, and the doctor's bright blue eyes were almost grave, yet Regan, the first lieutenant, who sat at his side, threw back his bullet head and roared, so that one of the messboys at the pantry hatch rolled his eyes with uneasy expectancy.

'A *mere* jg! By God I like that, Doc!'

The tiny web of wrinkles around Connell's eyes drew together in a secret smile. 'I had a feeling you might.'

The dishes vanished and the smell of fresh coffee, never far away, floated across the table.

Gunnar interlaced his fingers tightly below the cloth and tried to relax his taut muscles. Every movement of the deck beneath his feet, each sudden shudder of the props, made him stiffen, hold his breath and listen. He had purposely left the bridge to young Inglis for the quiet routine watchkeeping of a clear empty sea, and this was the first meal he had completed with the bulk of his officers. Deep down he was aware that he also wanted to break their clublike barrier, to feel his way into their code and find out what they were thinking.

About me? He stared at the sloping surface of his coffee and was caught off guard as the doctor asked, 'Do you expect a long assignment in Payenhau, Captain?'

Gunnar collected his scattered thoughts and felt his mouth obediently turn into a smile. The doctor's opaque eyes and quiet diffident manner could be unnerving. 'Hard to say. I have to contact the U.S. military adviser first. He's been there for some time. He should be able to put us in the picture.'

It was maddening the way small remarks continually laid bare the things which were uppermost in Gunnar's thoughts. The military adviser for instance. The orders stated in all but actual words that Gunnar and the ship would be under his orders and at his constant call until the operation was completed.

One side of Gunnar told him to get the job finished and then the hell out of it to Taiwan. The other, stronger, urge insisted that he stayed with the unwanted command as long as possible. For after *Hibiscus*, what then? This military adviser, like the many in Viet Nam, a Major Lloyd Jago, U.S.M.C., would probably be more awkward because of the complete isolation of his field of operations. What the hell was he doing in a penal settlement anyway?

Connell said, 'It might be a rest cure.'

Gunnar darted a suspicious glance at the man's smiling features, but Regan's harsh voice broke across them. 'At least it'll keep some of the hotbloods from chasing tail, eh?'

Maddox looked up from his pondering. 'Has someone been bellyaching again?'

Regan did not turn towards him but remained facing the captain. 'Just as I was coming down here Chief Tasker told me that one of the new dreamboats has been throwing his weight about.' His bushy, unbroken eyebrow lifted. 'Your yeoman, Captain!'

Gunnar leaned back. 'Oh? How come?' He fitted a small picture of Bella's dark head bent over some despatches that morning. A quiet, sad-looking boy, he had thought.

Regan continued with relish: 'I've read his folio. He was shot off the flat-top like a dose of salts apparently. Wanted to dip his wick into a bit of Chinese tail!' He grinned hugely. 'Can you imagine?'

Gunnar felt the colour rising to his cheeks. What did Regan know? Was there someone on the ship who had been in Viet Nam when he had been naval adviser at Qui Nhon? He tried to remain calm. Surely not here too!

The engineer spoke for the first time. 'The first girl I ever had was a Chinese.'

The others stared from the captain to him with surprise.

Malinski toyed with a doughnut as if it were a piece of delicate mechanism. 'Fifteen she was. A real picture.'

Regan frowned. The spring had gone out of his story. 'Christ, I thought only the swabs did that sort of thing!'

Malinski eyed him with faded, mild eyes. 'I was a stoker then. Nineteen. We don't all start with the silver spoon, you know.'

Regan looked confused and plucked at his hawk's nose. 'Hell, I didn't mean to imply——'

Maddox drained his coffee with a loud cluck. 'Like hell you didn't!'

Gunnar saw the immediate tension and said sharply: 'Okay, gentlemen. I think that flogs out that topic!'

Maddox said in a carefully controlled tone, 'We should hit Payenhau in forty-eight hours, sir.'

'Yes.' Gunnar saw the others relax. 'I'm afraid this detour has taxed the fuel a bit. We shall just have to cut down on unnecessary steaming. There are no bunkering facilities at Payenhau.'

34

It had been a drag, he thought. The first course had taken them many miles to the south-west before they had finally turned north-east towards the true destination. It was odd the way senior officers still believed in outmoded tactics, Gunnar pondered. In these days of Intelligence and active radio units it was hard to mask anything. That was even if anyone cared about the *Hibiscus*. What could happen? Even supposing for one crazy second that China took over the rest of the world during the second half of the week, the navy could blast Payenhau from the water without even surfacing its undersea cruisers.

A bosun's mate, cap in fist, peered round the curtained doorway. 'Captain, sir? Mister Inglis's respects but he thinks we've sighted a submarine!'

Maddox snorted, 'He *thinks*!'

But Gunnar was already halfway to the door. 'I'm coming up!'

Some of the others raised themselves on their chairs to peer through the shining ports. The sea was as placid and empty as before. Apart from a junk and two smudges of smoke on the horizon they had sighted nothing since leaving Hong Kong.

Regan said derisively, 'Young Peter Inglis would see a sub in his bath!'

But Maddox had seen the captain's face, the same empty eyes he had seen when the ship had careered sternfirst towards the flagship. It just needs something to go wrong, he thought. Just one stupid mistake and he'll rip apart.

He forced himself to remain seated, but his mind was already on the bridge.

*   *   *

Gunnar swung his leg over the bridge coaming and forced himself to walk quietly to the gratings. His palms felt moist as he lifted the powerful glasses, and he could sense the eyes of the signalmen on his back as he levelled them across the screen.

Inglis said hoarsely, 'It dived, sir.'

Gunnar had to squint his eyes against the blinding glare reflected from the flat, creamy water, and he was aware for the first time that he had left his cap in the wardroom so that the heat beat across his head with crushing force. 'Did you

35

get a good look at her?' His voice was controlled but sharp, and he knew that Inglis was staring at him. Almost savagely he added, 'Well, *did* you?'

Inglis was keen and eager to make himself into a good officer, but his obvious lack of confidence was already beginning to show itself. The quiet watch, the oppressive heat and the drowsy effect of the ship's gentle motion had been shattered, first by the lookout's report and then by the sudden appearance of the captain. It had seemed unimportant at first. The China Sea was open house for anyone who cared to explore its inhospitable vastness, and any nation which had the desire to push a submarine across it could do so. But there was something about this submarine. Shrouded in a long writhing layer of sea-mist it had come up to them almost unnoticed. The radar was out of action for three hours for some awaited repairs, and in any case nobody seemed to think another warship in this area mattered anyway.

Then Caslett, one of the duty signalmen, had remarked casually, 'She sure is cracking on speed, sir!' The submarine had turned away even as Inglis began to sort out his thoughts. Long and low like a basking shark, with a wafer-thin fin, she had shortened her silhouette and swung deeper into the mist. The sleek, rounded hull had been broken by a sudden upthrust of froth and spume, and she had begun to dive as Inglis had finally decided to call the captain.

He said: 'Steering almost a parallel course with us, Captain. I guess she was charging batteries, but made off when we started to come up on her.'

Gunnar dropped the glasses on to their rack and banged his hands together. 'Did you call her up!' He saw the mounting concern on the younger man's face but this only made Gunnar more impatient. 'Christ, man, what nationality was she?'

'I don't know, sir!' Inglis looked at the deck while everyone else stared at him and the captain. 'We didn't get time to flash her. She was off like a rocket!'

Caslett cleared his throat and held up the intelligence log like an offering. 'None of our subs in this area, sir.' He looked helpfully at Inglis's wretched face. 'Could be a Limey.'

Gunnar swung on the signalman, his face tight. 'When I want your advice I'll ask for it!' Then to Inglis: 'You should have called me at once. Get me a despatch blank, and as soon as I've written this down I want it coded and sent off at once.

36

Tell Lieutenant Kroner to come to the bridge and deal with it personally. I want every last detail about that submarine you can remember. Course, speed, description, the lot!' He ran his fingers across his hair, aware that his hand was shaking badly. 'And in future I want a good watch maintained *at all times*!'

Inglis lifted his chin, his eyes hot and angry. 'The radar is out, sir.'

'When this ship was first commissioned in 'forty-two, Mister Inglis,' Gunnar's tone was dangerously low, 'they didn't have it aboard at all. What d'you suppose the Germans did in the Atlantic? D'you imagine they came and signalled their positions before they attacked?'

'I'm sorry, Captain.' Inglis's embarrassment and anger were slowly giving way to open amusement. 'We're not at war now, sir.'

Gunnar took a pace towards him, his eyes hard and without pity. 'If you think that you should not be here!' As Caslett held out the despatch pad he added, 'By God, you'll not live long if you believe *that*!'

Gunnar wrote rapidly on a blank and thrust it into Inglis's hands. Then without another word he strode into the charthouse and stood for several minutes in the cool gloom of the small space, his eyes fixed unseeingly on the glass-topped table.

It was happening. In spite of his quick flush of anger at Inglis's stupidity he could feel the rising excitement like the stabbing of an old wound, which indeed it was.

There was more to the *Hibiscus*'s mission than they had told him. The vague orders, the deception of course and destination, it all added up. The submarine was probably Russian. It was quite likely one of their new atomic-powered ones, which would explain the speed and silence of its engines. Aiding their doubtful allies the Red Chinese no doubt. Helping them to do what? Gunnar leaned on the cool glass and stared at the clean chart between his hands.

He felt his breathing returning to normal, and plucked the moistened shirt away from his chest. Perhaps after this Inglis might learn to keep alert. Not at war indeed! What in God's name did he think they were doing out here otherwise?

There was a discreet cough in the doorway and Maddox peered in at him. 'All okay, sir?' He looked wary, but calm.

'It was a submarine right enough.' Gunnar relaxed slightly. 'I'd like to have had a crack at it with the d.c.'s.' He frowned slightly and did not see Maddox arch his eyebrows with surprise. 'You'd better tell Regan to check all the armament again when we have drill this afternoon. I want the whole lot at first-degree readiness in future.'

Maddox moved his feet uneasily. 'I'm not quite with you, Captain. Young Inglis seemed a bit too flustered to explain.'

Gunnar nodded. 'Shut the door.'

Maddox closed it obediently and moved closer. It was easy to sense the excitement in the captain, although Maddox was baffled as to its cause. But Gunnar's new appearance was infectious, and he felt that he had been allowed into some new and fast moving development.

Gunnar said quietly: 'I think we're being shadowed, Bob. Somehow the Reds are on to us. I don't know how much, but I'm hoping that the reply to my signal will explain things a bit.'

'Signal, sir?' Maddox was getting confused.

'I sent one off just now.' Gunnar leaned against the table and folded his arms. For the first time since he had taken command, for the first time since . . . He shook himself. It was useless harping back to other things. This was now. It was real and it was a new chance.

Maddox said slowly, 'I thought the orders specified no despatches, sir?'

Gunnar's mouth parted in a smile. Maddox noticed how that one action transformed the man into an excited boy, and he was strangely moved.

'This is different, Bob. This sneaking submarine will change things a bit. It'll change it for the other side too of course!' He grinned. 'The Reds don't like being caught out at their own game!'

Maddox rubbed his stomach as he always did when his thoughts refused to drop into the right order. Red submarines, deceptions, depth-charges, and a strung-out conspiracy with the far-off admiral seemed somehow out of character for a clapped-out little ship like the *Hibiscus*. He said carefully, 'It might be interesting.'

Gunnar bit his lip. 'You've said it. I'm just waiting the chance, just *one* chance to get even with——' He looked up sharply as the door slid back.

Lieutenant Kroner's handsome features stared in at them. 'Reply to your despatch, sir.' He darted an apprehensive glance at Maddox.

Gunnar stood up quickly. 'Well, let's have it.'

The lieutenant licked his lips. 'To boil it down, it says to disregard the sighting report, sir.'

Maddox said, 'That means it was one of our——'

But Gunnar waved him down. 'Go on, Kroner!'

'It refers you to section three of your orders, sir.'

Gunnar nodded with mounting impatience. 'Yes, yes, about maintaining radio silence, go *on*, man!'

'Message ends, sir!' Kroner looked dazed.

'*Ends?*' Gunnar tore the pad from the man's fingers and stared at it for several seconds. 'What the hell are they playing at?'

Kroner stared woodenly at the deck. 'Is that all, Captain?'

Gunnar did not answer, but walked instead to the chart table, his brows drawn together in a deep frown. Maddox gestured briefly towards the door, and Kroner, with a shrug, withdrew.

Maddox said evenly, 'Perhaps the stupid bastard didn't see *us*, sir?'

Gunnar looked up, his eyes wild. 'Hell, they saw us all right!'

'But if it was one of our own?' Maddox noticed how the captain's hands were gripping the table, as if he was afraid to let go. 'Anyway it was a good idea to check up.'

Gunnar stood up, suddenly quiet, even subdued. 'Yes. Yes, it was.' He turned towards the rear door. 'I'm going to have a lie down, Bob. Just snatch a minute or two.'

Maddox answered, 'I'll keep an eye on things, sir.'

But the door slid shut, and Maddox was left alone beside the chart table. He tried to dismiss what had happened, to bring back his old attitude of not caring, not demanding the voice of reason, but instead he could sense only fear at the enormity of his discovery. Gunnar was driving himself mad. He might be halfway there already.

Inch by inch Maddox could feel his own security being stripped away, and his reeling thoughts were mixed between resentment and pity. No wonder Inglis and Kroner looked so dazed and vacant. That would soon give way to bitterness or amusement. Either way it would spread through the ship, and then anything could happen.

He jammed on his cap and banged open the door.

Happen? Jesus Christ, it was happening right now!

*   *   *

39

Mark Gunnar awoke with a start and lay staring wide-eyed into the darkness. The rapid beating of his heart slowly returned to normal as his ears and thoughts became tuned to the quiet, reassuring shipboard sounds which filtered through the closed charthouse door from the bridge beyond. After a moment Gunnar reached out and switched on the small lamp above his bunk and peered at his wristwatch. A mere half hour before dawn, and he knew that he had hardly slept for more than a few minutes at a time. When once he had fallen into an exhausted sleep he had been visited yet again by the ever-recurring nightmare in which only his own suffering was real and stark, and the other figures and happenings vague and all the more threatening because of their size and featureless horror. He had awakened shivering and dazed, his body chilled in a layer of cold sweat, his eyes probing the darkness of the tiny sea cabin as if he expected to see a continuance of the nightmare.

He could hear the muffled movement of feet from the bridge and the persistent creak of the steering mechanism from the wheelhouse below. The bridge structure itself kept up its own grumbling chatter of squeaks and vibrations in time to the engines, and once he heard a man laugh, the sound indistinct and unnatural in the darkened ship.

What would the new day bring? Gunnar pushed his hands behind his head and stared at the riveted steel a few feet above him. Some time in the forenoon would see them groping their way into Payenhap, where an entirely new set of circumstances would be awaiting his attention. He checked the immediate impulse of excitement and interest which still dogged him like an old instinct. What did it matter any more? The despatch from the admiral in response to his information about the strange submarine should have been enough. A slap in the face. An empty but nevertheless definite rebuke.

He half wondered why he should feel hurt and surprise. He had seen it happen to others. One slip was all an officer required. He bit his lip, knowing that he was only concocting the beginning of another excuse for himself.

How Janet would have laughed! he thought. She had tried everything she knew to get him to leave the navy. Looking back it was almost comic how he had clung to the one job he knew well because it was the only thing in which she could not dominate him.

It had been all right at first. Naval life at its very best. Lon-

40

don, Paris, for the two years of their marriage they had managed to see most of the civilised world together. But when he had been singled out for staff training he had seen the change come over her, had sensed the difference between them. It was as if she had only tolerated his career like some women put up with their husband's hobbies.

Her father, a big timber man with several interests in Canada, had openly sided with his daughter on every possible occasion. 'Come in with me, boy, and stop wasting your life.' Now it was obvious he had been more interested in his daughter's life than Gunnar's. The navy was good enough for its social side, and as far as Janet was concerned that was all she could see of it. Attentive ensigns, flattering senior officers, even they could pall after a time.

Gunnar could no longer find one reason for his marriage, nor could he imagine what she had seen in him. She had no service connections, unlike his own family which had given its blood on more decks than he could remember. There had been a Gunnar in the navy since the War of Independence, and before that there had been Gunnars ferreting out the world's trade secrets in merchantmen and men-of-war since the time seamen had first bent a sail.

His father had died shortly after the Second World War, broken in health from the wounds received at Normandy, but his mother still lived in the same old timbered house on the outskirts of Boston. Living a quiet, well-ordered life of one bred and born to the ways of menfolk earmarked through the generations for service at sea. She had not approved of Janet, although she had never shown her anything but kindness. Gunnar had sensed her disapproval but had put it down to the usual parents' mistrust of anything or anybody new and different. And Janet was certainly different.

Gunnar could still remember her first visit to the Gunnar house. It was almost as if Janet had decided her own role from the beginning. Everything was larger than life, from the Cadillac her father had given her for her twenty-first birthday to her leopardskin pants. Gunnar, of course, had hardly noticed the challenge, but had been carried along with the tide of events he could not have controlled even if he had so wanted.

It was when he had been sent away on sea-duty for the first time after their marriage that the change came about. Upon his return she had seemed distant and cold, and she once more opened her attack on the one thing in life he held dear.

'Stop playing this stupid game!' Looking back he wondered how he had tolerated that first display of rage on her part. She had pushed him away, her mouth ugly with temper. 'I'm sick of playing second string to your damn ship!' And so on.

Each time it got a little bit worse, but when Gunnar had been posted to Viet Nam as an adviser he had believed that the sudden prolonged absence in hostile territory would change her. It did. In her letter she told him in cold, almost insolent, style that she had decided to leave him. There was someone else. This someone was apparently on another plane, a man of drive and energy who made Gunnar seem like an idiot child. He later learned that the man was in fact Jack Fenton, a flabby, fast-talking business representative employed by Janet's father, who lived, it seemed, entirely to grant Janet's every wish and desire.

It was from that moment Gunnar started to make a series of mistakes. He had still failed to grasp the essential fact that Janet had made up her mind, just as she had when she had decided to marry him, that she did not *want* him any more. Furthermore, if Gunnar had been less busy with the day-to-day effort of helping to build up the South Vietnamese defences against the impending communist assault from the North, he might have understood that she had made her plans long ago, had probably even selected her new partner with the same clear-thinking efficiency which made her so much like her father.

Gunnar had, of course, helped her by accepting the difficult assignment in Viet Nam. By taking the one challenging job which, if successful, would certainly earmark him for promotion and advancement, he had in fact given her the opportunity to act. In Janet's view distance was a great healer, and who knew what might happen in Viet Nam?

The next mistake he made was to plead with her. Most of his letters went unanswered, and in any case her replies became more vague and fewer as the weeks dragged by. He still wondered why he had started the affair with Laya, the Vietnamese girl in Qui Nhon.

She was tiny and black-haired, almost like a child compared with Janet's bright worldliness. After each hard, nagging day Gunnar returned to his quarters and found her waiting for him. No word of love was ever spoken, no promise or plan for the future even hinted at, yet from this strange acceptance Gunnar derived some happiness in those months before his world finally fell apart. He still asked himself if he had in fact found love in the strange, quiet-spoken Laya, or if in fact he had only allowed the affair as if by so doing he would hurt Janet and make her repent.

All this inner unrest and more beside was tearing him apart that day when he had been ordered to arrange the shipment of ammunition and stores by way of a small coaster which the local forces used for that purpose. Laya had been rather withdrawn for a few days, and Gunnar had believed she was sickening for something. She came of a good local family, her father being a merchant of high repute who was very pleased with his daughter's social progress, and Gunnar suggested that she stay with her family until his return.

She had become excited, tearful and wretched as he explained that he would be out of town for two weeks at least. He had to go some fifty miles inland to contact the commander of one of the montagnards, who in turn would be responsible for making a final collection of the coaster's cargo once it was shipped on to road transport. There was so much terrorist activity on the roads and railways at night that every precaution had to be taken. Security was at a premium, and the hard-pressed American advisers could never afford to lose patience with the slap-happy arrangements enforced by the South Vietnamese. All this he had tried to explain to Laya, more like a father to a daughter than a man to the girl whose bed he had been sharing. But she was like that. He felt protective towards her more than anything else, just as he found a kind of peace in her desire.

One week later the small convoy with which he was travelling was ambushed by the Viet Cong. There were three trucks of Vietnamese soldiers and one of stores for the journey. All were soon ablaze, and the dusty road was running with blood as the hidden machine guns cut through the unsuspecting guards.

In a daze of pain and apprehension Gunnar had been dragged through one jungle path after another, urged on by blows and curses even as searching helicopters prowled above the interlaced branches overhead.

The Viet Cong took no more prisoners from the convoy. The blackened, mutilated and stripped corpses still guarded the road when an army patrol stumbled across them two days later.

But Gunnar was special, and was to be afforded the full

treatment. Even now he did not understand what last physical barricade had held him together under the torture. There had been other prisoners in the jungle hideout. Peasants and soldiers, grey-faced and terrified victims of a war they did not understand. Slowly and methodically the Viet Cong went on with their interrogations and executions, only falling into silent watchfulness when a patrol or a prowling aircraft was reported.

The chief interrogator was young and sleek, and Gunnar suspected he was Chinese. His English was flawless, with an almost British accent.

He only appeared on the second day after Gunnar's capture. After two days of beatings and humiliations. The softening up.

He had sat in a small canvas chair, his jungle-green uniform clean and well pressed in spite of the squalid surroundings, a warm smile on his bland features.

'Well, Commander Gunnar? Time is very short, so let us get down to business.'

Gunnar had been kept in a small wooden cage, too small to lie, sit or kneel in. Every muscle ached, and his body felt raw and racked with pain. They knew all about him. His background, the men under his control, even the hours he worked in Qui Nhon. There was just one thing they were not sure about.

The nameless interrogator had smiled almost apologetically. 'I must have the exact inland route of your ammunition convoy and the pick-up area.' He had watched the surprise on Gunnar's bruised face with open amusement. 'Surely you did not think my group would betray its position merely to wipe out your little convoy the other day for nothing? It was *you* we wanted!' The man's casual air had vanished. 'Time is short. You will be killed very shortly, Commander, so we must get on!'

Gunnar had forced a smile. 'If I am to die there seems little point in continuing with this argument!'

'On the contrary! Tell me what I require and I promise you a bullet in the neck. I will even do it myself if you wish.' He sounded cool and reasonable. 'Otherwise you will be praying for death for a long long time. My men are experts. They have to be. If they kill a man under torture their own lives are forfeit!'

And from that point Gunnar's life had changed into a liv-

44

ing hell. With small breaks the torture went on hour by hour. The agony, the white-hot horror of the bamboo knives and the sounds of his own screams. He did not remember telling them the secrets of the ammunition convoy, but at the same time he knew he must have done so. The agony stopped, and like a bloody carcass he had been thrown into a pit on top of a pile of torn bodies like an animal in a slaughterhouse.

Then something quite unforeseen even to the vigilant Communist guards had happened.

A sentry had reported the sound of an approaching aircraft. Through the mist of pain and despair Gunnar heard someone order the dousing of the cook's fire, as had happened several times during his captivity. What happened next he could not be sure. Possibly the camp cook in his excitement upset some oil or petrol amongst the scattered embers, but without warning a great gout of flame seared through the shadowed trees, followed immediately by a tall column of thick blue smoke.

With every last ounce of his fading strength Gunnar had pulled himself blindly over the edge of the pit in which he had been thrown to die. The cold dead hands of earlier victims clawed at his torn, naked body, but he still struggled and tugged until he was across the trampled earth and hidden in the first barrier of bushes. He had heard the changing note of the aircraft's engines, had guessed what would happen next. He had so often heard the tired pilots complaining of their fruitless patrols, of the wasted napalm bombs which always hung ready in the hunt for terrorists and their invisible camps. That column of smoke would be all that this particular pilot could dream of.

Stubbornly, desperately, the breath choking through his pain-clenched teeth, Gunnar had crawled on. He did not even look back as the holocaust broke behind him, and he no longer felt the searing heat which scorched the very air in his lungs. He was past fear and beyond the pain of death. That was why he survived, if survival it was. Some hunters found him days later and took him quickly to the nearest army post. For charity or reward, he never knew or cared, nor did he ever see the faces of the men who had found him.

When the hospital restored his sanity and did its best with his lacerated body he heard the other half of the story. The ammunition convoy was safe, because it had been delayed inadvertently by the old coaster having an engine breakdown. A brother officer who visited him briefly before he was flown back to the States for more advanced treatment told him about Laya. On the day Gunnar had gone on his mission, she had disappeared.

Gunner could still not believe what he knew must be true. She had been planted on him, and, love or not, had betrayed him to the terrorists. Over and over again he tortured his mind with the knowledge that hers was not the real blame. Because of his own stupid personal troubles he had been the one to make betrayal possible. He had dropped his guard, left open the one gap which men like the sleek interrogator were always seeking.

The medal had been the final mockery. Heroism in the face of the enemy, making his escape in spite of his wounds, devotion to duty, etc. etc. God in heaven, how he hated the very sound of the citation!

It was incredible to remember how swift and easy he had made his own disgrace and downfall. The fact that he had not kept silent under torture, the knowledge that the convoy *would* have been destroyed but for an accident, helped to rip away the last of his inner strength.

And now, in spite of all that happened, he was still not to be spared. He was being thrown straight back into the thick of the unseen war, with even more lives resting in his hands.

The admiral's last despatch did not fool him any more than the bald context of his orders. There was something in the wind, and *Hibiscus* was to be the bait.

He sat up violently on the bunk, the sweat trickling down his bare chest and arms. They did not trust him with the full details of the operation, that was why he was entering Payenhau like a blind man. They needed his services and experience, but no longer believed in his judgement.

He thought of the resentment amongst his own men, the unspoken attacks on the constant drills and exercises he had made them all carry out. Well, let them complain! If anything went wrong this time it was not going to be because the ship was unprepared. It would not wipe out past events, but it might help to ease the pain of them.

The telephone buzzed discreetly.

He heard Regan's harsh voice: 'Captain, sir? Just picked up the Payenhau Group on the radar.' He paused and Gunnar heard the sigh of the bow-wave close in his ear. Regan continued, 'Dawn coming up now, sir.'

Gunnar nodded. 'I'll come up.' He dropped the phone and

46

swung his legs off the bunk. It was all starting again. He felt
for his small box of tranquillisers and reached for a glass of
water.

There was no past. The future was uncertain, but it was
there.

3

The Island of Tin Gods

Lieutenant Robert Maddox paused for a moment on the top
rung of the bridge ladder and leaned backwards on his heels.
It felt strange to hold the handrails and not feel the engines'
steady vibrations, and stranger still to see the unattended
wheel and the bare chart table. He sighed and heaved himself
on to the upper bridge.

The captain was standing on the gratings, and Maddox felt
that it was as if Gunnar had always been there, would remain
there until the ship broke up around him.

He saluted wearily. 'Ship secure, Captain.' Maddox was torn
with the desire to drop into his bed and sleep away the ten-
sions of the trip from Hong Kong, yet something stirred him
to come alive again from the moment but fifteen minutes earlier when the anchor had shattered the flat stillness of
the Payenhau anchorage. Now, as the *Hibiscus* swung gently
at her cable, glittering like a toy ship in her own reflection, it
was indeed hard to recall the nerve-jarring approach in the
dawn's half light, the captain's sharp helm orders, and the wild
impression which Maddox knew he had shared with others
on the silent bridge that the ship was heading straight for disaster. The channel between the first tiny group of islets which
surrounded the main hump of land like broken fragments
seemed invisible, and now in the first glare of morning it was
even more difficult to see how Gunnar had groped his way
to the centre of the placid anchorage. It was more like a giant
lake, with the surrounding islets overlapping and concealing
the narrow slivers of burnished water and the open sea beyond.

Gunnar was speaking to Lieutenant Kroner, who beside

the captain's rumpled and weary figure looked out of place and unnatural in a new crisp outfit of fresh khakis, a pistol prominent at his hip.

'And while we are here I want a good lookout maintained at all times.' Gunnar's tone was still terse, still on guard. Across his shoulder Maddox caught Kroner's eye and saw the communications officer blink like a disapproving owl. The captain continued: 'The gangway watch will always be in undress whites, and each O.O.D. must see that the flag is a good one when it's hoisted each day. Not some ragged old relic used for sea purposes.' He glanced quickly at Maddox. 'Anything to add, Bob?'

Maddox swallowed, caught off guard. Gunnar seemed so alert and wide-awake, although Maddox knew he had hardly closed his eyes since joining the ship. 'Sounds okay, sir.' He forced a grin. 'Seems more like a courtesy visit to see the ship dolled up like this.'

Gunnar's eyes were invisible behind his sunglasses but his mouth remained stiff. 'They'll be watching us from the shore no matter what we're doing.'

Kroner grunted. 'I'll carry on then.' He paused by the ladder. 'Any liberty, sir?'

Gunnar shook his head. 'Negative. There'll be time enough when I find out exactly what's happening ashore.'

The three officers looked towards the broken line of white buildings which swept down the sloping side of one of the hump-backed hills which rolled over the island like a green and brown desert. What Maddox had first assumed to be a line of white surf around the base of the hills was in fact a strip of narrow beach upon which lay a few grounded boats, and as he watched, Maddox could also see a few tiny figures standing motionless as they stared at the anchored warship.

There was a crude, spidery-looking pier constructed of weed-covered timbers and a slatted boardwalk which looked as if it had been there when the island first appeared, and a few moored fishing boats seemed to make up the total vessels of Payenhau. Except, that is, for a gaunt, rust-covered wreck which lay in solitary decay on a long sandspit below one jutting headland. Maddox guessed it had once been a small coasting steamer. There were still hundreds of such craft on the China Seas, scraping a living from any odd cargo or freight left unwanted by the more opulent companies. The wreck's bridge sagged in the middle where scavengers had long since

48

ripped out the sparse fittings and woodwork from the wheelhouse, and the stack had crumpled with rust and weather until only a short stub protruded above the buckled plates like a decayed tooth.

Maddox eyed the simple derrick mounted on the narrow pier and guessed that too had been filched from the abandoned coaster. It seemed to sum up the whole place, he thought grimly. Decayed and forgotten, bare and uninviting. There appeared to be no trees on any of the islands, just small stunted vegetation with the usual lush green of forced growth and parched roots. What a place for a penal settlement. He noticed also the long low buildings above the town which he had first taken as the prison. As he lifted his binoculars he could see it was a fairly new structure of rough concrete with deep shadowed slits at regular intervals which were probably gun mountings. Jesus, what a dump! He heard Gunnar say, 'I understand that the island's prison population is housed on the other side of that big hill above the headland.'

Kroner replied sourly, 'I'd imagine a cemetry'd be more in keeping!'

Maddox kept silent. There was no point in adding to the tension which daily seemed to mount within the small ship. Just get the damned job over and then the hell out of it. It would probably hurry things along once they could start this stupid assignment. He tried to visualise the giant whaleback of a nuclear submarine basking in the still anchorage. The modern world alongside this wilderness of a past life. Crude buildings, ancient sailing craft, matched against the self-contained power of the most terrible force controlled by man. Maddox mastered his gloom with an effort. The Free World. What a mockery it appeared at this particular moment.

Gunnar said: 'I'm going to shower and change. Have the boats lowered and awnings rigged.'

Kroner hitched his pistol belt. 'Both the boats?'

'Yes. We don't want the seams opening in this heat.'

Kroner looked as if he was past caring if the *Hibiscus*'s own plates cracked open, but he clattered down the ladder and could soon be heard yelling for Anders, the chief bosun's mate.

Gunnar took off his glasses and rubbed his eyes. They looked tired and filled with inner strain. He said, 'It looks quiet enough.' Then he glanced round the deserted bridge and climbed on to the ladder. Something made him add: 'Keep

49

the men on their toes, Bob. We don't want to be caught out!'
Then he was gone.

Maddox pulled a grubby handkerchief from his pocket and dabbed at his chin. A lookout? Keep them on their toes? Did the captain still believe that outside forces were deployed for the sole purpose of destroying the *Hibiscus*? At any other time it would have been funny. But all the humour had gone from this situation.

Maddox climbed down to the maindeck where already the duty watch were rigging the awnings. It would be hot enough soon, Maddox thought gloomily, anchored in the centre of a sheltered, shadowless bowl with not even a breeze to fan away the unwinking sunlight. He had earlier suggested that anchoring nearer the headland at the mouth of one of the channels would be better, also it would be closer to the pier where the boats would be tying up. Gunnar had merely said: 'Too risky. We'll keep well out from the land so that *we* can make the decisions!'

Although the captain always kept himself under control, there was the constant impression of some inner struggle, some tearing force which shadowed all of them like a cloud. Like that moment when the ship had entered the first channel merely an hour or so earlier. An islet on the starboard side had momentarily plunged the hull into darkness, except for the topmast which held the new sunlight like a golden crucifix, and Maddox had been conscious of the tremendous strain he was feeling as the little ship dug her sharp stem into the swirling water with angry contempt. A lookout, a seaman called Cummings, had said suddenly, 'Shoal on the port bow, sir!' His voice had been broken with tension and the concentration of the ship's eager approach. Gunnar had hardly moved but his voice was merciless. 'Mister Maddox! In future see to it that we have lookouts who can *see*!'

The shoal showed itself to be a shadow cast by a blunted pinnacle of rock by the water's edge, and as Maddox had sought for something to say in favour of the wretched Cummings, the captain had added, 'This one needs a white stick!'

Maddox hoped the story would not follow the others around the ship, although he knew that it would. A lookout who reported unnecessary sightings or even false ones was far better than a man who held his silence for fear of a rebuke.

It was that sort of incident which had confirmed in Maddox's troubled mind what he had earlier come to believe.

Gunnar was only half under control, yet it was his decision which held them at every turn.

At first it had been easy to imagine the ship being handed over to the Nationalist Chinese, the wardroom and bridge dominated by bland, expressionless faces. Now, Maddox could see no such future. It was as if he was tied to the *Hibiscus* for ever.

He found himself thinking about Mary, and no matter how he fought it he found a nagging worry growing within like guilt, which was for him an almost unknown sensation. Repeatedly he told himself it was merely because he needed some anchor, some outer force to fix his attention, but why her? He tried to remember other moments in his colourful past, but only Mary's picture remained. And it was always the last moments he recalled so vividly. Her pale, anxious expression as she watched his reaction when she had told him the news.

Maddox tore his eyes from the distant buildings and swore under his breath. Damn her! It was just that he was on edge like everyone else. Perhaps there was something or somebody in this godforsaken place to take his mind off the past. It seemed unlikely but there was always hope.

* * *

When Maddox returned from a hasty and unsatisfying shower he found Connell, the doctor, already stretched out on his upper bunk an unopened book lying on his stomach. He grinned down at the exec's flushed face. 'Cooled off yet, Bob?'

Maddox smiled ruefully. He wanted to like Connell, yet he was a difficult man to know. His friendly, bantering manner always seemed to make a barrier rather than open the way to real understanding. Maddox knew little more of him than he had learned when he sauntered aboard at Hong Kong. He came from Sioux Falls, a town about which Maddox knew nothing except that it could hardly be further from the sea. He often wondered why Connell had not stuck inland and slogged away at a family practice.

Connell stared up at the deckhead. 'Don't let him get you down.' he added quietly.

Maddox groped for a clean shirt his hair still dripping with water. 'I'm not worried,' he answered unconvincingly.

'Good boy. The first twenty years are the worst.'

Maddox stood up and began to twist the shirt between his strong hands. 'You've been around, Doc. What d'you make of him?'

It was strange that neither of them had mentioned the captain by name, Maddox thought afterwards. Again it was this sensation of guilt. As if they all shared it in some way.

Connell said after a few seconds, 'He has problems.'

'Don't we all?' Maddox felt cheated.

'It goes deeper than that, Bob. How would you like to be handed an old bucket like this if you had his record?'

'I don't know much about him.' Maddox was losing control of the conversation and added, 'Or you either for that matter!'

The doctor laughed shortly. 'Me? I'm just a quiet, degenerate quack. All I want is a place to lay my head, and a few bodies to heal!'

Maddox stared at him wearily. 'Jesus! You're like the rest!'

'I hope not.'

'How in hell's name did you get lumbered for this ship, Doc?' Maddox gripped the bunk his face creased in a frown. '*Seriously*, I would like to know!'

'That's an easy one. I asked for it.' He grinned at Maddox's obvious disbelief. 'I've been out here for two years, yet for all I've learned of the place I could have stayed in the States. Have you any idea what it's like to serve in a flat-top?'

Maddox shrugged. 'Just a ship I guess.'

'Just a ship.' Connell rolled on to his side and Maddox saw with surprise that there was a small crucifix around the doctor's neck. 'It was like a prison. The men were all so healthy I had nothing to worry about except the stock of contraceptives! If a guy was stupid enough to put his head under a rotor blade, or get sucked into a jet, it was a hospital case, or one for the morgue!' He laughed scornfully. 'And when I was off duty it was expected that I should go to the officers' club or to some stupid party.' He flopped on to his back again. 'In the navy everyone likes to have a doctor around. Senior officers can confide in him without weakening their pedestals of power and the junior ones want to show him their tremendous knowledge.'

Maddox flushed. 'Thanks a lot!'

Connell showed his white teeth. 'A pleasure!'

'What's the book you're reading?'

'Psychology.' The doctor thrust it beneath his pillow. 'But don't change the subject, Bob.'

'What's the use!' Maddox pulled on his slacks and tore angrily at the buttons. 'I'm the exec, so I guess I'm stuck with it!'

'We're all stuck with something.'

Maddox wheeled round. 'I'm worried, Doc. I shouldn't be shooting my mouth off like this, but there's a lot at stake.' He had started and the words poured out in a steady flood. The doctor lay quite still, his blue eyes fixed unwinkingly on the rivets above his face as Maddox unburdened himself in a low, hoarse whisper. Everything. The captain's behaviour, the resentment of the crew, even his own fears about a possible disaster if Gunnar cracked under the strain.

At length Connell said quietly: 'Thank you for telling me. I could not ask you outright, it's not my place.'

Maddox glared at him. 'Is that all you're going to say?'

'For the moment, yes. He interests me, but I'm only a doctor not a qualified head-shrinker.' His serious expression vanished. 'But we must be careful. We don't want to get charged with mutiny!'

Maddox stared at the open port. 'I wish to God I was a Norwegian dentist!'

For once Connell showed his surprise. 'Why, for Pete's sake?'

Maddox jammed on his cap. 'Then I'd be in Norway and not in this damned ship listening to *you*!'

Maddox almost cannoned into Bella, the captain's yeoman, who was just coming along the passageway between the cabins. 'What d'you want?'

Bella immediately looked resentful. 'Captain sends his compliments an' he wants you to accompany him ashore in fifteen minutes.' Bella jerked his dark head. 'And the doctor.'

Maddox dismissed him and stuck his head back into the cabin. 'Up you get, Doc! We're going to meet the rulers of these free islands!'

Connell smiled gently. 'I think it's *you* I shall have to watch.'

Maddox grimaced. 'Get knotted!' All the same, he was glad he had confided in someone.

* * *

The footsteps of the three officers rang loudly on the pier's crude wooden boards as they walked carefully from the steps at the far end where the *Hibiscus*'s gig had tied up. Maddox tested each board before he put down his feet, and once sidestepped hastily as the sun-dried wood gave an ominous creak.

'Not meant for my weight!' His words were apparently lost to Gunnar who strode ahead of his exec and to the doctor whose eyes were fixed on the shore end of the pier where a green painted jeep waited surrounded by a small crowd of watchers. A Chinese soldier in camouflaged green carrying an American carbine saluted sloppily and gestured towards the jeep where another soldier waited behind the wheel. Maddox noticed briefly that the jeep was extremely old, its tyres worn smooth with age, and carried a vertical piece of angle-iron fixed in front of its scarred radiator. It must have been fixed there many years earlier, he thought, for cutting barbed wire snares across roads in campaigns already forgotten.

The driver said in fractured English, 'I take you to Major.'

Gunnar sat beside him and Maddox climbed into the rear with Connell. The latter said quietly: 'Look at these poor devils. If the local inhabitants are like this, what must the prisoners be like!'

The small crowd did indeed look wretched. They were neither excited nor curious, but stared apathetically at the three newcomers with blank, empty eyes, their patched, sack-like clothes clashing with the officers' fresh khakis and the uniform of the driver.

The gears crashed, and with a jerk the jeep lurched on to a rough unmade road and gathered speed towards the top of the hill, where already the grim concrete citadel seemed bigger and more overpowering than it had appeared from the ship.

Maddox saw Gunnar look back towards the anchorage where the small submarine chaser lay alone and distorted in a dancing heat haze. He caught his eye, but the captain said nothing and turned away in his seat.

Maddox clung to the side of the jeep as it skidded round a corner in the road and began the final climb. It almost ran into a small party of labouring figures beside the track, and with sudden apprehension Maddox saw that the thin, emaciated men were in fact linked together by a slender chain, and two armed guards were watching them from beneath the shelter of a bush, their rifles trained casually as they enjoyed a quiet smoke. One of the prisoners who was trying to level a piece of roadway with a crude rake slipped and stumbled, his half-naked body pulling up short against the chain so that his companions leaned and staggered like dumb marionettes.

54

Instantly the guards dropped their rifles and began to pelt the whole party at random with pieces of jagged stone which lay in readiness to repair the road.

Mercifully the scene was swallowed up in a cloud of dust from the jeep's wheels, and Maddox heard Connell say hotly, 'Is this what we've come to see?'

Over his shoulder Gunnar said sharply, 'Wait until we've heard the whole story before you pass judgement, Doc!'

They passed noisily below a deep gateway in the concrete wall and slewed into a courtyard where the air seemed almost frigid after the heat and dust of the open road.

Although fairly new, the fort reminded Maddox vaguely of his boyhood and the first time he had read *Beau Geste*. There were even firing-steps on the high rampart for riflemen, and the deep concrete cloisters below doubtlessly housed the artillery which from this position could dominate the anchorage and the sea approaches beyond.

Several soldiers lounged in the shade and others were busy stripping and oiling a machine gun. They looked hard and well cared for, Maddox thought, and their American clothing and weapons marked them apart from the villagers by the pier.

Still hardly a word was spoken as another soldier came to guide them deeper into the fortifications which appeared to be cut into the side of the hill itself. The rough walls on either side of the entrance passage ran with moisture which glinted in the harsh electric light as they followed the small soldier past steel doors, piled ammunition cases and unused bags of cement.

The guide tapped on the final door and it was immediately jerked open to reveal a long, low room in the middle of which stood a tall, motionless figure in impeccable green fatigues and combat boots, a major of the Marine Corps.

The door closed with an echoing boom, and the room's other occupant, a marine sergeant, walked indifferently to a littered desk in the far corner with hardly a glance at Gunnar and his companions.

Major Lloyd Jago had a narrow, leathery face which like the rest of his wiry body gave the impression that everything superfluous had been sweated from it. His skin was more than tanned, it was seasoned so that his pale eyes looked out of place, flat and steady like a shark's.

Maddox watched him narrowly. He had met many marine

55

officers and had tolerated most of them. He considered that every marine had a more difficult time than his other service counterparts because of the additional burden imposed by supporting the great myth of toughness and perfection which was drummed into each and every one of them from the moment of entering the training camp. But not this Major Jago. He *was* the myth. Maddox watched him hold out his hand to Gunnar. But even that act was impersonal, like a drill movement.

Jago said: 'So you got here, Captain. Well, let's get started.' He offered a curt nod to the others. 'Maddox?' And to Connell, 'You might be useful, I guess.' He shrugged his square shoulders. 'We shall see.'

The walls of the bunker were lined with complicated-looking graphs and rotas, the coloured lines neatly marked with numbers and times, names and duties. But Maddox's attention was immediately caught by a larger-than-life reproduction of the famous photograph from the Second World War which depicted a small group of marines hoisting the Stars and Stripes after the bloody victory at Okinawa. There was also a picture of General MacArthur and one of the President. Like the major the long room was spartan and unwelcoming. The uneven floor was partly covered by rush matting, and Maddox observed a camp cot beside the humming radio set at the far end, and he wondered if Jago ever left his underground headquarters.

Gunnar said, 'I thought you might like to come out to my ship, I——'

The major interrupted with a quick wave of the hand. 'Sorry, no time.'

The sharpness of his tone was like an additional insult, and Maddox saw Gunnar's fingers grip imperceptibly at his sleeve.

Jago hurried on: 'You can forget most of your written orders. I'll give you a fresh bunch. I've been in contact by radio with the admiral and he's left it to me to fill you in.' As an afterthought he said, 'Take a seat, although I won't take long.'

He spoke in fierce, staccato sentences, and although his body remained rigid his eyes were never still. 'This is Payenhau, twenty-miles by twelve, with eight attendant islets. The present population is about eight thousand; peasants, fishing families and so forth. In addition we have several thousand convicts, men and women, who have to be guarded twenty-fours round

56

the clock.' He broke off sharply as Connell coughed. He continued in his flat, unemotional voice: 'The Nationalist Government on Taiwan are keen that this place should become a habitable place in its own right, so the convicts are used a great deal to clear road, plant crops and any other goddamned thing. Also we are building an airstrip. It'll be useful one day.'

Gunnar said evenly, 'Where do I come in?'

'I'll show you.' Jago strode to a wall map of the island and tapped it with a paper-knife. 'You can patrol the islands while you're here and keep an eye on things to the south and west. There have been a lot of suspicious craft around lately. Could be a Commie attempt in the wind to spring some of their boys from the prison here. I shall find out, and when I do——'

'Who is in charge here?' Gunnar's voice was just a little sharper but Jago did not seem to notice.

'The commandant is Colonel Tem-Chuan. He does more or less as he's told but can be quite useful. The real wheel is his second-in-command Major Yi-Fang.' The corners of the marine's mouth flickered upwards for a brief apology for a smile. 'He's good. He's really good. A soldier through and through. We have a good rapport, and he's got the right ideas about these bastards!'

'So they more or less take orders from *you*?' There was a distinct edge to Gunnar's tone now, and Maddox shifted uncomfortably in his steel chair.

'You could say that.' Jago nodded his cropped head as if he was considering the suggestion. 'I am military adviser, and what I suggest goes!'

'A lot of us thought that in Viet Nam,' Gunnar stood up and walked slowly to the map. 'We were wrong.'

'Not *me*, Captain!' Jago seemed to be enjoying himself. 'The Viet Nam circus went wrong in the first place because of outside interference and stupid politicians. No *guts*, d'you understand?'

'I don't believe in senseless brutality, Major.' Gunnar turned to face Jago, his eyes cold.

'You don't have to. All you've got to do is obey orders!' The insolence was not masked, and two spots of colour showed on Gunnar's pale cheeks. 'You can do your survey job but you'll also carry out the admiral's instructions as passed by *me*. Got it?' Jago moved to his desk and banged it with his knuckles. 'This is no Viet Nam, Captain. Here we call the tune without interruption!'

Maddox cleared his throat. 'Surely the prisoners can't escape from *here*?'

Jago eyed him as if for the first time. 'This isn't any navy college, mister. This is a tactical zone where anything goes.'

Jago tapped his holster. 'And wear sidearms when next you come ashore. You can't be too careful when you're dealing with these slope-headed bastards!' All at once he smiled. He spread his hands and said calmly: 'Look, you're under orders, so relax. I've arranged a couple of places for your men to enjoy a bit of liberty, though there's not much more than rice wine to drink! There are a few girls available, but I would advise the doctor here to keep a weather eye open!' The smile vanished. 'I'll arrange for you to see the colonel this afternoon, Captain, just to show willing. He lives in style in the other half of this place. He'll probably stay out here to die!' He laughed shortly so that he momentarily reminded Maddox of Regan.

Gunnar said, 'Is that all?' He sounded beaten.

Jago did not seem to hear. 'Just remember we've got to be little tin gods with these sort of people if we're going to get anywhere. They like discipline, furthermore they expect it!'

Connell said evenly, 'We saw some of it on the way up here.'

Jago leaned on his hands. 'What in Jesus' name did you expect? Goddamned fairies?'

He beckoned to his sergeant who had been watching the little scene with some amusement. 'Rickover! Bring that folder!' He passed it to Gunnar. 'I've put all the crap down there for you. Who to see, who to avoid, the lot!'

Gunnar answered quietly, 'I must get the survey started.'

'Jesus, a tug could do that!' Jago grinned unexpectedly. 'Still, I guess they couldn't spare a tug!'

Maddox did not remember leaving the fort, nor did he recall getting into the jeep. All he knew was anger and disappointment. He knew that Gunnar could not start a fight with his new superior, but all the same . . .

Connell whispered. 'I think the captain and Major Jago are going to get on like a house on fire, eh?'

For once Maddox could not think of an answer. As the jeep squealed down the road he watched the distant shape of the *Hibiscus* and wondered what he should do next.

Gunnar interrupted his brooding thoughts: 'A remarkable man, Jago. Like something out of a nightmare!'

Connell stared hard at the captain. 'The nightmare is right *here*.'

Maddox thought of what the ship's company would say when they heard of the extra work expected of them, and knew that the real nightmare had not even begun yet.

*　　　*　　　*

It was strange that the commandant's quarters could be so different from his U.S. military adviser's when they were in fact hewn from the same concrete structure. The main room into which Gunnar was ushered with such deference by a small Chinese servant was about the same size as Jago's bunker, but being built on a higher level it overlooked the whole anchorage by way of a wide, horizontal window, yet so thick was the outer wall that none of the sea's glare nor the powerful heat itself seemed to penetrate it. Gunnar could see his ship framed in the window like a scale model in a giant showcase, the small green islets, and even some of the interlacing channels between them. The room itself was impressive in its simplicity. The walls were covered with pale wooden panels and the floor with a cunningly interwoven pattern of mats. Some heavy chairs of old and exquisitely carved designs were placed around a centrepiece of marble which served either for a table, or as was now the case, as a support for a large bowl of tiny, transparent fish.

With a nagging irritation Gunnar saw that Jago was already in the room. It seemed this would be the pattern for the rest of his stay in Payenhau. Jago obviously did not trust Gunnar to make any personal contacts alone and thereby upset his own balance of authority. When he had returned to the ship after the morning visit ashore Gunnar had been unable to eat or rest. The insulting manner of Jago's reception had been bad enough. His folder of fresh instructions left Gunnar in no doubt as to his own position under the marine's over-all command.

Colonel Tem-Chuan made no effort to rise from his wide, carved chair, but Gunnar was neither surprised nor offended. The colonel looked incapable of movement, like a carving in his own right. He was gross, so that his circular head seemed merely a continuance of his fat body rather than a separate entity. He was either nearly bald or had once shaved his head, Gunnar thought, and the scalp was covered with a fine black fuzz, almost like down. His grotesque and unreal appearance did not end there. His eyes were hidden by the thickest pair of glasses he had ever seen, like bottle-top windows, which gave no clue to what lay behind them. But he was smiling, and one small plump hand gestured towards a chair directly in front of him. Gunnar guessed that it was so placed to save the commandant any unnecessary movement.

Another officer stood beside Jago, tall and slim, the marine's Chinese counterpart, whom Gunnar imagined was the 'perfect' Major Yi-Fang. He too was smiling with his mouth, but his deepset black eyes were hard and impassive.

The commandant settled his vast bulk in his chair and the two plump little hands smoothed down the soft olive-green cloth of his plain, ungarnished uniform.

'You are very welcome, Captain.' The mouth turned upwards in a small crescent. 'I hope your stay will be a pleasant one.'

There was a sudden movement and the soft flutter of feet across the matting, and Gunnar saw a young Chinese girl, covered from throat to ankle in a white smock, putting a tray of slender glasses and a tall decanter beside the fish bowl. With downcast eyes she stood beside the colonel's chair, as if waiting for some command or instruction.

The colonel wheezed comfortably. 'I think we will enjoy a drink to celebrate your visit, Captain.' He reached out as he was speaking and moved his hand down the servant girl's back to toy with a long plait of black hair. She kept her eyes down, but Gunnar saw her body quiver as if from pain as the commandant touched her. Like a possession, he thought. Like Laya!

He felt a glass thrust into his hand and realised that Major Yi-Fang had crossed the room with a hardly a sound. The drink was pale and therefore dangerous, he decided. Nevertheless, Gunnar downed his in one gulp, conscious of its immediate power and strange comfort. Probably made locally, he thought. The Chinese were good at that sort of thing.

Jago was staring at him strangely, but said in his flat, cold tone, 'The captain will start his surveying work tomorrow, Colonel.'

Tem-Chuan nodded equably. 'Quite so.' His English was perfect but for a slight lisp. 'I have put a boat at his disposal as you suggested.'

Jago said off handedly: 'It's a fishing boat with an old diesel. I imagine it'll be more suitable for your officers to get around the channels for soundings and measurements?'

Gunnar nodded. It was irritating him almost to breaking point the way that Jago took it upon himself to decide everything without any consultation. It might be because he had been in the habit of making all the decisions in Payenhau for so long. Or it might be something worse. Little tin gods, he had said himself. He must certainly be the most senior. Gunnar tasted his second drink and stared at the sunlit window. 'Thank you.'

Jago added with a tight smile, 'It'll leave your ship free for more important things, eh?' He and Major Yi-Fang grinned at each other like a pair of conspirators.

Damn them, Gunnar thought, they had it well planned before I dropped anchor. It made it worse to realise that Jago was probably right in his motives. Payenhau was many miles from the mainland, yet less than two hundred from another tiny island group which lay directly to the west. Owned by Red China, they were geographically useless except as a very temporary shelter for fishing boats and the like. But if some plan was afoot it might be a good jumping-off ground. He asked, 'What sort of people are detained here?'

The colonel shrugged, the effort bringing a rash of sweat to his smooth forehead. 'Scum. Political, maniacs, or just people who have lost their way in our society!' He chuckled. 'So many refugees are escaping from the mainland by way of Hong Kong that we have to watch out for the fellow-travellers. It is too easy for the Communists to smuggle agents and spies into our midst.' He took a delicate sip at his glass, and the movement made Gunnar think of a hippopotamus trying to drink from an egg cup. 'So my command here acts in two ways. It is a good place to sort over the rabble before we let them go in to Taiwan. The good we send on, the rest we keep to work.'

He had obviously seen the frown on Gunnar's face. 'We must play by the Communists' rules, Captain. They use a similar method, I believe?' He patted the girl beside him. 'It has its small rewards, however!'

Jago showed his teeth. 'She's the daughter of a real political agitator they caught in the net. He's in the prison camp here, so it pays her to be a nice girl!'

The colonel did not interrupt but chuckled even louder. 'Quite so!'

Gunnar felt sick and took another mouthful of wine. It was odd that everyone thought his problem was different out here.

Yet exactly the same mistakes had been made in Viet Nam. Corrupt and stupid officials backed up by sincere and dedicated Americans. Jago knew all this too. He must have some other scheme in mind.

'I hope you don't get bored by this place, Captain.' Yi-Fang was watching him fixedly. 'We have no other sailors for you to meet.'

Gunnar wanted to laugh. This wretched little cluster of land and rock, of poverty and suffering, yet its governors spoke to him as if he was the unwordly interloper from some backward land. He tried to think of home or of Europe and the smiling Mediterranean, but all of them seemed to elude him in the distance of time and memory.

Jago said with a grin, 'There is *one* other navy man, surely?'

They all laughed, and Jago continued in a steadier voice: 'You may meet Commander Jack Burgess, late of the British Royal Navy.' He spoke out the words as if reading an illuminated address yet the contempt was obvious in his tone. 'You'll find his details in my folder, so be warned!'

Gunnar said, 'What is he doing here?'

'This and that.' Jago seemed indifferent. 'He runs a boat for the commandant, stores and so forth. Bit of a comedown for a Limey officer!'

The commandant's thick glasses flashed as he turned his head with obvious petulance. 'He is a good fellow! A bit simple, but very useful!' To Gunnar he added severely: 'Burgess had some trouble and I helped him from the kindness of my soul. He is a solitary man, but he fights his inner battle with great fortitude.'

Jago grinned wider. 'Do anything for a drink too!'

Gunnar tried to think clearly and wished he had not hurried with his first drinks. He had met many R.N. officers when he had served with N.A.T.O. For the most part they were courteous, friendly and extremely competent. This Burgess was probably neither a commander nor even an ex-navy man. However, it would probably not matter.

Jago seemed to come to a decision. 'Now look, Gunnar. Let's get down to the matter of security. The commandant has okayed your boys using the town for liberty, but all else is off limits. Except the local beaches that is. We don't want any of them getting shot by my lads, do we? We can do without accidents at the moment.'

62

Gunnar eyed him thoughtfully. 'If you say so.' With the present mood of the crew about hanging around Payenhau it was hardly likely that anyone would be very keen on long walks over the hills anyway.

'Second point. Keep your boys away from prison working parties. I didn't like your doctor's attitude this morning, and if he's typical you'd better watch all of them!'

'I am quite capable of handling my ship, thank you, Major.' Gunnar kept his voice under control, but the growing pain behind his eyes was making him weary of Jago's assumed importance.

Jago stared at him. 'We shall see, Captain. This isn't Viet Nam, you know. You've not got a hundred jets ready to scream to your damn aid here! We're out on a limb, isolated, which is how I like it! I'm not losing my appointment here because some snotty-nosed sailor can't keep his lip buttoned!'

The commandant breathed out noisily. 'What he means, Captain, is that Payenhau is part of an experiment. We will build it up into another Nationalist stronghold. You may think it is small, yet it has the same area as Hong Kong, has it not? Who knows, one day it may become the jewel of the China Seas!' He frowned. 'But that is enough, I am very tired. Perhaps you could continue your discussions elsewhere. This morning I had to witness some executions and I am weary.' The servant made to leave but he tugged chidingly at her plait. 'Not you, my dear. Not you.'

Gunnar tried to catch her eye, but her face when he saw it was empty of everything but despair.

Outside the door Jago said quietly through his teeth, 'For Jesus' sake try to look as if you believe the old idiot! Let him dream of his jewel of the Orient if it makes him easier to get along with! He can go on TV for all I care if it'll ease the way to opening this place as a base!'

Gunnar looked at him bitterly. 'Is that what we depend on now?'

'We always have, Gunnar. He may look a fat slob, but he is well connected in Taiwan. The poor relation of a very influential family, so be warned!'

Yi-Fang, who had been listening, said, 'Fresh flowers often grow from old trees, Captain.'

There was no jeep to take Gunnar back to the pier so he began to walk down the hill alone, the sun beating across his shoulders more fiercely at each step. The wine was even more powerful than he had imagined, and he began to wish he had found time to eat something.

Someone fell in step beside him, and he looked round to see the big marine sergeant, Rickover, peering at him. 'Here's a good map of the island for you, sir. I guess the major forgot to give it you this morning.'

Rickover was a typical marine, Gunnar thought. Big, guileless and hardy. Beneath his soft cap Gunnar could see his cropped blond hair, almost as fair as his own, and he had the same well-fed sturdiness as Maddox.

The sergeant brushed away some yelling children with the well-practised ease of a man removing flies from his salad. 'Helluva dump, eh, sir?' Then he got to the point. 'I remember you, sir. I heard how you got your decoration.' He smiled with obvious admiration. 'Bloody good show, as Commander Burgess would say!'

'D'you know *him*, Sergeant?'

Rickover nodded vaguely as he watched a small squad of soldiers marching down the road. 'He's a nut, sir. But a nice nut.' After a while he added: 'Well, here we are, sir, the good old pier. Hell, it'll fall down one day, that's for sure!' As they watched the little gig curve towards the pier Rickover added uncomfortably, 'Just wanted you to know that all marines ain't enemies, sir!' He grinned with embarrassment. 'My major's a damn good officer all the same. Trouble is he doesn't think he's Jesus Christ any more. He *knows* he is!'

He was still laughing at his joke as Gunnar climbed into the gig and started back to the ship.

In the solitude of his cabin Gunnar began to sort out the faces and names of Payenhau. Added to what he already believed, Payenhau certainly seemed open for something, but even Jago must know more than he was telling. Then with quiet dedication which he thought he had lost for ever, he began to study the map of Payenhau, the Island of Tin Gods.

64

4

First Blood

The old fishing boat loaned by Payenhau's commandant to assist the *Hibiscus*'s survey had stood up to three days of almost continuous use with hardly a complaint. About thirty feet in length, flush decked and devoid of mast or deckhouse, it looked to the American seamen like yet another of the island's relics. On the third day, as it chugged noisily between two of the northern islets, the engine began to make an additional sound and almost as suddenly started to overheat.

Heiser, a tough little mechanic from the *Hibiscus*'s engine room who had been given charge of the ancient diesel and who had watched it with something like hatred since the survey had begun, hurried on deck where Lieutenant (jg) Peter Inglis stood with Anders, the chief bosun's mate. With four enlisted men they had been detailed to complete an investigation of the northern approaches, although because of the main island's high cliffs and scattered shoals it was more a formality than an aid to future navigation.

Inglis, slim and tanned in a pair of stained shorts, was peering at a chart while Anders held his sextant and watched the officer with faint amusement. Inglis took his task very seriously indeed, but unknown to Anders and the others his interest was genuine. The rough beauty of the islands, the complete isolation, affected him deeply, and even the remarks on his chart filled him with excitement. The last recorded survey of the Payenhau group was noted at the foot of the chart, carried out by a Captain Brooks, Royal Navy, of H.M. frigate *Nimrod* in 1778. In his mind's eye Inglis could easily imagine the weather-beaten frigate, sails aback, idling perhaps where his own battered boat was now while oared longboats toiled up and down the glittering water, pigtailed sailors and red-faced young English officers busy with the mysteries of lead lines and soundings while they recorded the particulars of this neglected collection of islands for posterity.

He heard Anders say, 'Well, Heiser, an' what's wrong now?' Like most professional seamen Anders was intolerant of this sort of work, and showed it.

Heiser looked at his officer and rubbed his grubby hands

with a piece of rag. 'Engine's overheating, sir. Water inlet's probably choked.'

They waited while Inglis folded his chart to cover his uncertainty. He said cautiously, 'What can you do about it?'

Heiser shrugged. 'Stop the engine. It'll seize up otherwise.' He jerked a thumb towards the nearest islet, a tilted slab of grey rock about a mile in length which rose slowly to a cliff end some two hundred feet above the sea. At the foot of the cliff, almost concealed in a deep cleft, was a heart-shaped patch of sand. 'We could beach her, I could have a good look at it then.' Heiser rocked back on his heels and waited for a decision as he listened to the engine's painful beat.

Inglis was undecided. 'Is there nothing else you can do?'

It was very hot, past midday, and Heiser was weary and irritable. 'I'm not a flamin' magician, sir!'

'That's enough of that!' Anders glared at him. 'Get back to your pit and wait for orders!' Anders was also in a bad mood. In his view Inglis was too easy, to damn soft with the likes of Heiser. The other enlisted men were lounging about either sleeping or shooting dice. It was always the same with these young officers. They wanted popularity and did not know when to get tough. Regan, the first lieutenant, had he been in charge of the party would have had everyone doing something. Right now, aboard the *Hibiscus*, he was probably drilling his gunners or supervising a massive hunt for cockroaches.

Inglish said resignedly: 'Okay, Chief. We'll run her into that cove.'

Anders grunted and yelled at the seaman by the scarred wheel: 'Head for the beach, Pirelli! Nice an' steady now!'

Pirelli, who had been half asleep in the unwavering glare, showed his teeth so that the livid white scar shone on his face like a streak of paint. 'Good as done, Chief.'

The cliff loomed overhead, and with a gentle groan of protest the boat surged up the shallow beach and came to rest with one final shudder.

Inglis said: 'Get the men ashore and leave Heiser to do his stuff. Better run out a bowline too in case she slips off.'

Anders looked at the crudely repaired hull with its obvious patches of dry rot and smiled. 'What a way to run a navy!'

The seamen jumped over the bows and wandered aimlessly up the beach. There was only a tiny patch of shade in one corner, and three of them threw themselves down with hardly a murmur.

Pirelli kicked off his shoes and paddled in the small wave-lets, his dark face bored and restless. How much longer was this stupid business going on? he wondered. The sense of drag-ging time was more evident than ever, and with an officer like Inglis it was getting worse. Baiting an officer was part of every-day life to underprivileged sailors, but with Inglis it was differ-ent. The men whined and grumbled and Inglis gave in too easily, so that for Pirelli at least all the fun had gone out of it. Even the few trips ashore in search of other distractions had only added to the general misery of the place. Two barnlike buildings had been put at their disposal, with drink, of a sort, to be had in plenty. Instead of easing tension it had sparked several open fights, and small grudges had broken out into fierce conflict. The trouble was, Pirelli decided, you could not get away from the very people you were cooped up with in the ship. Everything beyond this apology for a town was off limits, and the few roads were constantly patrolled by grim-faced soldiers armed to the teeth. Occasionally they saw groups of haggard women with hand-carts loading sacks and crates from the town's central store. They were all dressed in rough smocks and were said to be women prisoners or the wives of some of the island's detainees. It was also rumoured that in the centre of the island there was a giant prison camp which consisted of squalid huts and miles of barbed wire. Pirelli was not sure if this knowledge bothered him or not, but it did nothing to help either.

Now this poxy engine had folded. It was somehow typical of the whole thing. Before, in the *Hibiscus*, events had moved from day to day with the pleasant if dull routine of a normal ship. Until the new plans had been put into practice and the fresh captain had taken charge. Then there was Bella. . . .

Pirelli kicked moodily at a pebble and marvelled at the change which had come over the young, dark-eyed yeoman. Bella had tasted popularity as if for the very first time in his life. He used Pirelli's protection in the crew space to enlarge his own position, but worse, he seemed incapable of keeping his mouth shut about the captain. The crew were dissatisfied enough without Bella adding to their gloom. He appeared to enjoy nothing more than when he had an audience and he could enlarge on something the captain had said or done, or something overheard amongst the other officers. Pirelli openly scorned authority of any kind. He had been promoted and busted himself with faithful regularity and cared nothing for

67

advancement. Yet he cared very much for his own private backwater, and this new form of 'treachery' on Bella's part made him uneasy.

He stared upwards towards the top of the cliff. It was jagged and patterned with countless bird droppings. Above it the sky was bright blue and the cliff's shelter held the sun's heat like the walls of an oven.

From the fishing boat's hull came the intermittent clang of metal, and Pirelli guessed that Heiser, now he was alone, was more than likely reading one of his lurid paperbacks while he occasionally slammed the old engine with a spanner to make it sound as if he was working. Then, when it was too late to do any more buggering about with his stupid chart, Inglis would be told it was okay to get under way and so return to the ship.

Pirelli climbed over two sharp rocks, and after relieving himself amongst the green weeds by the water's edge he began to saunter round the narrow strip of sand. The hammering from the boat faded behind him, and once when he looked back he saw Inglis staring at the listing hull as if he expected a miracle to happen. Pirelli grinned in spite of his discomfort and pulled on his shoes. Perhaps a climb up this stupid cliff would pass the time. Not too far in case Inglis decided to shove off without him. After about ten minutes he found a possible path up the cliff, more like a goat track, but it was better than nothing. It was like being a castaway with nothing and nobody for hundreds of miles. Nothing moved, and even the sea was muted as he climbed steadily up the rock face, the sweat pouring down his strong, hairy arms.

* * *

Inglis threw the bowline over the stem of the boat and stepped back on to the beach. He should have roused the three drowsing seamen to do this job but he could no longer be bothered with their grumbling. Heiser, his face streaked with grease, peered down at him. 'Put her astern, Heiser.'

The mechanic was about to point out that it was hardly a task for an engineer when he noticed the edge to the lieutenant's voice and decided to obey without query. It had taken three hours to fix the engine, although he had to admit he could have done it in about fifteen minutes. 'Then what, sir?'

Inglis frowned. 'Back off and run it ahead and astern a

couple of times to make sure it's running okay. Then beach her again.'

Chief Anders looked up from his sitting position on a slab of rock. Who cares? he thought. It'll probably break down again tomorrow. Why the hell doesn't Inglis yell at these lazy bastards? Anders toyed with the idea of doing so himself but decided he had already carried the young officer quite enough. He saw the bowline fall untidily into the water just as the engine wheezed into life and began to move the boat clear of the beach. With a growl Anders struggled to his feet and sloshed into the water to gather up the rope before that fool Heiser allowed it to foul the screw when he pushed back up the beach. A loop of rope caught his ankle and with a profane curse he was dragged into deep water before he could free himself. Spluttering with fury he swam after his cap and heard someone laughing from the beach.

Only Inglis saw what happened next. There was a soft thud in the sand by his feet. Immediately he looked up, blinking at the sunlight above the cliff's ragged crest. He imagined he saw a brief movement, like a head being quickly withdrawn. Frowning, he looked at the thing which had narrowly missed him, and then fell back with horror.

Chief Anders had just reached his sodden cap when the hand grenade exploded. At first, in those fractional seconds his reeling mind imagined that the engine had burst, and he instinctively ducked below the surface to shield himself. The action of being pulled into deep water by the bowline saved his life, the last movement saved him from the actual sight of the explosion.

When he eventually waded ashore the beach was quiet as before. Only a black hole and the thin haze of smoke betrayed the passage of death, and with sick horror Anders staggered up the beach, his eyes mesmerised by the great scarlet patches around the three sailors who still lay in their attitudes of rest, propped up as they had been to watch the chief swimming after his cap. Their bodies were glistening with a dozen gaping wounds, and without going to them he knew they were already dead. Inglis lay on his back, and without thought for any further danger Anders tore off his shirt and began to twist it into a tourniquet. Anders heard himself sobbing with angry desperation as he attempted to hang on to the life in the poor torn thing at his feet. Inglis's face was a mass of blood, and he could see his teeth gleaming through a great gash in one cheek. But

69

he had lost an arm below the elbow and one of his legs lay at a nightmare angle like part of a rag doll.

Anders wheeled round as he heard the scuffle of feet behind him, the vomit thick in his throat as he waited for another explosion. With a gasp of relief he saw Pirelli's stricken face, watched the dazed incredulity in the man's staring eyes.

'Quick! Call Heiser!' Anders' voice was harsh. 'Don't stand there gawping!'

The boat beached once more, and stumbling with their bloody load Anders and Pirelli levered Inglis's body over the bulwark. Heiser refused to show himself, but between the engine's heavy beats they could hear him whimpering like a frightened child. But the boat glided astern, and after what seemed like an age edged its way clear of the shoals so that Pirelli was able to put the wheel over and head for the open water.

Anders stayed with Inglis, unable to help or even to speak as the young officer tried to move beneath his grip. Once as a spasm of pain lanced through him Inglis twisted free, and the chart he had so meticulously guarded fell blood-spattered and torn on to the deck. Anders threw it overboard and peered astern at the silent island. Like stiff spectators he could still see the three dead seamen, and wanted to call their names, to find the right words.

Pirelli said nothing, and he was aware for practically the first time in his life that he could not see because of the mist across his eyes. One of the dead seamen was Grout, his friend. Lying back there like a freshly slaughtered pig. In those brief seconds he changed from a man to a nothing. No recognition, no shape. Just a thing. Torn, gouged and broken. Pirelli dashed his forearm across his eyes and cursed between his teeth. He did not know or understand what had happened or why it had been done, any more than he realised what had made him take that lonely walk along the beach away from the others.

Hours later as the little boat thudded round the headland beyond the anchorage Pirelli was still repeating like a prayer: 'The bastards! The goddamn bloody bastards!'

The boat ground alongside the anchored *Hibiscus*, and Anders stood back to allow the scrambling familiar figures to crowd aboard. He saw the doctor, Connell, bending over the body, heard him passing quick, urgent instructions to the pharmacist's mate. Later the doctor said, 'I think he might live.'

Anders watched the bandaged figure being handed up over

70

the ship's rail, his eyes hot and angry. 'D'you call *that* living?' Then oblivious to the men who lined the ship's side he walked to the bulwark and retched. Then he wiped his mouth and watched the gig as it roared from its parent ship and headed for the shore.

That's right, he thought. Start the wheels turning now that it's too damn late! What do they care anyway! Just another goddamn *incident*!

But Pirelli thought differently. Already he had found Regan who had been left in charge of the ship. 'I want to go with the landing party, sir!'

Regan, his face tight and grim, eyed him warily. 'Are you fit for it?'

Pirelli swayed. 'I'm fit for them bastards! Just you try me!'

Regan turned away to watch the fast-moving gig. We'll see what the new captain makes of *this*, he thought.

* * *

Major Jago sat stiffly behind his desk and watched Gunnar stride back and forth across the underground bunker. Maddox was in the same steel chair he had occupied on the first visit, and like Jago followed the captain's shadow, his face heavy with concern.

Jago said again, 'I understand your problem, but action of the sort you suggest is not going to help.' He jerked his head towards the wall map. 'I sent two L.C.I.s and a couple of patrols to the islet in question and we should get a report at any moment.'

Gunnar paused in his pacing his chest working painfully. 'What the hell do you expect me to think? Three men dead and an officer cut to ribbons!'

Gunnar hardly recognised his own voice. It seemed incredible that so much had happened and so quickly. He had been with Maddox on the headland where the exec's shore party had been marking out the possible site for a radar reflector, when a white-faced and breathless Lieutenant Kroner had stammered out the news about Inglis and the others. Almost without pause Gunnar had ordered Kroner to return to the ship, to tell Regan to prepare for sea at once, to assemble an armed landing party. Jago's summons should have warned him, but even now he could hardly believe that the marine was so indifferent.

71

In his mind he could still see the picture of Inglis's mutilated face above the splinted and bandaged limbs as they had ferried him ashore to the citadel's sick quarters. Connell was staying with him until he could be flown out.

Jago continued flatly: 'Men get killed every day. There are always incidents, even here. You've got to be on your guard.'

'Your guard seems to be less than useless!' Gunnar was standing over the other man his eyes blazing. 'What d'you expect me to do? *Apologise?*'

Jago frowned. 'I expect you to behave like a responsible officer, Captain! I'm sorry for your young lieutenant, I'm damn sorry for anyone who gets killed out here.' He shrugged. 'But you should know well enough that these Reds aren't playing games. But if you go pooping off your ship's armament every time some wandering sailors run into trouble, you'll get no thanks from me, and none at all from headquarters either!'

He watched Gunnar's pale face intently. 'We have to move cautiously. The British wouldn't be keen on us starting something on their doorstep in Malaysia, neither would Washington welcome a spread of action which might antagonise Taiwan. We've got to make the local garrison *work*, to do its stuff, otherwise we might as well pack up and go home. Hell, Captain, the commandant here has only got a skeleton battalion, plus a few locally recruited characters. The latter are a bit rough, not combat material as yet.' He seemed to make up his mind. 'Anyway, I've radioed for instructions and the admiral backs me one hundred per cent. So just tighten up your security and stand fast, Captain. You can help me by making a sweep of the islands to the north and west, starting tomorrow. Just routine, but keep your eyes peeled. Any boat you see that you don't have in your supplement is suspect. Stop and search it, detain it if necessary, but no goddamn punitive expeditions, got it?'

Sergeant Rickover said sharply from the corner, 'Here it comes, Major!'

The radio stuttered and a voice said in broken English, 'Hello, Dodger, this is Hunter calling!'

Jago was on his feet and had the handset in his fist before the others could move. 'Come in, Hunter, this is Dodger!'

The set crackled. 'Hello, Dodger. We are in position Four X-Ray. We have recovered bodies of three dead sailors and have taken two Reds. Over.'

Jago looked flushed. 'Have you got an interrogation going yet? Over!'

A short pause. 'Negative. Both Reds dead after patrol landed.' Another pause, and Maddox saw the bitterness on Jago's face, his guard momentarily dropped. 'The three sailors' bodies had been bayoneted after death. Request instruction. Over.'

'Return to base, Hunter. Over and out.' Jago dropped the handset. 'A couple of Reds, eh. Probably some of the guerrillas we've had dropped on the island over the past few weeks. There have been a few shootings and so forth. Things are hotting up.' He banged his fists together. 'What wouldn't I give for a hundred marines!'

Gunnar said coldly, 'When can we get Lieutenant Inglis flown out?'

Jago sounded distant. 'Tomorrow morning. I've radioed for a chopper. He'll be okay.'

Gunnar saw again the fresh, eager young lieutenant on the bridge as he had been when *Hibiscus* left Hong Kong, holding down the con as if his life depended on it. Now disfigured, with one arm gone and maybe a leg when the surgeons got going on him, he was being written off. He felt the muscles tightening around his waist like steel bands so that his breathing began to hurt him. The bastards! Not content with open murder, they had to mutilate the three dead seamen with their bayonets. He said aloud: 'I'll want another fishing boat, Major, or one of your L.C.I.s. I'm not trusting the lives of my men to any more clapped-out junks.' He paused, and Maddox almost felt the contempt in his voice. 'Especially as their lives don't seem to count for much around here!'

Major Jago leaned back his hands flat on the desk. 'See the Limey, Burgess. His boat is the only other one with a good diesel. I'll okay it with the commandant.'

Rickover interrupted quietly: 'You'll find it on the west side of the anchorage, Captain. He has a house of sorts there.'

'I'll find it.' Gunnar picked up his cap. 'I'm just saying this, and I'm saying it once only. If my men get fired on again, and I'm on the spot, I'll see that something is done about it, and damn quick!'

Surprisingly the marine major grinned. 'That's the stuff, Captain!'

73

Gunnar walked to the door. 'Go to hell,' he answered calmly.

* * *

The three dead seamen lay in another bunker shrouded in flags, side by side as they had been on the unknown beach. Barely feet away, two crumpled figures in camouflaged green uniforms, each with a crude red star sewn above the pocket, lay wide-eyed and grinning with unseeing eyes.

Captain Pak, leader of the patrol which had searched the islet, prodded one of the corpses with his boot. 'Pity we not catch them before they die,' he said sadly. He pointed at two Czechoslovakian burp guns and a pack of grenades. 'This is all they have.'

Gunnar took a last look at the other three draped bodies and saluted without really noticing his own action. They too would be flown out in the morning.

He heard Maddox speaking quietly behind him, and turned to see the exec whispering to Connell. The doctor glanced at the still forms and said flatly: 'Inglis has died, Captain. Never recovered consciousness.'

Gunnar could only stare at him. Not even Inglis had been spared. This place was like the realisation of a curse from the past. He was bringing death and misery again, just as he had before. Thickly he said, 'I thought you said he would be all right.'

Connell shrugged. 'It was bad, sir. A sudden haemorrhage and that was it.'

You callous bastard, Gunnar thought savagely. Like all bloody doctors! Connell walked past him and peered at the remains of the dead guerrillas. Then without a word he walked after Gunnar and the exec out into the fresh mild night with its high stars and the reassuring murmur of the sea.

Over his shoulder Gunnar said harshly: 'Why the curiosity, Doctor? Did you want to perform on them too?'

Connell's face was hidden. 'I was curious, Captain. I still am.'

Maddox interrupted, 'Leave it, Bruce, for Christ's sake!'

The doctor said quietly, 'I am just curious to know how our men were bayoneted by those guerrillas we just saw.'

Gunnar wheeled round, his face white in the dim light. 'I see what you mean!' He gripped Maddox by the sleeve so that they all hung together in a small swaying group. 'Those machine guns which were taken off them don't *have* bayonets . . .' He paused uncertainly. 'Unless there was something else?'

Connell shook his head. 'No, Captain. Whoever did that to our boys, it wasn't either of those!'

Gunnar broke away and began to hurry towards the pier.

Maddox said, 'For God's sake, now look what you've done to him!'

The doctor shrugged. 'I know, Bob. But it's *us* I'm worried about now.'

Ahead of them Gunnar hurried along the rickety pier, heedless of the treacherous palings below his feet. It was all dropping into place at last. The Reds knew well enough the importance of Payenhau as a base for the Americans. They would not be fooled by the pretence of keeping it as a prison camp or anything else. It was the same old pattern of agents, spies and saboteurs. Ruse and infiltration by terror, and poor Inglis had stumbled on some of them by mistake. Where were the others, and how many were there?

It would be easy to land guerrillas by submarine or PT boat under cover of darkness, but the garrison was already aware of that fact. There was something else, something missing. He was still pondering as the gig nudged the piles of the pier and the coxswain called the boat's crew to attention.

Gunnar sat quietly opposite the other two officers and was aware how steady his nerves felt even with this additional burden. Yet he was more conscious than ever of the tightness of his command and the importance of mere individuals perhaps for the first time.

* * *

The wheelhouse of the *Hibiscus* was stuffy and humid, and only by constant use of the fans and clear-view screens could the watch-keepers see beyond the ship's corkscrewing bows. Heavy droplets of rain blew against the toughened glass windows, and black, heavy-bellied clouds scudded across the angry, restless rollers which broke with spasmodic fury into long, yellow-capped crests as they cruised to meet the slow-moving submarine chaser.

Mark Gunnar rubbed his knuckles across his teeth to stifle another yawn and felt the cold tiredness tugging relentlessly

75

at his limbs. He desperately wanted to sit down and rest his legs and body from the deck's vicious pitching motion. Several times he let his eye stray to the tall, uncomfortable chair in one corner of the wheelhouse which seemed more enticing with each passing moment.

For hours they had plunged and bucked their way towards the angry horizon which had suddenly faded into a pewter haze of rain squalls and broken water, with every rivet and plate groaning and jarring in protest. Occasionally an extra powerful roller would lift the ship's stern clear of the sea, so that the screws raced with released madness and shook the hull from end to end like a wild thing. The next instant the stern would bury itself, and the fantail and canting steel deck would sluice down with white foam and flying balls of spume. At this time of year storms were infrequent but sudden, widely scattered across the vastness of the China Seas but all the more savage in their search for victims. For two days the little ship had prowled round the islands, invisible from the land, but checking each blurred flash on the radar screen, and straining the nerves of every man aboard.

Out of the blue had come a radio message. A coded rendezvous, a small pencilled cross which had to be translated into a factual spot on the madly tossing water.

Hibiscus had sighted two junks heading for Payenhau and had stopped both of them. The weather had not worsened at that time, and Gunnar conned the ship directly alongside each vessel in turn, while helmeted gunners swung the slim muzzles of the twenty-millimetres across the much repaired and patched junks, covering the scurrying Chinese sailors as they manhandled the ribbed sails and peered curiously at the grey warship.

Each time Maddox had returned with his boarding party shaking his head. Food, fish and a few goats seemed to comprise the average cargo. Gunnar remembered how men and guns had been smuggled in similar vessels before, by way of false bottoms fixed in the holds of these ancient craft. The idea had first blossomed during the Japanese occupation of Hong Kong and Singapore, when friendly Chinese had smuggled refugees and stores for the starving and ill-treated British. The concept stayed with many a junk captain as one war and disaster followed another. It was easy to dodge the patrols, and far more profitable than bags of rice. But Maddox found nothing even after Gunnar had made him return, and the

76

weird, batlike craft had vanished astern. Gunnar wondered how they fared in the sudden storm, how in fact they managed to navigate at all.

He wrenched his wandering thoughts back to the coming rendezvous. Kroner had checked the coded numbers, and Gunnar knew that the submarine he was to meet was the *Grampus*, one of the navy's reconditioned subs which although conventionally powered was fitted with Regulus guided missiles. He glanced at his watch, it would be any minute now. The sonarmen had already fixed the submarine's steady approach, and no doubt her skipper had taken several looks at the pitching *Hibiscus*.

Gunnar tried to concentrate on what lay ahead rather than allow the lurking anger to blunt his judgement. He was neither trusted nor consulted, he and his ship were like underprivileged messengers. Jago must have known full well about this rendezvous when he dreamed up the island patrol, and probably jumped at the chance to arrange it if only to rid his small dominion of Gunnar's interference.

'Submarine surfacing on the port bow, sir!'

Gunnar hung to the rail and pulled himself out on to the unprotected bridge wing. The hot, stinging wind forced his clothes against his body, and the spray and heavy raindrops soaked him to the skin even as he levelled his glasses. With something like envy he watched the ugly black hull heave itself bodily from the depths and bury its snout into the first challenging roller. Spray ran from the conning tower where he could already see small oilskinned figures shining like seals on a sea-swept rock, and the jumping wire above the boat's whaleback which glittered with droplets like a string of diamonds.

Recognition signals flicked briefly across the pitching water, and within minutes a rubber boat was being shoved clear of the submarine's ballast tank to take its chance on the crossing. A hastily thrown heaving line was seized by one of the boat's handlers and within two more hazardous minutes it was squeaking against the *Hibiscus*'s pitted plates.

Gunnar gritted his teeth against the wind and lowered himself down the ladder to where Maddox and Regan waited by the rail. He had to shout above the wind, and saw that Maddox's face was apprehensive and set. All his good humour had vanished since Inglis's death, and the gloom in the wardroom had helped to add to the general air of watchful resentment.

Gunnar shouted: 'Stand off and rendezvous again as or-

77

dered! I'll be as quick as I can!'

Maddox tugged on his cap and bowed his head against the spray. 'Right, sir! The glass is still falling!'

Gunnar slung his leg over the rail and realised he had not brought his lifejacket. The tiny rubber dinghy rose level with his knee and then fell just as suddenly into another black trough. It would probably solve everybody's troubles if I drowned, he thought. No struggle, no fight, just sink into nothingness. He shook himself. 'Run for Payenhau if it gets any worse and lie to leeward!' Then he had stumbled into the rubber cockleshell amongst the straddled legs and straining seamen, and was just as suddenly clear of his own ship's side. It was strangely peaceful after the *Hibiscus*'s swaying bridge, only the motion was cruel and eager, the sounds and anger of the weather were muffled and indistinct as the boat swam through the high-sided troughs like a water turtle.

A lurch, curses from the seamen, and grabbing hands to haul him up the slime-covered ballast tank. More wind tearing at his legs, and indistinct figures pushing him to the unfamiliar ladder and the sheltered severity of the conning tower. Like a helpless prisoner he was pushed to one side as hatches banged shut and the O.O.D. landed on top of the retreating lookouts from the bridge party.

It was another world, and Gunnar tried to follow each precise movement and listen to every terse command. The slender depth needles began to move, while the planesmen spun their polished wheels and sat back in their chairs to watch instruments like tote operators at a racetrack. The captain, a small nuggety commander in a spray-spotted parka, grinned at Gunnar and gestured towards a swinging green curtain by one of the doors off the control room. 'The brass is waiting, Captain!' Over his shoulder he said: 'Steady! Up periscope!' With a hiss one of the periscopes slid from its bed, and after a preliminary inspection the captain said, 'Want a look?'

Gunnar lowered his head, sensing the other man's eyes on him, for a moment he could see nothing and then involuntarily he ducked as a giant distorted wave-crest reared towards him and burst over the lens. It was a weird sensation. Like swimming alone in a storm yet feeling nothing in a mad, silent sea. It was even hard to believe that the boat had dived to periscope depth, but for the gentle dials and the steady tilt of the deck. The lens cleared and then he saw her. At this angle she looked unprotected and strangely helpless. The *Hibiscus* held the

78

storm's grey light on her hull so that the spray-soaked steel gleamed like phosphorescence and the vessel's sickening motion became more apparent. One moment Gunnar could see her streaming deck and the lashed depth-charges, the next he could see part of her bilge keel and one brightly racing screw. Helpless she was too, he thought grimly, held in the periscope crosswires like an insect in a spider's web. He stepped aside and watched the periscope slide back to its bed.

The submarine's damp, musty air made him feel slightly sick, and he was conscious of the other smells of sweat and oil fuel, of food and men packed closely together. All around the world men were living and acting like this. Or dying like Inglis and the others. And for what? Most of the people at home were ignorant of what was happening, enjoyed their TV wars and the knowledge that 'someone' was doing the job of keeping the peace.

The other captain said quietly: 'You go on into the wardroom. There'll be coffee and a bite as soon as you've finished your conference.' He grinned so that his bristly face seemed younger. 'You must be in the top league to warrant this treatment!'

Gunnar forced a smile. If only you knew, he thought. Then with a nod to the other man he walked into the tiny wardroom, where a thin, hollow-cheeked officer sat staring at a chessboard. He was in khakis, but unlike the submarine's officers looked relaxed and well groomed. He was a rear-admiral, but had the grey-haired severity of a schoolmaster. He shook Gunnar's wet hand. 'I'm Sanders,' he announced crisply. 'I expect you've heard of me.' It was not a question or a boast. Merely a dried-out statement suitable for such a man.

Gunnar seated himself on a bench seat. Of course he knew Sanders. One of the C.-in-C.'s top intelligence brains. He popped up everywhere, and although he shunned publicity he sometimes appeared on the corners of impressive power groups in the newspapers of a dozen different countries. N.A.T.O., S.E.A.T.O., United Nations, or a top-level foreign conference, Sanders was never far away.

Now he was sitting at a littered table opposite Gunnar in a submerged submarine in the middle of the South China Sea. He pulled a manilla folder from a much used briefcase, and Gunnar observed that it was dog-eared and patterned with tiny pencilled notes.

Rear-Admiral Sanders stared at the open folio and said:

'I heard about your patch of bad luck. I was sorry to hear about young Inglis. He came of a good family. Might have done something with him one day.'

Gunnar remembered Inglis's nagging indecision and lack of confidence and tried to see him as the admiral was doing.

Sanders added: 'Still, that's how it goes. Might be killed by Red snipers or you could get flattened by a drunk driver! That's our advanced way of life, I guess.' He swivelled his eyes on to Gunnar's tired face. 'How are you finding things in Payenhau?'

It was a loaded question and Gunnar answered slowly, 'I've nearly finished the survey assignment.' As there was no immediate reply nor any change in the admiral's steady eyes he added, 'I expect to be ordered to Taiwan soon to hand over my command.' He kept the bitterness from his tone but saw the other man's face stiffen.

Sanders said, 'I'm afraid I can't promise you any changes yet.' He tapped the papers. 'Things are moving everywhere, and right now I need your ship in Payenhau.'

'I don't quite see——' Gunnar was cut short.

'Of course if you'd rather hand over command to another officer, I guess I could fly someone out?' The admiral's voice was casual. 'Naturally I'd rather keep everything calm and quiet, with you at the helm, so to speak.'

Gunnar tried again. It was useless trying to look for an opening. 'I just want to know what's going on, sir. It's obvious I'm not welcomed by Major Jago, and the place itself is as open as a prison!'

Sanders gave a small, wintry smile. 'I gathered Jago is not mad about you either!' He dismissed it all with a shrug. 'Can't be helped. He's a good man, and *you* are available.' He cocked his head. 'Hear that?'

Gunnar listened as the admiral watched him across the table. Faintly at first, and then more insistent above the purr of the submarine's electric motors he heard the steady beat of machinery, like the distant mutter of a freight train.

The admiral grinned. 'Your ship, Captain. She's up there, and every man aboard is wondering like hell what you're up to. Well, let 'em, it's good for their souls!' He wriggled in his seat. 'Now listen, my boy, and listen good. I know your record, and I know a lot more about you than many others do. And I can *guess* what I don't know for sure. You've a chip on your shoulder and you're bitter. The tangle will sort itself out, but I've not the time to worry about your personal troubles. There are more urgent things happening. Payenhau's fast becoming another problem. Something's brewing up and we don't know the whole picture as yet. But one thing is definite, the Reds have got their beady eyes on it, and they're not fooling. The trouble is,' he peered at his small chessmen as if looking for a solution, 'they have a good angle this time. Payenhau does not in fact belong to the Nationalists any more than to the Reds. It was merely a fishing community, a stopover for traders and so forth under the old regime. The Nationalists put their prison camp there without asking a soul, and then reinforced it with a military governor and so forth. *We* had to play along without much caring either way. But there was a self-supporting community there before the troops took over. Some say the old leaders are lying low and waiting for the troops and prisoners to go. You and I know that will never happen.'

Gunnar found that he was no longer tired nor even conscious of the strange surroundings. 'What can the Reds do, sir? The Seventh Fleet would wipe out any invasion threat surely?'

'It's not that simple. If the Reds can convince the islanders from within that their cause is just, that the commandant is merely a lackey of the imperialists, *and* that he intends to allow a giant U.S. base to be built, they might just be able to spring something.'

'I still don't see the problem, sir. We could swamp the place with men,' he remembered with sudden clarity Major Jago's words, 'give me one hundred marines', 'or the Nationalists could do it from Taiwan.'

The admiral touched a pawn and shook his head. 'Not now. Too tricky. We have already been approached by certain parties through the British at Hong Kong, warned if you like, that a build-up of our forces would be seen as a threat to security.' He shook his head more firmly. 'No, it's not on. Not for the moment, that is. We've got enough fuss in South East Asia and the damn offshore islands without adding to the mess. In addition, we've got two big fleet movements going on at present which leave our forces a bit thin on the ground round Payenhau. We must contain this problem not fan it into flame. We've got the nuclear subs and rocket conventionals like this one, but they are useless for this sort of caper. Like trying to kill a fly with a depth-charge!' He smiled and

81

added, 'They'll do when the "crunch" comes, but not until.'

Gunnar listened for the sound of *Hibiscus*'s engines but they had faded again. He wondered whether the storm had worsened, and if Maddox could cope with the ship. It was odd that he felt a sense of loss now he was away from the old *Hibiscus* and all her faults. They were not of her making, any more than they were his. Down here it was hard to imagine weather or even time. There was no motion, and little sound but for the motors' even purr and the tick of a clock in the damp, oil-laden air. He said, 'As I see it, sir, my ship is a sort of guinea-pig?'

'I like to think of her as my "feeler" in Payenhau. To be honest I'm not sure what's going to happen, but my British friends assure me that the Reds are afraid of our becoming wholly involved there. We are *not*, we must make the Nationalist Chinese stand on their own feet and fight for a belief and not just a nation. The United States is pouring billions of dollars into every country outside the Communist bloc. It therefore follows that we must occasionally bolster up countries and regimes which are otherwise unworthy. Countries whose only asset is that they are not committed to the communist way of life. We do not want total involvement out here, but we will not budge from our obligations.' He paused and drummed thoughtfully on the table. 'Go back to your ship and return to Payenhau. If the storm breaks we will help you all we can *later*. But at the first sign of trouble it may be your discretion which is all that will count in the long run.'

Gunnar felt unable to hide the sense of disappointment the admiral's last words had given him. If the Communists attacked the island, *Hibiscus* would be sacrificed to allow the Seventh Fleet's massive retaliation. If they did not, the ship would be kept hanging about until everyone was either used to her or sick of the sight of her, according to which side he was on. On top of all that there now seemed doubt as to the justification of their presence there at all.

The submarine commander poked his head round the curtain. 'Gale's moderating up top, sir. I think it would be as well for the captain here to get across to his ship before it changes its mind again.'

The admiral nodded as if it was all arranged. 'Very well.' He took a long look at Gunnar's drawn face. 'Be ready for trouble, boy, but keep out of it if at all possible.'

Gunnar asked the one question he had nursed since he had

joined the ship at Hong Kong. 'Was I specially selected for this job, sir? Or did it just happen?'

The admiral stood up and looked at the clock. 'The powers that be make many decisions about strategy and tactics, some of them excellent. Unfortunately they are eventually left to mere men to carry out.' He held out his hand. 'Good luck. When *Hibiscus* returns to the fleet I'll be there to answer your question. If there *is* an answer.' His tone hardened. 'But Payenhau is *not* going to be another Cuba!'

The air thundered into the ballast tanks and the deck tilted once more. Orders were shouted, and Gunnar heard a hatch slam open.

The admiral followed him to the brightly lit control room. 'There's just one more thing. Remember that Payenhau is one tight community. They've all got their own little axes to grind and they'll not like interference. If any trouble was sparked off by unnecessary friction it might leak out to the world press.' He smiled. 'If that happens, your popularity rating might fall considerably. Now get going, and watch the signs!'

Gunnar climbed up to the sea and the storm-filled clouds, a world he knew and trusted more than any admiral's half-truths. He tried to see himself as he appeared to the distant planners who had selected him for the vague task ahead. Taking it all round, he thought calmly, they could not have chosen a better man for a scapegoat. If Payenhau proved to be a satisfactory ending to some long-hatched plan then others would reap the credit. But if it did not, there was little doubt in his mind as to where the blame would lie.

5

Burgess

Robert Maddox licked a fragment of scrambled egg from the corner of his mouth and stepped out on to the maindeck, his eyes automatically squinting against the reflected glare. He had consumed a late breakfast, a lone diner in the deserted wardroom, and was now as ready to face another day as he ever would be. It was an odd sensation to look over the rail and see land alongside. Not the distant dried-up scrub of the Payenhau hills, but the pier itself.

Returning from the fruitless patrol and the rendezvous with the submarine, the *Hibiscus* had secured alongside the unsafe-looking piles with the delicacy of a man cracking eggs with a hammer. Whatever else Gunnar might or might not be, Maddox decided, he sure could handle a ship. Stern first, with hardly enough power to give the rudder steerageway, he had conned her straight for the jutting mess of timber and iron stakes until Maddox imagined he would ram it on to jagged bits of broken supports below the pier, or even worse, on to the beach beyond. Neither had happened. Gunnar had stayed immobile on the screen above the upper bridge his feet straddled, his eyes fixed on the narrowing gap of water. Then with a gentle nudge, a few curses and a hasty flurry of froth from the propellers *Hibiscus* had nestled alongside.

After a brief visit to Major Jago, Gunnar had retired to his quarters and left the ship's officers to their own devices and an uneasy night. Of the storm there was hardly a trace. Only one roofless hut by the beach and the tough hillside grass, ruffled like the coarse fur of some animal which has been brushed the wrong way, marked its passing.

Now it was another working day. Another day of confusion and mixed emotions, Maddox thought, as he watched Lieutenant Regan's stiff shoulders leading a crocodile of seamen down the pier and then right towards the headland. The ship felt listless and deserted, and Maddox had to brace himself to greet Chief Tasker who stood with his usual melancholy expression as he pondered over a list of working parties.

He saluted and said, ' 'Morning, sir.' His hollow eyes moved briefly over Maddox's frame as if in silent criticism for his late appearance. 'Both boats away, sir. Mister Kroner's gone with the gig, and Chief Anders has taken the other boat to the shallows by the West Channel with a sounding party.'

Maddox grunted. It was strange how they named places and positions with such casual indifference. It was as if they had been here for years. He peered at the small party of seamen on the pier who were rolling fifty-gallon fuel drums towards the town, their progress slow and unsteady because of the rough planking under their feet. When the ship had left Hong Kong the upper deck had been burdened with these drums which contained petrol for mobile generators which were required for supplying power ashore. Concrete and cement had to be mixed for firm bases upon which the crude-looking radar reflectors could be mounted at several vantage points near the main entrance channels to the anchorage, although Maddox secretly doubted if the captain of a super nuclear submarine would ever depend on such aids to navigation.

The reflectors, wrapped in canvas covers, were already lying on the pier, and the space they had left on the ship's narrow deck already seemed to make the *Hibiscus* quite spacious. Maddox knew that the captain was unwilling to allow the deck cargo to go ashore until it was actually required, but after the ship's behaviour in the sudden storm there was little choice. With the top hamper playing hell with the vessel's fine-edged stability the *Hibiscus* had rolled and bucked from one impossible angle to the next, and Maddox knew that had they been required to perform some extra manœuvre they might have been in real trouble.

'How many men left aboard, Chief?'

Tasker squinted at his list. 'Twelve engine-room hands and this working party of ten, sir.'

'Go and ask Mister Malinski if he can spare a few more, Chief. We want to get this unloading and stacking completed as soon as possible. They'll be flopping down in the heat otherwise!'

Tasker grimaced. 'Do 'em good,' was his sour reply, but he shambled away nevertheless, deep in his own thoughts.

Maddox walked aft to the fantail and looked towards the silent town. There was, of course, no traffic noise or the sound of industry, but all the same it did appear more deserted than usual. The soldiers who normally guarded the end of the pier were absent too, and Maddox wondered if they had gone to join with the bulk of the garrison in the manœuvres or whatever they were in the north of the islands. Gunnar had mentioned the troops' activity upon his return from Jago's H.Q., and Maddox imagined the marine major would by now be in his element. Playing at soldiers, he thought bitterly, like all the rest of his kind. He kept thinking of Inglis, and try as he might he could not drive away the idea that he had died needlessly and because of someone's stupidity.

He heard a scrape of feet and saw Malinski's sallow features peering at him around the gun shield of the forty-millimetre. 'I've sent up nearly all my men, Bob,' he announced wearily. 'There's not much for 'em to do here anyway.'

Maddox smiled. 'Thanks. It's this sort of life which demands a constant supply of beer, ice-cold and in very large bulk!'

Malinski nodded. 'Too right.' He wiped his greasy hands. 'What's the celebration ashore then? An election?'

Maddox grinned and turned his head. 'More like a day of mourning, it's just about——' He broke off, his jaw dropping in amazement. The wide dusty arrowhead of roads beyond the pier which had been so completely deserted had just as suddenly been blocked with figures. A silent, slow-moving crowd of townspeople, their shapeless, work-stained clothing binding them together into something sinister and somehow frightening.

Malinski saw Maddox's face and said, 'Trouble, d'you think?'

Maddox licked his lips. He felt as if he was losing control of something, but he could not clear his thoughts enough to decide. The mass of people approaching the pier seemed to mesmerise him, to hold him with its quiet, shuffling approach. 'Hell, I can't make them out!'

Malinski darted a glance at the small working party on the pier who were already standing upright and peering first at the crowd and then back at the ship.

Maddox said tightly, 'If this is trouble we'd better do something, and damn quick!' To the shore party the ship was a haven, a safe place. But Maddox knew what would happen if a mob like that reached it. He shook himself angrily. 'It's probably a demonstration or something!' Hell, what am I thinking about? No need to get in a panic! But his voice said, 'I think I'll call the captain.'

Malinski said slowly, 'I've seen 'em like this before.' Then more urgently: 'I'll get the skipper, Bob. I suggest you get that party of men together.' Then he was gone.

Maddox walked slowly down the gangway his heart thumping against his ribs. This was ridiculous, stupid, he kept telling himself. The menace was in his mind, made rotten and enlarged like everything else had become since Inglis's murder.

He waved to the seamen. 'Pull back, men!' Then just as quickly his racing brain connected with the pile of petrol drums and the cumbersome reflectors. 'Hold it!' He beckoned to Chief Tasker who stood like an interested onlooker by the edge of the pier. 'Take charge, Chief. Form the men in line across the pier between the stores and that crowd!'

86

'What the hell goes on?' Gunnar's voice sounded harsh, even nervous.

Maddox felt a wave of relief. 'I'm not sure, sir.'

'How many petrol drums are ashore?' The captain looked red-eyed and worn-out. He was unshaven and appeared to have slept in his khakis. To confirm this he said unexpectedly, 'Christ, what an awakening!' Then in a calmer tone, 'Just the day for Jago to be away.'

Maddox followed him through the thin cordon of sailors and halted a few feet from the inshore end of the pier. Quickly he worked out the possibilities. The line of unarmed sailors across the pier would keep the crowd from reaching the ship's fantail, but on the other hand the stern wires securing it to the big wooden bollards had already been reached and swallowed up by the crowd. Apart from cutting the wires, there was no quick way of releasing the ship from her moorings, and what might a hostile crowd be doing while the cutting was going on? Maddox was beginning to sweat. Now that they were closer, he could see the uncertainty on the faces of some of the Chinese, but there was also a hint of open anger and hostility. As if to fan his growing fears he heard a sullen rumble from the back of the crowd, which grew with surprising suddenness into a twittering chatter of shouts and what sounded like cat-calls. There seemed to be no leader, no set plan, and the crowd's front swayed and staggered as if pushed on by those behind. About two hundred, Maddox thought anxiously, with some more coming down the main road.

Gunnar said sharply, 'What the hell do they want?' Without waiting for an answer he stepped clear of Maddox and stood directly in the middle of the crowd's path.

Over his shoulder he said coolly: 'Send two men back to the ship to reinforce the gangway watch with rifles. Chief Tasker, tell the radio room to try and contact Jago, and tell him what's happening.' He looked up towards the distant citadel, above which a flag hung listless in the still air. 'There can't be anyone left up there!'

The crowd stopped so that their nearness and the noise of confused shouts seemed suddenly engulfing. Two or three had reached the pier itself, and Maddox could feel the timbers shaking under his feet. He felt an unreasoning fury replacing his fear, and was surprised to hear himself say hoarsely, 'The bastards!'

Gunnar said: 'That'll do, Mister Maddox! Keep still, and

87

stay calm!' Without turning his head to the ship he shouted, 'Gangway watch in position?' There was an answering shout, and Maddox heard the sharp clink of metal.

Gunnar sighed. 'Right then, let's get started.' Ignoring Maddox and the others behind him he took two paces towards the crowd. He could smell them, feel their confused anger and resentment, could have touched their patched smocks and work-roughened hands. Unlike Maddox, he felt neither fear nor anger. It was more like a cold elation, the sensation of a man committed to something he knows is terrible but already beyond his control.

He held up his hands. 'Get away from my ship!'

The crowd fell silent for a few moments, but shrill urgent voices began again from the rear, urging, jeering, insistent, like snapping dogs. Gunnar could feel the sweat gathering beneath his cap. It was happening yet again. Just like that other place. The senseless, headless mobs, the cool agitators using them like clubs to destroy the intruders. He remembered what the rear-admiral had so glibly explained about the 'Payenhau situation', left to mere men to carry out, he had said. From the corner of his eye he saw a stone flash through the air and heard a man cry out behind him.

It was a kind of signal, with one heaving push the crowd surged forward, and all at once Gunnar was surrounded, muffled and choking in a clawing, struggling mass of bodies. Someone punched him in the stomach he felt a strong grip on his arm pulling him down. A plank splintered, and a man screamed as his leg was trapped in the rickety pier and he was pushed hard down by the crush from behind. There was a madness, a blind urgency or purpose already replacing the crowd's earlier apathy, and Gunnar knew that within seconds it would be all over.

He kicked a man in the knee and pushed another away with the palm of his hand. He came up hard against the wooden bollard, and in spite of the water glittering below him he hauled himself up and on to the worn hump of timber, his eyes already seeking out his scattered seamen. Maddox was hatless, a streak of bright blood on his forehead. Two seamen were swimming in the water below the pier, but whether they had been thrown there or had chosen it as the safest place, Gunnar neither knew nor cared. One face was fixed in his stare, the one man who at that moment could be relied on.

On the fantail, an M-14 held in his fists like a toy, Pirelli stood quite still, his eyes watching the wave of destruction with something like eagerness. Pirelli had been kept aboard since the death of his friend Grout, in case he decided on some personal vengeance. It was well known that he had a record of violence, but at this particular moment Gunnar knew he was the man he wanted. A clawed hand pulled at his ankle, and from the edge of the crowd Gunnar saw another man aiming a stone at his unprotected body. Gathering his strength he yelled, 'Shoot over their heads, Pirelli!'

From the fantail the big seaman watched the surging mass of bodies with cold satisfaction. The rifle butt felt warm against his cheek and very slowly he moved the muzzle until the wooden bollard upon which the captain was struggling was dead in the centre. There was a single hand reaching from the screaming mob like a tentacle and already it was gripping at Gunnar's leg pulling him back and down. Once on the ground he would be a dead man.

Pirelli held his breath and squeezed. The whiplash crack cut through the air even as the unknown Chinese screamed like a tortured beast. The hand vanished, and Pirelli saw the drop-lets of blood had splashed across Gunnar's leg. He fired again and again, the kick of each bullet making his heart sing with desperate satisfaction. He saw Grout's smashed body through the smoke and Inglis writhing on the bloodied sand like a blinded animal. He was still firing when Chief Tasker knocked the rifle aside and pushed him back from the rail.

'That's enough, you goddamn maniac!'

But Pirelli's eyes were blank, empty of everything, and he allowed himself to be thrust aside. Crazed with sudden fear, trapped by the press of people behind, the mob started to break up. At the sound of shots they had fallen into a frozen silence, so that men stayed with open mouths and raised fists like those caught in the lens of a still camera. Then as the first screams of agony filtered through the smoke from Pirelli's shots the panic started. Within minutes the street was as empty as before, but for a wounded man who hopped on one leg, grotesque and terrified. Two still figures lay sprawled in the dust, one shot neatly between the eyes, the other crumpled but moving in short sporadic efforts to drag itself away.

There was a screech of brakes and two jeeploads of hel-meted soldiers spilled out on to the roadway above the beach. There were shouted orders and a short burst of firing.

Gunnar leaned against the bollard and rubbed at a bruise

on his arm. A sailor was vomiting on the pier, and two others were having their heads bandaged.

He heard Connell's voice, 'This one's a kid, Captain!'

Gunnar turned painfully to watch as a seaman lifted up the last victim of Pirelli's shooting. It *was* a child, a dark-haired girl of about twelve, her rough jacket glittering with scarlet in the harsh sunlight.

Connell said hotly, 'It was murder!'

'Would you rather lose the ship?' Gunnar eyed him coldly, conscious of the stillness which had engulfed the town like a shroud. The doctor turned his back and stooped down over the moaning child.

Maddox staggered across the pier dabbing his forehead with his sleeve. 'Jesus!' He peered at Gunnar's bruised face. 'A near thing, Captain!'

Gunnar ignored him and yelled to the deck, 'Put that man under arrest, Chief!' To the pier at large he said flatly, 'I'll have him court-martialled for this!'

He saw Tasker take Pirelli by the arm and guide him below deck and knew that he was really punishing himself. There must have been some other solution? Others might say that Pirelli had disobeyed orders and that it was not Gunnar's fault. But Gunnar knew differently. Deep down, he knew he had wanted the man to shoot as he had. Not over their heads, but into their stupid mouthing faces! He staggered and felt the old sickness sweeping over him. He heard the child whimper once more and knew that he wanted to go to her aid. Instead he said harshly: 'We'll have an armed guard in future, Mister Maddox. And when Major Jago returns I'll have a few words with *him* too!'

Maddox watched Gunnar walk back along the pier, his shirt torn, his face scratched and bruised. A slim, lonely figure who would have to answer for this and much more before they left Payenhau.

He heard the stamp of feet as Regan's party came marching down the slope from the headland, not a man out of step, no running and no panic. How typical of the man, Maddox thought savagely. He knew that Regan was right, but could only find hatred because of this knowledge.

Regan surveyed the dead man across his beaky nose and said shortly: 'Pity I missed it. I heard the shooting and thought the Reds were invading!' He eyed Maddox searchingly. 'Made a cock of it, did he?'

Maddox swung away. 'For Christ's sake shut it!' He heard Regan's short barking laugh behind him, and once when he looked back he saw with sick disgust that he was standing with one foot on the corpse while one of his men pretended to take a photograph to the apparent amusement of the rest.

Connell hurried along the pier and stood looking up at him. 'Will you give me a hand, Bob? I'm going to take this kid back to her home. She's going to live, but I'll have to keep an eye on her for a bit.'

Maddox took a grip of himself. In this whirl of madness only the doctor seemed the same any more. 'Where does she live?'

'The fishing village. I suspect she had nothing to do with the crowd.' He waited and watched Maddox's baffled uncertainty. Gently he added, 'You were ordered to go there anyway to fix up about using the commandant's boat, right?' Maddox nodded. 'Well then, we'll find it.' The doctor forced a smile. 'I need you to carry the kid!'

Maddox lifted his head to watch the soldiers on the road. They were back at their old posts, smoking and leaning on their rifles. A jeep rattled up the road to the citadel and a few townspeople wandered aimlessly in the dusty street. Was it possible? Was it only another nightmare? Maddox felt the lump on his face and saw the bloodstains on the wooden bollard where the captain had been swaying like some desperate gladiator. He made up his mind. 'I'll come,' he said thickly. 'I'll just tell the captain.'

Connell watched him go and then walked slowly back towards the shore.

Regan saw the doctor's face and kicked the corpse at his feet. 'Squeamish, Doc?' The men laughed, their voices unreal with relaxed tension.

Connell's eyes were cold. 'I was just thinking that is what they'll do to you when the time comes!' He walked towards the bandaged child, the anger boiling him alive.

Regan called, 'Not this chicken!' But his voice was tight and the men did not laugh in return.

*   *   *

The fishing village was within walking distance from the rest of the town yet the fragile-looking wooden buildings were so huddled together towards the water's edge that the com-

91

munity gave no doubt as to its complete separate aloofness from the other islanders. A tall-sided hill blocked the way to further expansion, so that the more recent dwellings clung to, and even overlapped, the sea itself, supported by tall stilts below which were moored numerous flat-bottomed boats bobbing amidst a jungle of drying nets, floats and handmade fish baskets. So closely huddled were the buildings that the winding streets were more like haphazard tunnels where window peered on to window, and chattering womenfolk had to step back into dark doorways to allow people to pass. There was a sickly yet inviting aroma of boiled fish and fried rice, of spice and tarred timber, and above all there was a sense of watchful activity which seemed denied to the rest of the town.

Maddox was sweating freely by the time he and the doctor had reached the fringe of the village, his arms numbed by the weight of the child who stared up at him with black, unwinking eyes. A bullet had passed cleanly through one of her thin arms, mercifully without breaking a bone, and the gleaming bandages and neat service splints clashed with her patched and bloodstained clothing.

Connell carried his first-aid satchel and was puffing thoughtfully at a thin black cheroot which left a fine trail of smoke to mark his passage like the stack of some busy freighter.

Maddox gasped: 'How much further, Doc? My arms are tearing out of their sockets!'

Connell squinted into the gaping mouth of the main street. Like branches of a tree other tiny avenues split away from the street and vanished into a tangle of leaning walls, rush mats and surprisingly delicate lanterns which hung from most of the cramped dwellings.

'Just follow the water, I guess. That must be the boat you're looking for,' he gestured towards a single thick masthead which swayed gently above the pointed rooftops, 'so we'll head for that first.'

People had appeared from several doorways, mostly women, as Maddox had expected. The fishing fleet, such as it was, spent most of its time away from Payenhau seeking whatever catch it could to help support the growing population as well as the unseen prisoners of the penal settlement. Nevertheless, there were many children, small and dark, who watched with open curiosity as the two navy officers entered the deep shadow and began to grope their way towards the centre of the village.

Maddox was tired and hungry, and the morning's fear and despair had also left him with a fierce thirst which he could not explain. But anything was better than staying in the ship where even the good food and fresh fruit could no longer give him pleasure.

Gunnar was ashore with Major Jago and Regan was left in charge. The latter had become impossible since the shooting, and it seemed as if the incident had opened some inner door on to the man's real nature. Regan was in fact in better spirits than Maddox could remember. Kroner and Malinski would have to bear the brunt of his cheerful brutality, Maddox thought. He felt a pang of guilt but instantly dismissed it as Connell said: 'They're all looking at us. I feel like someone from another planet!'

The village people were marked by poverty and the privations of their day-to-day existence, yet showed none of the servile ingratiation which Maddox had come to expect. Self-sufficient, he thought, and giving nothing away of their thoughts. Everyone on the island probably knew about the shooting and were quite likely aware of its real cause, even if he was not. Yet there was no open hostility, just this watchful curiosity reserved for interlopers.

The buildings fell back unexpectedly on to a small square, on the far side of which was a low-roofed, white painted dwelling with a deep veranda. It looked foreign and out of place, yet leaned across the lapping water on seasoned piles, conforming in this way only to its neighbours. Through its open doors and windows Maddox could see the sea beyond and the blunt black hull of a heavy work-boat. It was, he guessed, a motor fishing vessel of the type once used by the British as navy tenders, maids-of-all-work during the Second World War and now replaced by modern and more graceful powerboats. Its name, *Osprey*, was painted on the nearside of the tiny wheelhouse, and he could see two figures at work on the broad deck with buckets of water and long-handled brooms.

Connell said, 'We'll ask here if anyone knows where this kid belongs.'

Maddox nodded gratefully and leaned against the veranda. As if at a signal a raw-boned Chinese in an oversize drill jacket padded down the smooth wooden steps and bowed politely 'I take child,' his English was high and tinny, 'she belong down-street!' He bobbed his cropped head with serious importance and grinned. 'You go inside, yes?' His thin arms were all

93

muscle and he gathered up the girl with complete ease before Maddox could protest. The child immediately smiled and wagged her bandaged arm with something like pride.

Connell stepped forward frowning. 'I think we ought to make sure she gets home okay. I feel we owe an explanation to her folks.'

'Oh leave her alone, Doc.' Maddox fanned his streaming face with his cap. 'We can't do anything more, for Christ's sake!'

'I'm afraid I can't take that view.' Connell was unsmiling. 'Let us *try* to make up in some way for what's happened.'

The houseboy beamed from one to the other his teeth uneven and broken like an old dog's. In his arms the child seemed to have fallen asleep, so that the doctor was moved to say: 'Well, I guess she might be better with her own sort at that. All the same, I shall visit her and make sure——'

Maddox interrupted resignedly: 'Anything you say, *anything*! But just let me sit down, I'm bushed!'

A shadow fell across the steps and a thick bass voice said, 'So you finally decided to pay me a visit!'

Maddox stared up at the big man and again wondered what he had expected. Commander Jack Burgess was large and powerful in all directions at once. In his prime he must have been a giant amongst men, Maddox thought. Now most of his muscular body had given way to fat, and his heavy, grey-splashed beard added to his appearance of piratical improbability. He was wearing what appeared to be ex-navy shirt and shorts, which although spotlessly white were well darned and patched, and on his large feet he wore a pair of giant-sized leather sandals. Above the beard a pair of brown, sparkling eyes regarded the two Americans with cheerful welcome.

'Come in, boys! Come and take the weight off your feet!'

Apart from a lean-to, the building seemed to be all one room which opened on to an additional section at either end. The furniture was plain and unmatched, but there were some fine wood carvings on shelves and on the low tables, whilst hanging from one wall was a large faded photograph of a British destroyer at high speed.

Burgess threw himself in a cane chair which squeaked an immediate protest, and bellowed, 'Bring the drinks, you yellow ape!'

Maddox flexed his aching arms and stared at the English-man with both admiration and uncertainty. In Burgess he saw

94

a quick picture of himself in perhaps twenty years' time. If I ever get away from here I will start dieting, he thought vaguely. He noticed too how the early brightness in the giant's eyes was marred by a film of moisture, the sign of a heavy drinker, either now or in the past.

Another houseboy padded quickly into the room carrying a brass tray loaded with glasses and a bottle of whisky. Maddox licked his lips. He had stupidly visualised cans of iced beer running with condensation, or at worst some sort of local cocktail. Whisky, in the heat of the early afternoon, and on an empty stomach, was not quite what he had in mind at all.

Connell darted him a quick glance and Maddox forced a grin. It was probably the only bottle the bearded Englishman possessed, he thought, and the man's genial excitement seemed to fade behind something smaller and sadder. What in God's name had brought a man like Burgess here? he wondered as the whisky was splashed with the same abandon into three glasses. Loneliness, poverty, it was all apparent. The end of the line for a man who might have been something better.

Burgess lifted his glass. 'It's good to see you lads! I get so used to yapping at these twittering savages!' He glared at the hovering houseboy. 'Isn't that right, you bloody maniac?' The man grinned at his master and Burgess said cheerfully: 'Haven't taught him to speak the lingo yet. Plenty of time though. Not much else to do.'

Maddox hurried to break a threatened silence. 'About your boat.'

Burgess sat upright, his thick hairy legs straddled like capstan bars. 'Ah, the boat! A real beauty she is.' He patted his stomach his eyes suddenly distant. 'Bought her some years ago from a pal of mine in the R.N. dockyard at Hong Kong. He was in charge of Admiralty disposals and let me get her for a song.' He shook with silent laughter. 'Just as well, really, I didn't have much ready cash.'

Connell sipped his whisky. 'When did you leave the British Navy, Commander?'

Maddox saw the big man change yet again. Whether it was because of some sudden memory or because of Connell's addressing him by his old rank, he could not be sure. But the change was there, and it was immediate.

Burgess sat up in the battered chair his beard jutting and formidable. ' 'Bout ten years ago, Doctor.' His voice too was clipped and even formal.

He is reliving his past like an actor remembering some forgotten lines, Maddox thought uneasily.

Connell had noticed too, his face set and grave. 'What happened exactly?'

Burgess shrugged vaguely so that a droplet of whisky splashed on to his shirt. 'Bit of trouble, I'm afraid. One of our late colonies got its new independence a bit too early for me.' He laughed, but just as quickly frowned at his glass. 'I was in charge of some anti-terrorist patrols in inshore waters. I shot up a whole lot of the bastards only to find that independence had already been granted to 'em in that sector! Instead of terrorists they were patriots! Funny when you think of it. A stroke of a pen and everything's changed!'

Maddox heard himself ask, 'Couldn't you explain?'

Burgess faced him with a mirthless grin. 'Explain? *Me?*' He threw back his head and bellowed with laughter. 'Old Jack Burgess explain to a pack of bloody wogs! That'll be the day! I told 'em what they could do with the bloody navy! They didn't like *that*, I can tell you!'

Maddox swallowed hard and tasted the whisky clawing at his throat like fire. The houseboy was standing at his side, the bottle half empty in his brown hands. Jesus, I'll be passing out in a moment, Maddox thought.

As if jerking himself back to the present for Maddox's sake, Burgess said suddenly: 'What about a spot of grub, eh? You'll have to take pot luck, but it'll be a change, for you at least!' He counted on his thick fingers. 'Rice, and fresh prawns, and a few other bits and pieces my cook can dream up. Come on, what d'you say?' His guard had dropped and Maddox could see the eagerness in his eyes.

'I'd like that.'

Connell added, 'What about that kid?'

Burgess was on his feet, the floorboards bending under his weight. 'She'll be fine, Doc. They're used to hardship around here. They get enough of it!'

'I suppose you heard about the shooting?' Connell was holding his glass like a crucible.

'I heard all right. The poor bastards didn't know what they were doing! They thought you were landing nuclear warheads!' He frowned again. 'They're simple folk here. Goodhearted, but simple. Consequently they're easily led, or should I say *driven*!'

'Driven? By whom?' Maddox was leaning forward. He re-

96

membered Gunnar's face after the shooting and his own sense of failure and despair.

Burgess shrugged. 'Don't pay any attention to me. I'm just yammering as usual.' His tone was almost desperate, pleading. 'Let's forget it, shall we?'

Connell nodded. 'Sure. Let's enjoy a bit of real English hospitality.' But when he caught Maddox's eye the doctor's face was full of warning.

Maddox split his mouth into a grin. 'Yeah, we can leave the Chinese alone for a bit. As they say in Washington, we can keep pounding away at the Reds, and in another forty years we shall have whittled 'em down to a mere sixty million! You just bring on the food, Commander, and I'll willingly forget everything!'

Burgess swayed slightly and peered at the bottle. 'Seems we're running a bit short.' He smiled awkwardly. 'But if you gentlemen don't mind a drop of local stuff?'

The doctor fished in his medical bag and produced a flat flask. 'Vodka, officers for the use of,' he announced gravely, 'and strictly *not* for medicinal purposes!'

Maddox drained his glass and lay back, the strain and apprehension draining from him like sweat. He stared at the unlined roof and allowed his mind to wander as Burgess, chuckling and panting, moved rapidly from one end of the room to the other, his hands busy with plates and chairs. From the kitchen Maddox could hear his cook's voice raised in a vague song, while from the street outside came the gentle murmur of passing people. Just let go, he told himself. You've earned a break, so don't probe any further. The ship, Payenhau, even Mary seemed far away in the friendly, embracing whisky.

Only Connell seemed intent on his own thoughts. As if he was fitting together the pieces of some complex puzzle.

* * *

Major Lloyd Jago lowered the beer can and bared his teeth with cheerful satisfaction. Even without uniform he looked alert and somehow military, and his shapeless towel bathrobe had a lopsided slant so that Gunnar guessed that he carried a pistol in one of the deep pockets. Jago had listened attentively to his tight-lipped account of the shooting without comment, his cropped head glistening from a recent shower, his hands freshly scrubbed to remove any traces of the manœuvres which had evidently given him much satisfaction.

Then Jago had led the way through a small door, up a crudely fashioned spiral staircase and into a cool circular room which was apparently the highest point above the fort. Although about level with the hilltop at the rear of the concrete emplacements, the short, tower-like structure afforded an excellent view across the anchorage as well as giving a clear and unrestricted view towards the northern end of the island. Outside the sun blazed down on town and water alike, but inside the shaded eyrie it was cool, even chilled, and the air felt correspondingly fresher.

Jago squatted on an empty case and regarded the navy officer quizzically from beneath his greying brows. 'You worry too much, Captain.' He gestured towards another box where a small pile of beer tins stood in a plastic bowl of fractured ice. 'Dig in and help yourself.' He watched Gunnar's quick, angry movements and added: 'If you watch your step you can learn to cope with almost anything. I look on life as a series of achievements. I am not insensitive to failure, however. One muck up and a lifetime's achievements can go down the pan!'

Gunnar sat on a ledge feeling the concrete's damp coldness through his crumpled shirt. He felt strained and untidy, yet unable to take time to rest, to restore his outer calm. Jago seemed eager to talk, as if unlike Gunnar he had energy to spare.

Jago continued: 'I take pride in what I have done with my life. I had little education and had to get here the hard way.' He touched the old bathrobe as if feeling for his rank badges. 'I joined up as a rookie marine, slogged my way through Korea, and found my way up through dead men's shoes. In Korea our officers, youngsters like Inglis, were keen enough but as green as grass. There was no time, no quick way to find experience.' He shrugged. 'So they died just as eagerly. I grabbed my chance with both hands. I've never looked back.' His thin mouth twisted into a bitter sneer. 'I know I'll never rate a job in Washington, or a white-gloved detail with the top brass and their *ladies*, but I'll always be wanted where the fighting is, where the next trouble spot is getting started. And that suits me fine!'

Gunnar looked at him from a different angle. The man's sudden frank bitterness reminded him of Janet's comments and her contempt for men of Jago's calibre.

'And as for that business this morning,' the marine's voice

98

collected its normal sharpness, 'it couldn't be helped. It happens from time to time. They're ignorant and believe anything they're told. Nuclear warheads indeed! Did you ever hear such a load of crap?'

'I still believe there's more in it than that.' Gunnar stifled his earlier sensation of sympathy for this hard-bitten man. 'It didn't just happen. I know from experience that there is usually some justification for these outbreaks. *Or* there is an organised core to get them started. From what I've been told it seems that the locals are unhappy about this military "Occupation" of their own island. They don't want it, in fact they want nothing to do with either faction.'

Jago sighed. 'Then they'll just have to lump it! They happen to live in a bit of land which has become strategically important. Part of the pattern. It can't be helped. It was like that in Korea, in Viet Nam and all the other dumps. The Limeys had it all before us, and the Romans before them. Hell, the weakest will always go to the wall!'

'There's rather more at stake today——'

Jago waved his hand. 'Sure I know that. Before, it was a handful of guns to control a million spears and a stone age mentality. Today, these piddling little nations can bleat either to Washington or Moscow and they get all the weapons they want! Jesus, there never was a better world for testing modern arms!'

Jago punctured another can and regarded it moodily. 'And here we are, you and me! Washington and the fleet are a long way off, and we are the representatives of the power for peace.' It seemed to amuse him and he grinned. 'Well, we're stuck with it and that's that!'

Gunnar watched a gull slowly circling the tower. 'And somewhere on the island is our opposite number.'

Jago snorted. 'There you go again! My men can handle anything the Reds care to invent. The training is getting better all the time. We can cope!'

It was useless. Gunnar changed the subject. 'I'll get on with the survey tomorrow. My exec is organising the other boat now. How reliable is this Commander Burgess?'

'Reliable? He's predictable, and that's about all. Thinks he's in command of the whole situation here.'

Like you, thought Gunnar coldly. 'His position doesn't seem very clear.'

Jago chuckled. 'The commandant is a cunning old bastard,

99

whatever he may seem. He keeps a couple of Limeys here just in case we get difficult.'

'A couple?'

'Yeah.' Jago's eyes narrowed. 'I can see you've not read all my notes yet.' He continued: 'You know how touchy the Limeys are about this area. For generations the Royal Navy has run the whole shoot, now they're pinched out, except for Hong Kong. Even in Malaysia they're only tolerated because they're protecting the place from the Reds. It's like I said, a lot of piddling little nations calling the tune!' He took another drink. He was surrounded by empty cans but showed no sign of having taken a single swallow. 'But the Limeys don't like us as top dogs. If they guessed what we were doing here, for instance, they might start huffing and puffing around to interfere. The commandant knows that. If he keeps a couple of British nationals under his wing he could always drop a titbit of information in the right place and perhaps drag in a Limey warship to protect 'em!'

Gunnar was unconvinced. Jago's clear-cut thinking was too pat, too organised, like the man himself.

Jago added: 'Of course Burgess earns his keep. He knows these islands like the back of a gin bottle. Well, almost as well. He runs a good boat and would hate to lose his last little bit of authority. The garrison pays his keep and supplies him with hooch. That's about all he needs.' Jago grimaced. 'But don't rely on him in a pinch. Like all Limeys he thinks we're a lot of goddamned peasants!'

Gunnar looked thoughtful. 'Have you read my report about Inglis's death?'

'I read it.' Jago seemed impatient to end the conversation and glanced at his watch. 'A typical navy effort I would say.' He waved down Gunnar's unspoken protest. 'Sure, I know you feel rough about it, but it could have happened to anyone a bit green. The bayoneting you mention is just another typical bit of Red delicacy.'

'Why didn't your patrols find the men who did it? Or discover any boat on that islet?'

'Who knows? The Reds had a few hours. They might have been ferried over to the main island by a friendly fisherman or one of your *outraged* independent Chinese. Or they might have been lifted off by submarine. Either way we'll drop on them soon enough. Major Yi-Fang has promised to tighten things up here on in.'

Gunnar stood up, the beer already stale in his stomach. 'I hope you're right.'

'Sure I'm right. I'm not losing my own face because of them! Not for them, not for *anyone*, Captain!' He regarded Gunnar intently. 'The cards say you've got to stick around for a while. Just do that, Captain, and be ready if you're needed!'

'I'll be ready, don't you worry.'

'And tell your boys this is as much a war as anywhere else. What did they expect out here? Flags flying, and a front-line trench? Jesus, the flags go up only after the battle's over!'

As Gunnar picked up his cap Jago added casually: 'By the way, Captain. You can release that man Pirelli. Wrap it up in navy jargon, stop his leave for a bit if you must, but nothing violent, see? A court-martial would leak out, might invite attention.' He grinned at Gunnar's set face. 'And we don't want that, do we?'

Gunnar left without another word. The feeling of helplessness was firmer than ever. He was being controlled from outside like a puppet. Even his own ship seemed to elude him. Aboard the submarine the rear-admiral had said he could get another captain if required.

Gunnar walked blindly into the sunlight where the jeep waited to take him back to the *Hibiscus*. From now on I shall trust no one, he thought. If I am to be held responsible for what happens, then I shall act accordingly.

Surprisingly, he felt better for his decision, and when he met two armed seamen by the pier he returned their salute with unusual firmness.

6

You never know what's afoot

Leaving a rolling bank of white dust in their wake, the two jeeps raced past the fishing village and swung on to a right curve between two hills. The noise of the engines was immediately exaggerated and worsened by the enclosing land, and Gunnar, who sat stiffly in the leading jeep, was conscious too of the fact that the sea had been swallowed up behind him.

Sergeant Rickover was driving, his eyes squinting through the dust, his big hands swinging the wheel like a racetrack ace as he gunned the engine around the next bend in the road. The other vehicle was about twenty yards in the rear, and Gunnar wondered how they were faring in Rickover's dusty wake. The second jeep contained four soldiers, two of whom carried sub-machine guns and looked as if they were quite prepared to use them.

Rickover shouted above the din: 'Relax sir! You'll find it makes it easier on the rump!' He grinned without taking his eyes from the trail. 'The guys behind'd give their teeth to be way out ahead!'

Gunnar eased his legs and nearly fell sideways on to the road as Rickover cursed and twisted the wheel to avoid a small boulder. He looked back to where Connell sat wretchedly amongst his first-aid gear, his hands gripping the jeep's low sides like a rodeo rider.

He caught Gunnar's glance and gestured behind. 'Are they protecting us or just keeping a watchful eye in our direction?'

Rickover heard and shouted cheerfully: 'The commandant thinks it unsafe outside the town or between the villages. A couple of soldiers were knocked off here a while back.'

Gunnar looked up at the hills' rounded shoulders with new interest. It was a good place for an ambush. 'Did they catch anyone?'

The sergeant shook his head. 'Nah! Probably some local boys working off a grudge! You know how it is with these Chinks, sir. A bit of "squeeze" always gets going once the military moves in.'

Gunnar could imagine it well enough. As in Viet Nam, it was not possible to watch and check the ultimate destination of all the American aid, no matter what it was. Food, clothing, even arms, often floated on to the black market, the racket made easier by the unofficial army organisation behind it.

He wondered why he had come on this unexpected journey instead of leaving Rickover to look after the doctor as he thought fit. The wardroom had been in the middle of breakfast when the marine sergeant had been ferried out to the *Hibiscus* —which once more rode in solitary watchfulness at her anchorage—and had asked if it were possible for Connell to attend at the guards' quarters in the prison camp. One of the officers had apparently broken his leg. It was only then that

Gunnar had realised there was no medically qualified official on the islands. How in God's name they managed with closely packed detainees was open to the worst possible supposition. Perhaps this was the real reason for Connell being posted to the *Hibiscus* in the first place. Deep down Gunnar knew that he wanted to see and know more of the commandant's little kingdom, rather than worry about Connell's problems.

Rickover said loudly, 'They must be a tough bunch to live out here!'

Gunnar nodded and gripped his cap as the jeep sidestepped around a hairpin bend and started on a slight down-gradient.

Wherever they went, whatever they endured or attempted, the Chinese were tough all right. The vast millions of peasants through the mass of China had survived one crushing burden after another. The emperors and bandits, warlords and Japanese invaders, all had lived off their backs, whilst in constant attendance the climate and landscape defied their every effort to scrape a living from the soil. Most Chinese were content to survive. Hang on until the next frugal harvest. Hang on, no matter how much the privileged few in power schemed and manœuvred for more ambitious things.

Even in Hong Kong it was really no different, he thought. Crammed and crowded together under the protection of the British flag, watched and guarded by the distant power of the U.S. Seventh Fleet, the Chinese looked on their lot not as a salvation from the other side of the border, but as a mere incident in time. They did not really like the British, and in their minds associated American sea power with the gunboat era which had once controlled their ports and coastline and opened up trade to Europe and beyond. No, the Chinese were a power yet to be reckoned with. Seven hundred million of them. They did not really care which side of a border they lived or existed. They were first and foremost Chinese, and they looked forward to the time when their latent power would swamp all else. It was hard to understand that the whole pattern of China had happened in living memory for many, and in spite of their ageless traditions and patient calm the Chinese were constantly aware of this fact. From foreign gunboats to the present-day strife between East and West, each year had been marked with their own suffering and hardship.

The jeeps growled up another hillside, the road getting narrower and less stable. Rickover grunted, 'When the rains come these tracks are like waterfalls!'

103

'Have you heard anything about local dissatisfaction while you've been here?'

Gunnar's question made the sergeant chuckle. 'Hell, yes. You can't blame them really, I guess. These islands were self-supporting once, but the top weight of garrison and prisoners makes the balance a bit dizzy!' He dismissed it with a shrug. 'But it's the same everywhere, isn't it?'

The man's indifference was typical of today's fighting men, Gunnar thought. They no longer fought to defend home or empire. It was a loose, ragged battle, with the members changing sides as environment and wealth altered its substance and importance. Yes, it was the same everywhere.

Rickover braked slightly and allowed the jeep to idle forward over the top of the hill, so Gunnar could see that the centre span of the island was almost flat, like a flat dustbowl some five miles across. The whole area looked poor and starved of vegetation, but for the usual clumps of shrub and a few patches of wiry grass. The camp itself shimmered in a low heat haze, and the filtered sunlight glittered along the tall fences of barbed wire and the long-legged watch-towers which stood at every corner. It was a big camp, and appeared to be sub-divided again by a similar wired enclosure within, with more watch-towers and even higher fences. It was a hutted prison, with rank upon rank of low wooden shacks on both sides of the inner wire fence, above which floated a cloud of dust mingled with countless plumes of smoke from cooking fires. It was a tired, depressing place, where every ounce of life and hope seemed to have been ground down by time and situation.

Rickover lifted his arm. 'The inner camp is sealed off from the other one. It's for special cases. Red sympathisers and so on. The outer ring is for refugees, doubtful citizens from Taiwan and that sort of joker.' He released the brakes and the jeep shot forward again. Rickover said suddenly, 'I hate the goddamned place!' He then lapsed into silence until the jeep had reached the high wooden gates which started to open as the engine died into silence.

Rickover said: 'We don't take vehicles inside. A couple of prisoners made a break for it about a month ago in a rice wagon. But they were caught down the hill, poor bastards.'

'What happened?' Connell had spoken for the first time, his voice taut.

'Chopped 'em.' The sergeant put on his sunglasses and

104

hitched his pistol around his hip. 'Cut their goddamn heads off!'

Gunnar slid from the jeep and walked towards the guarded entrance. What was the point of explaining to Connell? You had to live with these people to understand their ways. Kind to children and old folk on the one hand, yet completely devoid of pity on the other.

A dapper lieutenant saluted and bobbed his head. 'Welcome!'

Rickover apparently knew him and said, 'Where's the injured officer?'

The lieutenant grinned. 'This way. You follow?'

Rickover pulled a pack of cigarettes from his denims and threw it towards the soldiers in the other jeep. As he followed Gunnar and the doctor through the gates he explained: 'Have to do that. The bastards'll milk my tank otherwise and then sell me back my own gas!' He chuckled. 'They'd pilfer the gold from your teeth while you were asleep and you'd never notice!'

Gunnar bit his lip as they followed the jaunty officer down the wide main road from the gates. He recalled Jago's summary when he had first arrived in Payenhau. 'Six thousand prisoners'. That estimate had obviously not included wives and children who stared listlessly at the passing Americans. Christ, to them we're just like the guards, Gunnar thought bitterly.

As if reading his thoughts Rickover said quietly, 'What have they got to look forward to?'

The lieutenant stopped outside a white, stone-built block of living quarters. Some flowers made a patch of colour by the entrance, and two Chinese women in worn clothing were busy watering and tending them with the concentration of priests.

The guide said, 'Here we are!' He opened a door to reveal a man lying naked on a military cot. His muscular, hairless body was taut with pain, and his face was likewise set with patient suffering.

Rickover said, 'This is Captain Han, sir.' And to the doctor, 'Can you manage?'

Connell looked at the two medical orderlies in outsize smocks who stood at the foot of the cot and said coldly, 'I can, thank you.'

A slight, dark-eyed girl entered the room and placed a dish of tea beside the cot. Gunnar expected the injured officer to make some attempt to hide his body from the girl, but he stared hard at her and kept her waiting for several minutes before he dismissed her with a brief nod. Typical, Gunnar thought. Like the commandant and the girl at his side. He saw the Chinese officer's face twist into sudden agony and heard Connell say conversationally, 'Keep still please.'

Gunnar moved to the door while Rickover slumped in a chair to watch the doctor get to work. Connell was highly competent, as he had already shown, but Gunnar had a feeling that Captain Han was in for a rough passage.

The hovering lieutenant saluted. 'What can do for Captain, sir?'

Gunnar pointed at the nearest watch-tower. 'I'd like to go up there and look at your gun.' It was strange how easily the lie had come to his lips.

The officer bobbed with obvious pride. 'Very good gun. Vickers!'

At the inner end of the long road from the gates Gunnar had seen the entrance to the inner camp. There were several armed guards outside the sealed entrance, although the watch-towers were obviously manned. The working parties inside and outside the camp were sparsely guarded, so why the extra precaution? Unless to stop Gunnar from getting too near. By asking to inspect the point furthest from the other camp Gunnar had obviously dispelled the officer's doubts. He had been hovering outside the guards' quarters with the sole purpose of stopping Gunnar from doing anything awkward and could now hardly conceal his relief.

He followed him up the sun-dried wooden ladder until they were under the conelike roof where a soldier stood beside the obsolete machine gun. Gunnar nodded. 'Very smart. Very good.' Then he patted his pockets. 'I seem to have left my sunglasses down there. Could you get them for me?' He watched the sudden caution in the other man's eyes, the slow, lip-reading uncertainty of a man caught off guard.

The lieutenant quickly weighed up the new situation. Gunnar could not leave the tower and walk back past the guards' quarters in such a short time that he could not be stopped. He smiled happily. 'Very good, Captain, sir!'

He scuttled down the ladder, and Gunnar unbuttoned the front of his shirt. With a quick wipe he smeared the dust from his hidden binoculars and then levelled them along the road. The watch-tower was just right. With startling clarity he saw

106

the faces of the soldiers, the grounded rifles and the big gates. Up and over to the low rooftops beyond. Not much sign of life, but for a few small groups of figures squatting in the shade. No women. Not much activity. He steadied the glasses on to the pale strip of concrete which was only just visible below the ranks of buildings. A road? He dismissed the idea instantly. It would be pointless to construct a road from this point. The one from the town was surely of greater importance, yet little had been done to that. Something Jago had once said . . . Gunnar heard the door bang below him and slid the glasses back into his shirt. He thought back over all the things Jago had told him about. An airstrip. That was it. Presumably the hard cases in the central camp were employed on doing just that. When it was finished they could move the whole camp away from the prepared site, and then . . . his mind refused to accept it. It *was* finished. He had seen the newly built concrete screen at one end, the wooden supports for possible landing lights.

He heard the lieutenant's voice: 'Sorry, Captain, sir. No glasses below.'

Gunnar looked past his baffled face. 'Well, I must have forgotten them!' He glanced briefly at the soldier by the gun. His face was blank and disinterested as Gunnar had guessed it would be. Soldiers of any army were rarely surprised by the antics of officers. He remembered what Rickover had said and handed his cigarettes to the one man who had seen him peering at the forbidden camp. The man saluted and showed his teeth.

The lieutenant said irritably: 'No need for whole pack, sir! One would do for common soldier!'

At the foot of the ladder Gunnar asked casually, 'Who do you have in the inner camp?'

The officer kept his face immobile. 'Communist agitators. Very bad, dangerous men!' He lifted his eyes skywards. 'Very bad men, sir!'

Gunnar walked into the shaded building. He felt vaguely satisfied and alert. Rickover had said that two escapees from the camp had been beheaded for merely taking a ride in a rice wagon. Yet everyone must have known that the likelihood of their really escaping was as remote as snow in Egypt. But the inner camp was full of potentially dangerous agitators, according to the beady-eyed lieutenant. Men who by these standards should have been executed before they even arrived! Someone was lying. But why? What was the point of it all?

Connell met him by the door. He was wiping his hands vigorously, his mouth set and angry. 'I've set his leg, sir. Can we get out of this place now?'

Gunnar eyed him thoughtfully. There was a lot to be found out in Payenhau after all. Perhaps the doctor might be accepted where others were not. 'Sure, Doc. I thought you might stop off at the fishing village to check up on that kid?' He watched the surprise show briefly in the doctor's bright blue eyes.

'Well, er, yes.' Connell seemed confused. 'Yes, I'd like that very much.' He nodded towards the door. 'I nearly forgot my oath with that one!'

Gunnar smiled quietly. 'I'll remember that when it's my turn, Doc.'

They remounted the jeeps and headed backtowards town. On the final hill Rickover's engine coughed and died. The tank was empty, as was the emergency can on the back. Gravely the soldiers from the other jeep gathered round and produced a full can of gas.

More cigarettes were exchanged and Rickover said wearily, 'I forgot that the journey took us *both* ways!' He grinned as the other jeep roared past them, the soldiers swaying with laughter.

Rickover tightened his jaw. 'Still, I will remember those jokers. Yes, sir, the very next time I have them on manœuvres I'll just about——' He never finished his sentence. With a dull crack the other jeep rocked sideways in a cloud of red-tinged smoke. One wheel spun crazily over the lip of the hill, while the jeep itself rocketed on to its side even as the tank exploded.

Rickover hauled on the wheel so that Gunnar thought for an instant that they would crash into the blazing inferno with its four writhing inmates. Somehow they missed the other jeep, and Rickover said hoarsely, 'Jesus, that was a mine!'

Gunnar shielded his face from the blazing heat and peered down at the road. A black smear in the dust told him where the crude mine had been hastily laid. 'It was meant for us,' he said calmly. 'They thought we'd be in front.'

Connell leaned against the jeep, his face pale. 'Thank God you forgot to pay those poor devils extra "squeeze", Sergeant!'

'Yeh.' Rickover, who had tugged his automatic from its holster, replaced the weapon and climbed back on the driving seat. 'I guess I'll never get my own back on them now!'

As they roared down the final slope Rickover said flatly:

'I've been here long enough to be blown up before, sir. The doctor is harmless enough.' He glanced sideways at Gunnar's impassive face. 'That leaves *you*, sir!'

* * *

Clad only in shorts, and sprawled in faded canvas chairs, the *Hibiscus*'s officers took advantage of the shade afforded by the fantail awning and of a too-brief breeze which stirred the water from its usual lethargy.

Regan was apparently asleep, an old newspaper across his head and shoulders, and Malinski was absorbed in a much-thumbed manual of machine spares. Maddox adjusted his sun-glasses and thrust his hands behind his head. Floating loosely on the stream, a narrow-gutted sampan, loaded to the gun-wales with important-looking water melons, passed slowly by the anchored ship. Like Chinese carvings the three crew members stood in a small, hopeful group by the sweep oar as they peered from beneath giant coolie hats at the warship's upper deck. There was no response however. The midday meal's greasy vapour still hovered between decks where most of the men snored in their bunks or idled their time before facing the afternoon sun and another round of work. Only the gangway watch, bored and listless, watched the passing boat, and their minds were elsewhere and not excited by the prospect of melon.

Lieutenant Kroner stretched his long legs and yawned languidly. 'The natives seem to be getting more friendly.'

Maddox grunted. It was true that more craft than usual had been passing nearer to the ship, but they still kept their distance, cautious and timid. Gunnar had left strict orders that no unauthorised vessel was to come alongside, but the warning was apparently unnecessary.

Maddox lowered his wrist to look at his watch. The captain should be back soon from his visit to the prison camp. What new ideas would he have? he wondered. It would be good to talk with the doctor again too. Malinski was a good guy, but his conversation was limited and he preferred to keep to himself. As for Regan. Maddox frowned so that Kroner remarked, 'Are you still yearning for the high life?' Maddox did not answer. It was plainer than ever how much they all missed Inglis. Alive he had been just an extra member of the mess. Shy, unsure of himself, and sometimes quite irritating. But now it was

109

obvious that he had made the right balance required for any small ship.

A radioman padded on to the fantail and peered down at Kroner. 'You coming to check the despatches, sir?'

Kroner stretched like a dog and yawned again. 'I suppose so.'

Maddox settled down to his thoughts undisturbed.

As usual his mind returned to the shooting on the pier and mostly to his own reaction. It was strange to view the incident with an almost clinical detachment. Even his own fear was like part of a larger pattern. But I *was* afraid, he told himself. Sick, unnerved, as he had never been before. He had felt out of his depth, shattered by the crowd's haphazard power and determination. It was like nothing he had experienced, and he did not know how he would react if it occurred again. The captain had been a different man under those circumstances. He had gathered some new strength, as if he had been expecting it all to happen, and had shown less uncertainty than he had over Inglis's death, when he was not involved. It was all very strange.

'Boat approaching from starboard, sir!' McCord, a quartermaster, poked his head round the forty-millimetre and looked at the silent group. 'It's the fishing boat, *Osprey*.'

Maddox was about to shake Regan, who was officially O.O.D., when he remembered that the Englishman, Burgess, would be aboard his boat, and anything was better than brooding over his own misgivings. 'Okay, I'll come.'

He slapped his cap on his dishevelled hair and sauntered along the deck as the sturdy M.F.V. putted alongside. He could see Burgess's bearded face in the small wheelhouse, and watched as a powerfully built Chinese threw a line from the bows to the gangway watch. One other hand was flaking down a rope with service precision on the canvas hold cover, and Maddox guessed there was probably a third Chinese in the tiny engine room. In spite of this small crew the boat wheeled smartly and coughed astern to creak obediently against her fenders.

Burgess barked another order, his voice unnecessarily loud, as if he were calling from the bridge of a frigate, and watched impatiently as the big deckhand hurried aft to secure the other line. Then he put on a white-covered cap and climbed slowly and carefully on to the *Hibiscus*'s deck.

Maddox noticed that the cap still bore a tarnished Royal

110

Navy badge, and something made him call the gangway watch to attention as the big man stepped aboard.

Burgess turned slowly aft and first saluted the listless Stars and Stripes, and then Maddox. The latter sensed that this was quite a moment for the Englishman. He could not guess how long it had been since Burgess had boarded a ship of war, or exactly what he was thinking at this moment. The man's dark eyes were steady and grave, quite unlike their bleary, excited restlessness when Maddox and the doctor had called at his shacklike house. He was an officer again. Reliving it, making every second count.

He boomed, 'Reporting for orders, Lieutenant!' Then his eyes twinkled. 'I thank you for your courtesy.'

Maddox felt embarrassed, although he could not say why. Several seamen had come on deck to see who had arrived, and the gangway watch still stood in attitudes of resentful attention. Maddox said hastily, 'Come aft and meet the others.'

Within minutes the other officers had returned to life. Malinski became quite voluble in his descriptions of London and the Portsmouth dockyard, and even Regan seemed pleasant and relaxed.

Maddox sat in his chair watching Burgess's features becoming more animated and less tense.

It's just that we're all sick of the sight of each other, Maddox thought. If we knew this was to be a three-year commission we would settle down and make the best of it. The uncertainty was more depressing than any stupid hint of danger and involvement.

Kroner stepped aft, and after a mumbled introduction to the newcomer drew Maddox to one side. 'Any sign of the captain?'

Maddox eyed the despatch pad in his hand and felt a rising knot of panic. 'Not yet. Why?'

Kroner held out the pad. 'Then you're in charge till he comes. This is a personal brief.' He smiled gently at Maddox's apprehensive face. 'Something for you to tell him.'

Maddox read the blocked words twice before they sunk in. Their content did not concern him personally after all, yet he felt a sense of anxiety, a feeling that he was called to do something. The message merely stated that the captain's wife had been granted a divorce, that the navy department were making the usual arrangement with reference to pay and allowances, etc., etc. A bald, matter-of-fact statement sent by radio

111

no doubt because mail was restricted by the ship's uncertain movements.

Maddox handed the pad back. 'Hell!'

Kroner grinned openly. 'Scenes behind the scenes! You never know what's afoot, do you?'

Vaguely he heard Regan say to Burgess: 'I have a picture of the place in my room below. Care to see it?'

Kroner had gone back to the radio room, and Malinski seemed content to resume his reading. Maddox decided that he would be well advised to think over the new piece of information and how it might affect him personally.

He slung his leg over the rail and stepped on to the M.F.V.'s broad deck. The big Chinese seaman was squatting against the wheelhouse. He smiled at Maddox and then went on with a task of wire splicing. He was a giant of a man, broad and extremely powerful. Maddox doubted if it were possible for him and Burgess to stand in the wheelhouse at one time.

His shadow fell across the other figure which still knelt over the wide coil of rope. Maddox took in the faded jean pants, loose canvas jacket, all surmounted by a giant straw hat as wide as a normal umbrella. 'Nice job,' he said companionably.

The figure stood up and turned to face him. Maddox stared transfixed at the upturned, unsmiling face. It was a girl. As the shocked realisation passed, Maddox realised two things simultaneously. She was young and extremely attractive, and she was obviously a half-caste. She had a fine, tanned skin, and but for her eyes and small, delicate mouth, she would pass as a European. Half Chinese without a doubt, he thought vaguely, a girl whose beauty was accentuated rather than marred by her shapeless, hand-sewn garments.

She said, 'When you've had a good look, just hand me the verdict!'

Maddox swallowed hard and was conscious of his own appearance. Never before had he been caught at such a disadvantage. Crumpled, grease-stained shorts, battered cap and an expensive wristwatch made up his inventory of clothing, and his broad chest was still streaked with the coffee he had been drinking with such careless ease in the depths of his chair.

He held out his hand. 'Maddox,' he said thickly. 'Bob Maddox.

Her small, neat hand merely touched his, then she stepped back a pace to look at him. Normally, Maddox would have basked in such a situation. Now he felt laid bare by those dark, unsmiling eyes.

She said curtly, 'Is my father enjoying himself?' A mere tilt of the head, yet the movement stabbed Maddox to the heart.

'Father? Enjoying himself?' he asked dazedly. Then it dawned on him. Of course . . . Burgess. A whole collection of distorted pictures floated through his mind as his brain sought to connect with his tongue. Of course, there had to be more to Burgess than he had supposed. Maddox knew enough about the rigid and monastic code of the Royal Navy to appreciate what Burgess's superiors must have made of his marrying a Chinese woman, no matter what her particular status might have been in her own right.

The girl sat on the rail and stared at her sandalled feet. 'Yes, he is my father.'

Maddox saw a watching group of sailors above him on the *Hibiscus*'s fo'c'sle. 'Come aboard. I'll rustle up some coffee.'

She looked up at the ship as if seeing it for the first time. 'No thank you.' She had a very English accent, which too seemed out of place and alien.

Maddox gained a little confidence. 'Come on, we won't bite!'

She took off the big hat, and immediately her neck and shoulders were enveloped in a mass of long, jet-black hair. 'I hear you've released that murderer,' she said in the same cool voice. 'I don't want to be near him, thank you. '

She meant Pirelli, Maddox thought quickly. 'It was an accident, you see——'

'I see very well. You know, you really are rather unbelievable!' She smiled very slightly, but there was still no invitation. 'You are always the same. You push in, throw your weight around, and expect everyone to fall flat on his face. You hand out candy and comics where there is no bread, and bullets where there is no understanding!'

Maddox flushed. 'Now *just* a minute!'

But she continued evenly: 'You point a finger and say, "That man is safe and pro-American, but *that* man is a comrade!"' She looked straight into Maddox's face. 'It must be wonderful to be so perfect!'

Vaguely Maddox could hear the distant mutter of the gig's engine. Gunnar must be coming back. He said hurriedly, 'The captain is returning.' He wagged a finger. 'But don't go away. I want to finish this talk and straighten out a few things!'

113

She replaced her hat. 'I thought you were the captain, you have such *authority*, such masculine sincerity!'

Maddox turned his back and climbed over the rail. It was a hasty and undignified retreat, and he imagined he could hear her laughing with the Chinese deckhand.

Chief Anders was leaning on the rail. 'Nice bit of tail there, Mister Maddox?'

Maddox glared at him. 'Shut your goddamned face!'

Chief Tasker joined his friend and stared after the bronzed figure of the exec. 'What's eatin' him?'

Anders turned to stare at the girl again. 'He's got a tile loose, I reckon!'

* * *

Maddox stood beneath an overhead fan as Gunnar sat on the edge of the wardroom table and read the despatch. When he looked up, Gunnar's eyes were still impassive, and he said, 'Does anyone else know about this?'

'Only Kroner, sir.'

Surprisingly, the captain smiled, the motion lighting up his strained face and draining away the weight of his inner thoughts. 'In other words, *everyone*!' He seemed to dismiss it. 'Well, it'll take their minds off their own problems for a while.'

Maddox said, 'I'm sorry, sir.'

Gunnar shrugged. 'Thank you. But there's nothing to be upset about.' Then in the same calm tone he continued, 'Somebody tried to blow us up just now.'

Maddox's jaw dropped. 'Who? I—I mean, where, sir?'

Gunnar leafed rapidly through the other despatches, a ray of sunlight showing the dust on his fair hair. 'By the village. A mine in the road. Sergeant Rickover is looking into it.' If he had remarked on the state of the ship's paintwork he could not have sounded more normal. Then in a sharper voice, 'Didn't you hear it, for heaven's sake?'

'No, sir.' Maddox wondered with sudden guilt if it had occurred when he was speaking to the girl. 'I was dealing with Burgess, sir '

Gunnar rubbed his chin. 'It's odd all the same. Just shows how careful we must be. Inshore sounds are muffled by that cliff. We'd not hear a thing out here. I think we'll move over to the pier again.'

114

'The pier, sir? I thought you said that after that affair the other day——'

Gunnar stopped him. 'I've had another think about it,' he said calmly. 'Did you know, Bob, that the French lost Indo-China because they shut themselves up into their forts like hedgehogs? We'll not make the same mistake.'

'You mean you want our boys to mix more with the locals?' Maddox was feeling past surprise. Inglis's terrible death, the shooting on the pier, and now this impossible attempt to kill American officers by mining the road, seemed to have steadied the captain rather than the opposite. Deep inside his mind a warning flashed and Maddox added: 'But if someone is trying to scare us off, sir? Wouldn't it add to their advantage?'

Gunnar smiled again. 'You've seen the picture, Bob. I'm glad I don't have to spell it out to everyone. Someone, some-where, is planning a coup of sorts on this island. I guess our arrival has been interpreted as something rather different than it was intended.' Then a touch of his old bitterness. 'If they only knew we were alone and on a limb here, we might see some real action!'

Maddox said hastily: 'The M.F.V.'s alongside, Captain. Commander Burgess is giving the ship a lookover.'

'So I see. Any problems?' Again that clear, penetrating glance which seemed to strip Maddox of his defences. 'What is the *commander* like?'

'Oh you know, sir.' Maddox spread his hands. 'A bit of the past. Rather pathetic in a nice way.' He faltered. 'He has a daughter, by the way. She crews for him.'

Gunnar stared past him at the open port. Half to himself he said: 'The second English national. I see now.'

Maddox did not see. 'She's a peach of a girl, sir.' He added awkwardly, 'Half Chinese, I guess.' He hurried on as if to cover his feeling of betrayal. 'Her father is a bit of a guy. Cashiered for knocking off some Africans during inde-pendence celebrations!'

Gunnar smiled but his face looked suddenly sad. 'I'm afraid not, Bob.'

'I don't quite follow?'

'I checked with the British at Hong Kong by radio.'

Maddox was feeling at a loss again. 'I didn't see any des-patches, sir.'

'I used Jago's radio this morning. Commander Burgess com-

115

manded a destroyer at one time, and he was discharged following a court-martial.'

'Well, that bears out what I said.'

'It was for embezzling navy funds, Bob. He's a hard drinker, and about as reliable as Pirelli's marksmanship!'

'I see, sir.' Maddox felt a sense of real disappointment. 'What'll we do about it?'

'Nothing.' Gunnar stood up and brushed the dust from his shirt. 'We need every ear in Payenhau we can muster.' He looked Maddox squarely in the eyes. 'Invite the pair of them aboard for dinner or something.'

Maddox moved his feet uneasily. 'The girl doesn't want that, sir.'

'Hmm. I might have guessed you'd already made an approach in that direction.' He smiled slightly. 'Right. Then get Burgess to invite us to his place. We'll take some drinks. Make it a party.'

Maddox looked at the despatch pad. 'Do you want to send a reply to that one?'

Gunnar seemed to have forgotten about his wife completely. 'No. Drop it.'

Maddox said suddenly, 'Do you think it's safe to go ashore just yet?'

'We'll soon know. But we can't find out anything out here. Anyway, Bob, you'll be in command if I set off another mine!'

As the exec left the wardroom he heard Gunnar humming to himself as if he had not a care in the world.

*   *   *

The party, which Burgess seemed only too eager to arrange for the *Hibiscus*'s officers, was a great success. Leaving a disgruntled Regan to take charge of the ship, they made their way through the narrow streets of the fishing village, between leaning buildings already alight with ornamental lanterns in the cool dusk. The meal was long and filling. Burgess's servants had prepared a mountain of food spread across countless dishes, each with its tantalising, delicate aroma, but all backed up with a base of fried rice.

Gunnar was used to oriental food, and watched each dish with careful anticipation, unlike Kroner, who before the meal was even half finished was sweating with exertion, his jacket open to the waist as he struggled through one piled bowl after

116

another. The wine which Burgess had insisted on providing was a ready thirst-quencher but too potent for casual drinking, and Malinski was talking with a fervour unknown to the others.

There was a lull at last as the servants began to remove the dishes, and Gunnar found time to study his new companions. Burgess was already full of drink, and appeared unable to deceive or betray anyone. As Maddox had said earlier, he was rather pathetic, yet showed a tremendous desire to hold on to his old world. Gunnar's eyes returned once more to Burgess's daughter. Lea Burgess was not a bit what he had expected. From the look on Maddox's face when they had all trooped into the low room, he had been knocked sideways too. Gone were the patched jeans and sloppy shirt, and she had not even made the pretence of clinging to her father's obvious beliefs in her choice of clothing.

Her simple, sheath-like dress was of bright kingfisher blue, high-collared, and slit at the thigh in Chinese style, so that her slim, tanned legs seemed to draw every eye as she moved around the room or sat quietly beside her father.

She was attentive and composed, yet gave little sign of warmth or welcome, even when Burgess repeatedly tried to draw her into the conversation. Once, when Kroner had unloaded a canvas grip of bottles brought from the ship, did she show some animation, and Gunnar saw her hand move quickly to her throat, and her eyes turned towards her father with something like fear.

Gunnar said: 'I noticed that the people here are at a disadvantage with their boats. It must be very difficult to unload fish at night or when the weather's bad?'

Burgess cleared his throat and moved his mind to the new subject with obvious effort. 'It is, Captain. In spite of everything else here, the fishing village was built after the town. They got the worst end of the anchorage.'

'I thought as much.' Gunnar pretended to take a drink. 'I think we can spare a couple of our mobile generators.' He gestured casually towards Malinski. 'The chief engineer would be happy to help the fishermen rig lighting and even a power winch for their boats, if they're interested?' They were all looking at him with mingled surprise and interest. Gunnar wanted to laugh aloud. He felt like a man in a trance, a being controlled by some mad outside force. It was all a game, a weird dance with no apparent ending. He tried to keep count

117

of the drinks, to stay ahead of the others in self-control and calm.

He saw Maddox glance sideways at the girl, watched the eagerness and hope in his eyes. Again he wanted to laugh, as he suddenly thought of Janet. Far off, delectable Janet, who had managed in spite of everything to show that she did not give a damn for him or anything he stood for. The divorce was a master touch. He still wondered if he had expected her to plead for release, to make some gesture of submission if only for her own ends. He had sometimes thought that he might offer to take the full blame, if only to feel a sense of superiority. But she had finished even that little dream. She did not need him, any more than she required his consent. No doubt when she was ready, or tired of her new love, she would take her father's powerful backing and look around for another.

Dimly he heard Malinski say: 'I'd like that, sir. It'll give my boys something to do to break the boredom.'

Gunnar nodded. 'There's a lot we might do here.' He noticed that the girl was watching him closely, her dark eyes hidden in shadow. Somehow he knew she was the one to be careful of. She seemed alone, apart from the others in her own contained world.

Burgess said vaguely, 'I'll see what I can fix, old boy!'

Gunnar moved in quickly. 'There's a headman, I believe?'

'That's right.' Burgess eyed the nearest bottle, and Kroner bent to refill his glass for him. 'Tao-Cho is his name. A funny old chap, as old as the hills!' His speech was slurred and his massive head was beginning to droop.

Outside the veranda Gunnar could sense the watching villagers, held at bay by the circle of bright lights like animals around a camp-fire. Any one of them could throw a grenade, fire a shot without fear of detection, yet Gunnar knew somehow that it would not happen. He was safe here. He was under observation even as he played through the game of discussion and planning with Burgess.

The doctor said: 'Perhaps I could fix up some sort of hospital here, Captain? Just to get them started?' He watched the captain uncertainly, as if waiting for Gunnar to talk him down.

Gunnar ground down the feeling of deceit and disloyalty Connell's question had aroused. This was the way it had to be played, and now the doctor was unwittingly falling into place.

118

'I think that's an excellent idea, Doc!' He saw the astonishment and relief on Connell's dark features. 'I expect they have a rough time of it here.'

Burgess laughed thickly. 'Your ship'll be taking root if you go on like this, Captain!'

He swayed and would have fallen from the chair but the girl seized his arm and whispered fiercely: 'Father! Please, you *promised*!'

Gunnar rubbed his chin. Promised what? he wondered. The drink most likely. She must have had a constant battle to keep him off the stuff in quantity.

'Just say the word, Captain, and I'll fix it with the old boy himself.' Burgess pushed the girl away, his eyes fixed on Gunnar's relaxed face. 'He owes me a few favours. I'll arrange a meeting for you!'

Gunnar stood up. 'Tomorrow then?' For the first time he looked directly at the girl's grave features. 'Perhaps you can remind him?'

She nodded, then looked away.

Gunnar made one more planned move. 'Well, if you'll excuse me, I think I'll walk back to the ship. No need for the rest of you to leave, but I've a few things to do before I hit the sack.'

Connell was the first to jump to his feet. 'Go alone, Captain? After what happened in the jeep?'

Maddox too was already halfway to the door. 'It's not safe, sir. Hell, you took a risk just coming here!'

Gunnar turned and looked again at the slender, black-haired girl. Your move, he thought coldly. 'What do *you* think, Miss Burgess?'

She stared from her father to Gunnar and then into the darkness beyond. Gunnar could almost hear her mind working, her clear, desperate thoughts which had tracked every part of their conversation like a recorder, so that she now knew exactly what Gunnar had done. One way or the other she must give an indication of her position.

'It is quite safe, Captain. Even for *you*!' Then she turned and walked out on to the other veranda above the sea.

Gunnar half smiled. The help for the villagers was the bait. She could not fail to see the difference such aid would mean to the impoverished villagers.

Gunnar walked out into the darkness, conscious of the silent, watching figures and the brooding shapes of the build-

119

ings around him. To win every sort of battle you must first split the potential enemy into as many parts as possible. Up to now they had had it all their way, had conformed in every detail to their normal pattern.

Tao-Cho might be powerful in his tiny kingdom, but he would make an equally powerful ally. It was only curious that men like Jago had failed to grasp that attack, when it came, started from within.

It was only just starting, he thought, but as yet Burgess's daughter was the only one who had showed a real sign of understanding.

7

A Name from the Past

Major Lloyd Jago stood straddle-legged on the bluff above the fishing village and stared down at the overlapping rooftops. In the slit-like gullies between the houses he could see an unusual bustle of activity, and even from his lofty vantage point his nostrils recoiled from the powerful stench of fresh fish.

Payenhau's fishing fleet was in once more. Jago had not got used to the excitement this event aroused. It was a combination of emotions shown so rarely by these stoical people, and he had not seen such jubilation even in San Francisco when the U.S. Navy had pounced on the port for liberty. This small fleet meant many things. It represented food and survival for a certain period ahead, and therefore a continuation of birth and growth. It also meant a reunification of split families and loved ones. Some boats were crewed entirely by the menfolk of one family, and the loss of such craft meant the finish of life itself. The boats were mostly old and much repaired like everything else on the islands. Few were longer than thirty feet, and none looked as if it could survive even a moderate squall.

Sergeant Rickover chewed on a cigar and kicked a small stone over the bluff. 'They'll be going wild for a few nights, Major.'

'You can say that again.' Jago's voice was tinged with contempt. Like most professionals whose path to the top has been hard, he was suspicious of anything untidy and undisciplined. 'There'll be another fifty kids started tonight!'

The *Hibiscus* shone in the far distance, the awnings shimmering in haze, the bridge and upperworks glittering with reflected sunlight. Small, white-capped figures moved slowly about her decks, and Jago noted that several working parties were meandering towards the town itself. He bit his lip and tried to dismiss the gnawing dissatisfaction the sight gave him. *Hibiscus*'s presence had been unwanted in the first place, but her sleek outline in the centre of the anchorage had nevertheless been a small hint of the power he represented. But now, after three weeks, the situation had changed, and he could not decide if it was for the better. He had tried to pump Gunnar, had even hinted at his uncertainty in his regular messages to his far-off superiors. But the usual curt replies from the latter had soon left him in no doubt that they were disinterested in his problems. The cold war was simmering elsewhere, and his own problems were an unwanted burden. Jago was quick to appreciate that any sign of uncertainty on his part might be interpreted as weakness, so he decided to handle the matter alone as was his normal approach.

He should have felt quite satisfied. Or so he kept telling himself. The islands were quiet for the present. Gunnar seemed to be toeing the line, and had certainly made peace with the inhabitants of the fishing community. The ship's influence had partly affected the town too. The doctor ran a regular sick parade in his makeshift hospital, while some of *Hibiscus*'s officers and enlisted men added their weight and know-how to repairing and maintaining the waterfront installations. Gunnar was a cool bastard, he thought. He knew a few tricks about how to get in with the Chinese, yet he shared nothing with either Jago or, it seemed, his own officers. He was a sort of influence, a brain which made moves and enforced ideas like an outside force. That part Jago certainly did not like.

Major Yi-Fang, the commandant's second-in-command, had remarked on the change several times, had even questioned Jago's power over events. He had pointed out more than once that Gunnar's assistance to these people might influence their desire for independence *against* the Nationalist Government rather than make things simpler in the long run.

Jago guessed that Gunnar was more interested in improving the American image than he was about the commandant's status. It might follow that he was right, of course. If Gunnar was able to smooth the relations of the townsfolk with the U.S. sailors, then the next move might be even easier. The arrival of a bigger, more modern ship to replace the *Hibiscus*, then a nuclear submarine and all its attendant supplies and facilities, would infiltrate the Chinese reserve with hardly a ripple. Then if anything went wrong it would be too late for protest. The commandant could be replaced, Jago conceded, just as he could. Although he could not admit it, Jago knew he was more concerned with his own appearance and relations with Yi-Fang and the tough fighting garrison he had helped to train and form into a formidable unit. He knew that the Chinese soldiers had long enjoyed their sense of importance and superiority over the islanders. It had been a suitable bribe to make up for their isolation and sense of separation from their own homes in Taiwan. They were better fed, even pampered by Chinese standards, and Jago knew that the uneven balance was necessary to preserve their unity and sense of purpose.

As a youth Jago had almost shipped overseas to join the French Foreign Legion. It had been a kind of symbol to him, and now, years later, the Legion's old magic stayed with him and often affected his judgement. But he also knew that the Legion had failed in North Africa because it had grown careless of its responsibilities. Loyalty was not enough. It was useless to allow the men to soften and take root, to intermarry with the locals of their garrison towns, to see the other side's point of view. A soldier, or for that matter a marine, had no point of view but his duty. That was clear to Jago, and should have been just as clear to Gunnar.

Still, if Gunnar wanted to play at diplomacy, Jago decided he would give him his head for a while. It seemed to have taken his mind off Lieutenant Inglis's death and the bungled shooting when a Chinese labourer had been killed. The latter incident had annoyed Jago more than somewhat. The only reason he had been so casual with Gunnar about it was because of his own sense of annoyance. The fact that the garrison sentries had been absent from the pier on that day had done two things. Gunnar's own guards now controlled that vantage point, and it showed also that the Chinese soldiers still had a lot to learn about continuity of orders. He had banged

122

home this point to Yi-Fang, and had felt a cooling in the man's attitude towards him. Yi-Fang had explained that an N.C.O. had been to blame, and seemed to think that covered it.

Jago glared at the nodding fishing boats and wondered if Yi-Fang realised the menace they represented. Once at sea they scattered to the winds, and no one could be sure what individual craft got up to. Any single boat could make contact with ships at sea, or, if required, touch land at the Red-held islands to the west.

It had taken Jago weeks to get the commandant to register these craft, to log and number the boats and crews alike. A simple enough precaution, a matter of military clear thinking. But Jago had nearly gone mad with frustration as he had forced the point home. The Chinese way was not for him. The long-drawn-out formalities, the endless tea-drinking, hardly seemed to fit in with the picture of an efficient administration. If only he had more help, he had told himself so often. Rickover was a damn good marine but was strictly a nine-to-five man. Outside his duties he took little interest in Jago's tiny empire. He could hear him now, tapping his foot and sucking contentedly on his cigar as if he were in Florida, not on the unhappy soil of Payenhau.

Rickover was more of a thinker than most marines, and Jago suspected, far better educated than himself. He was prepared to see Gunnar's point of view, and even hinted that he thought the islanders had a genuine grouse about their situation.

Rickover watched the back of Jago's bullet-head and smiled to himself. He knew exactly what the major was thinking, and how worried he was becoming. He suspected that if Gunnar had been killed by the mine Jago would have been more pleased about that than concerned about the death of his sergeant in the same jeep. Jago had gone on about it at some length, but Rickover, who saw most of the radio messages, knew there was another, more pressing, reason for Jago's behaviour.

If everything went well, with no extra strain thrown on the distant U.S. administration, Jago's chance of promotion was very promising. Every so often a helicopter flew in from a passing carrier with mail and despatches, and Rickover wondered with secret amusement if Jago had already sent for a new uniform and the much coveted eagles. If Gunnar, or anyone else for that matter, fouled up this chance of glory for

123

Major Jago, Rickover pitied him very much indeed.

Still, that was service life, he thought philosophically. The enlisted men fought each other in the open, but officers schemed and back-stabbed. It was always like that, and as far as he could see it would never change. A sergeant's life was the best. Enough authority to be comfortable, but insufficient to be bothered by the brass.

Jago suddenly said aloud: 'If I could just persuade Washington to give me one hundred marines, *fifty* even, I'd show these bastards!' He turned and looked directly at his sergeant. 'It would take some of the weight off your shoulders too!'

But Rickover stood firm. You can't draw me, Major, he thought cheerfully. You stay your side of the fence and I'll stay mine. Aloud he answered dutifully: 'It'll come, Major, It'll come.'

* * *

Mike Bella sat unmoving in his canvas chair, his elbows propped on the littered desk of the tiny ship's office where he carried out his duties as yeoman. A fan whirred overhead, making the papers and files flutter and the dust to swim in the filtered sunlight from the open port. Apart from the foremost part of the ship's hull, only the superstructure was higher than the pier alongside, so that Bella's small room was in deep shadow and pleasantly cool. If he thrust his head through the port he could look straight down into the green water below the pier, shadowed by the barlike structure of the planks above, and so inviting as it lapped and sighed around the piles. It was very clear, and Bella had seen the shelving sandy bottom, the rusted metal and fossil-like pieces of wood which had crumbled from the pier over the years. It was as if the ship was a permanent structure, actually sitting on the deceptively near sand and shells.

Bella stared at the notepaper and the few lines of his round handwriting. How could he go on? What was the point? The letter had been started when the ship had weighed from Hong Kong, and he had painstakingly added a little each day. They had been in Payenhau for three weeks and showed no sign of leaving, ever. The anchorage and coastline had been mapped and recorded several times over, and the concrete bases for radar reflectors had long since dried in the unwavering sunlight. The ship's energy was now expended outwards, like arms

124

of a central being. Some of the men actually seemed to be enjoying it, especially the crew replacements, some of whom were getting away from routine shipwork for the first time. As most of the replacements were misfits like himself, Bella knew that they were escaping minor persecutions, also for the first time.

He licked his pen and stared hard at the paper. Each time he ventured ashore with some message or other for the marine major, Bella had peered into the smooth Chinese faces of the islanders, seeing in each a tiny agonising memory of the girl he had left in Hong Kong. Even her name, Peach, which he had laughed about in those early days, rang in his mind like a distress call.

Her English had been poor, and she was one of a refugee family newly settled in the Crown Colony. But with patient happiness Bella had coaxed away her shyness, and even broken down her family's caution with his gifts and readiness to help. For the first time in his life Bella had been needed, had become an essential part of a family life. He rarely thought of racial difference, and when he did so it was more with understanding than concern. He knew enough about his own family struggle to feel a common bond of trust and love.

Now she was hundreds of miles away. When *Hibiscus* left Payenhau his chance of seeing her again was nil. Taiwan, back to the fleet, and then Stateside, back into the melting pot of sameness, the endless, boastful, empty life of enlisted men and their unreal dream-world of women and personal conquest.

He closed his eyes and tried to hold her face in his mind, but felt again the pang of fear as the outlines became more fuzzy and unsure. One day he might be completely unable to remember her sad, childlike beauty, let alone hold the touch of her hands in his mind as he had once done without effort.

'You busy, Mike?' The rough voice behind him made him start from his thoughts. Pirelli slouched in the doorway, a mop and bucket held loosely in his big hands.

Ever since that first meeting and the fight which had nearly ended in disaster, Bella had nursed a grudge against the big seaman. Pirelli had symbolised all the things he disliked and feared, and he had found real pleasure in usurping Pirelli's place in the small, tight world of the mess table. Yet after the shooting he had found a kind of sympathy for the man. Grout's death had changed Pirelli from a grinning, take-it-or-leave-it sailor to a grim, in-looking shadow. A man with a

125

grievance who was watched with caution by chiefs and enlisted men alike.

'Yeh, come in and squat.' Bella kicked some files from a seat and watched as the other man laboriously began to roll a cigarette. He saw the big fingers, strangely gentle, and wondered how a man like this could kill with such hatred.

Pirelli had been confined to the ship, had grown more morose with each day of activity ashore and the simple delights of some of the other men when they had returned from patching some boat or building a hut for a worn-out old villager. Like a lot of crawling Boy Scouts, he had once said, but the others had ganged up on him in a way they would have once never dared. Deep down Bella knew he had helped to cause Pirelli's loss of power, but it no longer gave him satisfaction.

His mind began to tick over. There was no work in the afternoon, and two-thirds of the crew would be ashore. Some of the officers were going sailing in a borrowed boat, no doubt suitably accompanied by a case of Scotch, and only Lieutenant Kroner would stay as O.O.D. Bella's dark eyes strayed to a pack of leave cards which had been introduced for the ship's stay in Payenhau. A run ashore would do Bella good, but he knew it would be fatal to go alone. His misery would grow rather than disperse with only his own company. He picked out a card and began to fill it in. They were already signed by the first lieutenant, as Regan was a great believer in time-saving, and the rest would be simple. Kroner spent most of his duty in the wardroom, reading and sleeping, and the gangway watch could not care less provided a card was produced.

He said carefully, 'What about a walk in the town?'

Pirelli picked up the card as if it was a piece of delicate porcelain. 'Did you do this?' He turned it over. 'Jesus, what a break!' He stood with sudden determination. 'I shan't forget this, Mike. I know a place where it's quiet, we can get a fair drink an' then we——'

Bella was embarrassed. 'Hell, get a move on then! Go and change and I'll meet you on the gangway in ten minutes.'

As predicted, it was too easy. The gangway watch took the card, winked at the captain's yeoman, and allowed Pirelli to pass without a word.

Fifteen minutes later Kroner checked the cards as he mustered the duty watch. He saw Pirelli's name and almost decided to make enquiries. Still . . . if Regan had signed the card

126

. . . that was good enough. You never argued with *him*.

Soon the figures of Bella and his tall companion dwindled and were swallowed up within the sun-bathed town, which from the ship appeared so peaceful and uncomplicated.

* * *

Maddox winced as his water-softened feet took the weight of his body on the sloping rocks. Below him the borrowed boat floated above its shadow in the clear water, the faded sail carelessly furled on the bottom boards, the food basket half empty. He stepped quickly off the rocks, which were hotter than he had anticipated, and stood in a tiny patch of cool sand. He shook himself like a dog, the exhilaration of his swim and a rare sense of freedom making his skin quiver. He plucked at the waistband of his trunks and then sat down heavily on the sand. It was a sheltered place at the western end of the anchorage, beyond the headland which halted the fishing village and directly opposite one of the small islets. Regan was drinking thoughtfully from a plastic cup, his eyes hidden by dark glasses, and Malinski was squatting on the crown of a rock like a contented gnome. There was a splash, and Connell lurched panting from the water, and pausing only to grab a tin of cheroots and his lighter from the boat he joined Maddox on the sand.

Maddox took one of the cheroots doubtfully and watched the blue smoke hover motionless above them. 'I enjoyed that swim,' he said.

Connell nodded. 'It was great.'

Payenhau was such a small place when one compared it with world events, Maddox thought, yet they had been here long enough already to appreciate its variation. Here, for instance, swimming and relaxing, perhaps for the first time. It felt safe, its isolation unmarred by the threat of danger. Yet only on the other side of the island Inglis and the others had died in similar, innocent surroundings.

Although the ship and the town were invisible around the headland, Maddox knew the area was well patrolled, yet he noticed that Regan carried his pistol and occasionally glanced up at the cliffs. But then he was like that. Contemptuous and arrogant one minute, cautious and watchful the next. A man wasted by inaction.

Connell said quietly: 'What d'you make of things now, Bob?

127

The skipper seems to have calmed down a bit, wouldn't you say?'

Maddox thought about it. It was true that Gunnar was more approachable, yet at the same time he seemed preoccupied with his own thoughts. Whereas he was keen to leave Maddox to deal with day-to-day routine, he checked and vetted the outside operations and changed them if he desired without giving any reason.

'He seems better,' he admitted, 'but he doesn't give much away.'

'I was wondering if we were all beginning to imagine things a bit.' Connell idly watched a gull hovering overhead. 'When Peter was killed I must admit I felt the captain might be right. But now I'm not so certain. They might have given him this command just to break him in again after his experiences and hospital treatment, and nothing more than that.'

'Maybe.' Maddox's thoughts returned to Burgess and of course to his daughter. The Englishman had seemed a bit quieter during the last week. He had apparently been unable to arrange a meeting between the headman, Tao-Cho, and the captain as he had promised, and seemed afraid to meet them socially. Gunnar too was keeping his distance, as if he understood that the revered Chinese leader was watching to see if American deeds matched their words.

'I keep thinking about that mine,' continued Connell thoughtfully. 'It shook me up I can tell you. To see those poor soldiers dying like that, it was horrible!'

Maddox twisted sideways. 'I know. But I'm surprised you're not hardened to that sort of thing, Doc.'

'Not to unnecessary and violent death. Perhaps I joined the navy to beat that weakness, if weakness it is.' He touched the little crucifix about his neck. 'I was amazed the skipper took it so calmly.'

Maddox said, 'Did he?'

'Like a cop at a road accident. Like ice. I guess his own experiences have hardened him.'

'Perhaps it's as well for us, Doc.'

'You can make steel brittle by hardening it too much, Bob!' Then Connell laughed. 'Never mind, there'll be a chopper flying in tomorrow they tell me. That means mail. I could sure use some.'

Maddox lay back and pretended to doze. Mail. He wondered if there would be news from Mary. Either from her direct or from a helpful friend. He wondered too if a letter would be less worrying than the lack of one.

He heard Connell ask, 'What would you do if you were asked to die for a place like this?'

But Malinski answered from his rock, 'I'd never forgive them!'

Regan called thickly, 'Open another bottle, somebody!'

The doctor laughed to himself. In a way they had both answered correctly.

* * *

The commandant's long room was just as Gunnar had remembered it from his first visit. When he looked across the window's wide sill he had a momentary sensation of loss at the sight of the empty stretch of inviting water. Only by leaning right out into the harsh glare could he see the *Hibiscus* at her shore mooring, and even then the bulk of her was hidden by an outcrop of rock below the window. Colonel Tem-Chuan still sat in his giant carved chair his eyes magnified and broken by the massive lenses, but he was no longer smiling.

Gunnar had answered the commandant's unexpected summons with a feeling of relief. Something had to break, someone must speak soon.

The colonel said, 'I think you do too much for my people here, Captain.'

So it's *my* people now, Gunnar thought. 'Little enough, Colonel. It's mainly to keep my men occupied.'

The colonel weighed up this piece of news. 'I see. Well, I am pleased to hear it, very gratified indeed.'

Gunnar kept his eyes steady and impassive and tried not to reveal the inner revulsion he experienced by the colonel's appearance. Tem-Chuan was naked but for a short, sarong-like cloth, his vast, sagging body made up of countless fleshy circles like the Michelin tyre advertisement. He must weigh a ton, Gunnar thought, probably only moves about for the basic requirements.

'Anyway, Captain, there is another matter I wish to discuss.' He sounded as if he had only just made up his mind, and Gunnar half expected him to broach the subject of his proposed meeting with the headman.

'I have certain information for you. I shall be interested in your enlightened comment.'

129

Here it comes. Another effort to hold his flimsy world in one safe piece. Gunnar waited, his fingers gripping his pockets.

'There is a terrorist on the island, Captain. My information is sparse, but reliable. This man came to Payenhau before you, whether by coincidence or design I do not yet know. But he is here. He is called Bolod.' The commandant fell into sudden silence as Gunnar sprang to his feet and walked quickly to the window. 'Do you know him, Captain?'

Know him? Bolod? Who did not know of this notorious Chinese organiser and terrorist? The months rolled back and the shaded room seemed to fade into the distance of time itself.

Viet Nam again. Could he never free himself of the horror and the treachery? Cameo after cameo coursed through his brain. The derailed trains, their butchered passengers lolling like bloody dolls, the mined roads, the despatch riders decapitated by snares of barbed wire; all these and countless more atrocities had been engineered by the man, Bolod. A mere name, in fact no one could be quite sure if the name covered several men. But every work of cruelty and destruction, every 'execution' bore his mark. And now he was here. It was again personal, a real and definite battle.

When he turned his face was composed but taut and pale. 'I have heard of him, Colonel. He is a professional. Have you confided this with Major Jago?'

'This morning, Captain. He has gone off with my second-in-command to alert all the posts. He suggested that this man might have killed your officer and laid that mine.'

The mine, yes. The murders on the lonely islet were more by chance, Gunnar felt quite sure of that. 'Perhaps. But how did your informant find this out?'

The colonel rubbed his protruding belly with irritation. 'That is my affair!'

One of the fishermen most likely, Gunnar thought quickly. It was too much of a coincidence. It was more imperative than ever to meet the headman. But it could not be forced. Experience had taught him the folly of pushing your ideas on such people. He felt the sweat on his arms. Bolod of all people! He tightened his fists at the prospect, just one more chance of finding the man.

The colonel said just as suddenly: 'And how are you feeling these days, Captain? More rested in yourself?' The man's face was bland and empty, the small mouth like a flower. 'You miss your wife perhaps?' He hurried on as if to mask the astonishment on Gunnar's face. 'I did hear something. News is all we have here.' He made a small gesture to a curtained doorway. 'But if you are lonely? I could arrange a young girl's company to pass away the slow-moving wheels of time.'

Gunnar swallowed hard. 'That will not be necessary, thank you.' He wondered who had spread the news ashore, but knew he was wasting valuable effort. The colonel was right. News of any sort was welcome amongst strangers.

The gross Tem-Chuan went off at a tangent. 'And Commander Burgess, has he been of use to you?'

'His boat has been a great help.' Faintly from the pier he caught a spasmodic burst of jazz from the ship's loudspeakers. Kroner was evidently treating the inhabitants to a little culture of his own. In fact, everyone was occupied elsewhere. The officers sailing, the men stretching their legs or hunting out spare women. Perhaps he was the only fool after all. Through that curtained door might lie the one thing he lacked. He half smiled at his own uncertainty. 'I must go now, Colonel.'

Tem-Chuan shrugged weightily. 'As you wish. Will you watch for this man, Bolod?'

'I promise you that, Colonel!' Gunnar's eyes filled with Arctic brightness so that the colonel regarded him with interest.

'That is reassuring.'

Gunnar paused at the door, his voice carefully controlled. 'I see that you are building an airstrip out at the prison camp?'

The great glass lenses flashed in the sunlight as he turned in the chair. 'Like you, Captain, I keep my people occupied!'

Gunnar walked down the cold corridors and out into the main courtyard. He waved aside the jeep driver and walked alone into the sunshine beyond the gates.

A man moved from beside a barrow of melons, a giant, muscular Chinese with a flat wrestler's face. Something familiar made Gunnar frown as the man shambled towards him. Of course, it was Burgess's deckhand. Gunnar wondered how the man enjoyed working for an erratic failure like Burgess.

'Do you want to speak to me?'

The man bowed slightly but was still almost a head taller than Gunnar. 'My name is Tsung, Captain. I am from Commander Burgess.' His English was clear, but slow and schoolroom style.

'I know you, what does your master require?'

131

The man's lips moved soundlessly, then he smiled faintly as if at some joke. 'The meeting is tonight, Captain. It will be aboard the *Osprey* at sunset.' He tilted his head to one side. 'O-kay?'

Gunnar stifled his excitement. 'That'll be fine. I will be there.'

Burgess had apparently enough sense to arrange the meeting in his own boat. Away from prying eyes. Or did he just want another bottle?

Tsung loped away, his mission accomplished. In the distance he looked like any other Chinese, and Gunnar wondered who amongst all these people was the man who had informed on Bolod. Now *he* would be a real capture. The key to the whole mystery.

From his high window the colonel watched Gunnar's slim figure striding down the hill and then waddled crablike towards the curtained door. He saw that the girl was still waiting, and he was glad he had roused the American captain into leaving so hurriedly. With a contented chuckle he dropped his sarong and closed the curtain behind him.

* * *

The place which Bella and Pirelli eventually found to be alone with their thoughts was certainly quiet enough, even quieter than either had expected. Bella thought they had walked for hours, mostly uphill, and all the time in the blazing heat of the afternoon. They had passed small groups of sailors and plenty of off-duty Chinese garrison troops, although most of the islanders seemed content to laze within the shadows of their doorways.

Once, Bella had pulled Pirelli into a side street as an army jeep growled past, its occupants darting glances in all directions as they carried out a town patrol. Conspicuous in navy uniform complete with white, shore-patrol gaiters, Chief Tasker sat stiffly between the soldiers, the *Hibiscus*'s one representative of law and order.

Then they had continued their search, until more from weariness than set planning they had found this place. It was in the last jumble of buildings on the hillside, so that through the open side of the room they could see the other dwellings below them, layer upon layer, like steps to the sea at the foot of the headland.

It was a wooden building, high-roofed and comparatively cool. Two sides were open to the weather but for rolled bamboo screens, and the beams were hung with faded, painted mats like battle flags. Some old men were squatting at the far end, smoking and playing a seemingly meaningless game with black ebony counters, which appeared to have few rules and very little movement.

A big Chinese in a canvas jacket regarded the sailors with apprehension until they slumped into two bamboo chairs in a corner away from the other occupants, and then he attended to them with quiet and dignified respect.

The drink, as to be expected, was a local brew, a cross between beer and wine, and tasted bitter. But it was fairly cool and left the mouth fresh and demanding more.

An hour passed, and but for an occasional remark each man was immersed with his own problems.

The sun moved over the island towards the distant sea and with surprising suddenness passed below the brow of the hill, which was higher than Bella had at first realised. Immediately the surroundings seemed to lose their shabbiness and poverty as lanterns were lit, and from another section of the building came the cheerful clatter of pots and dishes.

More Chinese filtered into the place. All were subdued at first, but upon realising that the Americans were harmless broke into a noisy, bird-like chatter which soothed rather than irritated Bella's rapidly fogging mind.

He noticed that Pirelli's eyes were red-rimmed and angry, and that he was drinking as fast as the proprietor could refill his cup, until at last the Chinese left one giant earthenware jug so that he could attend to the other customers and bring out the appetising bowls of rice from the other room.

The elation began to die, and Bella's mind seemed to cringe from the cheerful talk around him. The fact that Pirelli was past speaking and the Chinese tongue was unintelligible, added to his sense of despair.

There was a brief lull in the din, and for an instant Bella thought some more of the *Hibiscus*'s crew had arrived. He was vaguely pleased at the idea and felt inwardly crossed by Pirelli's apparent lack of gratitude. But it was no one he recognised.

There were two Chinese in similar leather coats, strong and competent looking. They looked around until one of them

133

saw the two Americans and then they started to push through the room towards them.

Bella felt an edge of alarm. They were far from the ship and any help if something went wrong. With his finger and thumb he groped under his waistband for his short-bladed knife which he had owned since his dockside childhood. He kicked Pirelli's ankle under the table. 'Pull yourself together! We've got company!'

Pirelli straightened himself with effort and glared angrily at the two strangers who now stood beside the table. One smiled and said in careful English, 'May we join you?'

There was something about these men, Bella thought. The other Chinese had treated them with respect not as mere equals. What was there to lose? 'Sure, take a seat.'

The first man had to translate to his friend and said to Bella: 'He has no English. I do talking.' He snapped his fingers and the owner hurried across wiping his hands nervously with a cloth. The man said unhurriedly: 'We have a real drink, eh? Not this *poison*!'

He gabbled again in Chinese and within minutes the table took on a different appearance. Good wine, a dish of seafood, even finger bowls appeared as if by magic. Through the haze of smoke Bella heard someone playing quietly on some weird stringed instrument. The total effect was pleasant and soothing, and Bella noticed that the new benefactor was treating him with great respect, like an old and trusted friend.

He said, 'My name is Shou-Chin, I am captain of fishing boat.' He beamed at Pirelli who was already sampling the wine with new energy. 'Your friend has great thirst?'

Pirelli eyed him coldly. 'I gotta great appetite too!' He made a violent obscene gesture but the Chinese fisherman shrugged. 'I not understand.'

Bella felt weary of Pirelli. 'He wants a woman, goddammit!'

The man rolled his eyes and spoke rapidly to his companion, who broke into sharp, chirrupy laughter.

Pirelli lurched to his feet his face contused with rage. 'Don't you laugh at me, you slope-headed bastard!'

Bella said anxiously: 'Sit down, you ape! They're all looking at us!'

But Pirelli had made up his mind. In his state of fuddled resentment and bitterness, his desire to hurt, to shock anything Chinese, had given him an idea. If poor Grout had been here it would have been different, but then so would everything

134

else. He snatched the bottle and glared at Bella's face. 'I'm goin', you can do what you friggin' well like!'

Bella felt a hand on his wrist and the man said quietly, 'Let him go. He is trouble I think.'

Bella was undecided. Pirelli on his own might upset everything. But even as he was about to follow Pirelli's swaying shape through the silent Chinese onlookers the man added in a tight, insistent voice: 'I have been looking for you. I have a message from Hong Kong. From a girl!'

* * *

Lieutenant Alan Regan walked slowly along the pier his eyes moving restlessly over the moored ship. The wires were taut and secure and the upper deck looked almost yachtlike under a line of electric bulbs. It was dark, the sunset having come and gone in breathtaking swiftness. There were little lights glowing up the hillside and the headlamps of a jeep probed soundlessly down the steep cliff road from the east. In a weak moment Regan had stood in for Kroner so that he could join them ashore where Connell was having a small celebration at his makeshift hospital. Regan did not want extra duty, any more than he had any desire to help Kroner, but he had not forgiven the doctor's scathing comment on the pier after the shooting, nor would he.

He peered at his watch. Time to check the dutymen. Routine had to run no matter where you were. Quarters, evening colours, testing guns, nothing could be changed.

A jeep thundered on to the pier so that it vibrated like a mad thing. Regan scowled as he saw Chief Tasker leap from it and run towards the gangway where already one of the watch had picked up his rifle with startled confusion.

Regan barked, 'I'm over here, man!'

Tasker blinked away from the harsh lights and saluted. 'I was lookin' for the O.O.D., sir!'

'Well, as from one hour ago, I'm it!' Regan balanced on his heels. 'Now what have our liberty boys been up to that makes you get in a sweat?'

Tasker controlled himself with an effort. 'It's Pirelli, Lieutenant!'

Regan lost his temper. The whisky drunk in quantity under the sun, the unsatisfactory boat trip and swimming party, and now this. 'What in the name of Jesus are you bellyaching

135

about? Pirelli's restricted, I'm just going to check on him!'

Tasker eyed him stonily. 'He's ashore, sir. With a pass signed by you!' He took a breath. 'He's just raped a Chinese girl and beat up a couple of soldiers! Apart from that, all's well, Lieutenant!'

Regan threw his cap on the pier. 'Christ Almighty!' He remembered vaguely that he had signed the cards in rather a hurry. An idea crossed his racing thoughts. 'Is Bella with him?'

'He was, sir. Not now. He's up the hill looking for him.'

'I'll *bet* he is!' He quickly made up his mind. 'Go and drag Mister Kroner from that tumbledown sick bay and tell him to take over again. You hold the gangway until I get back.' He beckoned to the quartermaster. 'Bring that rifle to me!' With a slap he grabbed the weapon and peered at the vibrating jeep. 'Take me up the hill, quick!' The Chinese driver's eyes glittered in the gangway light, and before Tasker could utter another word Regan and jeep had roared away towards the town.

Tasker looked at the other seaman. 'Fetch Mister Kroner,' he said wearily. 'It looks like being a long night!'

8

The Facts of Life

The hold cover of the Motor Fishing Vessel *Osprey* had been removed so that the velvet sky and the high bright stars formed a natural ceiling above the seated figures below. The hold was well lit by the vessel's own electric lights backed up with a powerful, hissing pressure lamp, and the small, crowded place was warm and humid in spite of the late hour.

Mark Gunnar was never surprised by the East's ability to make any gathering or event seem important and grave. Even in this converted fishing boat the formalities were observed, with neither a show of surprise nor an admission of discomfort. Tea was brought down the deck ladder by one of Burgess's messboys, and the silence was only broken by an occasional grunt or the careful sip of the transparent green beverage. Burgess too seemed subdued and watchful, although when he had ushered Gunnar across the closely packed tilting decks of the newly arrived fishing boats he had been careful to align himself with the American in the face of his strange, dignified Chinese visitors.

Tao-Cho was like somebody from an old painting. He was of great age, his thin, biscuit-coloured features criss-crossed with tiny lines, his chin decorated by a flimsy but venerable beard. His clothing was plain and without character, but draped itself around his erect frame with a kind of dignity. His companions were also elderly men of the same stamp, yet who hung on their leader's every word and waited with something like subservience for him to complete his tea drinking.

Gunnar had walked straight from the ship and through the village, constantly aware of patrolling soldiers and the feeling that he was expected. The troops faded away when he entered the village itself, and Gunnar had the impression that it was an island within an island, a forbidden place but to those who were chosen. Near the small square a child had stepped from the gloom and without a word had plunged his hand into Gunnar's, and with the confident sureness of an old man had led him down to the jetty across the first moored boat to where Burgess waited like an anxious mother to welcome him.

Tao-Cho slipped his hands into his sleeves and made a brief signal for the basins to be removed. He watched Gunnar with impersonal interest and said, 'Well, Captain, what is it we have to say to each other?' His voice was fragile without being weak, and Gunnar imagined that he must have been a ruthless leader at one time in his long life.

'I require your help.' Gunnar heard his voice magnified and distorted by the tall sides of the hold and sensed its insincerity. He added quickly, 'I think you know of my mission, but much more has happened lately to make me believe that this island may be in danger.'

The headman made no sign if he was disappointed or surprised by Gunnar's opening. 'But why come to me?'

'I am told you are the leader of these people. That you once controlled the whole group of islands and are regarded as a just and loyal man.'

'Loyalty? What is that?' A hand moved upwards to stroke the small grey beard. 'I was once what you would call a pirate. I led ships which were based here. Imperialist powers made honest trade impossible for the likes of us. They had the knowledge, the skill, *and* of course the gunboats!' He bobbed his

137

head with silent amusement. 'Eventually, of course, we had to give way to your Western "progress". We withdrew to these islands. Some of the younger men stayed with their trade until killed or captured by foreign warships. Others went to the mainland or to Taiwan to seek other work.'

He gave an eloquent shrug. 'They were of course unlucky. Like crops on bad soil they endured much and eventually were swept away. The Kuomintang, the Japanese, the new Nationalist Government, all exacted their toll, until our small community here remained alone. But we are resourceful people. We protected our children and our elders, we dragged a livelihood from the sea in a way unforeseen by our ancestors. We raised small but sufficient crops, in short, we survived. We had no riches but one. We had *freedom*!' The last word was spat from between the thin dry lips, and the other old men bowed and murmured agreement. 'Then the commandant, Colonel Tem-Chuan, came with his troops and his barbed wire. We had had a bad season, we listened to his promises of help and supplies. Before we realised the falseness of his words, more men came, more guns, and then the fort was built to control us all!' He glared with sudden anger at Gunnar. 'Now you want to finish what he started! To drive us out, to blanket our hopes with your false promises!'

Gunnar began again. 'I have heard that there is a Communist agent among your people.' He watched for some sign of alarm or guilt but there was nothing. 'If he succeeds in his task your people will be worse off than before.'

'So *you* say, Captain. But how can a man like you really understand us and what we suffer? Either way we lose our independence. Communist China or an American-backed Taiwan will hold no love for us. We are in the way, but we must find our path back to the light. If this man you mention can offer us hope, why should we not accept his word instead of yours?'

Gunnar felt his limbs relaxing as if from surrender. It was hopeless, particularly as the old Tao-Cho was right. Yet why should the commandant, for whom he openly expressed his hatred and contempt, tolerate him outside a prison camp? Whichever way you looked at it, it did not make sense.

Tao-Cho continued in his dry, flat tone: 'Do not take offence, Captain. I have watched you since your arrival and I think I understand your ways. You were worried about the man killed by your rifleman, yet what could you do? In your

138

position I might have had the right hand lopped from every grown male in the crowd, as an example! Who can tell? But you must understand that whereas you will soon return to your way of life, *I* shall be left behind as before. You will forget, but I must stay to hold the responsibility of my people no matter what comes to pass.'

'I just want to know where your sympathy lies. I will be content with that.' Gunnar leaned forward as if to force his sincerity across to the other man.

'I see.' His face became a mask for several minutes. 'I will tell you this. I will urge my people to resist a further occupation unless it is with our consent, and not developed by separate arrangement with the commandant and his government.'

Gunnar said calmly. 'You must realise that any outside power could subdue you in days without the protection of a great sea force.'

'You saw the old freighter wrecked in the bay, Captain?' The hooded eyes flicked upwards in the lamplight. 'It was Japanese. A small force of troops, but heavily armed and battle trained. Yet we killed them like pigs and destroyed their ship! We were not attacked again! A man who knows these islands can hide, fight and survive long after a stupid soldier has given up hope!'

Gunnar felt lost. 'But to the outside world you *are* part of Taiwan!'

'No one has ever asked us. We have been told what we must do by others! If we can regain our freedom through your side then I will give you all the help I can. If not, then we must look elsewhere, Captain. But while you are here I will watch over you. If you are true to your words within the limit of your own responsibility then I will think again. If not,' once more he shrugged, 'then I must think first of our own survival yet again!'

'You know that there was an attempt on my life?'

'I know that and much more. There will be more blood and suffering before the future is clear. We are not mere pebbles to be trodden down to save the faces of your leaders, Captain! We are people, we matter very much, at least in our own eyes!'

Gunnar stood up. 'I understand. Thank you for your patience and your concern.'

Tao-Cho allowed himself to be lifted by his companions. 'We will meet again whenever you wish, Captain. Yours is not

139

a happy task. No matter how thick the paint, the boat beneath remains the same!'

* * *

Connell's hurriedly arranged celebration party was in danger of ending as suddenly as it had begun. With Regan staying aboard the ship and Kroner getting suddenly called away to resume his duty as O.O.D., the others were left in that awkward frame of mind which could influence any party one way or the other. It was still early, and the cool night sky outside the brightly lit shack which the doctor had grandly labelled 'hospital' was far too inviting, too restful to encourage a hasty return to the crowded confines of the *Hibiscus*.

Connell stood with hands on hips, shirt open to the waist, as he puffed a cheroot, his eyes bright as he surveyed the spartan, whitewashed interior of his new possession. The makeshift operating table was covered with a flag, upon which stood two enamel dishes of melting ice and an ambitious selection of bottles, most of which were two-thirds empty. He levered the top from a fresh Coke and drained it without effort. The tiny hospital seemed to symbolise his other self, so that in Maddox's eyes he appeared larger, and perhaps more willing to share his thoughts with his companions.

Malinski squatted on a box of dressings swilling a tall glass with thoughtful, precise movements, his face dull and contented, and seated together like two white ghosts, the doctor's new Chinese assistants which he had lured or bribed from the town seemed quite happy to drink in complete silence and watch their new masters with placid but interested calm.

Maddox poured another stiff measure of whisky and groped for some ice with his fingers. It was just like Regan, he thought, to summon Kroner back to the ship without prior notice. For that reason alone Maddox felt determined that the party should continue to its bitter end.

Connell waved his Coke bottle. 'Aha! Another guest I see!'

Maddox saw the great bulk of the Englishman, Burgess, framed in the open door, his face fixed in his normal expression of hopeful determination. 'I'm glad you could make it, Commander.' Maddox looked hopefully beyond the other man in case the girl had relented and accepted their invitation. But he was alone. He added hurriedly: 'Grab a drink, Commander! There's plenty left.'

Burgess took a bottle, his big hand trembling noticeably. 'Just left your C.O. with the headman wallah. They are going great guns down there.'

'Anything useful?' Connell squatted on the table, his dark hair falling over one eye. 'Have they decided to kiss and make up, or fight?'

Burgess grinned uncomfortably. 'Come now, we mustn't be cynical, eh?' He passed down his drink and poured another, larger one. 'I think your captain has a lot on his plate at the moment. By Jove. I remember when I was in his shoes.' He shook his head gravely. 'But that's another story.'

Malinski sat up sharply as if awakened from a deep sleep. 'What was that? I thought I heard a shot!'

Burgess had an empty glass again. 'Maybe it was. There's always shooting of some sort going on. Might be fireworks on the other hand. The Chinks love 'em at any time.'

The engineer yawned and reached shakily for the table. 'Fill me glass then!'

Burgess lay back in a chair and allowed the tide of whisky to wash completely over his tired mind. He had been on edge all day and had allowed himself to betray his own set rule about drinking. In the tiny wheelhouse of his boat was a deep locker, used originally for signal flares, but now a glory-hole for anything unsightly or out of place in a well-run vessel. Beneath some carefully rolled flags and unused bundles of canvas, Burgess had secreted his store of bottles. Between his rare runs to Hong Kong or Taiwan, when he did his best to restock his small hoard, he sampled the bottles in order of importance. He always saved the whisky until the end. Shared with no one, unless with a suitable visitor, which, God knows, was rare enough.

Today he had been tested to the full. Three visits he had made to the wheelhouse, and then in addition he had been pleasantly surprised by a half-bottle from Gunnar when he had come aboard to meet the old Chinese headman. Burgess had not eaten, and his inside seemed to swell with fiery power. It was like old times, he thought vaguely. The mess parties, the noisy laughter, and antics which were so meaningless to any outsider. By a stretch of the imagination he could picture Maddox and his companions as some of his own officers in the past. Reliable, unworried men who cared nothing for the meanness and base stupidity of those outside the service.

He sighed and massaged his sagging stomach. Although

141

only fifty, he felt every bit of his age. Every hour seemed to drag and clog him down nowadays.

Whatever anybody said, these Americans were good fellows, he thought. One of them was already filling his glass, and they all seemed quite happy just to let him sit there, as if they too were short of company. He liked the senior one very much. Maddox, for all his cheerful brashness, seemed reliable and intelligent. Burgess had noted the academy ring on the exec's hand, the careless way with the man, which signified one not relying on service pay. He tried to picture Maddox beside his daughter Lea outside some grey-stoned church with green fields beyond. There would be a navy guard-of-honour, crossed swords and gay, sincere speeches. He could see himself also, somehow returned to service life, proud and magnificent in his best blue uniform which he still kept hidden in an old tin trunk at his house on the quay. If only *she* would be reasonable, try to understand what he was attempting to do for her, for both of them. Every day she seemed to move further away from him, to immerse herself in a different and forbidden way of life.

The spirit scored across his throat and his eyes misted over. One day, very soon now, he would show her. All the privations, the lies and the uncertainties would be forgotten, and she would be proud of him once again. He frowned to himself. Proud of him? Had she ever been?

It was too easy to recall the distant past, but more difficult to trace its threads up to the present day. Like Maddox, he had once been second-in-command of a small ship on the Far East squadron. But that was long ago, in another world. A lost, unobtainable sphere when everything had revolved around the majesty of the Royal Navy, which he had entered at the age of twelve. As for his father, and his grandfather, there had been no question, no choice. It was duty, it was their way of life.

He could remember the lines of sloops and destroyers, the tall grey superstructures and waving flags. Faces flitted through his mind like ghosts, like the distant memorials they had become.

Burgess had been in Singapore when the Japanese had invaded. The select, private world he had understood and cherished had reeled and fallen almost with the first bombardment, the first salvo of death which was unleashed by the confident Japs.

142

Burgess's ship had been sunk at her anchor without ever firing a shot. With some of the survivors he had tried to help in the frenzy and panic ashore, his service mind rebelling against the stupidity and fear of the authorities, the mounting confusion and the sure knowledge that defeat was unavoidable.

His wife had already returned to England, and Burgess still realised that her departure and not the fire of battle was the beginning of his own destruction. With effort he could still picture her dried-up face and aristocratic mouth curved in anger and disdain, her contempt, and what Burgess now knew to be her only attempt at pity.

At first it had been more of a game. Many of the officers had secret Chinese mistresses. It was a joke, something one did, nothing more than that. In Burgess's case it might have ended just as quietly, but for his wife's sudden arrival and discovery of the girl her husband had made pregnant.

Burgess had found her in the blackened and smoking hospital even as the Japanese troops had forced their way on the peninsula, and as the real horror of Singapore had begun. The birth of their child had been careless and hurried, with no one really caring about just one more life soon to be sacrificed with all the others. Burgess could not ever recall her saying a word to him. Only her eyes had spoken. He had seen the small, desperate hands pushing the wrapped baby towards him, like a dying lioness will try to find sanctuary for her cub even in her last moments. Then she had died, and Burgess had run with the child in his arms, run for the sea, the only thing he really understood.

With a handful of other escapees he had watched the death pall rise above the harbour, like the token of an old way of life. For days the listing ship had dodged the bombers and the hunting ships, but only when Burgess had reached safety did he realise what he had done.

The child, Lea, grew up almost as an orphan. From home to home, from school to school, while Burgess continued with his interrupted career in a navy which was fighting for its existence.

Then, at the end of the war, when he was once more looking forward to a return of something firm and familiar, life changed again. He soon found that things were not the same. At first it only showed when officers were promoted above his head, or when appointments became fewer and less important. He had no wife to control his path, no woman's voice to carry his case to the places where it counted in the clubs and at the admirals' parties. He started to go down, but made the final mistake of trying to buy his security with drink.

There had been one occasion when Lea had been brought to a shore establishment in Plymouth where Burgess had been serving as an instructor. She was eight years old, with the dark, vivacious beauty he had once seen in her mother. Looking back it now seemed likely that the 'friend' who had decided to introduce the child to Burgess's world had done so with the cold deliberation of an executioner. The secret smiles, nods and unspoken comments filled him with an all-destroying anger. He still did not know if it was because of the cruel amusement, or because of Lea herself.

After that he had given way completely. He had not intended to steal the money. It was just a loan from the mess funds, which he had intended to replace. The axe had fallen, and the court-martial had been merciless. Even the president of the court, an officer who had joined with Burgess, was not slow to ram home his bitter contempt. Burgess had broken the rules, betrayed the code. There was no reprieve.

Since then it had been a long journey. Strangely enough, Lea had helped to save him in those early days. She depended upon him so completely, looked to him for everything. When there was no longer money for schooling, no work for a cashiered officer, Burgess had taken it upon himself to go back to the East, although he had no idea what he was looking for. Burma, Malaya, Siam, he had been to them all. Yet in spite of everything he seemed unable to find success.

When the Korean war had started he had written to the Admiralty offering his services. Also during the Suez crisis, and even to the Americans when Viet Nam had exploded upon a war-weary world. His replies were hardly more than acknowledgements. Nobody wanted Jack Burgess.

Outwardly he still continued to play a part, to act the role he still understood. Time washed away memory and recognition, and fewer faces came from the past to torment him. He built a fresh image, a new personality which he offered to the world around him. Deep in his soul he desired to hit back, to humiliate the very ones who had wronged him into behaving as he had. As the years passed he could see little beyond that, and as one barrier after another presented itself he became more desperate, more hopeless.

144

Just one more try, he repeatedly told himself. There has to be a break somewhere. A lump sum of cash, and we'll show the lot of them!

When he had been offered the job in Payenhau he had seen it as the beginning of a breakthrough. The orientals always needed men like him, were hopeless organisers on their own. It was not much of a job, but it was a start, and he was in charge of his own boat!

From now on he would fight his battles *their* way, no holds barred. What did a few lies count? What did it matter if someone else got hurt for a change?

The glass rolled from his hand and his big frame slithered sideways against the wall. His mind was no longer fighting, and had become subdivided by the whisky so that he could only see faded, indistinct pictures which no longer menaced him.

Maddox stood looking at him doubtfully. 'Shall we leave him here, d'you think?'

Malinski grinned. 'He's enjoying himself for once!'

'All the same . . .' Maddox's blurred thoughts moved into sudden focus. 'I think I'll just pop down and tell his daughter.'

Malinski coughed. 'You do just that, Bob!' He winked. 'Wish you luck!'

◆   ◆   ◆

Some of Maddox's eagerness gave way to uncertainty on the darkened veranda of Burgess's house, and he stood for several minutes to regain his breath and get his bearings. Shutters had been drawn across the big windows, but through the sun-dried slats he could see the girl sitting cross-legged on a rug, her hands spread across an open magazine as she studied it with obvious concentration. The shaded oil lamps seemed to show dark blue shadows on her long hair, and once more Maddox was struck by her beauty, her sense of enchantment.

Suddenly she looked up, her calm giving way immediately to an alert watchfulness. She seemed to see right through the shutters, and Maddox knocked unnecessarily on the screen door, his voice awkward and loud. 'Sorry to crash in on you, Miss Burgess, but——' He broke off, feeling slightly foolish, and by the time he had opened the door the girl was already on her feet, her back to the wall as if expecting an attack.

Maddox took off his cap and blinked in the lamplight. 'I just

145

wondered if I ought to help your father down the road.' He saw her dark eyes watching his face. 'He's a bit merry, you know how it is!'

She did not smile. 'I suppose you've got him drunk again?' She passed one hand across her forehead. 'I will send the houseboys or Tsung for him as soon as you leave.' It was curt, almost a dismissal.

'I expect he finds it a bit lonely here.' Maddox stood his ground. He had got so far, it was too early to admit defeat. He only wished he had not had so much to drink. It made him feel clumsy and juvenile in her presence, and the realisation of her contempt made him suddenly angry. 'I didn't *have* to come, you know!'

She smiled, the brightness of her mouth completely transforming her face. 'No, you did not have to come. I suppose you meant well.' She gestured towards a chair. 'Rest for a moment if you like. I promise not to attack you.'

Maddox sank gratefully into the cane chair and peered at the open magazine. It was a tattered *Esquire* that he guessed Burgess had taken during his visit to the *Hibiscus*'s wardroom. The page was open at one of the giant, glossy advertisements, and from his chair Maddox could see well enough the usual scene, the impeccable women, the expensive car, the hint of riches and perfect contentment. All at once he was deeply moved. Several thoughts came crowding in on him simultaneously, each made more obvious by the old magazine's unwitting comparison. Burgess's false life, his self-deception built to cover his miserable failure to recognise the things which really mattered. And his daughter, this perfect, black-haired creature, dressed once more in faded jeans and coolie shirt, who was a prisoner of past convention, a girl prevented from enjoying all the things which others had denied her.

With shock he realised she was staring at him with anger. 'Always you stare, Lieutenant! I can guess what you are thinking!'

'You'd be wrong, I can assure you.' Maddox had never known himself to be so long on the defensive. 'I am trying to be a friend, if you'll let me?'

She relaxed slightly, and as she lowered herself on to a bench seat, Maddox saw a strip of tanned skin reveal itself below her rumpled shirt. He tore his eyes away and said in a strained voice, 'I understand how you must feel here, it can't be much fun.'

She smiled faintly. 'It is sufficient. We were managing before your ship came, you know. It must not be allowed to spoil things for us.'

Maddox was not quite sure what she implied, but said quickly: 'We can do a lot of good for these people, your friends. We don't spoil everything we touch, as some people seem to think!'

'I would like to believe that. But from what I have seen I think your hopes are soon to be dashed. There is rarely aid given freely, without strings. Always there is a catch, a bargain. And always the weak must get the unfair side to that bargain.'

Maddox said jokingly, 'Look at me, do I look like an exploiter of the poor?'

She jumped up again and dashed a piece of hair from her eyes. 'You see? You are making fun of me already!'

'Not really, believe me. It's just that I hate to see you like this, cut off from everything you deserve.'

She stared at him in surprise. 'You meant that! Just for an instant you were being sincere!'

Maddox grinned uncomfortably. 'It does happen. And believe me, I do apologise about your father. It was my fault. We had this party, and it seemed to misfire somewhere.'

'I see.' She studied him gravely. 'Would you like some tea?' As Maddox started to rise she said: 'It's no trouble. I was just making some.'

'Thank you.' Maddox crossed his legs to control the excitement which was coursing through his body. 'I'd like that very much.'

She walked through a curtain saying as she went, 'Keep talking, I can hear you quite well here.'

He looked round at the long, shadowed room. 'There are some nice pieces of carving here.'

Immediately her head appeared round the curtain, her eyes watchful as before. 'Let me see if you are mocking me!'

Maddox stared from her to the small, delicate carvings with pleasant surprise. Quite unwittingly he had stumbled on her weakness. 'Did *you* do these?'

She put her head on one side as if to gauge the sincerity of his astonishment. 'I did.' She came into the room, a tray of dishes in her hands. 'I learned how to do it when we lived in Malaya. They are not very good really.'

Maddox picked up a small figurine of a stooping water-carrier and examined it carefully. 'I'd say they were damn good!'

When he turned, her head was lowered as she poured some tea, but he could see the pleasure at the corners of her mouth. He sat down on the bench at her side, conscious of her smooth arms and the tantalising tilt of her head. 'You see, we can be friends after all!'

She handed him a cup and frowned. 'Please do not misunderstand me, Lieutenant. I am not really hitting at *you*. It is what you stand for, what you have to do whether you like it or not!'

'But I do understand. And I'm just as sure that it's not right for a girl like you to be in this position.'

She gave a small, sad smile. 'And what would you have me do? Go to Hong Kong or Taiwan? Or perhaps start a new life again in England?'

The last word seemed to resurrect the whole bitterness of her early years, and Maddox said hastily: 'Forget it. That's all over.' He spread his hands expansively. 'You could go anywhere, do anything. With your looks you could crash Buckingham Palace if you wanted!'

She threw back her head and laughed. 'Perhaps flattery is good for me after all, Lieutenant.'

'The name's Bob, if you don't object.' He grinned at her. 'I could be here for a long time, so you might as well get used to it.'

'Well, *Bob*, let me ask you this. If your government ordered you to fire on these people would you refuse?'

'That's a hell of a question! In any case, no such order would be given unless . . .'

She sighed. 'Unless it was considered necessary, right?'

'I suppose so.' Maddox sensed he was getting out of his depth once more.

'Like in Viet Nam, or in the Dominican Republic, all in the name of justice and freedom!' She smiled at Maddox's set face. 'You are not smiling, Bob? Are you surprised that I am interested in all these things?'

'It's not that. I suppose I hadn't really thought about it before. I mean about the little guys in the middle of all these campaigns and battles. But what can a man do?'

'We shall see, when your captain has made up his mind.'

'The captain?' Maddox almost dropped his cup. 'He's just a small cog like the rest of us.'

148

'I think not, Bob.' She stared past him in the far distance, as if seeing another place and time. 'I have met his kind before. He seems cold and hard, too dedicated to his own beliefs to see room for deviations or retreats. He is a lonely man, I think.'

'I guess that's so.' Maddox found to his surprise that it was easy to speak about Gunnar to this girl. It was as if he had wanted to tell someone and now could not stop himself. 'He has had a very bad time I think it shows in many of the things he does. Yes, I guess you're right, he is a lonely man. But in his position it's hard to be otherwise.'

She grimaced. 'You sound loyal.'

Maddox grinned and changed the subject. 'You ought to think about him as a prospective husband! I reckon you'd soon have him eating out of your hand!'

She did not share his joke. 'You sound like my father. He always talks of this man and that, like a marriage broker!'

'Your father is quite a guy.'

'You think so?' She shrugged. 'He is much changed from what he used to be.'

She sipped at her tea her eyes thoughtful. 'I am interested in what you say about your captain.'

Maddox gulped. 'I was only pulling your leg.'

'You mean, he wouldn't lower himself to mix with a girl who is neither East nor West?' Her mouth quivered with sudden anger. 'Not politically or racially perfect enough for a captain, is that it?'

Maddox grinned with relief. 'Hell, you know I didn't mean any such thing! You're a proper little spitfire, d'you know that? Just unbend and come out from behind that nettlebush long enough for me to get a word in!' He reached out impulsively and took her hand. It felt small and cool, and strangely reassuring. 'Will you do that?'

Very gently she withdrew her hand, but she met his eyes with a quick smile. Maddox noticed that her breathing was a little faster and she had lost some of her built-in composure.

'Very well, Bob. So long as you do not try to alter my views. They are all I have.'

Maddox swallowed hard 'We shall have to do something about that, my girl. It's just as well I came to Payenhau, I can see that!'

She shook her head in mock sadness. 'Always you joke. It must be wonderful to have no fears, no uncertainty.'

He watched the smooth skin of her spine as she leaned for-

149

ward to replace the cup, and felt the blood singing in his ears. He almost reached out to touch it, but controlled himself with a real effort. Not yet, not here.

She said: 'I am so sick of sham. It is hard to take things and people at surface value.'

'I guess so.' Maddox tried to concentrate.

'Here, they all wear masks. The commandant, Major Jago, Yi-Fang, and now your captain. They are afraid of losing face, so they hide their every thought, repress each simple ideal. It is very sad.'

There was the sound of shuffling feet on the dark roadway, and Burgess's voice raised in thick protest.

She touched Maddox's arm. 'The boys are bringing him back.' For a moment the sadness returned to her features. 'If only he could find the strength to fight it, or even to admit that we will never find the old ways again.'

Maddox saw it as the moment to leave. 'Can I see you again, Lea?'

Her eyes widened, caught off guard by the sound of her name. 'If you wish.' And as he backed towards the door. 'Thank you for your tolerance!'

Maddox gave his old grin. 'Thank *you*, lady!'

Whistling, he walked through the village, which now seemed a friendly place.

Things were getting better after all. Better than he could ever have dreamed. It had been a near thing over Gunnar, he thought.

For one dreadful instant he had nearly smashed up the affair before it had begun. Gunnar was the captain, and that was all. He was strictly not included in Maddox's personal plans for Lea Burgess.

● ● ●

The air in the small wardroom seemed almost cold, stale in the remaining hours before the dawn. Slumped around the table, their faces grey and strained, the ship's officers stared at Gunnar's pale features with mingled expressions of anger or dulled submission. The brief party which Connell had given to celebrate the opening of his shore hospital was forgotten, although the drink had done nothing to ease this pre-dawn gathering.

Gunnar's shirt and slacks were smeared with dirt, and in his

150

tired, angry face his eyes shone with feverish life, like windows on to the torment of his thoughts. He looked down at Maddox's slumped figure. 'Well, we've lost him! He's up there in the hills somewhere, and God knows what he'll do next!'

Regan licked his lips and touched the long strip of plaster across his high forehead. 'I'd like to get my hands on the bastard!'

Gunnar stared at him with open amazement. 'You really get me!' He began to pace across the frayed carpet, his hands moving in time with his words. 'You of all people should have known better, Regan. Pirelli is a gunner, one of your own men. It seems to me that none of you has done a damn thing to find out about your particular sections, you've not even tried to drag them together as a crew!' Each word was like a lash, and Maddox stirred in his chair as if he was feeling the sting of every sentence from the captain's tight mouth. 'I've knocked myself out trying to get this job properly organised, and when I'm away from the ship for one hour what happens?' He glared again at Regan's grim face. 'You go haring off into the hills after this deserter, armed with a rifle like some cop in the movies! What the hell were you going to do, *shoot* him?'

Regan shrugged angrily. 'I wish I had!'

'Well, he got you instead, didn't he?' Gunnar's voice was devoid of pity. 'What is even worse, he took the damn rifle off you before he made good his escape!' He lifted one hand and counted off each item on his fingers. 'So here we are. Pirelli's laid out an officer, deserted, and put the whole mission in jeopardy, simply because of your incompetence!'

Maddox said hoarsely, 'That's a bit hard, sir.'

'I don't give a monkey's damn what you think!' Gunnar eyed him coldly. 'It's the only word for it! Quite apart from raping a local girl, Pirelli's filled the book as far as I am concerned!'

'Perhaps he'll give himself up when he's had time to think about it, sir?' Malinski's quiet voice halted Gunnar in his pacing. 'He's got a lot to lose.'

Gunnar gave a small, bitter smile. 'Is that what you think? Would you hand yourself over in his shoes? Pirelli's facing ten years at least for what he's done already. God knows what he'll do before he's caught. *If* he's ever found, that is!'

'He can't get far, Captain.' Maddox sounded resentful, his face crumpled and weary from the night's unexpected developments.

'He's a seaman. Right now I'll bet he's thinking about hijacking some fishing boat, or making a deal with one of the junk skippers. He's no fool. But what gets me is the way you've all shown yourselves in this!' He scanned their faces with cool contempt. 'The man is allowed to walk off the ship because one of my officers is too damn lazy to attend to my standing orders. You just don't care, do you? You're so wrapped up in your own little worlds you still can't see what we're supposed to be doing.'

Maddox stuck out his jaw. 'It's not clear what *is* going on here, sir.'

'And it never will be until you learn a bit of discipline!' Gunnar ignored the exec's flushed face. 'Hell, you didn't even know about this until you chose to wander back to the ship!'

Maddox opened his mouth, and then closed it again like a trap.

'I'll not have this ship's reputation wrecked because of your damn laziness, do you understand me?'

The doctor opened his cigar case and then changed his mind. 'Will this business make any difference to our acceptance here, sir?'

'They'll not be laughing about it, if that's what you mean!' Gunnar ran his fingers through his hair. 'Just when we're feeling our way into their trust, this has to happen. I can just imagine what Jago'll say when he gets back. It makes a mockery of everything we've tried to do.'

There was a silence, and none of the officers looked at his neighbour. Outside the water lapped gently against the plates, and overhead they could hear the slow pacing of the quartermaster on watch.

Gunnar seemed spent, as if he could find no more words to goad the grim-faced officers. 'Well, have you no comment?'

Regan said flatly, 'If it's my fault, then I'll take the blame.'

'Like hell you will.' Gunnar's voice was shaking. 'I take the responsibility for everything, as you well know. Every stupid, thoughtless act, each piece of lazy indifference and incompetence is laid at the captain's door. One day you'll know what I'm talking about, if you live that long!' His shoulders slumped, as if the life had gone out of them. 'I'm going to turn in now.'

Maddox moved noisily to his feet. 'What do you want us to do?'

'Right now I don't care if you commit mass suicide. Just

152

remember that we start afresh in the morning. From now on I'll be watching each one of you. Our orders are to hold on here until told otherwise, and until relieved. Payenhau is important, otherwise there would be more open protest about what we're doing. Things are happening well enough, and when you find the time from enjoying yourselves or testing your manhood, perhaps you'll realise that there's more to earning your money than just carrying the uniform.' He looked through an open scuttle at the darkened hills beyond. 'That's all. Carry on, Mister Maddox.'

Maddox made a last effort. 'I think I should be the one to explain, Captain.'

Gunnar eyed him without recognition. 'I said, that is *all*! There'll be time enough for your explanations later on!'

He strode from the wardroom, and the others stood or sat in silence, listening to the captain's sharp footsteps on the steel decking.

Regan said at length, 'I guess the party's over.'

Maddox sat down again, aware that his limbs were shaking as if from a sudden fever. It was a fierce mixture of guilt and anger, or hurt pride and bitter resentment. He wanted to say something, to put back the clock, but he could find no more words. He could still feel Gunnar's cold anger, which had been like a wedge driven between them.

Kroner said in a small voice, 'I don't see that he needed to blow his top like that.'

Regan felt his bruised head once more. 'He's a nut, just like I said he was! There's no reason in a crackpot!' He turned defiantly towards Maddox and showed his teeth at the exec's brooding silence. 'What, no defence? No paths to glory, *Mister* Maddox?' He spread his bony hands. 'That proves it then! When an exec won't back up his boss, things must be very bad indeed!'

The doctor walked quietly to Maddox's side. 'Take it off your back, Bob. Words can't hurt you.'

But Maddox answered as if the doctor had not spoken. 'He spoke to me like a goddamn cadet! Like a first-year rookie!'

Regan paused on his way through the door. 'And you *took* it! Surely that must prove something?' They heard him slam his door and the sound of falling furniture.

Soon only Connell was left in the wardroom. He looked at the empty, discarded chairs around the table. Even their angles and posi:.ons seemed to reflect the anger of their recent occupants, yet Connell still felt more like an outsider than before. He wanted to share their drama, even to feel some of the humiliation which had grown with the captain's attack.

He decided to wait for a while to give Maddox time to turn into his bunk. But as he picked up a magazine his head lolled and he was soon asleep.

Like penned animals the other officers lay awake or asleep in their respective rooms, each wrapped in thought or in the constant world of dream and speculation.

Only Gunnar remained on his feet. Standing in his cramped room, his shadow crucified on the bulkhead by the desk lamp which played across the piled folios and despatches as if to mock him. Once, he reached out to touch the cool steel of the cabin wall, conscious of its gentle vibration, the inexplicable movement and life which ran through every ship, even when resting. He knew he would not be able to sleep, yet dreaded the loneliness of waiting for the first light. He felt ashamed, sickened by his own behaviour, the more so because he knew he was driven by necessity. There was no sharing, no passing off blame or responsibility. A ship could be welded into a single unit by tradition or environment, by its task or by the trust of others. Or, it could be drawn together by the mutual hatred for its commander. Gunnar sat down and rubbed his eyes, then he began to read his despatches with slow, concentrated effort.

If that was how it must be, then that was how it would be.

Somewhere outside the sleeping *Hibiscus* other men would be planning and preparing. Up on the hillside amongst the gorse and scrub. Pirelli was probably peering down at the glittering strip of water and at the shaded gangway light. He had his rifle. He was no longer just a man. A *mere* man, as the rear-admiral had said.

And Bolod. Was he out there too? Waiting to finish off his career of bloody victories with one final coup?

If anything was going to happen, it must be soon. The hidden enemy knew that there was an airstrip almost completed, probably knew about the proposed base and everything else.

When it came it would be swift and sudden.

Gunnar touched the riveted steel again with something like love. The tired old ship, which had seemed to sneer at his hopes and ambitions, had become part of his life, in spite of all else. Perhaps they had to prove their worth to each other. Like Bolod, every man looked for something.

154

9

Death Wears a Hat

It was a change to see another ship in the anchorage. The long-stacked freighter had wound its way through the Western Channel with ponderous confidence, the siren keeping up an intermittent squawking like an ageing banshee. Now she lay at anchor, hemmed in by local boats and buzzing with frenzied activity.

Gunnar stood alongside Major Jago's stiff figure at the top of the beach, where three landing craft snuggled in the shallows, their ramps lowered to receive the long procession of figures which had waited with murmuring patience since before dawn. Soldiers checked and re-checked their lists, junior officers waited by the ramps, almost the last barrier to the prospect of freedom.

'How many?' Gunnar shaded his eyes in the harsh morning sunlight to watch as the procession began to shuffle forward. There seemed to be countless children, but few old people amongst the crowded figures. Old people would survive least of all, Gunnar thought, in the long struggle of endurance faced by each refugee from Red China. At first, getting across the border would be enough. Then the long list of disappointments and dangers would really begin. The bribes required for each painful stage, the parting with the few valuables saved for that last journey, the separations and deaths along the way. Then Payenhau, herded together in that camp where it was said that they vetted and checked for fellow-travellers. In fact, the commandant was profiting in every direction. Before each rare visit of this ancient freighter he would more than recover the price of the refugee's keep by labour and unpaid skill. Now, some of them were leaving at last for Taiwan, the ultimate haven. Gunnar wondered if in fact they as strangers would find it much different after all. If too their eagerness and hope had been blunted by the commandant's short-sighted policy of greed and power.

Jago said at length: 'There's about two thousand leaving today. Good riddance to 'em!'

Gunnar's eyes narrowed as he watched the distant khaki shape of Regan, accompanied by two enlisted men, as he strode grimly along the lines of Chinese, peering into each face, his attitude of watchful belligerence visible even from the head of the beach. He was obeying orders at least, Gunnar noted coldly. Checking in case Pirelli was attempting to leave amidst the press of refugees. Alongside the waiting ship he had also seen the *Hibiscus*'s gig bobbing at the companion ladder, where Maddox was also keeping a close watch. Gunnar's harsh words had borne fruit of sorts, he decided. Two days since Pirelli had escaped and not a sign of him. There had been a distinct change in the *Hibiscus*, however. Orders were carried out promptly and without question by the officers, but in spite of this fact, Gunnar knew that they had drawn together only in their combined resentment of him, were only biding their time.

The first two L.C.I.s frothed astern and then swung away towards the freighter, their low sides seeming to bulge with crammed Chinese. Only the children waved and shrieked, their parents seemed content to watch the approaching ship with mesmerised fascination. No doubt more 'squeeze' would be waiting for them aboard, and more when they landed. It was what they had come to expect. One day it might be their turn, and only that made it bearable.

Major Yi-Fang, sleek and competent, strode along the sand, his boots black and gleaming in the sunlight. He saluted and said, 'They will soon be away now.'

'You've crammed them in a bit, Major.' Gunnar regarded him steadily, wondering why he should dislike this man more than usual.

'It is good enough, Captain. They have grown used to much worse.'

'There is such a thing as charity, Major!' In spite of his guard Gunnar felt angered by the man's amused arrogance.

Yi-Fang shrugged. 'Charity is the conscience of scoundrels, Captain, nothing more!'

Jago interrupted, 'Here comes the damn chopper at last!'

Gunnar checked the angry words in his throat and turned his back on the smiling Chinese officer. Faintly at first, and then with growing power, the helicopter flashed in the sunlight and then turned on the last leg of its flight towards the town itself. Like a giant mosquito, flying above its shadow on the placid water, it filled the anchorage with violent sound, so that the people in the landing craft shaded their faces and cowered their heads as it rattled above them. With a great

156

swirl of sand and dust it alighted with precise dignity at the top of the beach, while Gunnar and the others pulled down their caps and coughed in the miniature dust storm.

It was two days overdue, but no one seemed surprised. Payenhau seemed to slide further and further from the sphere of operations, and even within the island itself things had stayed very quiet. No more incidents, although Jago's men took care to maintain constant patrols and road checks around the clock. But there had been no softening in the attitude of the islanders, no olive branch or even a hint of what they were thinking and preparing.

Gunnar watched the shining rotor arms swing to a halt and then droop as if the life had gone from them. The doors slid open and several khaki figures lowered themselves to the land. There were official sacks, mail and fresh instructions no doubt. He saw Sergeant Rickover talking with the pilot and then collect a small parcel which he lifted in the sunlight, a great grin on his brown face.

Whatever it contained, it seemed to please Jago, who said in a surprisingly friendly tone: 'We'll have a drink together, Captain. Right now I must go and collect my parcel. Okay?'

Major Yi-Fang smiled as the marine strode up the beach. 'Promotion at last, Captain. We now have a marine *colonel*, I think!'

Gunnar grunted and walked slowly down towards the water's edge. So that was it. No wonder Jago was anxious to keep things smooth and unruffled. The thought of Inglis's death fanned through him like a searing flame, and he kicked at the sand with sudden fury. Of all the bloody-minded way of doing things!

He looked towards the bluff and the jagged outline of the fishing village. It was quiet again, the boats having left once more for the open sea just as quickly as they had arrived. The old headman would know by now of Jago's promotion and would arrive at the same interpretation as himself. A colonel would have to be backed up by a larger command Rickover would hardly be a sufficient force for one so senior. Tao-Cho would have his own ideas about that!

At the far end of the beach he sat down on a flat rock, suddenly tired and conscious of the unwavering heat. Across towards the nearest islet the sea looked flat and inviting, the green water almost milky in the sunlight. At the top of the islet the glare touched one of Jago's guard posts, giving the

157

hidden machine gun a sudden lethal glitter.

Gunnar looked around at the deserted beach and at the tall, sedate rocks behind him. It was still and quiet. Everyone was either in town or out trading with the freighter. It was too rare an event to miss. He made a sudden decision and began to strip off his shirt and slacks. With distaste he removed the heavy pistol from his belt and covered it with his cap on the top of his pile of clothing, then clad only in his underpants he stepped gratefully into the clear water and launched himself into its friendly embrace.

* * *

Lieutenant (jg) Don Kroner stood angrily on the fo'c'sle, his long, handsome face dripping with sweat. Ten of the ship's seamen, in undress whites, carrying carbines and ammunition, submitted to Chief Tasker's slow inspection as he moved along the untidy line, his gaunt features set in concentration.

The man at the right of the line, a tall, gangling gunner named Chavasse, banged his rifle butt on the deck and peered at the officer. 'What's the point of it all, Lieutenant? Pirelli's well away by now!'

The others swayed and murmured in agreement.

Chavasse had a nasal, whining tone, and sensed his unexpected importance. 'It's goddamn unfair, sir! Like some of the others, I was due for transfer when we delivered this can to the Nats in Taiwan! 'Stead of that we're stuck here like a lot of rookies!'

Kroner eyed him coldly. 'You'll do as you're damn well told, Chavasse! You'll patrol the outskirts of the town, *on foot*, and watch all the dives in case he shows up there.'

Another man, Robbins, a flat-faced ex-truck driver from Cleveland, laughed and pointed at his companion. 'If there's any dives in this dump, *he'll* wind up like Pirelli!'

Chief Tasker glared at him. 'Stow it! You're like a lot of whores waiting for a weddin'! Call yourselves *seamen*!'

Kroner turned away in disgust. It was always the same. The whining, the complaints, with every man seeming to drag his feet at each damn order. They all seemed to think it was some sort of game. Well, perhaps it was, but Kroner was sickened by his own apparent lack of control over these tough professionals. Without Inglis his own position seemed to have changed too. Now he was the junior officer, and was treated accordingly.

The helicopter took off from the beach and roared crabwise above the pier and then curved away towards the shining cleft between the islands. Soon its pilot would be back in his spacious wardroom in some carrier, the *Hibiscus* and this stupid place forgotten. This was not the navy. It was nothing! He swung back towards the chattering seamen. 'Silence there! Remember where you are!'

Tasker barked, 'Right turn!' The men shuffled rebelliously on the hot steel and then marched in single file towards the gangway, where Kroner saw with surprise that another officer was standing amidst a pile of suitcases, staring around him as if he had never seen a ship before in his life.

McCord, the duty quartermaster, ambled across and saluted. 'New ensign reported aboard, sir. Replacement for Mister Inglis.' He sucked his teeth dubiously. 'Newer than a fresh dollar, I should think, sir!'

Kroner stared past him with sudden happiness. 'Keep your opinions to yourself, McCord.' A new officer, and an ensign at that! It was too good to be true. He saw the ensign was holding his fistful of orders, looking for someone to drop them on so that he could join the ship officially. Kroner hitched his gunbelt and stepped aft to greet him, his face set to mask his unexpected pleasure.

The young ensign saluted. 'Come aboard to join, sir.'

He was a round-faced, cheerful-looking youngster, with a humorous mouth and remarkably innocent eyes. There was something vaguely familiar about him, but Kroner made a point of keeping his voice casual and unfriendly. He skimmed through the crumpled flimsy and grunted: 'Replacement for Inglis. Well, he was killed out here, so you watch your step.' That was just right. Knowing and tough. Just right.

But the youth merely smiled shyly. 'What a mess, eh?'

Kroner was confused. 'I'm Kroner, the exec is out on the freighter, and the captain's ashore someplace.' He stared irritably at the ensign, who was looking around the deck with amused candour.

'*Well?* Who the hell are you?' Kroner tapped his foot impatiently.

The ensign looked down at the folded papers in Kroner's hand as if to say that all his necessary information was there

159

contained. Instead he said cheerfully: 'Maddox, sir. Keith Maddox.'

Kroner groaned. 'Not another. There'll be a bigger mix-up than ever now.' He ignored the puzzled expression on the newcomer's face and said off-handedly, 'The exec's name is Maddox, you see.'

The boy nodded with sudden gravity. 'Yes, he's my brother.'

Kroner's jaw dropped. 'Hell! Does he know about this?'

Maddox junior shook his head. 'Not a thing. I changed places with the ensign who should have come. I thought it might be fun.'

'Fun?' Kroner grinned. 'Oh, brother!'

'What's the captain like?'

'You'll see.' Kroner's mind was busy. The atmosphere between Maddox and the captain had grown steadily more strained and brittle. The arrival of another member of the Maddox family might take the weight off the other officers in several ways. The O.O.D. rota would be better, and the exec, who was like a bear with a sore head since his conflict with Gunnar, might work off his rage elsewhere. Kroner beamed. 'Welcome aboard, Mister Maddox!'

The boy regarded him with wide, innocent eyes. 'My friends call me Pip,' he said.

Kroner swallowed hard. Pip would get along just fine. Like hell he would. 'Well, follow me and I'll show you around, er, Pip.'

McCord watched them go and then looked down at the young ensign's expensive leather cases. If they were still prepared to send officers to replace gaps in the ship's strength it meant that the *Hibiscus* was available for duty for some time yet. McCord kicked at one of the cases and spat over the rail. This piece of information would go down well in the fo'c'sle, he thought glumly.

●   ●   ●

Mike Bella stood quite still at the top of the salt-encrusted ladder and listened hard for several minutes. The old wrecked ship which lay across Payenhau's sandbar hung at a greater angle than it appeared from seaward, so that Bella had to keep one hand to steady his panting body as he waited and listened on the broken and crumbling bridge deck. He could hear his own breathing and the pounding of his heart, whilst the sea

160

noises seemed lost and muffled beyond the old and rusting hull. He had made quite sure he was not followed, and now that he had reached his objective he felt unsure and even frightened.

It had all started after his meeting with the Chinese skipper on that run ashore with Pirelli. This feeling of being doubly trapped, a man in a web of his own making.

That night, after he had left the strange Chinese eating house, with his brain buzzing with fresh hope and half-frightened schemes, he had met Chief Tasker and some of the men from the ship, and heard what Pirelli had done. Without enthusiasm he had joined in the search, for his mind had been elsewhere, with the girl in Hong Kong. But Pirelli's sudden and violent departure had been one thing, this new turn of events was something else. There was vague and garbled talk of rape and assault, of Pirelli's half-crazed dash up the hillside after his discovery by a military patrol, and that could be dangerous. If it was proved that Bella had given him the leave pass, things could get worse in that direction. And right now Bella needed to keep out of trouble.

The Chinese skipper had told him that he had friends in Hong Kong, among whom were the girl's own family. He had heard all the details of Bella's fruitless attempt to get married, had even met Peach and promised her that he would find Bella and try to help both of them to come together.

Bella had been dazed and confused by this sudden change of events. He had tried to find out more, to gain the man's real confidence. When he had asked outright how the skipper had discovered his whereabouts and matched up the scanty information, the big Chinese sailor had merely shrugged and said: 'Our world is small. We survive on our knowledge.' Bella had had to be content with it.

Then that night on the hillside Pirelli had stepped calmly from some bushes, without a sign of panic or surprise, smoking a cigarette and with a rifle beneath his arm like an amiable hunter. Bella had lost his temper, had yelled at Pirelli to return to the ship with him, before anything else happened.

Pirelli had squatted on the roadside and stared up at him with calm amusement. 'Save yer breath, Mike. I've done it for sure this time!'

'That girl, the one you——'

'Oh *her*!' Pirelli showed his teeth in the darkness. 'A nice bit of tail she was.' He became strangely excited and confi-

161

dential. 'I let on that I was goin' to let her go, you see?' He then bellowed with laughter, so that Bella peered anxiously down the quiet road, half expecting to see a startled patrol. 'Then I took her some place behind them shacks and knocked some sense into her!'

Bella's voice had been shocked. 'She was only a kid!'

'So what? She was ready for it, and I gave it to her good!' He had leapt to his feet and gripped Bella's jacket with sudden force. 'Come back to the ship did you say? Why, you stupid little bastard, they'd skin me alive!'

Then he had told Bella about Regan and the rifle. The lieutenant had jumped from a jeep and come blundering up the hillside, shouting Pirelli's name and cursing every bush and boulder which had blocked his path. He had been so angry that he had not apparently heard Pirelli's stealthy approach until it was too late.

Pirelli had said proudly: 'I clobbered him with a rock. Pity I couldn't have had a few words with him first!' Again that loud laugh, a gust of madness in the cool darkness.

But Bella had been strangely relieved by the news. After all, if Pirelli had done half of these things, it was enough to take everybody's mind off a mere leave pass. Rape, assault, desertion, they clicked into line like tombstones. But then Pirelli had dripped his bomb.

'They wouldn't have known about me, 'cept for you!' He had shaken Bella playfully by the jacket, a big dog worrying a puppy. 'I went back to that swill-joint to look for you an' your Chink friends.' He laughed more quietly. 'But I went round to that window, behind the screen. I didn't want to be seen.'

Bella had licked his lips, suddenly cold. 'So? Where do I come in?'

'I heard, Mike. I *heard*! Them bastards offerin' to smuggle that Chink broad of yours from Hong Kong, just for little old you, right?'

'What of it?' He had tried to sound unworried.

'That's a very good question, old friend. *Why* are they doin' it for you? What do they want in return, hey?'

'Nothing. I—I mean, not much.' Bella's nerve almost cracked as he realised the full implication of Pirelli's hard questions. To think of him outside that quiet window, listening and scheming, with his face still scratched by the girl he had dragged up the hillside, stripped and raped within yards of her own home. He was mad, suddenly and terrifyingly, with

162

the suddenness of a shock or a shaft of light.

Pirelli had continued almost soothingly: 'Be yer age, Mike. You are the captain's yeoman, you see despatches, hear things that no one else does.' He had twisted the jacket viciously. 'What are they after?'

'Just a few details. They want to know if the *Hibiscus* is sailing or not, and things like that!' He had wriggled like a pinned rabbit. 'Hell, it's nothing really! They're probably doing a bit of smuggling on the side!'

Pirelli had released him. 'Could be. I couldn't care less if they're smuggling Hitler in their lousy boat! But you can let me know *too* what's goin' on, see? If they can get your broad in, they can get me *out*!'

Then they had heard a jeep grinding up the hill, and Pirelli had grabbed up his rifle and made ready to go. Then he had paused. 'Finally, Mike, don't forget what I know about you. You meet me in a couple of days aboard that wreck in the bay. If I'm not there, leave some food in one of the bridge cabins. Call there every day until I meet you, got it?' His eyes had gleamed fiercely in the distant headlights. 'Otherwise, Mister Bella, I'll do for you too! It's a very *small* island!'

Bella had returned fearfully to the ship. It had been alive with scuttlebutt and speculation, but nobody had gone for him. Even Regan seemed unwilling to bring up the question of the leave passes, and appeared to have worries of his own.

Bella had been torn between informing on Pirelli's proposed meeting place and doing as the man had told him. But his mind refused to cope with Pirelli's sudden change, and revolved instead around the possibility of being reunited with Peach. The Chinese skipper had been quite cheerful about the prospect. 'When you know when and where your ship is going, I or my friends can smuggle her after you, see? Take her to Taiwan, and you can get married, or do what you will!' It sounded so simple. All the same, he would have to be careful. But the thought of touching her again, even in secret, made the other problems seem faint and unimportant.

Until now, that is. The old wreck seemed alive with creaks and tiny movements. Weed and fungus trailed from passageway and stanchions alike. Even after the years abandoned and picked clean by scavengers, it was still a ship. A ghost ship, with mocking, empty doors and buckled plates, but a place still alive from its long dead occupants.

This was Bella's second visit. Almost terrified he stepped

163

into the first cabin, once used by the vessel's master. It was now merely a big tin box, red-rusted and stained, its only port clouded by dirt and blown salt. He peered around in the semi-darkness and then almost fell as he heard a sharp, metallic click beside him.

Pirelli stared at him without speaking, his stubbled, dirty face devoid of welcome. Then he grinned and lowered the rifle almost reluctantly to the deck. 'You got here then.'

Bella put the small parcel on a ledge and said, 'It's getting difficult.'

Pirelli tore open the bundle and rammed a wedge of beef loaf between his strong teeth. 'So what!' He ate like a starving animal, his eyes red-rimmed and savage.

Bella regarded him emptily. He's mad, he thought. Completely up the creek! Aloud he said, 'They're still looking for you.'

'Let 'em! I'll be okay if you do your whack. If you don't . . .' He nodded towards the rifle. 'I'll fix you good!'

'There's a new officer come aboard today.' Bella racked his thoughts for something to say. 'A green ensign, but he's the exec's kid brother!'

Pirelli chewed thoughtfully. 'So he wouldn't recognise me, that's something!' Then he added, 'What's the captain doin'?'

Bella shrugged. 'He went ashore this morning. Nothing new there.'

'The lousy bastard!' Pirelli stared hard at the port. 'I'd like to kill that one!' He continued muttering as he searched through the parcel. 'Wanted to court-martial me, did he? Get me shut away!' He gave a wild laugh which seemed to re-echo through the listing ship as if all the old crew members were joining in the joke. 'Just for killin' a goddamn Chink! A pity the bastard didn't do somethin' about my mate when they killed *him*!' He nodded vigorously. 'Yes, Mister bloody Gunnar, I'll fix your hash for you!'

Bella stirred uneasily. 'I must get back now. The old man'll be asking for me.'

'Sure, sure. You carry on, Mike.' Pirelli was quite calm and reasonable once more. 'You're a good kid. I shan't forget.'

Bella smiled weakly. 'I hope you know what you're doing.'

'I'm not going to some stinkin' jail, I can tell you that!'

Bella walked through the door, his eyes darting down the sun-dappled passageway to check that all was clear. Behind him he heard Pirelli ease the safety catch, and said hastily, 'I'll be here tomorrow then?'

164

Pirelli laughed quietly. 'Yeh. And for Christ's sake get me a bottle!'

'I'll do what I can.'

Bella's sliding footsteps rang around the ship as he groped his way back to the maindeck. A rotting ladder enabled him to lower himself down to the cool sand, where he was hidden by the bulging hull from the rest of the anchorage and the haze-covered town beyond. He began to walk along the narrow sandspit as the tide crept slowly forward towards his shoes.

He was caught in a double blackmail if either party required to use such pressure, yet the thought of Peach, and the fact that she might already have started on her journey towards him, made him feel almost lighthearted.

* * *

Maddox lowered his arm from shading his eyes as the old freighter's siren screamed out for the last time as she began to swing towards the outer channel. The decks were crammed with faces, and some of the released refugees had even climbed into the rigging to stare back at Payenhau. Maddox sighed and climbed from the bobbing gig to the warship's deck, where Kroner waited to receive him.

'Don't tell me!' Maddox glared at Kroner's smooth face. 'World War Three has started, and they want me to parachute on to Peking!'

Kroner smiled gently. 'No, nothing but good news. We have a new ensign as replacement, which means less duty for the rest of us.'

'*And* it means we're taking root here!' Maddox was unimpressed. 'Anything else?'

'I don't think so.' Kroner stared at the freighter's slow progress. 'The skipper's ashore, and I understand that the formidable Jago has received his promotion from a grateful nation!'

'Jesus! That's all we need!'

A dull crack echoed across the anchorage and sent the dozing gulls soaring from the cliffs. 'What was that? Another mine?' Maddox snatched the glasses from the quartermaster and peered shorewards. A few soldiers were looking towards the hills, but otherwise nothing moved.

Kroner said, 'Perhaps it was a firework.'

Maddox grunted unconvinced. 'Well, it's not our worry. Yet!'

165

'Shall I send the new officer to see you? He seems anxious.'

'I'll bet.' Maddox thought gloomily of the shower he had been anticipating. 'Yes, I'll give him a couple of minutes below. Go and get him.'

Kroner smiled smoothly. 'A pleasure.'

Maddox threw himself down into his chair. He felt rattled, and at the same time mentally stifled, as if he wanted to dash ashore to let off steam. To drink, or just walk in the sun until he dropped with exhaustion.

Aboard the freighter all morning he had scrambled through musty-smelling holds, feeling foolish and unwanted, watched with open amusement by the ship's Chinese crew.

It was like playing at soldiers, yet without the satisfaction found by Jago under similar circumstances. And *he* was a colonel now. Maddox wondered how that might affect the balance of power in Payenhau.

He answered the small knock at his door without looking up. 'Come in.'

Then for a full minute the two brothers looked at each other, the young ensign with cheerful pleasure, Maddox with astonished wonder.

Maddox exploded: 'Is this some sort of joke? What in hell's name are you doing here?'

His brother removed his new cap and laid it thoughtfully on the table. His dark hair was shorter than his brother's but almost as unruly. 'I thought it would please you.' His mouth spread in an innocent smile. 'Mister Kroner made me very welcome when I told him you were my big brother!'

Maddox leaned back and stared at him. 'I'll bet he did, the deceitful bastard!' Then he ran his eyes slowly over the ensign's slim figure. 'Hell, Pip, you've grown a bit since I saw you last!'

His brother perched himself on the table and looked around the small room. 'Not much for an exec, I'd have thought?'

They both laughed, the ice was broken, although Maddox felt uneasy and worried by Pip's unexpected appearance.

'How are things in New York?' He felt like a foreigner, and saw Pip's generous mouth twitch before it became serious.

'It's still big and busy, Bob.'

'And Mother?'

'Not big, but even busier.' He opened his wallet. 'I've got some pictures I thought you'd like.' He watched as Maddox laid them face down on the table. 'Well, don't you want them?'

166

Maddox smiled uncomfortably. 'Later. I'm a bit pushed.' After all this time he could no more open up the memory of home in front of an audience than fly. Later, when the ship was quiet for the night, he would study each one.

Pip said casually, 'I'm getting married, by the way.'

Maddox staggered to his feet. 'You're nuts! At your age? You're crazy!'

'Thanks for your good wishes, Bob!'

Maddox slumped down again and stared silently at his brother. It was like looking at an old photo of himself when he had left the academy. Slim, self-assured, eager. And yet there was a difference. Pip seemed more determined in some strange way. He said carefully, 'What does Mother say?'

'Oh, she agrees, naturally.'

'You *know* it's a problem to get hitched when you're only a junior officer! The women don't like it, the travelling, the separation, and everything!'

'No I don't. And neither, I suspect, does my big, wise brother!' He smiled gently. 'You'll like her. How is Mary, by the way?'

Maddox flushed. 'That's all over.'

'I'm surprised. I thought you'd hit the right one there. Mother read more into your sparse letters than usual, I guess.'

Maddox sighed. 'Have you settled in yet?' The talk of Pip's proposed marriage had shaken him badly. He did not feel jealous as he might have supposed, merely a sense of loss, like a man who has suddenly noticed that age has overtaken him with nothing to show for its passing.

'Yes, I'm all fixed up.' Pip waggled his legs. 'It's a crummy ship by the look of it, but from what I can gather they can't spare much else. I got a lift in a carrier from Taiwan, and they seem to think things are hotting up in the Formosa Strait. There are a lot of units heading up there just in case. But me? I'm safe and snug down here with my old guardian.'

Maddox grinned uncomfortably. 'Not so much of it! Remember, an exec can make life hell for a greenhorn ensign!'

Pip looked suitably impressed. 'I'll complain to the captain!'

Maddox waved him down. 'Watch your voice. The ship is undergoing a touch of the Blighs at the moment!'

'Tch, tch! I can see I shall have to put things right. What's he like by the way?'

'The captain? He's young, he's keen, and he's a bit worried at the moment.'

167

'That's a marvellous description, Bob. It sounds as if you've never even met him!'

'That's how I feel at the moment! Seriously, it is a bit tricky just now.'

Pip nodded. 'Kroner told me about the deserter and the officer who was killed. Is there more to it than that?'

'I'm not sure. The captain thinks so, but he's a bit prejudiced.'

'I was doing a short gunnery course when he was in the States.' The ensign looked distant, as if aware for the first time the meaning of joining a ship some twelve thousand miles from home. 'I read all about his medal which he got from the President. He must be quite some guy.'

Maddox watched his brother with something like love. 'I guess he was once. I'm not sure what he is right now.' He stood up and added awkwardly: 'I'm not sure that I should say this, Pip, but it's damn good to see you. It seems like years.'

Pip picked up his cap and dusted it severely. 'It *has* been!'

There was a tap at the door, and Bella looked in at the two officers. 'I've got some orders to be signed, Lieutenant. I can't find the captain.'

Maddox pulled out his pen. 'It's just routine. I'll do it.' He glanced importantly at his brother. 'Just one of the burdens of this job!'

Pip smiled at his brother's broad back. 'I can see why the captain can stay ashore with *you* around!'

Bella waited nervously. 'Anything else, sir?'

Maddox eyed him wearily. 'Should there be?'

'Any sailing orders to copy out, or anything like that, sir?'

'Hell, no. We're here for ever at this rate!' They watched the yeoman walk slowly back towards his office.

'He seems a bit down.' Pip's brows were raised questioningly. 'Is he okay?'

Maddox shrugged. 'We've all got troubles here, my friend.' He glanced at his watch. 'But come and meet the other inmates. I'll be interested in your reactions.'

Maddox wondered what Pip would think of Lea Burgess, but decided almost immediately that it might be unwise to make an early introduction. He himself had only met her once more since the hospital party, and that had been for less than an hour aboard the *Osprey*. Still, it was a beginning, and she was getting more attractive each time he saw her.

Pip said suddenly, 'What *did* happen to Mary?'

Maddox pushed him in front of him into the wardroom. 'You mind your own affairs, my lad. There's more to life than just getting married!'

Regan looked up from a magazine and stared at the newcomer. 'So this is the other half of the Maddox family?' He sounded angry and hostile.

The ensign went across to him. 'I've been looking at the three-inch on the fo'c'sle, sir. I wonder if you could explain a few points about it to me.' He shrugged helplessly. 'I'm afraid I'm a bit green on that gun.'

Regan dropped his magazine and pulled up another chair. 'Sit here then.' He cleared his throat. 'Well, it is a bit of a sticker. But these are the points to watch for . . .' He broke into a technical but friendly discourse.

From across the wardroom Malinsky winked at the exec's amazed face. There were obviously no flies on the new ensign.

*   *   *

Mark Gunnar floated on his back, his eyes closed against the glare, hardly moving on the slack water. The enclosing warmth of the sea seemed to soothe him, to relax every aching muscle and penetrate the confines of his mind. He felt drowsy, yet able to think more clearly than for some time, and he allowed his thoughts to drift in the same way as his body.

Jago had got his coveted promotion, and the island's administration had not altered from its course by one degree since the *Hibiscus* had first dropped anchor. Only Gunnar himself seemed to have been singled out for attention of one kind or another. They all wanted rid of him for mixed reasons, and in this quiet, peaceful sea Gunnar could see their points of view well enough.

What had he brought them but trouble? Even the far-off headquarters staff seemed aware of his early mistakes and stupid pessimism. Yet he still felt sure there was danger, even if it was as beyond his own control as before. What would another captain have done? Gunnar half opened his eyes to watch an anxious cormorant circling above him. Another commander might well have done the bare bones of his assignment and been content. A dull routine task was nothing new. It was the rule rather than the exception.

Viet Nam's memory had tainted him, had warped his judgement so that he could no longer accept anything as just ordinary and routine. He smiled bitterly. Even Bolod might be a figment of someone's imagination, a necessary scapegoat for those who had been unable to destroy the terrorists and their works.

He tried to think of the distant future. In a few months I shall be thirty. What then? There might be a series of possibilities. Return to the States, or accept another appointment out here. If any was offered. Like Payenhau, he was being passed by, overlooked gratefully by those who knew his record but kept quiet. Wearily he rolled over and began to swim slowly towards the beach. Whatever else happened, he was here, and things had to be done. Back at the ship they would be waiting for him, ready to obey him with as much resentment as they dared.

He blinked the water from his eyes and stared hard at the beach and his small pile of clothes. A figure moved along the sand, a small, familiar figure in a patched smock, the child with the enormous white bandage which Connell watched over in his hospital. Gunnar struck out more strongly. It was the girl whom Pirelli had shot on the pier. The incident everyone seemed eager to forget for varied reasons.

She stopped and shaded her eyes to watch him, and did a slow sort of dance from one foot to the other, her round face beaming expectantly. Gunnar smiled to himself in spite of his troubled thoughts. This child had become quite a character, if only because of her bandage. Members of the crew gave her candy, or took her for rides in the borrowed jeep. It seemed only right in this mad situation that she should stumble across the captain who had ordered the shooting, swimming in his underpants!

He stumbled and then began to wade hurriedly up the beach. The child smiled broadly and ran to head him off. She wanted to help him, but was confused by the jumbled pile of clothing. Gunnar slipped on the loose sand, and she beat him to the heap, her hand grasping Gunnar's cap as if for a first offering of friendship. Gunnar sighed, and then stood stock-still with horror.

As she lifted the cap there was a sharp snapping sound, and as the child looked down with surprise, a shining new grenade rolled slowly off Gunnar's shirt to land at her bare feet.

In a split, agonised second Gunnar's shocked mind relayed the facts. Someone had placed the grenade beneath the cap,

170

delicately balanced so that even with the pin withdrawn the
lever would be held shut merely by the cap's weight on top.

With one desperate sob Gunnar hurled himself forward, so
that his dripping body actually passed across the bomb as it
lay snugly in the sand. The child screamed in terror as Gunnar
gathered her frail body in his arms, and without losing momentum crashed forward and down into a slight dip.

He did not hear the grenade explode, but was conscious of
a great pounding pain in his lungs. His eyes were still open,
and he knew vaguely that the child pressed below his body
must be screaming, yet he could hear nothing. He wanted to
placate her, to make things right, but could no longer fight
back the darkness and the feeling that he was being carried
through space.

Someone was running towards him, but the sunlight had
faded and he could not see who it was. The pressure in his
lungs was too much. He could fight no more. Mercifully he
received the darkness and lay still.

10

Towing Job

The nightmare was even more intense, more vivid than usual.
Framed against the swirling red and orange background the
interrogator remained stark and motionless, like a silhouette,
whilst the walls around him appeared to merge, to gather
speed, like the inside of a tornado. Gunnar wanted to cry out,
to move, but remained as always mesmerised and helpless,
blinded to all else but the black, unmoving inquisitor. He could
never hear him speak, yet the pounding, merciless questions
were always there, fixed in his brain. It was the same as waiting
to plunge down a steep cliff, to be trapped between two flashing wheels, every phase of the nightmare carefully spaced,
exact in its toll, and awful in its finality. But this time there was
a small difference. The inquisitor had a personality, a name.
It was Bolod . . . and although he had no face, Gunnar recognised him as clearly as if he had been confronted by a portrait,

171

But it was time for the pain, the bamboo, the horror to complete the cruel torture.

It was only a dream, the usual one, from which Gunnar freed himself with the desperation of a man escaping a sudden, fast-moving death. It was sheer physical effort which allowed him to pull himself clear, to drag his racked body back to the reality of life. But again there was a difference. This time he could not move, and he heard himself scream as pressure was exerted on his straining shoulders to hold him down to await the torture.

Somewhere, as if from the end of a long tunnel, he heard a voice say, 'He's coming round, hold him!'

The dark mists began to clear, the nightmare tumbled into obscurity, and Gunnar opened his eyes. He was still surrounded in darkness, but for a shaded lamp, and two pale shapes which hovered above him, merging and fading, and then finally becoming real and distinct. Both faces were tight with concern, and as Gunnar again tried to move he realised that part of the dream had followed him into consciousness. The young, tight-lipped youngster with the sweat-stained shirt was pressing down on his bare shoulders, holding him firmly on to some sort of bed. The girl, her mouth moist in the lamplight, her hair hanging down in long black waves, was equally tense, her face clouded with anxiety.

Reluctantly the mist parted, and Gunnar allowed his streaming body to relax. He was presumably in Burgess's house. His daughter and this stranger had obviously found him on the beach. The memory flooded through his mind with horrifying reality, and he struggled to sit up.

The youth said: 'Easy, sir! Just take it steady for a bit.'

Gunnar blinked. 'Who the *hell* are you?'

Lea Burgess moved above him, and he felt her hand, cool and smooth on his forehead. She said quietly: 'You have had a bad time, Captain. You were calling out.'

Gunnar lay back and stared at the ceiling. 'God, how long have I been here?'

She replied: 'Six hours. You were hit in the back by a piece of stone. You will be better soon.'

Gunnar's mind wandered and fumbled with the bare facts. The bomb, the child's mouth wide in a silent scream, then nothing. Hoarsely he asked: 'The child? Is she all right?'

The girl's mouth moved in a quiet smile. 'She is very well, Captain. Thanks to you.' She held a damp cloth against his

172

forehead. 'I was on the beach, looking for her, when I heard the explosion. I saw what happened. It was a fine thing you did.'

Gunnar tore his eyes from her face and stared at the young man by her side. He was, he realised for the first time, an officer.

The latter said awkwardly: 'I'm your new ensign, sir. Arrived today in the chopper.'

Gunnar fell into a brooding silence. I must have been screaming and fighting like a madman, he thought. Watched and held by these two as he relived each horrifying moment.

With sudden terror he saw the neat set of fresh khakis lying on a nearby chair, and another realisation made him struggle on the sweat-dampened bed. 'Let me get up!'

But the young ensign immediately held him more firmly, his face filling with determined apology. 'It's okay, sir! Really it is.'

Gunnar stared at him with speechless pain. A thin sheet covered him from the waist down, he knew that apart from it he was naked. The sweat flooded down his face as he realised that these two must have seen his *back*. With helpless anger he gasped: 'Leave me alone! I must get out of here!'

The girl's dark eyes were clouded and grave. 'Do not worry, Captain. There is nothing to be ashamed of!' She turned and the light shone on the fine, upturned tilt of her cheekbones. Her voice was gentle but persuasive, and seemed to rob him of his determination.

The ensign flashed her a quick, grateful glance. 'Anyway, sir, there's no ship at the moment.'

Gunnar could only stare at him, and he continued quickly: 'There was a despatch from the old freighter, sir. She lost her propeller and was getting into difficulties. *Hibiscus* sailed to take her in tow. I understand a salvage tug has left Taiwan to rendezvous.' He gave a quick grin, making him seem vaguely familiar in Gunnar's pain-filled eyes. 'I reckon her passengers will be darn glad to get to their destination after all this.'

Gunnar heard himself ask, 'What is your name?'

'It's Maddox, sir. I guess you must be thinking you're getting bogged down with our relations.' He shrugged helplessly. 'I'll try to live it down, sir!'

'Maddox, eh?' Gunnar lay limply and looked past him at the girl. 'Thanks,' he said simply, 'I've been a lot of trouble for you.'

173

She smiled, the relief flooding across her tanned features. 'Men are always trouble!'

Maddox junior added: 'They left me behind to look after you. The doctor went with the ship in case of trouble.'

'Quite right.' Gunnar pulled the sheet up to his chin and saw the other two exchange a quick glance. The thought of the ensign, let alone the slim, dark-eyed girl, seeing his mutilated back made him feel sick and unsteady. When he moved he could also feel the powerful throb of the bruise, which coupled with the grenade's blast had laid him unconscious for nearly seven hours.

During that time, as his exhausted mind had floated in unreality and horror, the *Hibiscus* had got under way, had sailed without him. Even now, Maddox would be coping with all the intricacies and dangers of deep-sea towing in the face of God knows what hazards. A ship without a screw was a great, lumbering juggernaut which could smash or maim even the most experienced vessel handled by any hardened professional.

Pip Maddox could follow each emotion on Gunnar's pale face, and said suddenly: 'It'll be okay, sir. The weather's good, and they'll have made contact before nightfall. It'll be a copybook exercise!'

Gunnar felt drained and empty, but the boy's grave confidence made him feel suddenly calm, even relaxed. In spite of everything he felt his face twist into a smile. 'You're just like your brother. I wish I had half your optimism!'

The girl had gone and returned just as quietly with a tall glass. 'Some whisky, Captain, it will make you feel stronger.' She showed her teeth in a white smile. 'This one is called Pip. Did you ever hear such a ridiculous name?'

Gunnar allowed the neat spirit to move down his throat and felt its power coursing through his spent body. 'Pip, eh? That's good. Can't have two Maddoxes in *my* ship!'

Pip stood up and ran his fingers through his hair. 'What'll I do now, sir?'

Gunnar sighed deeply. 'Has Major Jago been around?'

Pip grinned widely. '*Colonel* Jago has been and gone, sir. Heaps of noise and bluster, and a whole lot of military preparation!' He waved vaguely. 'He's got patrols all over the place, and there's a guard outside here, just in case.'

Lea Burgess said: 'That won't be necessary, Captain. The people in the village will protect you from harm.'

174

Gunnar regarded her intently so that her eyes dropped from his stare. 'You trust them, don't you?' he asked slowly. 'I guess you know them pretty well at that.'

She nodded simply. 'They are good people. They despise invaders, but they respect you for what you have done.'

'It was automatic.' Gunnar tried to remember his exact reactions. 'I guess I nearly killed that kid with my weight!'

Pip said quickly: 'Lucky it wasn't my brother! He would have flattened her!'

The girl smiled. 'Do not let him hear you say that, Pip. He would be very upset!'

They both smiled like conspirators, and Gunnar felt a strange pang of jealousy. Again he was acutely aware of his own position, of loneliness, of being on the outside, even here. He heard her ask: 'What will happen now, Captain? Will there be reprisals against the islanders?'

'I think not. That grenade was a mile from the village. Anyone could have done it. It was meant for me, like the mine on the road. Someone wants me dead.' He laughed quietly. 'I'm used to that feeling.'

She said, 'I thought I would hate you, but it is not so.'

Both Americans looked at her with mixed astonishment and surprise, and Pip replied, 'I guess I'd take that as a compliment!'

But the girl looked directly at Gunnar, her lips framing the question: 'And you, Captain? What do you think?'

Gunnar propped himself on his elbows. 'I'm glad.' He was surprised to know that he meant it. 'But right now I guess I'd better get on my feet again. There's still a lot I don't know.'

Pip Maddox stood up and looked at the girl. 'Come on, we'll wait in the next room.'

Through the curtain Gunnar could hear them speaking in low tones as he struggled into his clothing. He caught sight of himself in a tall mirror and turned so that he could see the criss-crossed scars which enfolded his back like an obscene web. Viciously he tugged on his shirt, blotting them out. But she had seen them, had even touched them. The thought made him sink down on the edge of the bed and press his face into his hands. It had almost been enough to hide his disfigurement before, now things seemed different. In the past it was in some way connected with his wife and the girl who had betrayed him and broken his mind. He had told himself that it was over, unimportant compared with the task in hand and the rebuild-

175

ing of his career. He had always known it was a lie, but it had helped. This strange, exciting girl, whose simplicity matched her perfection, had somehow seen through his defences. Her quiet 'There is nothing to be ashamed of' had stripped away his pretence, laid bare his weakness with a gentle certainty which had been more of an encouragement than a rebuke.

For a few moments longer he let his mind wander through this new field. It was hopeless, of course, for in spite of everything else she would soon discover that his duty left little room for personal concern. Payenhau must not be allowed to blunt his judgement yet again. It was just a place, as Jago had pointed out. One day world power might allow the great forces to withdraw into few but all-enveloping positions. Until then, places like Payenhau would always be in demand by one side or the other. Soon every single rock which jutted only a few feet above sea-level might carry a man with a rocket! He grinned stiffly at the stupidity of his thoughts. He was dead tired but there was still a lot to do. It was no longer a mere guess that someone was out to kill him. Either he or the ship, or both, represented a link with the outside might of a foreign power which could not be overlooked. *Hibiscus* was small and puny, but she was still a force, a lever which could open the floodgate upon any aggressor.

The thought nagged at him as he sat staring into the shadows around the bed. He called through the curtain, careful to keep his voice steady and casual, 'Does anyone know I'm ashore?'

Pip Maddox answered, surprised but alert: 'No, sir. Colonel Jago thought it best, in case of more trouble.'

Gunnar pushed through the curtain and blinked in the lamplight. 'Is there any chance of getting the M.F.V. under way, Miss Burgess?' He saw her eyes flicker in the lights, the quick tightening of her chin.

'My father is not well, Captain.'

He noticed the two bright spots of colour rising to her cheeks and said: 'A pity. I was hoping to take a quick trip up the coast.' It was pitiful to see the way she sprang to her father's defence. He was probably blind drunk in some dive in the town as no work had been allotted his precious boat.

She said with a touch of defiance: 'I can manage the boat on my own, Captain! I could take you.'

Gunnar knew that he should not agree but said quickly, 'If you're sure?'

She turned away, her hair swinging, hiding her face. 'I will get Tsung and the engine boy.'

Gunnar watched her go. 'There's a good moon and we might spot something.'

'Er, what, for instance?' Pip looked blank but eager.

'I don't know.' Gunnar smiled at the young ensign's surprise. 'I see you had the sense to bring an M-14 with you, and plenty of ammunition I hope?'

Pip grinned like a schoolboy. 'Sure did. I also drew a new pistol for you, sir. Your other one got slightly bent in the explosion!'

Gunnar smiled tightly. Another couple of seconds and he would not have been in a position to do anything. He pushed the thought to the back of his mind as the *Osprey*'s engine coughed into life. Everyone on the island would know of *Hibiscus*'s hurried departure, and most people would find it hard to draw the line between ship and captain. If there was any chance of looking around the islands it was now. He touched the ensign's arm. 'This is where we stick out our necks!'

He led the way into the cool evening air and watched the silver path left by the moon with quiet satisfaction. If anything went wrong he would have himself to blame. But then, if he had been killed by the grenade as intended he would already have been replaced, so what the hell?

The boat squeaked clear of its fenders and headed out into the stream. A searchlight flashed down from the nearest islet, but Tsung the deckhand signalled a brief reply with a hand-lamp and they were left in peace.

Gunnar leaned against the thin wheelhouse and watched the dark headland coasting past, and once when he lifted his head he saw the girl's face faintly illuminated in the compass light as she steered the cumbersome boat with easy familiarity towards the narrow eastern channel.

He bit his lip with sudden irritation. Forget it, he told himself. She is none of your business, so clear her from your mind! If anyone's, she belongs to Maddox. He'll use her and leave her, like all the others. He found no comfort in the thought, and when Pip Maddox climbed up beside the girl he found himself hating even him.

* * *

'Coffee, sir?' The mug came out of the darkness and stood vibrating on the ledge below the bridge screen. Maddox grunted and picked it up as the *Hibiscus* took another slow roll to starboard, her frames protesting as she wallowed heavily in a shallow but dragging trough.

He rubbed his eyes and tried to concentrate his thoughts completely on the mocking black shadow which swayed dimly across the submarine chaser's narrow bows. He was dead wretched tired, yet he knew he had to act, to make this thing work, or else . . . He barked into the darkness, 'Send for Mister Regan!'

A voice said almost at his elbow: 'No need. I'm right here, staring at that goddamned sonofabitch as I have been for the last lousy watch!'

Maddox flexed his arms and peered at the sky. It was unusual to see the fast scudding clouds, the only occasional glimpses of distant stars.

It had all started well enough, with Maddox feeling a sense of freedom as the *Hibiscus* under his own hand had opened up her old jets and poured on the power as she dashed towards the glittering horizon line on her errand of help for the disabled refugee ship. The sudden shock of seeing the captain, whitefaced and murmuring in his state of unconscious exhaustion, had made him realise yet again how close was his own burden of responsibility. He had seen the rebellion well in his brother's eyes when he had ordered him to stay ashore with Gunnar, and afterwards wondered why he had made such a decision. Was it really because he was unused to the ship, or was it because he was so unsure of himself that he did not want Pip along as a witness?

It had been harder to locate the old freighter than he had imagined. The radar was confused and obstinate in spite of Kroner's constant attention, and when at last the ship was sighted, the weather had already started to change. The wind had risen from the east, long intermittent gusts of humid breath which had turned the swells from lazy, sullen rollers into long, ragged crests of dirty yellow spume which broke across the *Hibiscus*'s eager bows so that Maddox had to order a reduction of speed. Twice the warship circled the stricken freighter while the lamps blinked across the tossing water, and Maddox tried to remain calm as one crisis rose after another. On exercises with the fleet, towing was a dreaded affair, even with trained personnel and drill-book regulated equip-

178

ment. This ancient freighter had very little of either. The master was a half-caste, mainly of Dutch extraction, but his mate was a pure-blooded Chinese.

Several times Maddox had looked at the sky and peered at his watch. Time was getting short, and with wind and current against him he fully realised that the helpless ship was drifting very rapidly towards the west, where there was always the possibility of more danger than mere weather.

The freighter was drifting beam on to wind and sea, and Maddox knew full well, if not from actual experience, that a ship disabled or not under control will drift to leeward faster than a ship having way on her. With infinite caution he had conned the ship into what he estimated to be a favourable position on the freighter's port quarter. Several times he had peered aft to the fantail where Regan and Chief Anders appeared to be knee-deep in a fantastic tangle of wires and grass hawsers, while leather-gloved seamen fought to connect the complicated puzzle of slips and stoppers which to Maddox's anxious eye looked beyond hope of any sort.

Cautiously the *Hibiscus* had cruised diagonally past the other ship, and with a double crack the line guns sent the thin ropes snaking towards the countless heads which lined the freighter's rails. One line fell short, but the other was seized and passed forward to the freighter's blunt bows where even more men waited to heave the makeshift hawser across the narrowing gap. The freighter's master had managed to cast his port anchor, and as far as he could make out from the frantic signals, Maddox understood that as soon as a good wire had followed the hawser across the Dutchman would begin to veer out his cable towards the *Hibiscus*'s corkscrewing stern.

Now, hours later, Maddox peered into the darkness at the helpless ship with bitter hatred. It had been hopeless. *Hibiscus* was not suited for towing a ship of the freighter's massive bulk, and three times the tow had parted so that the whole nerve-racking business had to begin again. Only once had the operation nearly succeeded. Heaving lines had hauled across the grass hawser, and then, like a reluctant, shining snake, the freighter's towing cable had started to jerk across the pitching wavetops. Soon its weight began to take effect on both vessels, and as the actual cable vanished below the surface in a deep loop the *Hibiscus* swung viciously off course, until by constant helm orders Maddox managed to steady her again while the tow was shackled to the big slip on the fan-

179

tail. Then the towed ship seemed to go beserk. Caught by cross-currents of wind and tide she veered away on the cable, carried like a mad thing until she was steaming almost parallel to the little warship while the deep loop of cable hung between them like a life-giving cord, yet which threatened to destroy both of them.

The next instant would find the freighter careering down towards the *Hibiscus*'s beam, her high, rust-dappled stem cleaving through the water and holding the men on the bridge mesmerised with shock and horror. It had been on one such occasion that the cable had again parted.

The freighter had seemed to stagger as an extra powerful gust caught her high superstructure, and without a second's warning she began to pay off sideways towards the other ship.

Maddox had gripped the rail, his sore eyes trying to gauge her speed, to estimate the rate of drift. But all he could see was the towering stem, the frantic hand-waving Chinese and the vessel's twin anchors looming above the swaying *Hibiscus* like two malevolent eyes.

Maddox had torn his eyes away. 'All engines ahead full! Right standard rudder!' He hardly recognised his own voice.

Kroner shouted, 'Christ, she'll cut us in two!'

The *Hibiscus* stubbornly refused to swing, although the engines thrashed and shook the bridge as the revolutions mounted. Kroner yelled: 'Slip the tow! For Jesus' sake *slip*!' His face was white like an old man's, his eyes fixed on the towering freighter as it bore down on them.

Maddox licked his parched lips. 'Bring your rudder *hard* right!' He no longer knew what he was doing. He just had to get away.

The *Hibiscus* yawed violently and staggered. Men yelled and cursed as the deck tilted so that some skidded towards the boiling water, gripping and scratching for handholds as the ship went over and stayed over.

'Slip the tow!' Maddox was pressed against the rail by two of the signalmen, held transfixed as the maddened freighter lifted her shadow over the bridge itself. There was a muffled clang and the *Hibiscus* rolled back on to even keel, still swinging in response to the full rudder. But the freighter seemed to take on a new lease of life. Almost skittishly she swung clear, hampered by the great dangling weight of her anchor cable, yet once more free to move as the mood took her.

Regan had panted up the bridge ladder as Maddox dazedly

180

brought the ship back on course. 'What were you trying to *do*, for Christ's sake?' He peered round the bridge as if surprised to find it still intact. 'You nearly scuppered my lot down aft!'

Maddox said thickly: 'Shut your yap! I had to do it! She'd have mashed us!'

Darkness had soon followed, and as one cup of hot coffee followed another Maddox and Regan stood side by side watching the dim shadow like an adversary. It had drawn them together, but little else.

Regan said wearily: 'We'll wait till dawn, eh? What d'you think?'

Maddox nodded. 'God, that tug'll never make contact after this lot. There'll be merry hell to pay!'

Carkosi, a radioman, shambled through the darkness. Finding the exec he reported, 'She's sendin' an S O S sir!' He shrugged, as if contemptuous of such stupidity.

Maddox gripped his jacket to stop his hands from shaking. 'What do you mean?'

'Well, sir, as far as I can make out her master is askin' for help. He gives his position as accurately as he can, which puts him less than a hundred miles south-east of the Chinese mainland.'

Maddox heard Regan's quick intake of breath. 'Christ, no wonder he's in a panic. If the Reds come out to take a look it'll be curtains for those poor refugee bastards!'

Kroner interrupted quickly, 'He's fifty miles out, the stupid bastard!'

Maddox rubbed his chin. 'Right or wrong, he'll bring the whole pack down on our heads!' He thought rapidly. 'I'll ask instructions. Yes, I'll send a despatch and inform the fleet of our position. That should clinch it.'

He jumped as Regan's hand fastened on his wrist. 'Forget it! They'll eat you alive if you start doing that. We've got to hang on here and take that maniac in tow at first light. Flash that idiot and tell him to stop signalling.'

Maddox said, 'And if he refuses?'

'Tell him I'll blow his friggin' radio shack straight into the drink!' Regan grinned in the darkness as the lamp began to stammer once more. 'I will too!'

Maddox stepped shakily from the gratings. Regan was taking over. But he was right, of course. The admiral would have little time for anyone aboard if he was asked for help before anything actually happened. He listened to the faint buzz of morse and static from the radio room and wondered if the Dutchman had heeded Regan's tough message.

Carkosi reappeared, his jaw moving steadily on a wad of gum. 'She's piped down, sir.'

'Good.' Maddox took a deep breath. Right along the line he had fouled it up. There was a little time left. He would have to make sure he made full use of it.

In a strained voice he said, 'Stand by to commence towing at first light.'

Regan rubbed his hands in the darkness. 'If we drift much nearer the mainland we'll be able to *walk* across to that bucket!'

* * *

'Dawn comin' up, sir. Mister Regan's respects an' would you come to the bridge?'

Maddox groaned and rolled dully out of the charthouse bunk. There was a stale taste in his mouth, and he had the impression that it was less than minutes since he had fallen asleep.

The upper bridge was already bathed in an eerie orange half-glow as he staggered to the gratings where Regan was watching the crippled freighter with levelled glasses.

Regan said flatly, 'It'll be clear enough soon.'

Maddox took a mug of coffee and drained it without speaking. The sea looked brightly angry in the strange light, and even the old ship ahead glowed with a fresh, copper-coloured light. It was still blowing but the waves were less violent, and the crests only broke with occasional power, as if they too were newly awakened.

Regan rubbed his stubbled chin. 'We ought to make another turn around her and try to drift a line across. If only we were in shallow water we could both drop the hook and pass a line over at leisure.'

Maddox stifled his irritation, and watched the masthead turning in a wide circle as the slow-moving *Hibiscus* rolled painfully in each trough. 'Hell, the weather looks weird. I've not seen a sky like it before!'

Regan grinned as Kroner staggered drunkenly on to the bridge, rubbing his eyes and yawning hugely. ' 'Morning, Don!'

182

Regan eyed him with an unpitying smile. 'Got over your little batch of nerves yet?'

Kroner scowled. 'You can talk!'

'Tell the master we're going to start towing operations in fifteen minutes.' Maddox shook himself and turned towards one of the bridge signalmen, who like the others was clinging to a support to stop his body from being knocked stupid in the steady, gyrating motion.

The signalman said sharply: 'There's a ship fine on the port bow, sir! You can see her just below the freighter's stack!'

Maddox swore and fumbled with his glasses. The lenses swept across the rusty sides of the other ship, and then he caught his breath as he saw a thin, wafer-like shadow just below the horizon line. It was still merged with the night sky, lost in a welter of spray and fast cloud, but a ship nevertheless. Even as he watched, his numbed mind tearing between the possibilities of calling up the fleet or putting *Hibiscus* between the freighter and the newcomer, he saw the big, ice-blue projector begin to flash, as if from the sea itself.

There was absolute silence on the open bridge as the signalman said, 'Her Majesty's destroyer *Bosworth*, sir!' He went on reading as another man filled in the message pad.

Regan laughed shortly. 'A Limey, for God's sake! Must be out of Hong Kong.'

Maddox snatched the completed pad and read the scrawled pencil very slowly. He said at length: 'The *Bosworth* has a navy tug in company. She's closing in to give us assistance.'

Regan grunted, 'Sticking his goddamned nose in more likely!'

As the angry bronze sunlight spilled over the horizon it held the converging ships like scale models and lit up the creaming bow-wave of the big destroyer to give an added impression of power. The British ship was a radar picket destroyer, its trim outline marred and disfigured by the giant mass of revolving radar frames, yet with easy grace it swung in a full circle and then reduced speed to run parallel with the *Hibiscus*, which rocked suddenly in the disturbance thrown up by the destroyer's screws.

Maddox noticed that the British ship had placed herself between the freighter and the *Hibiscus*, and as he watched he saw a tall, immaculate, white-uniformed figure with a cap heavy in gold leaf climb on to her bridge screen, and heard the squeak of the loud-hailer. The destroyer's captain had a crisp, authoritative voice, and Maddox was vaguely reminded of Burgess.

'Good morning, *Hibiscus!*' He sounded cheerful and refreshed, and Maddox imagined that the British officers had probably just completed an excellent breakfast. He tried not to think of the picture his own ship must present. Her decks littered with wires and ropes, her dungareed and unshaven crew lounging wearily, too tired even to look at the glittering newcomer.

The metallic voice continued: 'Heard the S O S and decided to look in on your problem, old boy.' A pause. 'There's just one thing . . .'

Regan swore. 'Here it comes!'

'This freighter is on our lists as being concerned with the smuggling of illicit refugees from the Crown Colony. My tug will take her in tow, if you have no objections?'

They all looked at Maddox. The British captain was no fool. What could Maddox say? *Hibiscus* was not an official escort. She had merely been attempting to take a disabled ship in tow. What the Nationalists were doing on the side to ensure a flow of new blood to Taiwan was none of their concern. He bit his lip and looked helplessly at Regan's uncompromising features. 'What do you think?'

Before he could answer the loud-hailer added, 'Of course, I could stand by until your people decide to take over the tow.'

Regan said sharply, 'Tell him to go to hell!'

Maddox forced himself to say, 'Give me the mike!' The set buzzed to life in his hand and he felt the *Bosworth*'s captain staring at him across the surging mass of trapped water between them.

'The freighter is from Payenhau. Lost her screw yesterday and we tried to take her in tow.'

'I see. Bad luck.' The voice sounded noncommittal. 'Still, it's not really your problem, is it? Hong Kong is the nearest port, and I do have a tug right here.' As if to back him up a siren hooted dismally, and Maddox saw a bobbing mast appear briefly above the freighter's swaying hull.

The doctor had arrived on the bridge, his eyes red-rimmed but alert. 'You *can't* let them take over from you, Bob! Those poor devils will be thrown back into Red China. The British haven't got room for all of them in Hong Kong!'

Maddox gritted his teeth. Into the speaker he said flatly:

184

'Very well, Captain. She's all yours!'

He watched unhappily as a smart launch shot from the destroyer's hidden side and curtsied towards the freighter. The Britisher had been very confident. The launch must have been ready to slip from the start. The packed Chinese on the crippled ship's maindeck were not slow to understand their change of fate. The agony and suspense, the privations and sufferings had all been in vain. There was a great sigh, 'Aiya!' which seemed to represent all the misery of refugees everywhere.

The destroyer fell away, her guns swinging to cover the small boarding party. In spite of the choppy sea the tug was already fumbling around the bigger ship's stem, and Maddox could see the professional ease with which the British salvage crew were getting to work.

Regan said between his tight lips: 'You fool! You stupid, gutless fool!'

Maddox swung on him. 'What d'you know about it? What did you expect me to do under the circumstances?' He controlled his voice with a real effort, aware that some of the bridge party were watching him. 'The British might have got here first and the question of towing would not have arisen!'

Regan sneered, the truce was over. 'Well they didn't, and it did!'

Kroner watched the freighter begin to turn obediently on its new halter. 'Poor bastards.'

Maddox flared up, unable to stop himself. 'Poor bastards? I like that! Yesterday you were squealing like a stuck pig for me to cut the tow, you couldn't stop yourself from going pop-eyed when you thought your precious skin was in danger! Now it's over you want to be noble, play the big hero! Well, not me! I take the responsibility and that's all there is to it!'

A signalman shouted excitedly, 'One of the Chinks has jumped for it, sir!'

Spellbound they watched the frantic, desperate strokes of the man who had appeared below the freighter's counter. Every so often the sleek head was hidden by the waves, then he would appear once more, swimming more strongly than before towards the *Hibiscus*.

The destroyer's launch idled clear of the ship's side and gathered way, a man already in the bows with a boathook.

Some of the American seamen had forgotten their weariness and were yelling encouragement. 'Swim up! Come on, Tarzan!'

The swimmer reached the *Hibiscus*'s side, and Maddox saw his wide-eyed, streaming face as he peered up at the ship's flat side and at the curling Stars and Stripes which blew gaily from the gaff.

Chief Tasker bellowed: 'Get a heaving line! Give him a hand there!'

But Maddox said tightly: 'Hold it! He's not our concern!'

The man seemed to realise that even this sacrifice had been in vain. He paddled clear of the side, his eyes still on the flag, as the destroyer's launch swept towards him. Then with a sob he lifted his arms and vanished. The launch turned in a slow circle, then one of its crew semaphored back to the parent ship. Maddox noticed that one of the British sailors was sitting in the boat's cockpit rolling a cigarette. To them it was just routine.

The doctor stayed looking over the heads of the silent men on deck. 'He was looking at the flag,' he said at length.

Maddox walked hotly towards the chartroom. 'Send a despatch, Mister Kroner. We're returning to Payenhau. Give them our E.T.A.'

Regan called after him, 'I wonder what that poor bastard was thinking just then?'

Maddox slammed the door and tugged the chart from its folder. When the signalman had reported the other ship he had imagined for a moment that it was a Red Chinese warship. The thought had chilled him in the same way as the baying crowd on the pier when Pirelli had opened fire. But now he wished it *had* been an enemy. Anything was better than the humiliation of defeat which he now felt.

Soon the *Hibiscus* had the sea to herself. But some of the tired seamen still looked around as if they expected to see the fated refugee ship, or even the swimmer who had looked in vain at their flag.

11

Conflict

As the dark clouds momentarily parted across the moon's path the slab-sided islet glowed white and silver and seemed to change shape as Gunnar levered himself upwards in the dinghy to get a better view of it. It was a bleak, hostile place, and now that he was committed to his sketchy plan Gunnar could well imagine Inglis's men dying there.

The clouds blotted out the moon once again as Tsung, the *Osprey*'s massive deckhand, tugged easily at the oars and sent the small craft leaping beneath an overhanging rock. Already lost in the darkness of the uneasy water astern, the *Osprey* seemed far away, and Gunnar checked the automatic at his waist as if to reassure himself. What did he expect to find here anyway?

It had been an uneventful trip so far, with only the fishing boat's steady diesel to break the silence. Near the northern side of the main island the weather had taken a change for the worse, and the gathering cloud banks had been broken into long, angry streamers in the freshening wind, so that the full moon laid them bare in its cold eye for mere seconds and then allowed them to be plunged into impenetrable darkness. Lea Burgess certainly knew her ship, he thought. Skilfully she had steered the heavy boat around unseen clumps of rock, and had allowed for the sudden and vicious tide races with the coolness of a navy coxswain.

The boat ground on to some shingle, and with remarkable agility Tsung leapt ashore and guided it on to firmer sand.

Gunnar said: 'Well, come on, Pip. This is where we use our legs.' To the big Chinese he added: 'You get back to the *Osprey*. I'll flash my torch when I want you.'

They waited until Tsung had manœuvred clear of the beach, then Gunnar said: 'Don't want him hanging around. He might fall asleep and allow the dinghy to go adrift.'

It sounded unconvincing although Pip said nothing. Gunnar knew that his real reason was for the girl's sake. Competent or not, he disliked the idea of her being alone at anchor but for the wizened Chinese engineer, who would be next to useless in an emergency.

187

Pip slung his rifle and said, 'Where first, sir?'

'According to my calculations we're just a few yards from the beach where my boys were ambushed. We'll climb up to the top of the cliff and see what it's like.'

They climbed in silence, occasionally dislodging stones or pausing to get their bearings. Gunnar pulled himself over the lip of the cliff and began to walk purposefully towards the centre of a small depression. It must have been here that the man with the grenade had hidden. Probably the same sort of man who had so neatly tried to dispose of him too.

Pip said thoughtfully, 'It's like solid rock.'

That meant that anyone would have great difficulty in hiding anything in such a grim place. Gunnar poked amongst some stones and loose boulders. They were encrusted with sand and blown grit, undisturbed for a century.

Together they began to walk down the smooth, open slope towards the other end of the islet. Eventually Gunnar said, 'There are steep rock faces along the other two sides, so if anyone wanted to land here it would have to be over there, beyond that pinnacle.'

They paused, and Gunnar squinted thoughtfully at the strangely shaped rock which glinted in the moonlight like the petrified steeple of some forgotten church. He knew from his chart and what he had gleaned from his survey teams that below it lay a small, sheltered cove, not much bigger than the one in which Inglis had met his fate.

Suddenly Gunnar wished he had not been so impetuous. If anyone was on the islet, his automatic and the ensign's rifle would be a poor match for anything really serious.

They reached the pinnacle and stared down at a small, darkly shadowed cove. The sea noises were quieter, and Gunnar guessed that it was well sheltered from wind and weather. But it was empty, and as bare and bleak as the rest of the islet. Suddenly weary, Gunnar scrambled down a slippery slope of loose stones, conscious of the throbbing bruise on his back and the feeling of disappointment.

What had he really expected? Perhaps he half thought Pirelli might have been sheltering here, although God knows it was a hard enough place to reach. Or perhaps a cache of arms left in some secret cave, waiting the landing of a trained Communist commando. But it was now painfully clear that there was nothing. There was not even the possibility of a hiding place which might warrant a closer inspection by daylight. Gunnar cursed himself and looked back at the islet's ragged outline. There was another cloudbank moving fast towards the moon. He could just make out the ensign's silhouette framed against the glittering water, and toyed with the idea of making some additional explanation.

Surprisingly, Pip Maddox's voice lacked both amusement or surprise. 'Gives me the creeps! I can imagine myself getting a bit scared up here!'

Gunnar looked at the clouds. 'We'll wait a couple of minutes until they've passed and then go back to the other side.'

Maddox gestured towards a black clump of gorse. 'Good idea, sir. We could stumble around in that lot!' He pushed at the nearest bush with the rifle, and then they both stood stock-still with shock. There was a strange, tinny rattling, like the discordant jangling of bells.

The ensign said, 'What in hell's name——' But as Gunnar tugged at his pistol he gasped, 'Christ, there's someone in there!'

Gunnar pushed at the boy's shoulder and sent him rolling down the slope, at the same time he threw himself sideways as the darkening sky was torn apart by a savage burst of gunfire. It seemed to come from right underfoot, so that Gunnar imagined the bullets had passed within inches of his face. Blindly he pumped the trigger of his pistol, slipping and reeling as his ankle became entangled in the thing which had raised the alarm. The oldest trap in the world, and he had allowed himself to walk right into it. Just a few cans tied on a length of wire which Pip's rifle had inadvertently brought to life, and with it the man behind the gun.

The young ensign was nowhere to be seen, and as yet his rifle was silent. Gunnar could feel the prickle of suspense between his shoulder-blades as he lay, holding his breath in the spray-sodden gorse. Perhaps the boy was already dead? He bit his lip until he could taste the blood on his tongue.

The pistol felt like lead in his hand, and with sudden panic he found he could not remember how many times he had fired. He had another clip in his pocket, but he knew from past experience that in the heart-chilling silence his hidden adversary was listening for just one movement to open fire again.

His eyes clouded with strain, and he wanted to cry out as the impossibility of his position became more evident with each dragging minute. He had brought it all on himself. In

189

spite of the warnings, the threats on his life, he had still wanted to be the big man. Now it was too late, and worse than that, he had sacrificed yet another life for nothing.

Then he heard Pip's voice from somewhere beyond his left shoulder. It was strained and frightened. 'I'm sorry, sir! I can't find the rifle!'

Instantly, the orange tongue of flame tore across the wilting gorse, the night again crazy with the sound of whining and ricocheting bullets.

Gunnar staggered to his feet, his eyes blinded by the muzzle flash. He shouted wildly: 'Run for it! Get back to the beach!' Then he lunged forward and down, his pistol jumping in his hand like a mad thing. Pip's sudden movement had drawn the other man's fire, had betrayed him for those few vital seconds. Teeth bared like an animal, Gunnar fired again and again until the hammer clicked against nothing, and in the very next instant he was rolling and kicking on top of the man who had tried to kill him.

Grunting and gasping they rolled and thrashed, struggling and fighting for a handhold until Gunnar thought his lungs would burst. He could feel the man's breath hot and foul on his face, could sense the eyes within inches of his own. Once they rolled across something hard and unyielding, and Gunnar felt a prick of savage triumph as he realised it was the man's sub-machine gun. A blinding pain made him cry out for the first time as the man brought his knee up into his groin. Helpless and sobbing, he rolled clear and saw the stooping shadow outlined against a faint beam of moonlight as it groped for the discarded gun.

Gunnar moaned and waited for the thudding agony of the first burst. Instead there was one solitary crack, almost puny on the open slope, and with the suddenness of an apparition the other man vanished into the gorse, his pitching body disturbing the jangling cans for the last time.

'Are you okay, sir?' Pip Maddox was already pulling him to his feet, his voice small and shaken.

Gunnar nodded and picked up his automatic. Without speaking he rammed a fresh clip into the butt. He switched on his torch and then rolled the dead man on to his back. In the flashlight he could see the expression of incredulity on the distorted face, the teeth bared in a final cry.

The ensign stooped behind Gunnar and then turned violently away. Gunnar heard him vomiting but forced himself

190

to continue with his examination. This must have been one of the men surprised by Inglis's landing party. Overlooked by Jago's troops, he had probably been kept alive by supporters from the main island.

He stood up and flashed the light around the small, sheltered foxhole. Just big enough to sleep two men, it was covered with rough planks and disguised by gravel and pieces of gorse. There were packs of ammunition which bore U.S. markings, and several tins of food. The man himself was big, and extremely dirty. He looked like a soldier, although he carried no marks of identification.

In another minute he would have killed me. Now in the flashlight the man looked fragile and pathetic, a mere dirty remnant which did not belong.

Over his shoulder Gunnar said quietly: 'You did well, Pip. Don't reproach yourself. You don't get a second chance in this game. You got yours, and responded better than most men put in your position!' He straightened up and put his hand on the boy's shoulder. 'War is okay when viewed through a gunsight or on the television. But this is the real war. Now you know.'

Pip said in a strangled voice: 'I just fired. I would never have believed it possible!'

Gunnar grinned in spite of the tension within him. 'Just as well for me as it turns out!'

The ensign took a grip of himself with obvious effort. 'What'll we do with—with him, sir?'

'Leave him. He's no loss to anyone.' Gunnar was surprised at the hardness of his own voice. He added, 'I'd give a month's pay to know what he was up to all the same.' He picked up the sub-machine gun. Grimly he said, 'Another bit of American aid which got into the wrong channel!'

Pip Maddox said in an awed tone, 'You *expected* to find something, didn't you, sir?'

Gunnar shrugged. 'I don't know what I expected. But this isn't the end. It's just part of the pattern. It proves I was right, that I was on the correct angle all the time. The doctor noticed it before I did. Two bodies were brought in by Jago's patrol after Inglis was shot. Both were in full uniform, as if they had just landed from some ship. This one tonight was in rags. I think those two men in uniform were already dead when the patrol found them. Just a couple of coolies snatched for the purpose of deceiving us into believing that it was a casual brush with a Red patrol from the mainland. The real killers got away, that was why neither of the bodies was wearing a bayonet. My men were bayoneted after they died and that was what the doctor noticed.'

They started down the cliff path into the face of the wind, and then Pip said, 'The dinghy's here already!'

Gunnar quickened his pace and almost collided with the girl and the towering shape of Tsung. Gunnar caught her by the shoulders. 'I said to wait till I signalled!'

But she did not seem to hear. He could feel the warmth of her shoulders under his hands and knew that she was shaking. She said: 'We heard the shooting! I thought you had fallen into a trap!' There was a sob in her voice. 'After all you have been through, and I thought—I thought——' Then she was pressed against him, and he was holding her tightly, with her hair brushing his mouth.

He felt at a loss. 'There was only one of them. He is dead.'

It was like a dream, like a world he had forgotten. They all stood crowded across the narrow path, yet he was conscious only of the girl's body pressed against his own, the fragrance of her damp hair as she cried uncontrollably into his shoulder. It was all so clear, as if made so by the nearness to death those few moments before.

Gently he turned her body towards the sea, so that the wind pushed the hair free from her face. 'Come on, we'd better get back to your boat.' She did not try to free her shoulders from his arm, and allowed herself to be guided back to the waiting dinghy.

Once aboard the *Osprey*, she allowed Tsung to keep the wheel while she sat silently on the deck in front of the wheel-house, her eyes towards the pitching bows.

The spray streamed back from the stemhead like tropical rain, and with the girl beside him Gunnar was soon soaked to the skin. When he suggested that she should go below she merely shook her head. 'No. I want it to last. I am afraid of tomorrow. But now . . .' She left the rest unsaid. Gunnar reached out and took her hand. It was damp with spray, yet warm within his own.

He did not know how it had happened, or even for sure what *was* happening. But he did know what had been lacking for so long and for the first time allowed his mind to consider the possibility of a future.

Pip Maddox stood beside the wheelhouse and allowed the

spray to soak his face as if to wash away the mingled feeling of fear and disgust. It had not been as he had imagined it would, but now that it was over he had to admit to a feeling of elation which filled him with shame. He had actually *killed* a man. The thought hammered through his brain again and again. He still did not know how he had done it. Desperation, fear, the draining sickness of self-preservation, each had played a part. That one action, whatever had prompted it, had saved them all. They were aboard this boat and the islet was lost in the black sea astern, as if it had never been. He looked across at the captain. He too must have felt as he did. The girl's head had fallen sideways and rested on Gunnar's shoulder, and in spite of the wind and the boat's uneven motion there was for a while a sense of great peace.

* * *

Colonel Lloyd Jago was rapidly working himself into an open rage. It was a violent, destructive thing which fanned across his hard features like the clouds which Gunnar had watched blot out the moon. His green shirt was darkly patched with sweat, and he looked as if he had not slept for twenty-four hours. As he paced beneath the bare bulbs of his bunker he seemed to grow in size, as if the place was no longer big enough for him and his immediate problem.

He stopped suddenly and stared fixedly at Gunnar's impassive features, as if to find some small detail which he might have missed. 'Jesus Christ!' he exploded again with the fury of a breaking wave, 'do I have to spell it out for you? It would be just the same if you were a four-striped captain in a task-force cruiser, *I'm in charge!*'

Gunnar's voice seemed quiet by comparison, but the spots of colour on his cheeks showed the signs of inner resentment. 'So you said when I first came——'

But Jago stamped his booted foot. 'Hear me out! God knows I was willing to tolerate your crackpot ideas at first, but this is the goddamned limit! You get yourself blown up, and then before I can get the thing organised, you're out on some crazy scheme of your own amongst the islands, and as near as hell get killed again!' He stared at the other man as if surprised by his own words. 'Then you come back here as large as life with this cock-an'-bull yarn about a conspiracy which is about to

193

pull us *all* down!' He paused for breath. 'Really, Captain, what do you take me for?'

Gunnar started once more. It seemed useless, but the marine's fury had fanned his own anger into the open. 'If you're not prepared to accept my suggestions, then I can only ask a higher authority, Colonel!'

'Like Jesus you can! I've already made my report, and your status here has been confirmed, *again*! You're not an adviser on political and military integration now, Captain, you merely happen to be here on sufferance as far as I am concerned. You command one small ship, a mere fragment of the Seventh Fleet, do I make myself clear? I'm not talking to you as a brother officer, or even as a fellow-American, such terms are too simple for a mind like yours. I'm speaking to you as your superior, a mouthpiece if you like. But even if you don't like it, it still goes!'

In a far corner Sergeant Rickover, earphones on head, cranked busily on a lever and spoke quickly into his mouth-piece.

'See him?' Jago waved his arm violently. 'He's trying to keep in touch. Since this fiasco started all hell has been let loose around here. Ever since that fool exec of yours balled up a simple towing job, our name is mud!'

Gunnar said tightly: 'It's all in my report. Maddox did what he could. He could not possibly have forced the British to keep away from that freighter.'

Jago eyed him coldly. 'He should never have been in charge in the first place. If you had stayed in the ship as I requested you would have been out there with the ship. Instead you were swimming.' He glared. 'Swimming, I goddamn well ask you!' He hurried on: 'In any case, Maddox did foul it up, and now the local Chinks are cutting loose in every direction. There have been a dozen incidents already since your ship crawled in!'

Gunnar bit his lip. Maddox's own explanation was pretty bad at that. It was the one weak link in his own argument with Jago. 'They're being incited by professional agitators, I expect,' he said quietly.

'Maybe! But they think we deliberately handed those refugees over to the Limeys as a matter of course, don't you see that? They think that all my efforts to form them into a unified group under Taiwan is so much crap, and that we only intend to take over as a base for ourselves.'

194

'Well, that's true, isn't it?' Gunnar was also shouting. 'If you had been more level with them, or tried to do something for the islanders instead of training a lot of stupid prison guards to form fours, you might have got results!'

'Is that so?' Jago's voice dropped to a dangerous level 'That's where you're wrong. If there *are* any commies, they are amongst the so-called islanders, see?' He stared at Gunnar with exasperated calm. 'How can I make you see that what you're doing is wrong? That man you killed on the islet may have been a commie agent, he might have been a bandit, or even an escaped criminal, who knows? It doesn't really concern me or you. What does concern both of us is the fact that your actions, plus this latest fiasco on the part of your ship botching the towing job, has put us in a new jam. Now I can't even call in marines without stirring things up worse than they are. These agitators will tell the mobs that is what we intended all along. I've only got my Chinese troops to do an unnecessarily difficult job which would never have arisen before you came.'

'What about the commandant?' Gunnar felt tired and bitter. All the feeling of rested hope had vanished within minutes of the *Hibiscus*'s return. It was true what Jago had said. Mobs had roamed the town, there had been outbreaks of stone-throwing, and several times the troops had fired above their heads to disperse them.

'The commandant? He's a useless slob!' Jago picked up a ruler and bent it in his strong hands. 'He can't ask for troops without good reason. Would *you* in his position?'

Gunnar did not answer, so he added with heavy sarcasm, 'I hate to think what you would do, Captain!'

Rickover looked across. 'They've just burnt down the hospital, Captain.'

Gunnar stood up. 'Is Connell all right?'

Rickover nodded. He too looked tired out. 'Yes. A platoon went there and took him back to the ship.'

Gunnar shifted uneasily. 'Thank you.'

'And another thing, Captain. No more despatches to the admiral. Your orders are to maintain radio silence until otherwise told. Just receive the normal traffic, and that's all. From now on leave this mess to me!'

Gunnar looked unseeingly at the wall map. 'And you don't consider that I'm right about a possible takeover by the Reds, by Bolod, for instance?'

'Of course I know they're up to something, but it's nothing I can't handle once this civil disobedience is checked. God, man, what did you expect here?' He wagged his finger. 'But this is not going to be another Cuba, it's not going to be another *anything*! Get that through your head, and just stay out of trouble.'

Gunnar turned towards the door. 'I'd like to see the headman, Tao-Cho. He might listen to me.'

Jago snapped the ruler with sudden impatience. 'That bastard! He's a mean-minded, self-important old swine who should have been thrown in the pen years ago!'

'I'm asking your permission to visit him, officially if you like.'

Jago snorted. 'Officially is right! No more of your cloak-and-dagger tactics here. It might have been all right in your outfit in Viet Nam, but this is a strictly military affair. Any buck from Tao-Cho and there'll be a massive retaliation which will put his nose really out of joint!' He breathed out slowly, aware that Gunnar's face was still unmoved by the outburst. 'Okay. You go and see him. But you'll take an armed escort, and it'll be official and above board, got it?'

Gunnar smiled tightly. 'Got it.'

Jago pushed back his chair. 'See here, Captain, I've got nothing against you personally; You've had a tough time, and maybe it's affected you worse than you realise. I admire your record, but that's all in the past. I got a medal in Korea, but I don't expect the admiral to kiss my arse because of it, see?'

Gunnar eyed him impassively 'I try to forget the past too.'

'Well, that's good. But we don't want any more killings, or the Senate will be asking what sort of an outfit we're running.' He smiled thinly. 'My lads can deal with anything from the outside. In any case long enough for me to call up a strike force from the fleet.'

Gunnar said: 'I happen to know that the Seventh is pretty busy elsewhere, Colonel. If this show goes dead on us, it'll be in our laps right here.'

'Well it won't. So do your job and be a good boy. As soon as I can I'll get your ship replaced by another. But until then we just have to manage.' He shrugged. 'If not, then I'll have *you* replaced!' He swung his chair, displaying his back to Gunnar. 'Give me Pak on the phone, Sergeant. I'll tell him what we're doing.'

Gunnar slammed the door and marched up the narrow corridor between the yellow electric bulbs. Outside the gates were still open, but the soldiers fully kitted and armed patrolled the ramparts and idled around the waiting jeeps.

Below the buff he could see the masthead of his ship. The poor, salt-stained and demoralised *Hibiscus*, which he had boarded as she had come alongside the pier after two attempts. Maddox had been angry as well as despairing, and Gunnar thought he knew why.

But right now time was short, and things had to be done, popular or otherwise.

*   *   *

Jack Burgess stood like a rock in the centre of his living room, his bloodshot eyes fixed and determined as he stared at the seated American officer. He cleared his throat and said awkwardly, 'I think you'd better keep away from here for a bit.'

Robert Maddox lifted his eyes from his glass and returned his stare with something like indifference. 'Suit yourself.'

Burgess seemed a bit taken aback, and after sloshing another full measure into Maddox's tilted glass he busied himself vaguely by adjusting the closed shutters and pumping one of the pressure lamps.

Outside the room the street was dead quiet, as it had been since sunset. Maddox knew that soldiers were in the small square and another jeepload were only at the end of the first street, listening and ready. But he was past caring. He could not remember when he had felt like this, or when he had been so drunk. But the drink was no longer a balm, and it left him neither elated nor angry.

For Maddox it had been one hell of a day. The humiliation and confusion over losing the tow had been only a beginning. He had rounded it off himself by nearly ramming the pier upon his return to the anchorage, and even after a second attempt had brought the long-suffering *Hibiscus* to roost with a sickening jolt which had made the teeth shake in his head. He had felt like a schoolboy as he had blurted out the facts to the captain, who had stepped aboard almost as soon as the first wires had gone ashore.

It had sounded bad even in his own ears, and as he had watched Gunnar's grey eyes hardening he knew that worse was to come. Surprisingly, Gunnar had said very little about the actual towing. This point Maddox took as a personal rebuke, especially as the captain did comment to some length on the appearance of the ship.

Maddox had been dog tired. 'Hell, Captain, the boys are beat! They've been on their feet for twenty-four hours frigging about with the tow! You can't expect the ship to be in review order!'

Gunnar had eyed him coldly. 'I do expect it! I want the ship in first-line readiness for anything. Another tow if necessary!'

Maddox had wanted to say that if the captain had been on the bridge the result might have been the same. Instead his voice had said, 'I suppose this'll go against me?'

'Or me,' Gunnar had replied quietly.

But it was only when Maddox had met his young brother that the explosion had really been sparked off. Open-mouthed he had listened to Pip's excited account of the night search, the frantic struggle in the moonlight, and finally the killing of a Chinese terrorist.

Blindly he had run back to the captain's cabin where he had found Gunnar still standing beside his littered desk. 'What the *hell* do you mean by taking that kid with you like that?' The words had burst from him in a flood. 'Isn't one medal enough, for Christ's sake? Do you have to get him killed too to prove what a helluva hero you are?'

Gunnar had looked for one brief instant as if he was going to strike him. Go on, hit me, you cold-blooded bastard, Maddox's maddened brain had said.

But Gunnar had sat down, suddenly ice calm. 'I'll forget what you said, Mister Maddox. But if I hear another word like that I'll put you under arrest!'

Maddox had felt as if he wanted to explode, so that the small cabin seemed to close in on him like a vice. All the frustrations and insults, the unexpected dangers and everything else, crushed his reason and rendered him speechless.

Gunnar added more quietly: 'Your brother is an officer. Just because he is related to you does not exempt him from danger. He did very well. If there are any medals going they should be for him.'

Gunnar had stood up, and only then did Maddox notice the strain, the dark shadows beneath his eyes. Calmly the captain had continued: 'Try to remember that this is a ship of war, not some yacht. And when I require your advice on

198

how to run this ship, I'll damn well ask for it!'

The next few hours had been too busy even for Maddox to find time to contemplate the damage his anger might have done. There had been riots in the town, and once a bullet had slammed against the pier within feet of the deck. The hospital had been fired, and Connell had returned smoke-blackened and quiet, and had spoken to nobody since.

His brother kept clear of him, as if remembering the old days when Maddox had been the controlling force in the home, the bastion between father and the rest of the family.

There seemed only one thing to do, and as soon as his duties permitted Maddox went ashore to find Burgess, or rather his daughter. He had sampled a bottle in his cabin before leaving, but now, a good many drinks later, he was beginning to feel the effects of the strain and the unexpected self-discipline of taking command even for a short period of time.

But the visit had soured. Burgess seemed on edge, moody and watchful. He said thickly: 'You know I like you, Lieutenant. It's just that it doesn't do my position any good in the village to have you dropping in all the time. It's taken a long time to build up a bit of mutual trust.'

Maddox grunted. 'Sure, sure. I understand, Commander.'

Burgess seemed intensely relieved and said in an almost ingratiating tone: 'It's bound to blow over. Perhaps then we can all get together again. I can see we've a lot in common.'

Like hell we have, Maddox thought. In a week perhaps, or even days, we'll be away from this rathole, and Gunnar's madness as well. He said, 'You're dead right!'

Maddox allowed his fuddled mind to drift again. What would become of them all? Whatever else happened he must see to it that Pip was prevented from risking his fool neck again.

The curtain moved and Lea Burgess stepped lightly into the room. She was wearing her old shirt and slacks, but in Maddox's eyes she could have been in a Paris creation.

Burgess asked: 'Where have you been, then? Not with your captain I hope? It's too late to be out on the streets!'

Maddox's sluggish mind stirred to life as he saw the quick smile on the girl's lips. Pip had mentioned something about her being with Gunnar on the boat. In his rage he had not waited to hear the rest of it.

Burgess added with a broad wink, 'Well, never mind, your lieutenant is here now!' He swayed and loosened his shirt collar. 'I think I'll take a stroll on the jetty to check the moorings.' He put a big hand on Maddox's shoulder and added with unusual sincerity: 'I'd give a lot to get out of this place! My time'll come. It may be soon now.' He looked across at his daughter. 'She'll make a good wife for someone, Bob. A *good* wife.' Then carrying a full glass he lurched out of the room.

Maddox watched the girl as she sat quietly on the edge of the bench seat which he had shared with her so long ago. He stood up and poured another drink, and then, without asking, another for her.

He dropped beside her and thrust the glass into her hand. 'Drink it, it'll do you good.'

He could feel the warmth of her body, could see the small droplets of perspiration on her upper lip. It was very hot, and the blood was pounding in his brain like a giant hammer.

'I think your old man fancies me as a son-in-law, Lea. He's a good judge of character.' He slipped one arm about her shoulders and squeezed gently. He felt her stiffen but said easily, 'You're quite a girl!'

She smiled strangely, her lips moist in the lamplight. 'I think that you have been celebrating?'

'Like hell.' Maddox eyed her fixedly, like a marksman measuring his target. 'I've been letting go a bit, that's all.' He watched her from beneath his lowered lids. 'That fool of a captain has nearly driven me up the wall!' He felt her shoulders move and saw her chin lift a fraction. Maddox knew enough about women to guess at her reaction.

Almost roughly he said, 'Have you gone and fallen for that stiff back?'

She turned away, her face partly hidden by her hair. 'That is an unfair question.'

Maddox pulled gently at her shoulder. He could feel the moist warmth of her skin soaking through the thin material and guessed that beneath it she was naked. 'He'll love you and leave you, Lea.'

With a sudden move she stood up, and Maddox cursed himself for his clumsiness. It was the drink, of course, but at least he knew how she stood. Hastily he said: 'I was only kidding. Now just you sit down again.' He pulled her down so that she lost her balance and fell against him.

In one swift movement Maddox had pinioned her body with his arm, and with his free hand caressed her neck and throat. She twisted violently but Maddox held her firmly

200

against his side. 'Easy there! No one is going to hurt you!' Then, deftly, he slipped his fingers into the front of her shirt and plucked at the buttons.

Something seemed to explode in his mind. It was more like resentment than passion, and he heard her cry out as he ripped impatiently at the shirt until his hand found the smooth straining skin beneath.

It was then that a violent blow across the side of his head sent him sprawling to the floor. He had a vague, distorted vision of the girl's tear-stained face as she pulled the torn shirt across her breasts, and then of Burgess's angry red eyes as he stood above him.

'Get out of my house, you bloody bastard!' Burgess looked on the edge of madness. 'Out now, before I kill you!'

Maddox felt as if he was going to be sick. Shakily he picked up his cap from the chair, his humiliation complete. 'Okay, I'm leaving!' He tried to recover his scattered wits. 'You can keep your daughter for another time!'

Burgess's face crumpled. 'She's a good girl! I'll not have you speaking like that . . .' but he seemed suddenly confused, as if he had lost his direction.

Lea spoke from the far side of the room. 'It's all right, Father. He didn't know what he was doing.' She looked across at Maddox's inflamed face. 'Do you still want to show me America?' Then she laughed, a brittle sound, torn from her very heart, and ran through the curtain.

As Maddox made to leave, Burgess mumbled: 'I had to hit you, d'you see? I didn't want to. You're a good lad really. You'd be right for her, I'm sure. Perhaps when you call again she'll feel differently.'

Sickened, Maddox turned away and walked blindly into the darkness.

12

Storm Warning

Gunnar paused outside Burgess's house and shaded his face
to look at the sky. It appeared washed out and pale, but was
in fact well filtered by a drifting bank of haze which spread
the sun's normal blaze into a shimmering, eye-searing glare.
The village was quiet, but in the stale wind Gunnar could de-
tect the odour of burned wood and charred mortar. He had
passed the gutted hospital building that forenoon on his way
to meet the headman, Tao-Cho. It had been such a contrast
to his other meeting with the old man. Without turning his
head he had walked into the labyrinth of narrow streets, aware
of the patrolling soldiers, the faces beyond the darkened doors,
and of the youth who had been sent to guide him to the meeting place. But he had been even more conscious of the stamp
of feet, the clink of equipment, and the deep breathing of
Lieutenant Regan who led his party of armed seamen behind
his captain.

The meeting had turned out much as Gunnar had expected.
Even the small spark of hope had been extinguished when
he saw Tao-Cho's masklike face and hooded eyes. He had
been seated with his elders in exactly the same group as before,
but this time, in the cool dignity of his own house, he seemed
aloof and unreachable. Jago too must have known what the
headman's reactions would be when he had ordered Gunnar
to go with an armed escort. If there was any more doubt left,
Tao-Cho soon dispelled it.

'I am meeting you under duress, Captain. There is nothing
to add to my last statement, nor do I think you have anything
to offer but further offence!' He tucked his thin hands into his
sleeves. 'I waited for you to show your heart. You gave us
gifts, but it was only for the sake of your own plans in which
we had no part. You made your choice. We have made
ours.'

Gunnar had remained standing, a solitary figure amidst
the faded hangings and worn wooden beams. 'You have made
a big mistake. There can be no understanding without trust.
If you think that by siding with the enemy you will regain your
old power, then you are mistaken.'

A thin hand flashed impatiently. 'We side with no one, Captain. Like all of your mind you cannot recognise the truth. We do not want outside help, nor do we expect it.'

And so it had continued for the best part of an hour. Probe and rejection, suggestion and counter claim. Until at length Gunnar had said: 'I command a ship, Tao-Cho. I am responsible for the men who serve in her. But compared with this, your responsibility is far greater, and more final! No one can exist any more merely for principles. There has to be co-operation, even if the ways of men are different and mistakes are made before understanding can be reached.'

Tao-Cho stared at him with empty eyes. 'Go your way, Captain. I can no longer offer friendship to a man who respects my house only with armed men. Soon you will learn that our paths can never cross. We will not become part of your battleground, whatever the price.'

Gunnar had left without another word. Regan had fallen in step beside him. 'What did the old goat say, sir?'

'Nothing we don't already know. I respect his ideas, but I think he is wrong. Dammit, I *know* he's wrong!'

Regan had said uncompromisingly: 'He can jump off then! It's nice to know we can whistle up the Seventh Fleet if he gets out of hand.'

Gunnar had lapsed into silence. It was amazing how men like Regan had such fierce faith in the outside help which always hovered on the end of a radio wave. It was not as simple as that, and never had been.

The armed party had tramped back to the ship, but Gunnar had made his way to Burgess's house alone.

Now, as he stood looking up at some tiny, specklike gulls which circled uneasily overhead, he thought of his words to Tao-Cho. Of his own responsibility to his ship and his men. He had not done very well with either so far.

A board creaked under his foot and he stood uncertainly on the veranda. His earlier eagerness had melted and he felt unsure and nervous. It was different from the *Osprey*'s deck after the mad struggle with the terrorist. The fear of death, the revulsion and the relief had joined with his own quiet exultation as the girl had laid her head on his shoulder. That was over.

The room was shaded and cool after the dusty street, and with shock he realised that she was standing by the far window, her body framed by the sparkling sea beyond. There

203

was tea on a small table, and he noticed that she was wearing a green dress and not her usual Chinese shirt.

'I was afraid you would not come, Captain.' Her face was in shadow but the catch in her voice made his throat go dry. She continued, 'I could have told you what you already know, but I thought it best to leave it alone.'

He crossed the room and stood looking down at her. Her small, oval face was grave and anxious, and she was watching him in a strange way he had not seen before.

'I thought you'd throw me out. All that I said, all that I hoped . . .' He shrugged. 'I guess I asked for it. Like you, I should have left it well alone. Instead I made one error after another. I pretended to myself that I mistrusted every Oriental ever born, but I know now it was something else.' His voice was bitter, but he could no longer check himself. 'I used it to cover up my own uncertainty.'

She moved one hand to brush a strand of hair from her cheek. 'Have you ever told anyone of this?'

He shook his head, surprised at himself. 'Never. Perhaps I should. But there was no one. He walked to the window, aware that she was watching him intently. 'Something my exec said to me yesterday made me think again. I've done all this, risked men's lives, even been responsible for their deaths.' He remembered Maddox's flushed, angry face with sudden clarity. 'He was right.'

He felt her hands on his own, pulling him round so that they were facing each other again. 'Do not speak like that! You will make me angry! It is untrue, and the lieutenant is a fool to hurt you when you need his help!'

Gunnar stared at her. Need his help? Had he ever needed anyone's help? In seconds she had laid bare his other weakness. His own stupid pride.

She led him to the bench seat and said gently: 'I have made some tea. You will feel better.' Then she smiled, and Gunnar felt the tension draining from him like blood. She added: 'I knew you would come here. You see, Captain, I am *half* Oriental!'

Gunnar watched her as she moved quietly to the small table. What am I doing? What is happening to me?

Just then Lea looked across at him, her dark eyes sad. 'Stop tormenting yourself. It is no good.' She placed a cup at his side and then surprisingly knelt on the rug by his feet. 'When you first came here I hated you.' She studied his face with

204

sudden warmth. 'I had never even seen you. It was just that you represented something bad, a force which could change everything.' She tossed her head as if to indicate the whole house and the village beyond. 'I thought this was the final home for me. I could even bear it if I was left alone. My father needs me. He still talks of getting away, of making that one big success which will change everything. But before your ship came his dreams were less frequent. Sometimes he was almost content.' Her eyes became distant. 'When you arrived I saw the change come over him, as it did over others here. He lives a life of make-believe. You are a clever man, you must have noticed?'

Gunnar nodded gently. 'He has had a lot to bear.'

She swallowed hard. 'Did you know that he was dismissed from the navy in disgrace?'

Gunnar saw her mouth tremble. 'Yes, I knew.'

She reached up impulsively and pressed his hand. 'And yet you said nothing. You are a good man. I was so wrong about you that I am ashamed.'

'I am the one who should be ashamed, Lea. But I am grateful for one thing only. Of meeting you.'

She shook her head violently so that her hair fell across his legs. 'You must not say that! Not because you think you have to!'

Gunnar touched her hair and answered, 'You know that's not the reason.' Cautiously he added, 'Your father cannot expect you to stay here for ever.'

'I would rather do that than see him shamed again in another country.'

Gunnar gripped her shoulder and eased her gently against his leg. 'He must think the world of you.'

She smiled sadly. 'I wonder. In his eyes over the years I have come to represent his downfall, the one indiscretion which ruined his life!'

'Would you leave here if I asked you?' He tightened his grip and knew he was hurting her.

She looked down at his fingers biting into her smooth skin and said quietly: 'I would do anything for you. I do not understand my own feelings, but I know what they mean towards you.'

Gunnar dropped on to his knees beside her, his eyes searching her face. 'But I've told you nothing of myself, of my own life?'

205

'I know a lot about you, Captain. The rest will find its own way.'

Gunnar felt as if he was spinning round in tight circles. 'You must not call me "captain". It's indecent!'

She touched his mouth with her fingers, her eyes moving across his face as if to search out the tension and destroy it. 'But you are my captain now!'

How long they sat together Gunnar could not remember, and the tea, untouched, grew cold on the table. Outside, the sky seemed paler and more angry, and Gunnar vaguely remembered the circling gulls above the village. Probably a storm blowing up. But it could keep. They both looked towards the window as a siren hooted impatiently in the distance. He felt her stiffen.

'It's my father coming back with *Osprey*,' she said quickly.

Gunnar pressed her close, conscious of the pounding of his heart which matched hers with its eagerness. 'I must see you again soon.' He looked into her face, aware of the complications and the barriers which Payenhau demanded of him.

'Soon. Very soon.' She was trembling, and added in a small voice: 'I trust you. I must trust you.'

He held her a while longer, feeling the power of love coursing through her, laying bare her innermost thoughts in a way he had never known before. He knew what she meant by trust. It was something real. A thing which nothing must spoil.

He heard the fishing boat squeak against the jetty and said urgently: 'The sandspit by the wrecked ship. Can you get there tonight? Tomorrow might be too late. There might be no tomorrow.'

She nodded and turned her face away. 'After sunset. It will be safe there.'

As Gunnar strode into the hot wind which stirred the dust in the square he felt her watching him.

When he reached the pier he saw Regan supervising a party of seamen in doubling the mooring wires. He said in his harsh voice: 'Storm warning, Captain. But we should be snug enough in here.'

Gunnar stepped aboard the ship, which suddenly seemed safe and friendly. He saw Maddox's broad shoulders disappearing around the bridge and knew he was deliberately avoiding him.

In the wardroom Kroner untwined his long legs and held out a despatch flimsy. 'Just decoded this one, sir.' He could hardly contain the excitement in his voice. 'Sailing orders!'

Gunnar snatched the paper and read it twice, his eyes misty as each word made itself felt.

Hibiscus would sail for Taiwan in one week. She would be replaced in two weeks' time by the destroyer *John Dundas*, which would assume the duty until plans for a new base were completed.

Kroner said brightly: 'That means we'll be paying off, sir. Back to home and beauty!'

Gunnar did not hear. 'This is confidential. But yes, I guess that is what it means.'

It also meant that Payenhau would be without immediate surface support for a complete week. He thought of the girl waiting back in the village and knew that it meant more than that.

He walked blindly to his cabin and sat for several minutes on the edge of his bunk and tried to compose his thoughts. Jago would do nothing, he had complete faith in his own arrangements. He might be right. But then again . . . Gunnar rang the bell at his side and heard a door slam in the passageway.

His yeoman, Bella, stood waiting in the doorway. 'Sir?' He looked ten years older, and his dark face was blotchy from lack of sleep. Gunnar did not notice and said quickly: 'I want you to type out some orders for Commander Burgess of the *Osprey*. When I have signed them I want you to take them to him yourself, and see that he reads them.'

Gunnar's mind began to recover from its initial shock. If Burgess could be sent to Taiwan on some pretext or other, he could carry a full report to the commander-in-chief. It would be natural and could not possibly offend Jago, who might not even hear of it. It was so simple that Gunnar almost laughed aloud. It would also mean that he and his daughter would be clear of Payenhau if the eruption came. Suddenly he was quite sure that it would come.

Anyway, tied as he was by the admiral's over-all strategy and his own radio silence, there was no other way. It would be the one last card. He couldn't explain his uneasiness any longer, but he knew now that the danger was there.

*   *   *

Bella drew heavily on his cigarette and listened to the wind

207

sighing against the hull of the moored fishing boat *Osprey*. It was snug in the small forward cabin, and he watched the big, bearded Englishman as he scrutinised the two typed sheets which Gunnar had signed only two hours before.

He had made his way to Burgess's house by a roundabout route, calling first at the wrecked freighter with a parcel of food for Pirelli. He had been shocked by the change which had come over the man. Dirty, unshaven, he had become a scarecrow shadow of his former self, and there was a kind of wildness which made Bella long to get away.

Pirelli, on the other hand, seemed unwilling to allow Bella's departure, even though every minute meant danger of discovery. He had rambled on about trivial things concerning the ship, the crew and day-to-day routine. All his outer belligerence seemed to have vanished, and had left in its place a pathetic hunger for the only world he understood.

Bella had told him about Gunnar's intention of sending the *Osprey* to Taiwan, more to fill in time than for any real information value. Pirelli had grasped it with something of his old eagerness. 'I know that boat, Mike.' His eyes flashed in the half light. 'I could stow away in her. Yes, I could do just that!' His lip curled in a sneer. 'It's no use waitin' for your Chink friends to get me off. They're goddamn useless!'

Bella had turned away in case Pirelli had seen the sudden guilt on his face. He had been right. The Chinese captain had met him on more than one occasion. That part had been easy, as Bella was one of the few people from the ship who had regular access to the shore with messages and so forth. Once the Chinese captain had vanished for several days with a vague promise that when he returned he would be bringing the girl with him. Now it was urgent. If she arrived after *Hibiscus* had sailed, he would never see her again, and what was worse, Peach might end up in the prison camp, isolated from her family and the prey of anyone who cared to adopt her. But at last he had something to tell the big Chinese sailor. With his new-found knowledge he could force an issue one way or the other. If he told the man that *Hibiscus* was sailing finally for Taiwan he would realise that Bella could no longer supply him with information. His quick mind had already plotted what he was going to say when he met him again. It would be easy to bring forward the *Hibiscus*'s sailing date by a few days for his benefit. Then by promising to arrange a similar information service through the yeoman on the relieving destroyer, he might get things speeded up. Anyway, it was worth trying. As things stood, he could be no worse off.

Burgess folded the message and asked, 'Any idea what he wants me to take?'

Bella shrugged indifferently. 'Just a despatch or something.'

'It could be important.' Burgess's mind was obviously working on a different tack. 'It could make all the difference.' .

Outside, the wind plucked more urgently at the stout hull, and Bella could feel the normally quiet waters surging around the piles of the jetty. 'Is it going to be rough, do you think?'

'We get a lot of storms here. They soon pass over. We're pretty sheltered in this anchorage.' Burgess seemed impatient, unwilling to prolong the conversation as Bella might have expected. Well, he thought, that suits me. It'll give me more time before dark.

Burgess smiled quickly as the yeoman stood up and jammed on his cap. He could hardly disguise his eagerness to guide him over the side, and once when he looked back Bella saw the Englishman already walking into the village, his head bowed against the rising wind.

Bella trudged through the swirling dust, his hands deep in his pockets as he prepared what he was going to say. He had one hundred dollars which he had carefully saved in Hong Kong, and he guessed it would help to smooth the paths of diplomacy which lay ahead. In his locker he had another roll, as well as the expensive length of red silk which he had been hoarding for Peach.

He thought momentarily of Pirelli. It would all work out very well after all. Pirelli would be away at last, and from then on he would be on his own. Pirelli asked all the time about the ship, yet it was strange how his name hardly ever cropped up now. It was as if he had died with Grout and the others. It might have been better if he had, Bella thought grimly. The *Hibiscus*'s sailors had enough of their own worries. In the navy you soon forgot broken friendships and old faces. Just as you soon cleared your memory of the dead.

He shielded his face from the miniature sandstorm and squinted along the coast road. It was empty but for a parked jeep, its occupants sheltering miserably beneath the canvas hood, and with a final glance he turned sharp left and made his way up the hill towards the meeting place.

* * *

209

Robert Maddox lifted his head to listen to the muffled twitter of the bosun's whistle. Evening colours, but instead of the usual grand sunset it was already dark and subdued, so that in the wardroom the messboys had switched on the lights, and from the quaking movement of the deck the ship could have been at sea.

Maddox toyed with his ballpoint and stared again at the blank sheet of notepaper which he had balanced across a magazine on his lap. He still did not really believe what he was doing. He tried to tell himself that it was an escape, an answer to the shame he had endured because of the girl, Lea Burgess. Every man needed an escape. Like the handsome Kroner, who kept a full-length photograph of a stunning girl in a bikini beside his bunk. Only a very close inspection showed that the girl was a part of an advertisement for camping equipment which he had filched from somewhere or other. Yet Kroner doted on that picture, and stared at it with unfailing fascination. It was his sea anchor, his brake.

Maddox lifted his eyes slightly to look at Regan who was sitting at the table his narrow head lowered over some new plan of gunnery mechanism. He was always studying his trade. Some day he might be a senior officer with a couple of stars on his collar instead of a tarnished bar. Heaven help his poor subordinates, Maddox thought savagely.

He looked down again at the paper. It was still there in his untidy handwriting . . . *Dear Mary.* How in God's name could he continue? Even if she forgave him, which was most unlikely, did he really *want* her?

He moved his mind away from the empty page and thought of Gunnar. The captain had called him to his cabin and told him about the despatch. Sailing orders, the magic words. Gunnar had been correct and cool, gave no hint of the tension between them. Gunnar would make him eat dirt when they touched Taiwan, he thought grimly. His angry outburst in defence of Pip, his clumsy handling of the tow, and all the other things he had omitted to do paraded across his troubled thoughts like spectres. On the other hand, Gunnar would find little praise for his own doings. The realisation gave him no comfort, however.

At that moment Pip Maddox entered the doorway, his khakis dripping with spray, and wiping the moisture from his unruly hair. 'Colours completed, sir.' He grinned at his

210

brother's gloomy face. 'You should see the water, quite big waves in the anchorage!'

Behind the pantry hatch they could hear the clatter of dishes as Slattery and his mates got ready for the last meal of the day. Pip sniffed hopefully. 'What's for chow?'

Regan said without looking up, 'Goddamn tinned ham again, I expect!'

Pip threw himself into a chair and stretched luxuriously. 'I pulled down my first flag tonight! It was quite a ceremony.'

The others looked at him with surprise, but he grinned and added: 'There was I, booted and spurred, saluting at the correct angle, and doing it by the book. And what happened? Chief Tasker is moaning because his rheumatism is playing him up, and the quartermaster was holding a cigar behind his rump while the flag was actually dipping!'

Regan grimaced. 'What, no mighty throng paying homage?'

Pip scowled. 'Only a couple of ancient Chinks who were gathering scraps from our galley chute!' He smiled uncertainly at his brother. 'I did see the Burgess girl, however.' He rolled his eyes. 'What a dish!'

Malinski said, 'Where was she going?'

The boy shrugged. 'I dunno. But the skipper bounced ashore a few minutes later, so I guess he's gone a-courting!'

Maddox half rose from his chair. 'The captain? Jesus, Pip, you should have told me!'

'Yeh, you must tell the exec when you're O.O.D., Pip!' Regan grinned with obvious pleasure. 'He likes to *know* these things!'

Pip looked at his brother uncomfortably. 'Sorry, Bob, but he did say it was okay. Said he didn't want to bother anyone.'

Regan nodded sagely. 'Oh sure, I can imagine!'

Maddox glared at his brother and then checked himself as Kroner lounged into the wardroom his despatch folder under his arm. He looked round, as if sniffing out the possible dangers, and drawled: 'Broadcast from Hong Kong. Fresh gale blowing up from the south-east. Looks nasty.'

Malinski remarked slowly, 'It's gone round then?'

'Sure has. It was due west a few hours ago.' Kroner sighed. 'All we need is a storm just as we sail for home!'

Maddox buried his face in his letter-writing. It can blow to hell for all I care, he thought savagely. Just let me get *out* of here!

So the captain had gone ashore after the girl. She would tell

211

him what his exec had tried to do. If her father had not come in at that moment Maddox could not imagine what might have happened. It made him sweat just to remember her tear-stained face and what he himself must have looked like. It was little removed from attempted rape. No better than Pirelli! He swallowed hard. It was no use trying to believe that she wanted him to do it. If he had been in a different mood, with less drink under his belt, it might have been different. But only *might* have' been. You could never be absolutely sure. With something like a groan he tried again . . . *Dear Mary* . . . Then after a few more minutes he began to write.

* * *

In the fast-fading light the waters of the anchorage surged angrily in a mass of broken whitecaps. The heavy, humid breath of the wind pushed at it and held back the receding tide, so that instead of sliding gently from the long sandspit it tossed and broke across the wrecked ship's counter and rattled the rusty plates with thrown pebbles as if to mock its dishonour.

The two lines of footmarks in the sand met and mingled as Gunnar reached the girl who was waiting in the lee of the towering hulk. Whipped by the wind, her hair floated like a black banner, and in the strange light from the angry water her eyes looked huge and bright.

Gunnar took her arm and called above the hiss of spray and sand: 'We must get under cover! I don't want you blown away!'

They found the sad, frayed ladder which Pirelli and Bella had already used, and after a moment's hesitation Gunnar led the way up and over the ship's buckled rail. In the dancing shadows the ship had regained some of its old dignity, and the scars and fractured plates merged together as a whole.

Gunnar took off his jacket and spread it on the canting boat-deck beside the chewed stack, and with a quick laugh the girl sat down, her hands pushing the rebellious hair across her shoulders, her lips parted and happy.

It was strangely quiet on the sheltered deck, and even the sea noises seemed far away.

He lowered himself to her side, and with a sudden, impetuous movement she turned to face him and was in his arms. He felt her face pressing into his chest and heard her say: 'Let me

212

keep it like this. Shut out everything else. I feel safe here, with you!'

Gently he stroked her neck and shoulder and said quietly, 'My ship is leaving in a few days.' He waited, conscious of her stillness, as if she had stopped breathing. 'I had to tell you, although it is supposed to be a secret.'

Far away, 'I shall never see you again.'

The words cut at his heart, so that he said with sudden fierceness: 'You must never say that! I can tell you now. I love you!'

She lifted her chin, her eyes shining in the darkness. 'Where will you go? What will happen?'

He looked over the rail at the maddened whitecaps. 'Taiwan for a bit, then maybe Pearl Harbour. I'm not sure. But I'm not going back to the States. Not yet, if I can help it.'

She whispered: 'I wish this was our ship. Just ours, sailing on alone for ever.'

He pressed her face against his own and said: 'You must leave here. I have made arrangements for your father to take his boat to Taiwan. You must stay there. I will give you an address I have and I'll be with you after that for as long as you like.'

'Will it be like that?' She was studying his face, her hands on his shoulders. 'Can I be lucky enough?'

He laughed quietly. 'Lucky? That's my privilege!'

He pulled her down across his chest and felt her spine quiver beneath his hands. She said: 'I can't bear to leave you. Not now.' She was speaking close against his ear, her face hidden. 'I cannot wait, I cannot tell you——' He felt her quiver as his hand moved and touched her breast. 'Please——'

Tenderly he slipped his arm beneath her shoulders and raised himself on his elbow. Her hair was a dark halo across his jacket, her arms and legs pale and unmoving as she stared up at him. Then as he bent over her she opened her arms wide and averted her face as he began to unfasten her dress, until as he tortured himself a moment longer she lay on the old ship's deck like a white crucifix.

She said with a sob, 'There has never been another—I have not done this before——'

Then he was pressing down on her, feeling her fingers gripping his shoulders with the fierceness of pain and want. Down, down, enclosing and enfolding, his mouth holding hers to smother that first delicious agony which neither wanted to end.

13

'She's Going Over!'

There was a harsh scraping of metal as a mooring wire was dragged along the deck overhead, and Gunnar looked up startled, pulled unwillingly from his brooding thoughts. The door of his cabin was closed, but seemed incapable of shutting out the sounds of a ship coming to life.

It was mid-morning, yet the sun had never regained its power, lost in the brief fury of the gale. The sea was still restless and sullen, and slopped against the slender hull in deep rhythmic waves. Everything creaked and muttered, and Gunnar could hear the bustle of movement, the clatter of feet and an occasional bark of orders. Without looking at his watch he knew it was close on sailing time. The mission to Payenhau was ending as it had started. Futile, empty, wasted.

Heavily he slumped down on to the edge of his bed and turned over the small carved figure in his hands. It was a newly finished figurine of an American navy officer. Of himself. She had given it to him almost shyly the day the *Osprey* had sailed for Taiwan. With a lull in the storm the fishing boat had sailed in sudden haste, and Gunnar realised how much he depended on her. But her absence made him realise something more. That he had nothing to offer her when eventually he reached Taiwan, and for himself there would no longer be even this ship.

There was nothing, absolutely nothing in his favour. In addition, there was much against him. The death and mutilation of the landing party, as well as Pirelli's mysterious disappearance. And now this other thing. Within hours of sailing time, his own yeoman, Bella, had vanished, as completely as if he had been plucked away in the gale.

Gunnar could well imagine how all these things would appear in the cold atmosphere of a court of enquiry. He knew he would not have cared so much but for his own sense of failure, of being dragged away before the real danger was unmasked.

By contrast the ship showed itself in different mood. An almost holiday air prevailed, the gloom and mutinous despondency of the past weeks wiped away with the announcement of sailing orders.

A bosun's mate poked his head around the door with only the briefest pause after a knock which Gunnar had not even noticed. 'The exec's respects, sir, an' it's five minutes to go.'

He vanished before Gunnar had time to answer. That was the way of it now, he thought bitterly. Every man aboard knew that it was almost over. The *Hibiscus* was no longer a part of everyday life. It was merely a passage-ship, a one-way ticket home.

He stood up slowly and then placed the little carving carefully beneath the pillow where it would be safe once the ship met the open sea. It would be a rough passage, and he knew he was unreasonably glad about this. He needed something to break the tension and the disappointment.

He waited a moment longer, his aching mind turning to that other memory for comfort. He could still imagine her smooth skin and feel the eagerness of their combined desire and love. But it did not help. Instead it added to the realisation that in her eyes he would soon be like her own father. A man forced from his set track, a failure impossible to live with.

Almost blankly he walked into the passageway and made his way on deck. The sky above the anchorage was high-clouded and angry, and a strong wind still ruffled the sparse vegetation above the town and blew the flag out stiffly from the staff.

He climbed the ladder, noting the quick glances from his men, the meaning looks which made him feel a stranger already.

Maddox saluted. 'All lines singled up, sir. Engine room ready to proceed!' His face was controlled and calm, and again Gunnar thought he was facing someone he hardly knew.

'Very well.'

He walked to the front of the open bridge and gripped the rail, allowing his lungs to fill with the hot, dusty air being whipped from the beach and the coast road.

Regan stood at the starboard wing, staring down at the pier and waiting to take over the duty of O.O.D. once the ship had left the protection of the land, and Kroner lounged negligently against the taffrail, his face turned towards the bridge as he awaited his orders.

Ensign Maddox climbed breathlessly on to the bridge and blinked round, seeking out the captain, his face flushed with excitement. 'Sir! They've found Bella!'

Gunnar swung round his face alert. 'How do you know?'

'I was just disconnecting the shore phone, sir. Sergeant Rickover told me.' Some of his excitement drained away. 'He's dying, sir.'

Gunnar balled his hands into tight fists. 'Get the doctor on the double.' As the ensign scurried away he yelled: 'Mister Maddox, hold everything! Stand by to receive a stretcher party!' The slow-moving jeep which he had noticed minutes earlier took a on a new and grimmer significance. The silent crowd fell away to allow the vehicle to lurch on to the pier at a snail's pace, and Gunnar could see Colonel Jago's stiff-backed figure beside the driver and the two Chinese soldiers in the rear with their covered burden.

It seemed to take an hour, but in fact Connell and his assistants were already easing the stretcher across the rail as Gunnar reached the deck. Roughly he thrust aside the murmuring sailors and laid one hand on the doctor's arm. 'How is he?' He hardly recognised the yeoman's white, pallid face. He looked dead already.

Jago climbed aboard and said shortly, 'He's been carved practically in half!'

Gunnar swayed, his eyes misting with helpless fury and despair as he stared past the marine's stony features towards the placid town and the humped hills beyond. Another one. Another victim of his own folly!

Jago stood aside as the still figure was passed out of sight. 'My medics have shot him full of dope, but I guess it's only putting off a certainty.'

Gunnar clenched and unclenched his fists. 'But why? How did it happen?'

'Probably one of the damned villagers working off a bit of hate. A patrol found him beyond the town. He was trying to crawl with half his guts hanging out!'

Gunnar's eyes were ice-cold and suddenly very still. 'You must change my orders, Colonel! You can do it. You could send a despatch right now and say you need my ship here!'

Jago eyed him strangely. 'But I don't, Captain. Frankly I'll be glad to see the back of you!' He looked at the clouds. 'There's another gale brewing, and you'd be wise to get clear and into a bit of sea-room.'

Gunnar swallowed his helpless anger. 'If that's an order?'

'It is.' Final. Nothing more.

216

'You're making a mistake, Colonel. I hope to God you realise that?'

Jago gave a thin smile. 'Forget it. Go back to the navy and leave this sort of war to the professionals, Captain.' He held out his hand. 'Good luck.'

Gunnar shook it briefly and walked back towards the bridge ladder. Over his shoulder he said quietly, 'Save it for yourself!'

He returned to his place on the gratings, aware of Regan's curious stare. He snapped, 'Take in all lines!' It was finished. Bella's return had rounded off the finality to sickening perfection.

'All engines back one-third.' The deck began to tremble, and he watched the pier begin to slide past the low hull where Maddox moved amongst the seamen with the rope fenders.

Gunnar found that he was shaking uncontrollably and his chest felt bathed in sweat. With something like fear he realised that the old feeling was coming back. The edge of collapse he had left in the hospital after Viet Nam. He forced himself to watch the ship's steady movement across the wide anchorage, her twin screws dragging her astern towards one of the sheltering islets. He was seeing it for the last time. The hills, the listing wreck on the sandspit where he had taken the girl's love with the same lack of consideration as he had done everything else.

'All engines stop.' He waited as the cross-wind made the bows swing slightly towards the western channel. It was as if the ship too was eager to be away and could no longer wait for the helm.

'All engines ahead one-third. Left standard rudder!' It was useless to prolong it. The ship began to turn away from the narrow beach, past the untidy cluster of the fishing village where so much had started and ended. Behind him a signalman clattered on to the bridge the Jack already rolled carelessly beneath his arm. It would not be needed much more.

An islet loomed large on the port bow as the little ship began to thread her way into the channel. There was a good quartermaster at the wheel, and this time he would need little help and encouragement. The sea looked grey and hostile, and the sun's path was silvery through the haze as the *Hibiscus* thrust her stem into the deeper water beyond the islet.

'All secure, sir.' Maddox had returned to the bridge. 'Shall I take the con?'

Gunnar nodded absently. 'If you please. I am going below to see Bella.'

The exec said uncertainly: 'I'm sorry about him, Captain. On top of everything else too.'

Gunnar eyed him coldly. 'Bring her round to the south-west as soon as we are clear. If there's to be another storm warning I want to be well clear before we turn north on to the final course.'

Maddox said, 'Yes, sir.' He looked across at his young brother, who turned away as if unable to watch Gunnar's despair. He added, 'It's better this way, sir.'

Gunnar swung his leg on to the ladder, his shoulders outlined against the green and brown hump of land. 'I'm glad you think so.' Then he was gone, and Maddox cursed himself for wavering from his decided course of action. The captain was done for. He should never have been sent back to sea duty so soon, if at all. He leaned his arms on the screen and turned his thoughts back to Mary and the completed letter which he would post in Taiwan.

* * *

Connell glanced up as the captain entered his small domain and stood swaying between the white-enamelled pipe-cots. Connell noticed how he did not appear to be holding on for support although the ship was already swinging through a rapid and violent series of sharp arcs.

Gunnar asked, 'Any change, Doc?'

Connell shook his head. 'Nothing.' He wondered why the captain was showing such concern over Bella. The poor wretch strapped in the lower cot had once been his yeoman, but that meant very little. If the ship had been on a long commission it might have been different. A commanding officer often grew very close to his yeoman, if only on a master/servant basis. But Gunnar seemed haunted and driven, and although the weather had worsened already since the ship had left Payenhau, he appeared to be unable to stay away. For hours the *Hibiscus* had flogged south-west away from the island group and its protective layers of reefs before turning towards the north on her new course. Now she had the bleak and tossing sea to herself. There was no longer an horizon, and in the grey half-light their immediate world was a tossing panorama of white and yellow crests, which crumbled into long streamers

218

of spray and drifting spume in the mounting wind. Connell had never heard wind like this before. It howled and whined, as if trying to shake the pitching ship apart. From the rattling signal halyards to the uneasy jolting furniture, it drove its gusts through every crack and opening until even the clothes on a man's back became sodden with spray and seeping damp.

Gunnar sat on a cot and stared fixedly at Bella's white face. Already it was sunken and skull-like, like that of an old man.

Connell said quietly: 'I'd give a lot to get him into hospital. This place is little better than a field ambulance!' He looked almost pleading. 'No chance of calling up help, sir?'

Gunnar shook his head. 'None. No chopper could find us in this gale, even if it could get airborne.' Bella stirred in his coma, and Gunnar said sharply, 'What's happening?'

Connell rubbed his lined face. 'Nothing. He's half conscious some of the time, but he doesn't know anything. Once he said something about a girl. I think it was that Chinese girl he wanted to marry.' He bit his lip. 'Poor kid.'

Gunnar watched his hand in his lap. What was the point of staying here? Bella would be able to tell him nothing. It was better to let him die in peace.

Connell said slowly, 'The storm seems to be getting worse.'

'It is.' Gunnar brought his mind to the present again. 'A Force Eight again, and worse to come before we get out of it.' He did not want to talk. There was no point in adding the fact that the glass had dropped with frightening rapidity even in the last hour. It could mean everything or nothing. In the China Seas tropical storms had few of the reliable symptoms of other areas.

A telephone buzzed at his side and he dragged it from its hook in one movement. 'Captain speaking.'

It was Kroner, his voice far away and distorted by the howl of the wind. 'She's not holding on the new course, sir!' He sounded scared.

Gunnar's mind stirred. 'I'll come up.' He added as an afterthought, 'How is it?'

'Bad, sir. Damn bad. The glass is still dropping, although not so rapidly, but the visibility is down to four miles.' The hull shivered and hummed like a mad musical instrument. 'Jesus, it's throwing us about like a bucket!'

Gunnar stood up and clung to the cot as the deck canted suddenly beneath him. 'Keep at it, Doc. Call me the moment he tries to say anything.' His eyes bored into the crouching doctor. '*Anything*, got it?'

With effort he forced open a hatch and almost fell on the streaming upper deck as a big breaker surged over the rail and thundered against a twenty-millimetre gun-tub. It was wild all right. With something like awe Gunnar realised that he had hardly noticed the storm's approach, nor had he read the signs with much interest. All at once it was real, and very close.

The small upper bridge had long since been abandoned in the face of wind and weather and as was normal on such occasions, all watchkeeping was carried out in the wheelhouse. It too seemed smaller and more crowded, crushed by the weight of the sea's fury which faced the ship on every side.

Gunnar had to grip the steel door to stop himself sliding backwards across the rail as the bridge canted above him, while over his shoulder he could see the water boiling alongside as if being heated from far below in some impossible cauldron. He waited until the labouring vessel had completed her upswing and, then pushed into the wheelhouse and slammed the door behind him. Already the windows were streaming with salt spray, whilst inside they were constantly running with damp and condensation.

Kroner skidded towards him and shouted: 'It's real bad, sir. The helmsman's having a job to hold her on three fifty degrees!'

Gunnar felt his way past the straddle-legged quartermaster, whose intent features shone yellow in the compass light, and stared back across the ship's yawing stern. The sea was cruising down in long, unbroken rollers and catching *Hibiscus* on her starboard quarter. Rank upon rank, some curving over in yellow-fanged crests, the others steep and black-sided like solid things. He watched one such mass of water reach under the narrow stern and saw the ship cant skywards. Like a toy she was pushed forward and down into a deep trough which buried the bows as far back as the little three-inch gun on the fo'c'sle.

Paice, the quartermaster, yelled hoarsely, 'She's payin' off, sir!'

The gyro tape ticked remorselessly round as Kroner shouted, 'Bring your rudder hard left!'

'Three five five—three six zero!' There was a sob in Paice's voice. 'I can't hold her!'

Gunnar wrapped his arm around a stanchion and felt his

220

ship tearing at his muscles, pulling him down. 'Back the port engine! Flank speed on the starboard!' He felt the hair prickle on his neck as the telegraph jangled, and imagined Malinski in the bowels of the engine room with his small world standing on end about him.

'Three five five—three five zero!' Paice let out a gasp. 'Comin' left, sir!'

'All engines ahead full!' Gunnar watched Paice's thick hands spinning the wheel as he met the swing of the bows against the corkscrewing stern. That was close, he thought. If the ship paid off and broached into those rollers he might never hold her. She would turn turtle and go straight down in minutes. It had happened before.

The door at the rear of the wheelhouse rasped back on its rollers and a radioman staggered drunkenly through the gap. ' 'Nother message from Hong Kong Radio, Captain!' His eyes rolled in the semi-darkness as he caught sight of the sea for the first time. 'Jesus, what a friggin' mess!'

Gunnar's jaw muscles tightened. 'This is it, Kroner.' He sensed the lieutenant's fear as together they sprawled across the chart table and Gunnar picked up the brass dividers. 'It's a typhoon. We seem to be running parallel with it!'

Typhoon. The word moved in the wheelhouse like an evil thing. Paice glanced briefly from the compass towards the man at the telegraphs and pursed his lips in a silent whistle.

Kroner watched the captain's hands moving the dividers deftly across the stained chart and said in a strangled voice, 'Bad, sir?'

Gunnar spoke half to himself. 'It's situated within fifty miles of latitude twenty north and longitude one hundred and twenty-two east, moving north-west.' He rolled the parallel rulers across the chart and marked off the calculations against the ship's track. 'It's coming right up the Luzon Strait.' He said sharply, 'How is she holding, Paice?'

Paice swallowed hard. 'Wheel feels as if it's made of glue, Captain, but I'm on course, three five zero!'

Not for long, thought Gunnar grimly. The sea was pushing ahead of the storm centre, forcing its combined might across hundreds of miles of open water to hit the only moving object, the starboard quarter of the *Hibiscus*. He tapped his teeth with the pencil and stared at the chart. 'A typhoon, Kroner, is a nasty thing.'

Kroner stared at him as if he had expected some kind of

miracle. 'How fast is it moving, do you think?'

Gunnar winced as another roller piled itself against the frail hull plates and made the deck cant at thirty degrees. Even at full speed the ship was only just keeping steerage way with little in reserve. If sea and wind ever matched the ship's passage through the water, then the rudder would become so much useless weight. 'Two to three hundred miles a day mostly. But with the storm we've already had, it might be speeded up a bit.'

His voice held neither fear nor hope, and Kroner's face seemed to turn green as he stared at the maindeck. On the lee side the rail was almost hidden, and he could see a small, motionless group of oilskinned seamen clinging to a lifeline as they tried to put an extra lashing on the whaleboat.

Gunnar said suddenly: 'Keep a good lookout on the radar while you can. There may be some other unfortunate under way!'

An extra big roller glided out of the mist of spray and rose leisurely above the starboard rail, but just as it appeared to be gathering itself for one more heave beneath the ship's canting bilge keel it began to curve over and break.

Gunnar sprang to the telegraph and jerked it viciously. The man who should have been awaiting his order was staring astern, his face full of fear like a mesmerised rabbit. 'Rudder hard left! *Hard* left, Paice!' Gunnar hung on as the mountain of water broke and fell across the fantail with the sound of an express train hitting a building. The port engine was already thrashing astern, but the ship began to slide, helpless on the edge of a trough which opened on her lee rail as if to swallow her whole.

Paice clung to the wheel, his legs kicking for a foothold, his face only inches from the compass. A signalman fell spread-eagled, and was held against the port door like a pinned insect, his terrified face contorted with pain as a heavy locker tore itself from its lashings and crashed into his body.

Paice yelled, 'I can't hold her, sir!' He blinked at the compass. 'Zero one zero! Christ, she's *goin'*!'

The deck was right over now, and Kroner seemed to be hanging at a forty-five-degree angle as he clung to an overhead lamp socket. The port wing of the bridge looked as if it was already touching the great mass of churning foam, and once when he looked down Kroner saw water actually spurting around the edges of the clamped door. 'Christ!' His voice

222

broke in a whimper. 'She's going over!'

Almost on her side, the stricken ship lay at the bottom of the giant trough, the whole world suddenly restricted to two great banks of shining black glass, above which the sky soared in long streaks of grey and silver. It was a world gone mad, of sudden silence as the wind passed over the small, hidden valley between the two careering rollers.

Gunnar felt a pain in his ribs as he was pushed harder and harder against the telegraph. Somehow he managed to jerk a telephone from its hook, and wondered if Malinski was able to reach his receiver. 'This is the captain!' Gunnar was still shouting, his voice suddenly loud in the tomblike stillness of the listing wheelhouse. 'I'm going to turn her!' He paused, and thought he heard the engineer coughing, like a man on the end of a coast-to-coast line instead of one hundred feet away. 'When I give the signal I want flank speed on the starboard screw. Put it full astern, and damn your gauges!'

'Okay, sir!' Malinski sounded tired.

'And the port screw ahead full!' Gunnar stared hard at the silent, clinging figures around him. Every eye was on his mouth, like a lot of deaf-and-dumb madmen, he thought wildly. 'Right, Kroner, let's get at it!' He heaved himself against the telegraphs and swung the brass handles with determination, between his clenched teeth he snapped: 'Bring your rudder hard right, Paice. *Now!*'

The ship began to vibrate and quiver as if the engines were going to tear loose from the shafts as rudder and screws fought against the ship's sodden, helpless length. Gunnar blinked away the sweat from his eyes as he stared fixedly at the gyro repeater. It did not move. The ship still lay beam on, her keel coming up to meet that one final thrust which would roll her over completely.

Paice said weakly, 'She's swinging, sir!' He sounded as if he no longer believed what he saw. 'Zero one five—zero two five!'

The trough seemed to fall away and the wind screamed into them once more. It sounded murderous and final, and with something like despair Gunnar watched a gaunt, high-crowned breaker surge over the starboard waist and explode against the stack, so that the wire guys thrummed and whined and threatened to tear themselves loose from the deck. The tons of water roared down the sloped, dripping steel and cascaded the full length of the vessel before dissipating themselves across the lee rail. When once the ship rose wearily to meet the next onslaught, Gunnar saw that the gig's davits were empty and the guardrail looked like a roll of twisted wire. But she was fighting back. She was trying with every ounce of her twenty-three years' experience and stubborn pride to turn and face her natural enemy.

Paice said: 'Still comin' right, sir! Zero nine five!'

Gunnar pulled the telegraphsman from his position of nerveless stupor and thrust his cold hands on the brass levers. 'Starboard engine stop!' He reeled away from the telegraph, rubbing his ribs as he peered through the clear-view screen. The bows were visible once more. A thin wedge of streaming metal almost lost in a welter of whitecaps and black rollers. Once heading into the sea she could take a second breath, mark time until . . . 'Bring her right to one two zero!'

He had done it. Already the ship was riding more easily, although the deck aft of the bridge was washed down continuously by the enraged water as it broke back from the bows. But anything seemed better after that moment of horror in the great hungry trough.

Paice was an experienced helmsman, and in his hands the Hibiscus swung on to her new course. Only then did Gunnar ease the engine speed, and felt a sensation of cold satisfaction for the ship as with one final roll she straightened her deck and pointed into the storm.

He watched the bows climbing skywards and felt his stomach tense to receive the shock as the ship plunged across and down into the next roller. Every rivet and fitting was jerking and tearing in a chorus of insane pandemonium, but she was holding her own. He wiped his face and noticed that his hand was shaking. He looked at Paice. 'Okay?'

Paice did not look up but his voice was shaky with relief. 'Hell, yes, Captain! Remind me to sail with you again!'

Gunnar smiled tightly. He felt tense, yet in some strange way cleansed, as if the life-battle had been a personal test.

The signalman pushed the heavy locker away from his legs and said sheepishly, 'Thought I was a goner that time.'

Kroner still looked sick and seemed to have difficulty in putting his words in order as he checked each phone and voice-pipe. Eventually he said dazedly: 'All systems checked, sir. A few cuts and bruises. No one lost overboard.' He shuddered violently as a big wave towered above the port wing and surged down the length of the ship to disappear astern in a welter of bursting spray. It must have been fifty feet high. 'What do we do now, Captain?'

Gunnar leaned on the chart table and stared at the pencilled lines. 'Too early yet for guesses. We can't head for Taiwan, that's for sure.' He felt the relief crowding in on him. Even the signalman knew it would be death to try to resume the earlier course. 'We can ride it out here and hope to dodge the storm centre, or we can run for cover.'

Kroner said weakly, 'There's no cover, sir.' He peered helplessly at the empty chart. 'Not a goddamned thing!'

Gunnar shrugged. 'You give up too easily.'

A telephone whistled impatiently, and Gunnar heard Malinski's voice in the far distance. 'Everything okay up top, sir?'

Gunnar half smiled. 'Sorry, I should have told you. Thanks a lot for your help just then!'

Malinski coughed. 'Yeh. I knew we were still afloat. The fish would have been in here otherwise!' His tone became formal and businesslike. 'I'd have asked to take on ballast, but,' Gunnar could almost feel him shrugging, 'I thought you might have other ideas, sir.'

Gunnar frowned. How did Malinski guess? Did he really know himself what he was about to do? He felt as if he was waiting for something, a sign, an outside hint of what step he should take which would commit himself and the ship yet again. He said, 'I'll let you know.' To the wheelhouse at large he added, 'See if you can rustle some coffee.'

He noted with surprise that several figures in lifejackets had been sheltering behind the wheelhouse, probably in the radio room. It was strange that even when a ship was sinking men climbed up to its highest point like rats before actually jumping. A pitiful, useless gesture.

One of the seamen called, 'I'll lay that on the line, Cap'n!' It was one of the men who had stared at Gunnar earlier with such casual indifference, even contempt, and now looked at him as if at some kind of super-god. For the first time since he had taken command he had been seen as the captain, he thought bitterly. Only when he was needed.

Kroner was saying anxiously, 'Call from the doctor, Captain.'

Gunnar snatched the phone, his mouth suddenly hard. 'Captain here?'

Connell sounded like an old man. 'Bella's dying, sir. He'll not live much longer now.'

225

Gunnar stared round suddenly impatient and gripped by a new feeling of urgency. 'Where's the exec, for Christ's sake?'

'Here, sir.' Maddox stepped over the coaming through the rear door and stood shaking himself like a big dog, his khakis black with spray and torn in several places. 'I couldn't come earlier, I was trying to fix the depth-charges and put them to "safe".'

Gunnar nodded briefly, then brushing past him said: 'Hold her on the new course. I'm going to see Bella.'

Maddox blinked vaguely around the disordered wheelhouse at the crumpled and weary figures and at the raging water ahead of the plunging bows. '*Now,* sir?' But Gunnar had already gone, and Maddox staggered to the compass and peered at it with disbelief. 'Jesus, we'll be back in Payenhau if we keep this up!'

He clung to the voice-pipes and watched the fast-moving wave-crests. Even when the *Hibiscus* had actually left the pier he had felt that it was not all over. Not then, not just like that. Something in Gunnar's eyes should have warned him, and he felt the grip of fear and uncertainty rising again inside him as if to jeer at his optimism.

14

Traitors or Patriots?

As darkness closed in across the storm-lashed waters and the *Hibiscus* met one gigantic roller after another with tired resentment, so came the rain. At first it was hard to tell the heavy drops from the great streamers of spray which drifted back from the bows with each savage thrust, until with sudden exuberance the black-bellied clouds seemed to burst open and the rain fell in a steady, unremitting downpour. It flayed the upper deck and rattled across the bridge windows like lead shot, and when a luckless sailor was forced into the open it reached and held him in long, diagonal fingers which left him gasping for breath as if he had been physically beaten.

Gunnar clung to the pipe-cot and listened to it sweeping

226

across the deck above his head. In the steel cabinets the medicine bottles rattled and clicked, and several times he heard the unexplained thud of some heavy object falling from its lashings in the next compartment. And, above all, the wind kept up its demented wail, drowning all else and leaving the dulled and prone to the worst fears of human imagination.

He tried to shut out the sounds of his ship's private battle and stared fixedly at Bella's twisted face. The skin looked transparent and shining with moisture, and his eyes, when they flickered occasionally beneath the long, dark lashes, gleamed like hot stones.

Connell said: 'I'll give him another shot. He can't stand much more of this!' He looked around at the vibrating, staggering shell of steel as if to blame the ship for Bella's predicament.

Gunnar crouched on the edge of the bunk and studied the dying face with sudden determination. 'Leave it!'

Connell stared. 'I can't. He'll feel the pain again if I wait!'

But Gunnar did not seem to have heard. 'I must let him speak. It's important!'

Even as the doctor opened his mouth in protest Bella began to writhe in his harness, his mouth contorted with the rising flood of agony. Gunnar reached out and held one of the yeoman's hands. It was ice-cold, and the fingers seemed to move independently like trapped animals in his grasp. 'What is it, Bella? What are you trying to say?' Gunnar squeezed the hand, his eyes boring into the agonised face. 'Come on, man! *Tell* me!'

Connell caught Gunnar's arm. 'For heaven's sake, sir! What do you think you're doing?'

The captain's eyes flashed in the lamplight, cold and hard. 'Leave this to me, will you?'

Connell stood up, his hair flopping across his face and making him look wild and angry. 'He's my patient! I *insist*!'

Gunnar shook his arm away. 'Be quiet! He's trying to speak!'

Bella opened his eyes and stared up at the two faces with shocked disbelief. 'My God, where am I?' His white teeth clamped along his lip until the blood showed bright and cruel on his pale skin. 'Christ, the pain! Oh, Jesus, the pain!'

But Gunnar squeezed his hand again and said in a low, fierce voice: 'It's me, Bella, the captain. Try and tell me what happened. I *must* know!'

Bella fell silent, and for one instant Gunnar thought he was dead. Then in a strange, childlike tone he said: 'They said they would get her from Hong Kong for me. They *promised*! They wanted to know about the ship and what we were doing here!' He broke off and his dark, feverish eyes filled with uncontrollable tears. 'Forgive me. I didn't know what I was doing!' He opened his mouth wide and screamed, the sound echoing around the small room and deadening the storm with its agony and terror.

Gunnar said quietly, 'Just tell me what happened.'

Connell was almost sobbing. '*Please*, Captain! Leave him alone!'

A hypodermic glittered in his hand, but Gunnar pushed him roughly aside. 'Be silent!' Then to Bella he continued, 'What did you tell them?' The yeoman's eyes were tightly closed and beneath the blanket his body was beginning to writhe as the pain closed in once more. Gunnar bit his lip and shut his mind to all else but Bella's words. Even the awful stomach-wrenching stench must not deter him.

Bella whispered faintly: 'I told them we were sailing. But I brought forward the date a couple of days.' He bared his teeth like a snared animal. 'They—they promised they would bring her from Hong Kong.' The tears flowed ceaselessly across his sunken cheeks. 'They lied! She never even *knew* about it!' His head lolled from side to side and Gunnar steadied it with his free hand. It was a nightmare, a scene from some forgotten torture chamber in which he was the chief tormentor. Yet he must not stop, not now.

'Who are "*they*"? Who did this to you, Bella?'

'I don't know. Chinese. Only one I knew by sight. That was on the last day, when I said I would report them to you unless they promised to keep their bargain!' He arched his back and screamed again, his breath hot and inhuman across Gunnar's face.

Gunnar felt the man's life ebbing away like water from a broken pitcher. 'Who *was* he?'

Bella lay very quiet and his face looked almost youthful again. 'He called himself the leader. The man of steel!' He broke down into a fit of choking sobs. 'Don't let him get at me again! Don't let him touch me!' He threw himself almost clear of the bunk in spite of the lashing, and a bright flurry of blood gushed from his mouth. Then he fell silent, his eyes fixed unblinkingly on the hidden distance.

228

Gunnar stood up and almost fell as the ship rolled violently beneath him.

The doctor caught his sleeve. 'You butcher! You mad, bloody *butcher*!' He hung on as Gunnar pulled at his arm. 'You couldn't even let him *die* in peace!'

Gunnar prised his fingers away. 'It was important. I didn't enjoy it.' Then as Connell clawed his way across the heaving deck towards him he seized the doctor's sweat-stained shirt and pulled him close like a rag doll. 'Listen to me, Doc! *Listen!* I don't give a damn what you think of me. You can report me when you get to base, do what the hell you like.' He held the limp man away from him, his eyes boring into his sickened face. 'You wanted adventure and excitement, right? You thought you'd come aboard my ship for a little experiment, didn't you?' He pushed the doctor down on to a cot. 'You patronising, hypocritical bastard! All you can think about is yourself. The whole world might erupt about our ears, yet you think you know all the answers with the power of God in your damned hands!'

He looked down at Bella's still face and said in a more controlled voice: 'He thought he knew the answers too. Traded a few bits of information for his own pathetic hopes of getting his girl from Hong Kong.' Bitterly he added, 'You can't trade with those bastards!' Then he reached down and pulled the blanket across Bella's vacant stare. 'Well, Bella, you did me a good turn without knowing it. You brought forward the sailing date, and I *did* sail early after all! If anything's happening on the island it'll be right now!' He looked across at the crouched figure of the doctor. 'Did you hear, Doc? Man of Steel he called himself!' He bared his teeth as if tasting the words. 'In Mongolian it would be translated as "*Bolod*"! Now do you understand?'

Then he turned on his heel and thrust his way through the door and back towards the bridge.

*   *   *

Maddox forced his body into a corner of the wheelhouse, his face set and determined as the public-address system squawked, 'All officers report to the bridge!' The words were torn away even as they were uttered, and Maddox thought that every bone in his aching body was bruised or broken by the constant, crazy tossing of the ship.

229

The captain stood on the other side of the wheelhouse, his face towards the streaming glass, his shoulders stiff and squared as if on parade. The other watchkeepers still remained at their stations as if they had never moved, and the compass line appeared to be welded to the same figure, one two zero.

First one officer and then another staggered and fell into the humid, streaming compartment, and each one seemed to forget the menace of the storm as he realised the tense atmosphere which awaited him. Only Malinski, excused because he held their lives in his hands merely by staying with his racing engines, was absent.

Maddox checked them over and said harshly, 'All present, sir.' He knew that it was now or never. 'I think I'd better tell them what's happening, sir.' He saw Regan's eyebrows lift with astonishment and noticed too that the doctor's normally impassive face seemed dazed and empty.

Gunnar nodded curtly. 'In the chartroom. I'll give you three minutes.'

They followed Maddox into the small, damp-smelling space and closed the door against the listening seamen of the watch.

'What the hell is going on?' Regan rubbed his bristled chin. 'Is this some new disaster?'

Maddox's eyes flashed warningly and for once Regan fell silent instantly. 'It's like this.' Maddox found that he was speaking fast, like a man short of breath. 'The captain intends to go back to Payenhau!' He saw the mingled stares of surprise and resignation and added sharply, 'He's got some crazy idea that there's a Red invasion coming off!'

Kroner asked nervously, 'When did all this happen?'

'Right now, that's when!' Maddox cursed as the deck swayed and threw him against the table. 'Bella just died. The doc says that the captain more or less made him die in agony.' He glared at Connell's lined face as if for support. 'Well?'

The doctor nodded wearily. 'It was dreadful. He refused to allow me to kill the pain. He just wanted him to talk!'

Brutally Maddox continued: 'So this is the picture. Gunnar expects us to drag back to the islands and sniff out the danger. He's got some crazy idea that it's now or never as far as the commies are concerned.'

Kroner asked, 'Has he asked permission?'

'No, he has not.' Maddox sounded triumphant. 'He says it would only be refused.'

Regan grunted. 'It would too. They probably expect him to run for shelter ahead of the storm. To Hong Kong perhaps.'

Kroner peered at the bulkhead as a big wave thundered against the hull like a hammer beating an oil drum. 'It *would* be a shelter in Payenhau?' His voice sounded weak and submissive.

The exec glared at him. 'You've not understood a word, have you?'

Regan raised his hand. 'Just a minute! Are you saying that the captain actually *asked* you to get our opinion?'

Maddox looked away, his eyes angry. 'No. I just wanted to let him know how we all stand. If we go back there, there is bound to be a court of enquiry. What with all the other things that have happened, Gunnar'll be lucky to keep his skin. But I want him to know that we're against the whole crazy scheme. If we make that clear now we'll not be held to blame.'

Regan rubbed his chin again. 'Hell, I'm in this for a career, I don't want my name lumped with his in a court-martial!' His eyes glittered across his big nose. 'But again I don't want to be charged with insubordination!'

Maddox shrugged. 'Suit yourself. I'm in too deep to pull out now.' He looked at his brother. 'I told the captain I'll not be held responsible if Colonel Jago tears *him* apart!'

Pip Maddox spoke for the first time. 'I'd never have thought it possible!' The others stared at him as he continued in a quiet, shocked tone, 'After all he's been through, after all he's done, and now you've not the guts to back him up?'

His brother said gruffly, 'Stow it, Pip, you don't know what you're talking about.'

'Don't I?' The young ensign swallowed hard. 'I think I know the captain better than any of you. He'd bust himself wide open for any one of you if you got in a jam, but *you!*' He searched their faces. 'You don't even rate a handshake from him!'

Maddox lifted a telephone from the rack and waited until he could hear the captain's brief acknowledgement. 'I've spoken to the officers, Captain.' He turned away so that he could not see Pip's contemptuous expression. 'I've told them what you intend to do. Is there no alternative?' He waited, his eyes on the streaming metal wall.

Gunnar must have had his lips close against the mouthpiece, his words seemed to ease their way into Maddox's bruised

231

mind. 'It's either my way or you take over the ship, Mister Maddox.'

Maddox stared round at the others. 'What did you say, Captain?'

'I shall place myself on the sick list as from now, and you can see the ship through the typhoon.'

Maddox gasped. In his mind he could see with devastating clarity the reeling deck when Gunnar had so skilfully swung the ship to face the oncoming storm. Even then the captain must have been planning and preparing, allowing the weather to act as his ally as he conned the ship closer to Payenhau and lengthening the last dash to Taiwan.

'Take over the ship?' He repeated the words aloud and heard Regan say sharply: 'Like hell you will! I'd rather sail with my old mother than have you in command!'

Maddox said quietly: 'Very well, sir. If that's the way you want it.' In a sharper tone he added: 'But this isn't finished, Captain. You've no right to put the ship in danger just to work off an old score!' But the phone was dead, and he slammed it on the rack with sudden fury.

Regan straightened his cap. 'Well, gentlemen, I have the deck. If you'll excuse me?' He grinned mirthlessly at Maddox as he passed. 'He's got you over a barrel at the moment, old friend.'

Maddox watched them troop back to their stations, his brow furrowed and dark with anger. To his brother he said thickly, 'The damn fools can't see I was doing it for *them*!'

But Pip brushed him aside, his face confused and embarrassed. 'Were you, Bob? It didn't sound that way to me!' Then Maddox had the chartroom to himself.

When he reached the wheelhouse it all seemed normal again. Gunnar stood loosely by the helmsman his arm crooked around the telegraphs, and Regan had his face pressed against the glass as he watched a white shadow coasting past the port beam. In the blackness beyond the wheelhouse only the wave-crests showed themselves as if to mock Maddox with their power and constant menace. He knew that he could never hold the ship in this storm, never in a thousand years. There was nothing in Gunnar's face to show his inner thoughts, or even if he would have carried out his threat. Maddox stared out of the windows towards the racing mass of water. Against the salt-caked glass his reflection floated across the tumbling waste like a spectre. But instead of himself he saw only the disappointed and ashamed face of his brother.

Behind him Gunnar said almost conversationally, 'Ease your helm, Paice, don't make hard work of it.'

Paice answered in the same vein: 'Sure thing, Captain. She's takin' it like a goddamn whale!'

Maddox felt a smarting in his eyes. What was the matter with these idiots?

Before he was finished, Gunnar would drive them all to destruction.

*   *   *

Once again the *Hibiscus*'s narrow bows began to climb towards the hidden sky as a challenging mass of water thundered down to meet her. Gunnar gritted his teeth and clung even tighter to the telegraphs, and mentally ticked off each nerve-stretching second. It was like fighting the sea single-handed, using the ship as a weapon, or a living, breathing force to smash through one barrier after another. His throat felt like a kiln, and he had to blink his eyes to clear away the sensation of blurred and dazed numbness which seemed to obstruct each painful calculation.

They were riding the edge of the storm's wild circle, fighting through the careering water and swooping cloudbanks almost blind in the face of a continuous downpour of torrential rain. Hours had passed since he had used his blackmail on Maddox, yet time appeared to have lost its meaning altogether. Only now was real, only the reeling, dripping world of the wheel-house was fact.

The wind which enveloped them and deadened their minds with its insane shrieking had moved up another notch on the scale, and Kroner's last garbled report stated that it had passed one hundred knots and still rising. Gunnar looked around him at the crouched, clinging figures, all of whom centred on the man at the wheel. McCord, the quartermaster, had replaced the indomitable Paice and was fighting his own private war with the shining wheel as he peered fixedly at the compass, his thin face streaming with sweat and exertion. Gunnar stiffened and tightened his grip as the ship began to stagger sideways, caught a body blow by a flailing crest which had broken every rule by cutting diagonally across the path of its companions to push savagely at the starboard bow.

'Right full rudder! All engines ahead flank speed!'

233

McCord cursed and then said shakily: 'Comin' right, sir! Zero eight five, zero eight eight!'

Gunnar released his hold and reeled across to the clipped chart. 'Meet her!' He peered at the rambling, seemingly haphazard pencilled lines of his dead reckoning. Sidestepping, checking, but always moving painfully towards the Payenhau group of islands which should now be lying somewhere ahead, lost in the screaming madness of the storm.

A door slammed shut and he felt Kroner breathing heavily at his side.

McCord yelled, 'She's steady, sir!' He sounded surprised.

Gunnar grabbed at the pencil as it rose in the air and floated from the table. 'Ease your helm, McCord, and come left to zero four five.' He moved again, painfully and carefully, not trusting a step without a handhold. One sudden lurch and he could smash himself senseless. 'Any luck with the radar?' He looked at Kroner's white face for the first time.

Kroner shook his head. 'Nothing, sir. Just distorted tangles!'

'I guessed as much. The waves are too high anyway to get much of a picture.'

Kroner said thickly, 'How are we making out, sir?'

Gunnar shrugged. 'We'll live.'

A phone buzzed and Kroner pressed it to his ear. 'Yes, I got that.' He nodded violently. 'I'll tell the captain.' He looked at Gunnar with a mixture of respect and dread. 'Radar reports a brief shadow of Payenhau, sir. He's lost it now, the scopes are clean again, but we're on course for contact, about ten miles.' He gulped. 'Jesus, Captain, I don't know how you found anything in *this*!'

Gunnar smiled tightly. Neither do I, he thought. 'Tell the engine room to reduce speed and give me a steady fifteen knots. We'll ride it out and head in at first light.' The ship shuddered and reeled tiredly on to her side, bringing the battered watchkeepers alive as if they had been touched with a naked power circuit.

'Hold her!' Gunnar joined the helmsman and pushed the wheel in the man's fumbling fingers. 'Come right again, meet her!'

Gunnar watched the ticking gyro and counted seconds. Through the soles of his shoes he could feel the ship fighting back, feeling her way through the surging criss-cross of broken water. There were still some dangerous moments ahead, but the worst might be over. Already he could feel the vessel's new confidence and prayed that his own strength would match it. He even found time to think back, to recall Maddox's angry face and Bella's last moments alive. They all thought him mad, and perhaps he was. But by now his despatch would have been delivered by Burgess, and no matter what had happened in Payenhau the admiral would be in no doubt of how to react. He would no longer be lulled into satisfied complacency by Jago's previous reports, and if any sort of uprising had occurred, a swift despatch by the *Hibiscus*'s radio would start the machine working. In this sort of war you had to plan, to be swift and to be sure. If he had learned nothing else in Viet Nam, Gunnar knew that it was better to act swiftly and incorrectly than not to act at all.

Again the door banged, and Maddox stood shaking himself in his shining oilskin, his face flayed red by the spray and rain. In a gruff formal tone he said: 'I've checked for damage, sir. Everything holding firm.'

Gunnar nodded. 'Good. Now go and make some arrangements to feed the men.'

Maddox eyed him cautiously. 'In *this*?'

Gunnar turned away, the destructive forces of exhaustion and mental strain tearing at his mind like claws. 'I don't expect a four-course meal! Tell the cook to do his best. Tinned peaches, anything, but keep them occupied! They're at low enough ebb already. I don't want them dead on their feet when we drop anchor tomorrow.'

Maddox looked at the captain. 'It was planned, wasn't it, Captain?'

Gunnar smiled gravely. 'Something like that.'

'You'll throw away everything just for an idea?' Maddox could not conceal the bitterness in his voice. 'Risk the ship as well!'

'If necessary. The ship is here for a purpose. While I make the decisions you'll just have to bear with it.' A shutter seemed to drop behind Gunnar's grey eyes, and Maddox knew it was pointless to continue.

Gunnar said sharply: 'Check the radar scopes again yourself, Mister Kroner. See if you can get something definite.'

Gunnar had kept Kroner continuously busy between radio and radar throughout the storm, and as he had suspected, the man was almost grateful for it. Kroner had almost cracked at the beginning. Bit by bit he was making recompense, if only by staying on his feet.

235

He said: 'It's amazing, isn't it? Earlybird and men in space, and we can't even get the goddamn radar to work properly!'

Gunnar looked at him with surprise, noting too the wide grins of the unshaven faces around him. Kroner had made a crack. Things had to get better now.

* * *

As the little *Hibiscus* eased her way painfully under the slight protection of Payenhau's south western approaches, the storm raged on across the hills and villages of the main island and flattened the rain-starved gorse and bushes along the high slopes like wet fur.

Sergeant Rickover lay on his side in his camp bed, a book angled to meet the yellow and wavering glare of his oil lamp. Some of the power cables had been damaged by a falling mast above the citadel, and the electric light had been halved throughout the honeycomb of passages and emplacements. This neither worried nor surprised the big marine. The generator was unreliable at the best of times, and lack of proper electricians made future improvements unlikely.

He was only half-reading the book, and his ears listened to the muffled wail of the wind and the swish of rain against the concrete walls. But the town and the anchorage were on the lee side of the island and well protected by the hills behind them. Rickover had seen one other typhoon hit the island, and had endured worse discomforts in other parts of the world. Here he was safe and snug, and a telephone would tell him if he was needed. Perhaps after the storm had passed Base would send a Red Cross team or some crackpots from the U.N. to repair the damage and patch up the mess. Either way they would be company, fresh faces to break the boredom.

Rickover thought about the *Hibiscus* and wondered how she was faring. He thought too of Gunnar's grave, determined face and decided that the ship had little to worry about. It was just that Gunnar took it all too personally. The big guys made the decisions, so what was the point of getting steamed up? It would all be different in a year or two anyway. With the way the world was shaping it would be just a matter of time before it was equally divided into two entirely different camps. The whites against the coloured races. It showed great possibilities for fighting men, and sometimes Rickover wondered if that was what really bothered his colonel. Jago was probably anxious in case he was too old to wait for the big, final crunch.

The phone whimpered in its leather case and with a groan Rickover rolled on to his back and pulled it from its nail. 'Sergeant Rickover. Who's that?'

It was a Chinese corporal, a small, round man who followed Rickover about like a faithful dog. The sergeant pretended to be disgusted by such servitude, but nevertheless he had taken a liking to the little man. The corporal was apparently in charge of the citadel's guard patrol. 'Big worry, Sergeant! All telephone lines down!' He paused, and Rickover could hear him breathing heavily.

'So what?' The marine wearily sat up and scratched his chest. 'Tell your officer!'

'No officer, Sergeant. All gone.'

Rickover swung his legs over the side of his bunk and stared at the phone with exasperation. All gone. How could that be? 'Okay, Seltzer, I'll be right down.' He waited for the man to chuckle with delight at his nickname as he normally did. His real handle was far too difficult for Rickover's uncomplicated tongue. But there was silence.

Rickover stood up and stretched. Phone lines down, that was one thing, but where the hell were the Chink officers? There were always a couple on duty at the very least. As usual, he would have to sort things out. Some 'adviser', he thought gloomily. More of a goddamn nursemaid!

As an afterthought he cranked the handle of another phone set and waited for the explosion of Jago's anger. Instead another fractured Chinese voice rattled in his ear. 'Colonel not here. He gone out.' Click, the phone died in his hand.

Suddenly Rickover was fully alert and anxious. This had never happened before. Jago always left a full statement for his sergeant, and *always* kept a Chinese officer in the bunker to stand by the radio in case of emergency.

Rickover began to throw on his green fatigues and then, quietening himself with an effort, he strapped on his pistol and equipment as if for patrol. Feeling rather self-conscious he jammed his helmet on his head and regarded himself thoughtfully in his mirror. He looked as if he was going to war. With a brief grin he picked up his carbine and torch and stepped out into the corridor.

Blinded by heavy rain he groped his way across the open square and into the gate office where he found Seltzer and two soldiers sitting quietly by the door. They stared at the giant American with his rain-splattered clothes and heavy helmet, but Rickover said shortly, 'Now, what goes on?' The corporal looked frightened, and Rickover noticed for the first time that he was unarmed, although the other two soldiers carried carbines as usual.

Seltzer seemed at a loss. 'All gone,' he said weakly.

Rickover looked through the door and listened to the wind. In the anchorage there would be waves a mile high in spite of the shelter. It was a pity it was too dark to see anything. 'Where's the colonel?'

'Please, I don't know, Sergeant!'

Rickover did not turn but watched the others reflected in the black glass of the window. There was only a small oil lamp but he could see the way that Seltzer was shaking. Jesus, what was going on? It was then that Seltzer moved. Small, fat and not very bright by Rickover's standards, but his loyalty was no longer in doubt. With one terrified gasp he sprang past the big marine, wrenching the carbine from his loose grasp in one frantic movement. The hut exploded with sharp cracks as he jerked the trigger, and as Rickover staggered wildly in the blue smoke he saw one of the soldiers throw up his arms, his face blossoming into an obscene scarlet flower. But the second soldier was firing too, and the hut became a madhouse of barking guns and the fierce ricochet of bullets.

Rickover pulled out his heavy pistol, aware that the firing had stopped and that he was somehow unhurt. He dropped on one knee beside the fat corporal who was clutching his thigh and whimpering like a child. As he looked up he seemed to drag upon a last reserve of courage.

'Get *out*, Sergeant! Run now or they will kill you!' His voice rose to a desperate scream. 'They *told* me to call you down here! They knew I was loyal to you! They were going to kill both of us!' Tears rolled down his biscuit-coloured face. 'They did not think you would come from your bed armed and ready!'

Rickover slipped the pistol into his holster and retrieved his carbine, then peered through the swirling smoke at the two dead soldiers. With a chill he recognised both of them. Two of the regular troops from Jago's carefully trained force. Gently he asked, 'What has happened?'

Seltzer closed his eyes. 'Mutiny! It is a revolt to take over

238

island. They say that the islanders are rebelling against the army!'

Rickover pulled the man's arm up around his neck and tugged him to his feet, gritting his teeth against the man's short cries of agony. 'Is there a jeep outside?' He did not wait for an answer but half dragging the writhing corporal he kicked the door aside and battled into the rain and wind towards the vehicle shed beside the main gate, which to his horror he saw was open and deserted.

There was a jeep, just one, and with something like a prayer Rickover heaved the wounded man into the back and goaded the engine into life. He felt the clang of metal against the side of the game little vehicle, but concentrated upon the curving road and the wind-torn buildings beyond. He tried to sort out what he knew, but half expected that in a moment he would come awake from a nightmare.

A rebellion, a mutiny, call it what you like, it was too terrible to contemplate. Where the hell was Jago? What would he do if there was no radio? It was over a week before another ship arrived, and by then . . . he cursed wildly as two running figures scattered across the dim headlamps, soldiers or townspeople, he neither knew nor cared. If Jago was a prisoner or even killed, there was only Yi-Fang. He would know what to do. Over his arm he yelled, 'Where's your goddamned major, Seltzer?'

He had to strain his ear to hear the corporal's pain-racked reply. 'He with rebels. He bad man, Sergeant.'

Rickover stopped the jeep on the side of the road and rested his head on the wheel. What was the point of running? Where to, and with what purpose? Wearily he asked, 'Jesus, has the whole garrison gone over?'

'Not know, Sergeant. Not know.' Seltzer's face was shining with rain but he did not seem to notice it. 'It all happen in one hour. First, officers go away, and then I am disarmed by my own men.' A touch of anger crept into his tone. 'But I not let them kill you!'

'Yeh, sure.' Rickover patted his arm encouragingly. 'I must get you fixed up.' He stared round through the sheeting rain. 'Where the goddamn hell shall we go?'

Seltzer clutched his sleeve. 'Take coast road. Make for west side. All quiet there!' He moaned. 'Yi-Fang is at prison camp. He has big lot of guerrillas there.'

Rickover steered the jeep back on to the uneven road, his

239

mind shocked and reeling. Holy cow, it was getting worse every minute! If Yi-Fang was behind all this he must be off his head! The prison camp was said to be full of suspected terrorists and commie sympathisers, and if that lot got loose it would be the end of Payenhau!

He could feel the fury knotting in his stomach like icy fingers, and he realised that he was driving almost blindly through the storm with his foot hard on the floor. So Gunnar had been right about the half of it, and now he was gone. Having realised the hopelessness of his position Rickover felt suddenly more relaxed, even lightheaded. He tightened his grip on the wheel and swung the jeep up on to the high coast road, the blown sand and pebbles rattling on his helmet with the rain. 'Come on, boy! Let's get at the bastards!'

It was happening. It was impossible, yet it was for real. Like all those other places where soldiers and marines had been killed and trapped by outmoded beliefs and stillborn ideals.

He thought of Jago and what he must be thinking if he was still alive. The headlights cut across an upturned cart and another jeep which appeared to have dug its nose into the bank at the roadside. In the few brief seconds before he jammed on the brakes and threw himself sideways from the seat with his carbine already cocked, Rickover saw the dim outline of several heads and the faint gleam of a levelled rifle.

Then to his intense surprise he heard Jago's voice cutting through the rain like a saw. 'Hell, Sergeant, I thought you'd *never* get here.'

* * *

The cave, such as it was, appeared more like a deep cleft in the hillside which made no allowance for the continuous and heavy rain, and Rickover began to wonder if it had been a good thing to meet up with Jago again. Worse still, Jago was wounded in the leg, and now sat, apparently unconscious of the rain, with his bandaged and splinted limb jutting in front of him like a white tusk. Piece by piece Rickover had managed to join together the sequence of events, and the result was not encouraging. As far as he could make out, Rickover understood that Yi-Fang had joined with the islanders in declaring some state of independence from all military occupation by the Nationalist government, the Americans, and any-

240

one else. Guard posts had been overcome, telephone lines cut, and arms and ammunition handed round to trusted parties. Overnight, under cover of the typhoon, a complete takeover had been arranged.

Jago had apparently been in consultation with Colonel Tem-Chuan when it had all started. He was reluctant to talk much about it, but it was obvious that but for the help of a small handful of loyal, or baffled, Chinese troops Jago would now be lying dead with the others. Instead he had shot his way out of the place and rallied his small force across the coast road to await developments.

It was quite inconceivable how such a thing could have happened. Yi-Fang had never shown any liking for the islanders, and the old headman in particular. He was a pure militarist, with prior loyalty directed to his leaders in Taiwan, or so it had appeared. Now he was probably in virtual control of the island, whichever way you looked at it. If the islanders declared their old independence, what, after all, could anyone do about it? Rickover had often heard Jago speak of the remote possibility of some sort of rebellion, but he had always considered it improbable in the face of his well-trained force of troops. Rickover pulled up his collar and grimaced. Well-trained force!

Through the gloom he could see Jago's quick, irritable movements as he waved away the attentions of one of the men. He seemed quite incapable of accepting the new situation. Even now he was barking orders at the crouched figures, some of whom were probably already planning to desert as soon as they were sure what was happening.

Jago said sharply, 'Well, Sergeant, what the hell are you moping about?'

'I was just wondering what we should do next.' Rickover was glad the colonel could not see his eyes.

'Do? *Do?*' Jago bobbed his head angrily. 'We'll counter-attack and knock hell out of the bastards, that's what!' He chuckled. 'They'll soon get the message when they know we're ready for 'em!'

Rickover tried again: 'But, Colonel, there's only us left. If there are any other troops loyal to us they'll be too scared to show themselves.'

Jago snorted, 'Rubbish!'

Rickover stood up, suddenly weary of the officer's stubbornness. 'You're deluding yourself, sir. The island's cracked wide open, and right now we've got to think of some way to stay alive! Did you know Yi-Fang's gone to the prison camp to release the Reds there?' He raised his voice, no longer caring. 'Well, didn't you? And don't you realise that all this means one thing as far as I can see? Yi-Fang's been a commie all this time and we just didn't realise it! He's been stirring up the locals into believing that they're due for independence, and when they agree to back him,' he clicked his fingers, 'bingo! He steps in and takes over the whole works!'

Jago sounded scathing. 'Even allowing for your being partly correct, what would be the point of that?'

'I'm only a goddamn sergeant, sir, but even I can see that! We've allowed him a free hand. We've trained and armed his men, and never once questioned *him*. He's been here for ages, he's had plenty of time to fill his inner prison camp with every guerrilla and agent he wanted. Each refugee ship must have carried a whole crop of them. He just kept them in that camp, safe and snug, and then shipped out the others to Taiwan! It's so simple it makes you spew!'

Jago said in a quieter tone, 'And we let him build an airstrip with convict labour!'

Rickover grunted. 'We did. So even if a proportion of your men had stayed loyal, Yi-Fang's boys could have held their airstrip in the middle of their own camp until help arrived!'

Jago tried to struggle up. 'Jesus H. Christ! We've got to do something!'

'There's nothing we can do, Colonel. Not a goddamn thing!' Brutally Rickover added, 'So Gunnar was right, after all, it seems!'

'You shut your mouth! I'm not finished yet!'

'We soon will be though. A handful of scared Chinks and a few wounded men, what the hell is that meant to be?' Rickover spat on the wet ground. 'How the West was won!'

Jago strained against the streaming clay. '*For God's sake stow it!* Yi-Fang wouldn't let me down! Not after all I've done for him!'

Rickover turned away, suddenly dispirited and beaten. 'Yeh, that's right, Colonel, he's a Democrat through an' through!'

Jago seemed to have forgotten him. 'Now let's see. We've got to retake the citadel, or at least the bunker, and get the radio going. We can call up a strike force and square these buggers up in no time at all.' He chuckled in the darkness. 'It'll be a feather in our caps then!'

Rickover squatted wretchedly on an ammunition case. Jago was off his head, either because of his wound or because of the unbelievable collapse of his little kingdom. Whatever the reason, the end was the same.

'If only Gunnar had stayed,' Rickover was voicing his thoughts aloud, 'we could have done something then.'

Jago's voice was scalding with sarcasm. 'Him? He's a do-nothing guy if ever I saw one! Talk, talk, talk, that doesn't win goddamn wars!'

Rickover banged his carbine savagely. And what'll you do, you big bastard? he thought. Stay here and be killed, I guess, if only to cover up your stupid mishandling of the whole flaming mess!

He leaned over Seltzer's inert shape. 'How are you doin'?'

The corporal nodded vaguely. 'Okay, Sergeant.' Then in a strangely determined voice: 'You wrong, Sergeant, most troops loyal. They just get confused, you unnerstan'?'

Rickover ignored Jago's mutterings and stared emptily at the rain and the fast-moving clouds. If I were the admiral, what would I do? Just supposing I knew what was going on, that is. He smiled bitterly. It was obvious really. Just send a nuclear sub and blast Payenhau to fragments!

Jago said reasonably: 'Still, Sergeant, I think yours is quite a good bit of supposition. Just supposing, as I said, that you are right, our people would be in a jam if Yi-Fang was a traitor and took over the island in the name of the islanders.'

Humour him. 'Why, sir?' Rickover stifled a yawn.

'Well, if we had to retake the island by force, *real* force, the whole goddamn world would know about it. And after the Dominican affair, Viet Nam and all the rest, the pinkies and the yellow-bellies'd soon be howling for blood! They'd say we were crushing the free peoples of Payenhau just to make a U.S. base. Trouble is, those sort of maniacs never look too deeply to see who's really behind it.'

Rickover breathed out slowly. 'Yeh, a smart angle.' It was too. And with perfect timing. Before supporting ships could arrive, and within hours of *Hibiscus* leaving, Yi-Fang had moved, and fast. How Yi-Fang and his cronies must have laughed at Jago behind his back. If the commandant had been another man it might still have been saved. But there was only Jago, and he had failed.

Jago added suddenly: 'But that is not the way I see it, no sir! As soon as it's light I intend to counter-attack and contain

243

this situation myself, have you got that? One good slam in the belly and we'll roll 'em over like tenpins!'

Rickover smiled in spite of his tortured thoughts. 'Sure we will, Colonel. You, me and poor old Seltzer, we'll take on the whole commie army if you say so!'

But when there was no reply Rickover turned to see that the colonel had apparently fainted from loss of blood.

That, at least, would give a little peace before the final storm, he thought.

15

Attack

Robert Maddox jerked open the wheelhouse door and stepped carefully outside on to the open wing. Although it was dark his eyes slowly became accustomed to the familiar shapes around him, and he found time to marvel at the sea change which had cast its spell over the whole ship. The bridge and superstructure seemed to give off a sort of phosphorescent glow, like some strange iced cake, and he saw that every inch of the steel plating was covered with a layer of plastered salt, stiff and petrified, as if it had always been so. But the greatest change of all was the sea itself. Still choppy and heaving with sullen anger, it was a poor imitation of the typhoon which had smashed them down, battered at their frail defences, and then left baffled and frustrated by their ceaseless efforts to stay alive. The surging, deafening anger was spent until another time, and it was hard to imagine that the storm still existed in another place, a giant, berserk vortex which even now was probably rolling some puny ship on to its beam ends, or smashing blindly against the last barrier of the Chinese mainland.

Soon the first hint of red-gold would peep over the edge of the world, would show what had happened and display their strength and weakness once again. The fatigue and the fear had left him drained and cold, and he knew that even if he were able to take the time, he could not sleep. Not like the captain. Gunnar was sleeping now, for the first time since Maddox could remember.

244

The storm had showed little sign of relenting, yet Gunnar had somehow tested its power, had sensed its parting. Quite suddenly, and without warning, he had remarked to the wheelhouse in his quiet, compelling voice: 'We're through. The ship has done us proudly!' Then without fuss or further comment he had handed over the con and retired to his bunk.

Maddox swayed unsteadily as a final broken roller wallowed against the hull and hissed around the foot of the stack. A foot scraped on the open ladder, and Maddox saw with surprise that it was Malinski.

The small engineer took off his cap and let his wiry hair ruffle in the stiff breeze. 'It's nice to be able to stand up straight again,' he said. A match scraped and Maddox saw the man's worn face illuminated above a glowing pipe bowl, and sensed the familiar tang of Malinski's rank tobacco. He added: 'I was in a can running out of Pearl some years back and we went head-smack into a beauty of a typhoon. It rolled the sticks out of us, an' we lost ten men overboard in the first five minutes. Christ knows how we stayed afloat, but we did.' He sucked contentedly on his pipe. 'It sure is one hell of a challenge for any skipper.'

Maddox thought bitterly of Gunnar's parting words: 'The ship has done us proudly.' That too was somehow typical of the man. A sort of old-world way of putting things which seemed to symbolise the endless line of seafaring men who had borne his name before him. It might have been the captain of a four-piper in the First World War, or of a square-rigged frigate. But he praised the ship for survival. Not himself. Maddox bit his lip, knowing that the truth pointed well away from that. Had he been left in command as Gunnar had threatened, the ship would have handled differently, of that he was quite sure.

'I wonder what's in store for us now?' He spoke in a half whisper, and Malinski cocked his head in surprise.

'Oh, I expect we'll just give that marine colonel a touch of colic.' The pipe bubbled cheerfully. 'And then start back for Taiwan once more!'

Maddox touched the rough bristle on his chin and felt the gnawing pangs of anxiety again. 'I hope it's as simple as that.'

'On the other hand, the captain might just be right. Nothing would surprise me any more. I've been in this navy a long, long time, but I've never started out on a survey job and ended in this sort of situation before.'

245

'Maybe.' Maddox shifted uneasily. 'But I'm right, I know I am. The captain's been a good officer, and he can handle this old scow like a dream, I'll give you all that. But, and it's a big *but*, he's been so steeped in this East-West brain-washing that he can't confine himself to his own, plain duty.'

'Perhaps too many of us have done just that in the past, Bob?'

'Oh Jesus, don't *you* lecture me!' Maddox walked to the rail and stared down at the neat, serried ranks of marching rollers. They seemed short and safe after the storm, like a well-trained rearguard following the conqueror.

The engineer chuckled. 'Forget it. You should have been down below with my boys. I thought the whole ship was falling apart.' He half turned. 'Hello? More company?'

They saw the familiar, thin shape of the doctor clinging to the rail as the ship rolled sluggishly and stayed momentarily at the same heavy angle. At the reduced speed *Hibiscus* was only marking time against the steady flood, and each movement was heavy on the stomach and dangerous for the unwary.

'Hi, Doc. Join the party.' Malinski kept his voice cheerful but nudged Maddox in the darkness.

Maddox said, 'What's your problem, Bruce?'

'It's Bella.' Connell sounded subdued, yet his voice hinted at the man's inner strain and uncertainty, so that it was hard to remember him as he had once been. 'He's got to be buried.'

Malinski nodded. 'Sure. It's not too good in this climate.'

'I'll tell the captain.' Maddox felt uncomfortable because he had in fact forgotten all about the dead and mutilated yeoman.

'You do that small thing.' There was a sting in the doctor's words, as if the mention of the captain had revived his earlier anger. 'No doubt he'd like to feed him to the sharks!'

Malinski watched the other man's shoulders outlined against the occasional whitecap. 'You feel things pretty deeply, Doc. I'm surprised, I suppose.'

Connell laughed shortly. 'I surprise myself. When I was in a carrier with the big boys I was uneasy, dissatisfied if you like. The thought of hundreds, thousands of people being wiped off the slate by one aircraft from our ship, if so ordered, made me feel we were on the wrong course. I used to listen to the men yarning about their girls and their adventures in the Chinese brothels, or about their folks back home and the latest movie. But no one said a word about what we were doing, what we could do if the button was pressed.'

'I guess we all think like that——'

Malinski faltered as the doctor continued in the same tense voice: 'No, it wasn't that. It was a feeling of helplessness, a sense of committal. I wanted to get away, to find out what went on closer to the problem. I put in to go ashore, but nothing happened. When the chance came up for the *Hibiscus* I volunteered straight away. I guess I imagined that some change would come over me, a clearing of vision, a sense of purpose.' He shrugged helplessly. 'I just don't know what I expected.'

Maddox interrupted harshly, 'Instead you discovered it's a dirty business here just the same, eh?'

'It's more difficult.' Malinski began to refill his pipe. 'The guy with the bayonet hasn't got time to ask questions, he just has to kill or get spitted himself! We've got to trust someone, but if the call goes out we've just got to do our best.' He looked directly at the doctor. 'I think you're wrong about the captain.'

Connell turned his face away. 'I think not. When I get back to sanity again I'm going to fry him alive.' He moved to the ladder and they heard him groping his way towards his quarters.

Malinski replaced his cap. 'He's probably got religion, Bob. The scalpel just doesn't mix with a crucifix, I'm afraid.'

The door opened half an inch and a tired voice intoned, 'The book says it'll be sun-up in ten minutes, Mister Maddox!'

Malinski grinned broadly. 'See? God sure keeps us informed of all the real important things!'

* * *

Mark Gunnar wrapped his fingers around the thick mug and felt the heat of the rich, strong coffee coursing through his body. It was curious, but in those few hours he had slept better than he could remember, and after a shave and shower and a quick change into clean khakis he felt almost rejuvenated and fresh.

He was never tired of watching the sun climb from the sea. To him it was the best of sights, yet one which always held some new excitement. The great, glowing mass which still found sufficient surplus to spill down a widening, calming path across the ruffled wavetops, the steady, strengthening warmth which already raised a haze of steam from the sodden decks

247

and battered upperworks. For the first time he saw the savage manhandling his ship had received in her fight against the storm, the twisted guardrails, the empty davits and raft racks. Somehow the whaleboat had managed to survive, and he noted with satisfaction that Regan was already bobbing around his gun mountings, checking and coddling his lethal charges and clearing away the salt rime and shredded canvas covers.

A party of seamen were gathered round the whaleboat's davits, and Gunnar felt a small twinge of sadness, or was it guilt? He could not be sure. The very first task in Payenhau would be to ferry Bella's body ashore and bury it quickly. It would no doubt be recovered and flown home at some later date, to be forgotten by all but the close few who knew the boy as he had once been.

He walked on to the bridge wing and looked narrowly at a working party on the forecastle. Hoses and brooms worked automatically but without enthusiasm, and he could see Chief Tasker lounging against the slender three-inch gun, a cigar stub in his jaw like an old tooth.

They were all thinking about him, talking about him. He wondered if they would have reacted differently with another captain. But another captain might have behaved in a way they could understand. When *Hibiscus* returned to Payenhau he would get short shift from Jago and from the over-reaching command of the far-off flag officer. He might even be required to hand over command, to await a court of enquiry.

The undulating, black mass of Payenhau seemed to sway across the bows as if pivoting on the jackstaff, and he thought it looked forbidding and unfamiliar.

He let his mind drift from the immediate problems and thought again of Lea Burgess. She was never far away in his mind, and without effort he could picture her dark eyes and feel the warmth of her embrace. It would be more sensible to realise that she might soon forget him once she was allowed to see that other world, once she realised that there was more to life than a dream.

The ship staggered noisily in a cross-current and he banged down the mug as if to show the readiness he did not feel. He called to the bosun's mate who hovered nearby, 'I shall want the cable party up forrard in twenty minutes.' He slung his glasses around his neck and began to climb the ladder to the upper bridge where Kroner and Ensign Maddox were already preparing the ready-use chart for the last run in.

When he looked again the shore was much closer, and the dull, smooth-backed hills were already bathed in gold as the sun felt its way across the storm-battered ground and threaded its colouring amongst the cliffs and gullies.

Maddox clattered up the ladder and paused on the wet gratings to stare at Gunnar's neat and alert appearance. The exec was still unshaven and crumpled, and seemed almost unnerved by Gunnar's transformation. 'Coming up to the main channel now, sir.'

Gunnar nodded. 'As soon as we enter the main anchorage I want the whaleboat lowered to deck level.' He added: 'I shall go ashore the moment we drop the hook. You can lie at anchor in our original position clear of the pier, and I want a full guard mounted until I know what's going on. I've already told Regan what I require, but it'll be up to you to see that the routine runs smoothly.'

'Who are you taking, sir?' Maddox sensed the tenseness which had crept into Gunnar's voice. 'A full burial party?'

'Negative. Six men and Ensign Maddox.' Behind him he heard the young ensign draw a quick breath.

Maddox clenched his fists. 'Is that necessary, sir? I mean, I think he's been put in enough danger already.'

'If you are right, there'll be no danger surely?' Gunnar's tone was cold. 'In any case I can't spare a more experienced officer.' Then in an almost matter-of-fact voice, 'Watch this approach now.'

Maddox stepped up beside the compass repeater his face bleak. He spoke sharply into the voice-pipe, 'Come right to zero one zero!' Goddamn him! It was almost as if the captain was deliberately goading him.

'Wreckage on the port bow, sir!' a man sang out from the wing as a wallowing tangle of broken timber bobbed slowly past on the ebb.

Gunnar watched it pass. The frail boats of Payenhau would stand little chance in the typhoon's speedy path, even in the anchorage.

The land reached out and encircled the slow-moving ship and the deep black shadows cast by the early sun seemed to chill the men on the upper bridge like a cold breath.

Then the first islet had fallen away and the bows were crossing a shallow path of bright sunlight. He heard Maddox say, 'Right standard rudder.' Then in a brief pause, 'Steady on zero two five.'

249

It was strange how well Maddox behaved when he was angry, Gunnar thought. He forgot the others as *Hibiscus* sliced clear of the first part of the channel and into a wider patch of ruffled water. Steadying his glasses he could just make out the distant shadow of the fishing village, but even at this distance he could see the loose piles of broken boats across the pale beach, the houses open to the sky. The storm must have found its way across the anchorage after all and ripped some of the flimsy buildings apart.

He heard Kroner say fretfully, 'Damn this haze, I can't see a thing.' No one answered.

It *was* a bad haze, Gunnar observed. The land was already giving up its moisture to the sun, so that even the hills quivered above the far-off town and the still-hidden citadel, as if the whole island was smouldering above subterranean fires.

Gunnar said, 'Reduce speed to ten knots, Mister Maddox.' He heard the bells jangle and saw the bows drop slightly as the ship cut across the last of the channel's unpredictable tide-race.

He stiffened, just faintly above a clump of buildings he could discern the slender white line of the citadel's flagmast. No flag flew, and he could not remember if it was normally hoisted at dawn or kept flying all day.

Ensign Maddox's voice broke with excitement. 'The wreck, sir! Look, it's moved!'

Caught by the unnatural high tide ahead of the typhoon the whole length of the rusted freighter had pivoted from the sandbar and slid into deeper water, so that only the bridge and forecastle remained above water. Unconsciously Gunnar plucked the shirt away from his skin as he remembered the girl on the listing boatdeck, her words about the peace and happiness of that one moment together.

Somewhere below he heard Chief Anders calling to the lowering party and the squeak of the whaleboat's blocks as it moved down the falls. We came back, he thought. Even Bella, the haunted and betrayed Bella who had never been given a chance by anybody, was returning like a ghost to the home of his murderers.

Regan called from the bows, 'Starboard anchor ready to let go, Captain!'

'All engines stop.' The ship glided forward, the stem hardly making a ripple as it cut gently through the sheltered water.

Gunnar swallowed and tried to clear his throat of the sudden dryness. It was all wrong. No people, not even a dog by the old pier. He felt naked and exposed in the open water, but tried to retain a sense of proportion. It was still very early and they were not expected. It was unlikely that anyone would be overjoyed to see the ship anyway. A sudden thought crossed his mind as he looked again at the roofless houses. The people would need help, even from him. 'Tell the doctor to wait by the whaleboat. He can come ashore with me.' He wondered how Connell would feel about accompanying his captain and the body of a man he had seen suffer so badly in his hands. He tightened his jaw. He can think what he likes!

'Coming on now, sir!'

'Very well.' He dropped his hand and saw a spark of rust as the anchor plummeted from the hawse-pipe. 'All engines back one-third!' The ship trembled and shuddered as the anchor dug its flukes into the deep, clear water which they had come to know so well. 'All engines stop.'

It was an anticlimax, and for several seconds the men stood quite still on the silent bridge, each wrapped in his own thoughts.

Then Anders yelled, 'Lower away there!' and the whaleboat splashed alongside.

Thank God there was one boat left, Gunnar thought. The pier was sagging at an impossible angle and one nudge, even from a junk, would have finished the job.

Gunnar glanced at the young ensign. 'Get down to the boat, Pip. Check that all the men are armed as instructed, just in case there's any trouble.'

Kroner said sharply: 'The citadel, sir. The gates are open!'

'Jago must be getting overconfident.' Gunnar climbed down the ladder. 'I'll be as quick as I can.' He tried to read behind the exec's troubled eyes. 'And I'll keep you informed of what's happening.'

Slattery, the steward, was waiting by the rail and handed Gunnar his pistol belt without a word, but he watched the captain with something like affection. They don't want me to go, Gunnar thought bitterly. They don't want me to make a fool of myself again.

He sat in the swaying whaleboat and took a good look at the ship. He could see the scarred paintwork, stripped bare by the pounding waves, the old patched plates bared for all to see. The oars dipped, and in seconds they were parted from the parent ship's side.

From his high vantage point Maddox watched the boat pulling away like a small water insect. He could still see his brother's head beside the captain and the bright patch of colour made by the flag across the dead yeoman between the cramped oarsmen. He remembered what Connell had said earlier and wondered what he was thinking at this moment.

Regan clumped across the bridge, cap in hand, and gnawing at a giant sandwich. 'Jesus, Bob, you look as if you'd slept in a bottle!' He grinned wolfishly at Maddox's unsmiling face. 'Even your ears are bloodshot!'

Then he tensed, and Maddox turned to follow his stare. High on a hillside, above the very channel they had just used, there was a small puff of brown smoke. In an instant it was caught by the breeze and blended itself with the drifting haze, but Regan said sharply, 'That was a shot!'

Even as they stared there was a thin, abbreviated whistle followed immediately by a loud splash right alongside. Then another, and yet a third which exploded on the water with a bright yellow splash and an ear-splitting crack.

Kroner gasped, 'What th' hell!'

But Regan was already starting back to the ladder, the sandwich still in his hand. 'A mortar! A goddamn mortar!' Then he halted and stared at Maddox's stricken face. 'Get going, Bob, for Christ's sake, they've got us zeroed in!'

Maddox felt unable to move. He opened his mouth but no words came.

Regan punched his arm. 'Come on, Bob!'

Maddox moved dazedly across the bridge, his heart pounding his ribs like a hammer, in a strange, unrecognisable voice he yelled, 'Sound General Quarters!'

Regan was already on the foredeck running like a madman towards the bows. Maddox was alone. It was his responsibility. Dashing the sweat from his eyes he shouted: 'Break the cable! Let it go!' But Regan was already herding his section back to the cable, his arms moving like flails as he pushed and kicked the dazed men to his bidding.

Maddox was suddenly ice-calm, as if he was under sentence of death. To Kroner he said harshly: 'Send off a despatch immediately. Tell them we are under fire. We require air assistance——' He broke off with a gasp as another pattern of mortar bombs exploded around the hull and sent a stream of white-hot splinters whining above the bridge. 'Get going, man, send it off!' Then he reeled to the voice-pipe. 'All engines

252

ahead full! Right full rudder!' He prayed that the cable was already broken, and stared wildly towards the shore to see if he could find the whaleboat. But the ship was already swinging, and the boat, if it was still afloat, was hidden by the wrecked freighter's bridge.

He suddenly found that he was lying on the deck, his eyes within inches of the neat rivets, an agonising pain in his ribs, his ears singing with the agony of an explosion he had not heard. Sobbing and gasping he dragged himself to his feet, retching with the stench of explosive and burnt paint. There was a funnel of black smoke pouring from below the bridge, and the stack was pitted with tiny shining holes from the bursting bomb. The ship was still swinging, and had he not been deafened by the explosion Maddox would have heard the chattering voice-pipes and the inhuman screaming from one of the signalmen who had been impaled by a strip of flying steel from the maindeck.

His hair had fallen across his eyes, and like a wounded animal he staggered to the voice-pipe. 'Steer straight for the channel! Give me maximum speed!' He ducked as another blast rocked the bridge and ripped the chart table from its clips like a piece of scrap paper. 'Get a fix on that mortar position and open fire!' He pounded the screen with helpless fury, he did not even know if the guns were ready. But from somewhere forward he heard the click of a breech block, and as his hearing slowly returned he caught Regan's harsh voice above the whine of the fans and the steady thresh of the engines. 'Stand by all guns!' Maddox peered over the screen and saw with amazement that some of the men were even wearing their steel helmets and lifejackets, so that they looked unfamiliar and stiff in their automatic movements.

The three-inch gun staggered back in its mounting and its sharp crack scraped the inner membranes of Maddox's ears. He did not see where the shot fell, nor did he care. There was so much to remember, so much to do, and all the time the ship was racing towards the twisting channel like a mad thing.

He climbed to the ladder just as Kroner appeared smoke-stained and wild-eyed on the wing. 'Did you send it off?' Maddox shook his fist at the land. 'We'll give those bastards something to remember when the planes arrive!' He realised that Kroner was gripping his arm and stared at him, his fist still in the air. 'Well?'

Kroner was shaking. 'That mortar bomb knocked out the radio shack! I didn't get a chance to send!' He turned and looked as if he was going to be sick. 'Jesus, it's like a slaughter-house down there!'

Maddox pushed the quivering officer in front of him and into the shuttered wheelhouse, where the men's eyes gleamed whitely at him through the thin haze of smoke. 'Hold on, Don! Hold on, for Christ's sake!' To the helmsman he barked, 'Keep her steady!'

Once the racing ship brushed an outjutting sandbar, and for one terrible moment Maddox imagined they would tear out the bottom, but with a nerve-jarring wrench *Hibiscus* ground over the sand and thrashed her way into deeper water, stack gas mingling with the smoke of her wound as it streamed away astern.

The gun had fallen silent, and after a few moments Regan joined them in the wheelhouse. 'Five killed and two wounded,' he reported flatly. 'I didn't stand a chance with that pea-shooter. If we could have caught the bastards in the open I could have cut them to pieces with the twenty-millimetres!'

Maddox rubbed his eyes, willing himself to think coherently. 'All engines ahead standard.'

Regan said quietly, 'Well, Bob, what do we do?'

Maddox watched the land sliding away on the beam and replied: 'So he was right after all. He was goddamn well right!' A nerve jumped in his cheek. 'My God, Pip's back there!'

As if he had not heard Regan continued evenly, 'We can hightail it for Taiwan and get help, or——'

Maddox studied the gunnery officer's deepset eyes with desperation. 'Or what?'

'Go back.' Regan gave a thin smile. 'Fight our way in and get your brother back.' He paused. '*And* the captain, of course!'

'I'm not sure—I mean, I don't know . . .' Maddox looked frantically around the wheelhouse. 'If we got in there again they'll tear us apart!'

'We'll be ready for 'em this time.' Regan was grinning like a wolf. 'Come on, Bob, do you want to live for ever?'

His grin changed to a sneer as Maddox turned away and said, 'I must think, I must decide what to do!'

'You sure must. You're in command as of now, God help us!'

254

Maddox wheeled round. 'And don't you forget it!'

Regan opened the door. 'I'm going to tour the gun positions. I've sent Chief Tasker to see to the wounded. I guess I'm exec, eh?'

Kroner interrupted, his face ashen, 'I've just remembered something.' The others stared at him. 'You remember when the captain took your brother on the chase in the fishing boat *Osprey*?' He gestured excitedly. 'When he went up to the northern islets?'

Regan rubbed his chin. 'What of it?'

'He went through the eastern channel!' He peered at their blank faces. 'Well, don't you see? That fishing boat is deep draught, at least eight feet.' He waved his hands violently. '*Hibiscus* only draws seven and a half!'

Maddox walked to the chart, conscious of the trembling in his legs. 'We'd have to keep the speed right down, and even then we're three times as long as that scow!'

'Even so, it's worth a try.' Regan was studying the chart. 'Christ, Don, I didn't know you had it in you!'

Kroner glared at him as he dabbed his mouth with his handkerchief. 'I want to live, that's for sure. But I reckon we stand a better chance like this than going in bull-at-a-gate!'

'He's right.' Maddox stood up slowly. 'If we go in slowly we might feel our way through that channel. It's narrow, but short.' He thought of his brother's look of disappointment and shame. 'We'll do it!'

Regan grinned. 'You're not such a punk either!' He paused by the door, his angular features and beaky nose making him look like a pirate. 'One thing, if we make a friggin' mess this time, no one will ever hear about it! We'll all be in the bone orchard by the time the brass gets on to it!'

Maddox controlled his breathing and said, 'Come left to zero nine zero.' By now the first shock was wearing off and the whole ship would know what he was doing. What was he trying to prove? It didn't make sense. They were all acting like strangers. Even Kroner seemed to have taken on a new being.

Paice spun the wheel. 'Steady on course, sir.'

Maddox picked up the p.a. and after a moment said: 'This is Lieutenant Maddox speaking. In a few moments we are going to re-enter Payenhau.' He stared emptily at the microphone, hearing the metallic echoes fading around the ship. 'Where we will, if necessary, engage the enemy.'

He dropped the handset and listened to the clatter of an ammunition hoist.

Engage the enemy? He did not even know who the enemy was.

* * *

'Pull like bloody hell!' Gunnar clutched the whaleboat's gunwale as the startled seamen dug their oars and then picked up the rhythm which had fallen apart with the first explosions. It had been a matter of minutes, yet already it seemed as if they had been crawling across the open water for eternity.

With sick horror Gunnar had watched the creeping barrage of mortar fire, the familiar pattern which he had seen before used against houses and troops, trains and children. Then as the slim grey hull had tacked round to break free from the confined anchorage he had seen the tell-tale orange glow abaft the bridge, the whirling dust-cloud of flying metal and belching smoke. Unlike small-arms fire or low-trajectory weapons, the mortar bombs were able to fall from directly overhead, and whereas their chances of success against surface craft were normally slight, on this rare occasion, with a slow-moving target in a predetermined and zeroed area, the result of that one hit would be all the more devastating. Straight down, like the bomb from a diving aircraft, missing the scanty protection of the main hull and carving deep into the heart of the ship herself.

Anders had shouted: 'Must have got the radio, Captain! There's nothin' much else there!'

It's enough, Gunnar had thought. Then as the ship gathered speed and the whaleboat had swayed in confused disorder, he had seen the new danger to themselves. Now the boat was within yards of the beach and the end of the sandspit. A few feathers of spray spattered alongside the wooden hull and Pip Maddox ducked involuntarily.

'Rifle fire, I think, sir!'

Gunnar shaded his eyes, conscious of the oarsmen's taut faces as they put their full weight against the slender blades. The bowman yelled and let his oar skid clear of the boat as he threw one hand against his shoulder. Connell started to scramble to his feet as the blood began to seep between the man's fingers, but Gunnar snapped: 'Sit tight! Time for him later!'

With a lurch the boat grounded in the sand and Gunnar

256

hurled himself over the side, aware of the cool water swilling around his legs, the indistinct, almost casual, crackle of small-arms which he knew was coming from the citadel. The gates were now shut and he could see a few small movements from the crude walls.

The boat tilted and Bella's shrouded body rolled forgotten across the thwarts. 'Hit the deck!' Gunnar tugged out his pistol and threw himself behind a small pile of rocks.

Anders was yelling. 'Spread out! Keep yer heads down!'

More firing, the danger only real because of the close whimper of bullets overhead.

Gunnar lay still, his heart pumping painfully against his ribs, his eyes watering with concentration. He tried to imagine what Maddox would do now. Probably made off to safety while the going was good. There was little else he could do.

Anders wriggled through the sand, his face red with exertion. 'What now, Captain?' He gestured towards the distant orange flashes. 'The bastards have got us pinned down well enough!'

Gunnar eased himself up on his elbows. The firing was dangerous but inaccurate. One good rifleman alone could have done the trick better than the hidden men on the ramparts. He thought quickly of the mortar fire and began to shape his vague plan. It was obvious that the ship's return had been a complete surprise to the enemy, and everyone appeared to be nearer the other end of the island. By the prison camp, for instance. So sure of complete surprise and overwhelming victory that they had left the citadel almost unguarded.

'Hell, here come the reinforcements!' Pip Maddox sounded shaken.

Gunnar's ear had already picked out the whine of a jeep's engine without really taking in what it meant. 'Chief! Three men on the double! Cover the coast road!'

But no shots were fired by the crouching sailors as the jeep swung into view, and they all saw the burly, helmeted figure of Sergeant Rickover behind the wheel. Bullets pattered in the dust beside its wheels, and some actually ricocheted from the flat steel by Rickover's hands, but like an uncontrollable chariot it plunged over the edge of the road and came to rest in a cloud of dust and smoke.

Rickover unceremoniously hauled Jago's body from the back and bawled something to the other three occupants who threw themselves down beside him.

257

Rickover blinked at Gunnar with cheerful surprise. 'Jesus, Captain, I didn't know it'd be you!'

Anders grimaced sourly. 'The President couldn't make it!'

Gunnar peered down at Jago. He looked old and grey, his face deeply lined with pain. 'Is he okay?'

Rickover unslung his carbine and said briefly: 'One in the leg. The bone's all splintered.' Then he squinted over the rocks. 'The bastards are all coming down the road behind us. We made a road block to hold up their transport, but it's a matter of minutes. I left the rest of my guys behind, dead or wounded.' He gestured to the wounded corporal and two Chinese troopers. 'This is the lot as far as I know!' He looked again at the citadel. 'It's there or nothing for us, sir. If we wait here we'll either get shot or drowned, if we're lucky!'

The marine's eyes were cold and professional. It was a military problem, no longer a matter for conjecture. 'There's only a few guards. The gate's the problem.' He grinned without humour. 'They're not too strong. More for show than anythin'.' He cursed savagely as a splinter of stone rattled against his helmet. Then he added quietly: 'The jeep would do it. Once there we could hold off the main rush for a few hours and get that goddamn radio!'

Gunnar said: 'I've already sent Burgess to Taiwan. At least I didn't wait to be told what might happen!' He wriggled higher along the rocks. 'If Maddox runs for Base we can expect the full works by tomorrow.'

Rickover was staring at him strangely. 'I don't get you, sir?' He cocked his carbine. 'The *Osprey* is still here! I saw it at first light. At anchor on the west side!' He gripped Gunnar's arm. 'Hell, sir, you look like you've seen a ghost!'

Gunnar looked away, his set face only half masking the despair and shock which welled up inside him like a flood. It was *impossible*! The *Osprey* had never sailed, it had been here all the time while the *Hibiscus* had been sawing her way through the typhoon's fringe, every hour which Bella had suffered, and he himself had schemed and plotted to make this one last gesture.

It was a pattern, and an exact copy of what had gone before. All that misery and suffering, the agony of disgrace and failure had taught him nothing, and his betrayal had been all the more complete.

He wiped his face with the back of his hand and tried to reassemble his tumbling thoughts. How they must have

258

laughed at him. It had been too easy.

The cold, consuming fire of anger suddenly flared into something wild and terrible, and with steel in his voice he yelled: 'Anders! We're going to rush the gates with the jeep! Full covering fire on the ramparts!'

Pip Maddox said breathlessly: 'I'll go, sir! I could do it!'

Gunnar regarded him searchingly. 'Not this time.' But they both whirled round as the jeep's engine roared into life.

Rickover stood up, his face no longer cool and unruffled. 'Seltzer! Come back, you mad bastard!' He shouted again into the noise of the tyres ripping at the roadway: 'Come *back*! You'll never make it!'

Anders threw up his carbine. 'Rapid fire!' He glared sideways at the seamen, his eyes red-rimmed with danger. 'Shoot, you goddamn bandits!'

The firing sounded puny, but Gunnar saw the grey splinters fly from the top of the ramparts, and then he was up and running after the jeep, followed by Rickover and the two remaining soldiers.

He heard the marine gasp as he ran: 'The poor bastard's wounded. He's already saved my hide, but it's his pride that he's after this time!'

With a shattering crash the jeep exploded against the tall gates. The wood splintered and yawed drunkenly, but held from the rear by strong chains it opened less than two feet. The jeep was on fire, and as Gunnar panted up the slope it blew up in one final detonation. Sickened he watched Seltzer's fat shape fall away into the holocaust and lose its meaning and reality.

But Rickover was past him, already kicking at the side of the nearest gate where it had been wrenched free from its rusted hinges. Between clenched teeth he snarled, 'One for you, buddy!' and fired into a small running group of soldiers beyond the guard hut.

Then, scorched by Seltzer's funeral pyre, they were all in the courtyard and running like madmen for the citadel. One of the Chinese soldiers at Gunnar's side fell without a murmur and Gunnar fired his pistol directly into the face of a man who crouched behind a pile of ammunition boxes. He screamed and rolled back into the shadows, the top of his head blasted away. Then they were running down that familiar passageway, their shadows leaping ahead of them in the faint glow of oil lamps. Gunnar felt mad, crazed beyond reason or

259

control as he tore headlong ahead of the others. A few more yards and they would be in Jago's bunker.

Rickover put his shoulder against the steel door and thrust it open. For some unknown reason the electric lights were working here, and the scene was all the more unreal because of it.

Jago's headquarters, his seat of empire, was a shambles. Even his giant picture of the marines under fire was defaced and crudely daubed in Chinese characters. A young lieutenant and two soldiers lay spreadeagled in their own blood by the far door, and in those frantic split seconds Gunnar realised that they must have been some of Jago's men who had, like Seltzer, stayed loyal.

Three panting, sweating Chinese leaned against the radio table, their eyes fixed on Gunnar's face, their expressions fearful but triumphant.

Rickover looked past them at the tangled ruin of the transmitter and said slowly, 'I guess we were too late, Captain!'

Gunnar dropped his arms to his sides. It seemed hopeless, as if there was a more powerful force available to counter every move he knew.

He looked up as Rickover said flatly: 'It's funny, isn't it? These Red bastards know every game in the book. They murder, cheat, torture and lie. Anything to get their ends.' He gestured towards the three soldiers who had carefully laid their weapons beside the radio. 'Yet when they get caught they immediately expect fair play in capital letters!' The carbine jumped in his hands, the sound deafening and metallic in the confined space, its echo mixed and blended with the other two shots, killing any cry or sound which the soldiers might have made. In the harsh light the blood looked bright and unreal.

Rickover crooked the carbine under his arm and looked at Gunnar calmly. 'I guess you can fix me for that, Captain? But the bastards had it coming!'

Gunnar shrugged heavily, hearing the distant scrape of feet in the courtyard and Anders' resonant voice. 'I never saw a thing, Sergeant.' He walked slowly out of the bunker, and without warning the current died and plunged it into merciful darkness.

Rickover slammed the door, shutting off the smell of cordite and death. My God, he thought, they even taunt us in

260

death. They brutalise us and make us like them in our efforts to survive and win.

Jago's voice echoed down the passageway. 'Put me down, you clumsy ape! I'm not dead yet!'

Outside in the early sunlight Gunnar stared round at his little party. It was not much, but it was a start. Chief Anders was dressing the wounded seaman's arm, and Connell was attending to a non-co-operative Jago.

One of the sailors, a giant Texan named O'Brien, held out his arms which were covered with the great, spilling colours of Old Glory. He grinned self-consciously. 'Just brought it along, Cap'n. I guess poor ole Bella won't be needin' it right now?'

Gunnar looked around at their strained faces and felt the prick of emotion behind his eyes. No regrets, not a word of complaint or fear for what he had done to them all.

Jago looked up, his face shrunken with fatigue and pain. 'Well, what are you waiting for, Gunnar?' He pointed impatiently to the ramparts. 'Hoist the flag, it's the least we can goddamn well do!'

Gunnar climbed the steps, feeling the sun on his neck, sensing their eyes following his figure along the rough concrete wall. He stared down at the panorama of destruction, the burned-out jeep and its charred driver. The few crumpled figures, and the distant, listing whaleboat with its canvas-sewn occupant. It was somehow a fitting place for such a useless gesture of defiance.

The big flag clung to the pole and then filled itself from the hill-top breeze. Gunnar looked up at it and saluted. It would not be there for long, but it was a sign of faith.

Like the murmur of an onrushing wave he heard the sound of a great intermingled roar. As yet unseen, the infuriated rebels were coming to finish what they had begun. What we all helped to begin, Gunnar thought wearily. By our trust and carelessness, by our clear-cut ignorance, we helped very well.

Jago croaked: 'You're running things now, Captain. So let's get on with it!'

Gunnar wondered if Jago saw the flag like the one in his bunker. He hoped that he did.

He reached the others and said evenly: 'The radio's kaput, but we hold the citadel. We've just got to stick it out until help arrives.'

Rickover gathered up a bag of magazines and looked at him

with open admiration. 'All we need now is the goddamn cavalry!'

Jago had seated himself awkwardly on a box beside the gate, a rifle and two pistols within reach. 'I sold you, Gunnar,' he said quietly, 'but I'll back you now, no matter what you do!'

Gunnar slumped by a weapon slit and watched the first running figures rounding the bend in the road. What are we doing here? What is the point of it all now?

He blinked to clear the mist from his eyes and said firmly, 'Wait till I give the signal!'

16

A Matter of Gunnery

Pirelli opened his eyes and blinked in dazed bewilderment. For several minutes he lay tense and still as his sleep-fogged mind crept unwillingly back to life, then he relaxed slightly and stared upwards at the small circle of bright blue overhead.

To anyone but a hardened and professional seaman, the *Osprey*'s cable locker was just about the worst and most uncomfortable hiding place imaginable. Situated right forward against the stem, it was sealed from the rest of the boat by a collision bulkhead, and received its only ventilation via some small holes above the bilges, and of course the circular outlet in the deck above, through which the cable was allowed to rattle on its way to the sea-bed. But now the boat rode easily at her mooring, and the shining links of the cable hung straight down beside Pirelli's makeshift bed and disappeared below him in the narrowest, sharpest point of the stout hull.

Pirelli had decided on this place almost as soon as he had planned to stow away in *Osprey* for her trip to Taiwan. He had slipped aboard in the darkness, feeling instantly with his inborn sailor's cunning that the vessel was deserted. Then going forward through the small living quarters he had released the narrow watertight door to the cable locker and eased himself inside to await events. There was a wide shelf which stretched from beam to beam just behind the sealed door, upon which Burgess had stored a roll of used and well-patched canvas, but to Pirelli's aching body it became the most comfortable bed he could remember.

Just as he had expected, *Osprey* had sailed, her heavy diesel muffled but steady as the boat chugged away from the anchorage and pushed her blunt stem on to the open sea. The motion was sharp and savage, and even Pirelli soon became aware that the weather was worsening. Strangely, he did not care, he had fooled them all, and was almost clear. In Taiwan he would complete the rest of his plan. Once in the busy dock area he knew he would be able to find shelter and make arrangements to find a berth on an outgoing ship. Anything was better than to be discovered by some Chief Provost and slung into the nearest cage to await trial.

He quickly worked out how many legal occupants there were in the pitching boat. He had heard Burgess's heavy step on deck and listened to him giving his orders to the Chinese deckhand. There was also an engineer quartered right aft. And of course there was the girl.

The first night out, when the wind had brought the spray hissing and sighing against the wooden sides, and salt water had even sprayed down from the higher seams on to Pirelli's hiding place, she had come down to the small cabin, so near to Pirelli that he could have touched her but for the bulkhead. As soon as she lit the gimballed lamp Pirelli had pressed his eye to the wall, and had soon found a place which had eluded both paint and filler. He quickly forgot the stench of the bilge water and diesel, the nerve-jarring shudder each time the stem plunged down into a trough, and everything else, as he watched her slip out of her clothes and sit on the edge of her bunk, combing her long black hair and watching herself in a small mirror. He wanted to confront her, to push her down on that inviting bed like that other girl, to make everything complete. He would have told her about the night she had met the captain aboard the old wreck, when he had listened to their furtive movements and waited for them to settle down on the boatdeck. It would have been easy to kill them both, but escape was more important. All the same, he would have liked to let her know that he had seen them together.

Pirelli had remained motionless behind the thick partition, his eyes gleaming in the narrow pointer of light as he had watched her every movement. How smooth and supple her shoulders looked beneath the lamplight, how full of promise her small, perfect breasts.

Pirelli sat up with a jerk. The foul air and exhausted sleep had dulled his mind. What did the girl matter now? Something had gone wrong. For some reason or other the boat had returned to Payenhau. He imagined at first it was because of the threatened storm, but like most seamen Pirelli could judge matters concerning his natural element very well without the benefits of navigational training. They could have reached Taiwan without effort before the storm could touch them. There had been no engine trouble, and Burgess had seemed quite happy about things, for Pirelli had often heard him singing from the wheelhouse.

He pressed his eye against one of the seams and peered again at the nearby land. It was unfamiliar, yet he knew it was Payenhau. Why should Burgess come back? And in any case, why return to a different part of the island? Anxiety began to gnaw at his insides, and several times he toyed with the idea of leaving his hiding place and swimming ashore. For hours he had laid jammed in the cable locker while the boat's new anchorage had gone berserk and thrown him from one painful position to another. The engine had kept running although the anchor was down, and Pirelli guessed that Burgess was taking no chances on dragging his hook as the storm raged and bellowed across the nearby hills.

Someone had left the *Osprey* in the dinghy even while the storm was battering at the moored boat, and Pirelli marvelled at the stupidity or urgency which would make such a trip necessary. Now in the early sunlight he could see that the beach was barely twenty yards away, so whoever it had been had known what he was about.

But what had awakened him? He tried to sit upright and cursed as the pain lanced through him. He could not stand much more of this, living in his own filth, and not even knowing what was happening.

There was a thud as a hatch was thrown open, and immediately Pirelli crouched on the alert, the rifle in his big hands. Sunlight streamed into the cabin where he had hungrily watched the naked girl, and he saw Burgess stamp down the ladder, and he noticed that he appeared to be dragging his daughter behind him. Burgess was very red in the face, while his normally immaculate shirt was soaked in spray and sweat. The girl was dressed in shirt and jeans, and appeared to have

264

been crying. She looked wild-eyed and defiant, and even as Burgess turned to face her she said: 'You lied! You *lied*!'

Burgess stepped back two paces, his bearded features angry. 'You hold your tongue! What's done is done!'

Pirelli blinked and squinted harder through the crack. Burgess was drunk, or very nearly so, but it was something else which had transformed the girl so suddenly. Gone was the quiet, secret smile Pirelli had seen in this cabin, and instead she looked on the point of hysteria.

Burgess glared round. 'This is my chance to get all the things I wanted. No more crawling and waiting, it's all *over*!'

She tried to plead. 'But you promised, you said you would go! Who told you to come back to Payenhau?' She moved her hands with quick desperation. 'Mark Gunnar is relying on you, don't you see?'

Burgess swayed and banged the table. 'Don't you dare to talk to me about him! He's finished as far as I'm concerned!' He faced her, his teeth bared like an animal. 'You dare to lecture me! You talk of that—that——' He broke off as she clung to his arm, her eyes shining with tears.

'Get away, and forget your precious captain!' He said in a quieter tone: 'He took your body, didn't he? Made you a whore just like your mother!'

She fell back as if he had struck her, her knuckles against her mouth.

'Did you think I didn't know?' Burgess's voice was getting louder. 'I tried to keep you clean, to save you for something better, but you knew best! All my life I have been dogged because of *one* mistake, you! But that's all in the past. With this money I'll be able to pick up the old threads or start again, just as I please!'

The girl seemed to have gained a small control of herself. Her body was motionless and very erect as she stood and faced her father. 'For the promise of some gold you sold the Americans? For the idea that someone else was to blame for your own faults you are prepared to let Captain Gunnar wait for help that will never come in time?' Her lip quivered. 'Do you really think you can *live* with these things?'

Burgess pulled a silver flask from his pocket and lifted it to his mouth. Pirelli could see the neat spirit running down his beard like spittle.

Then Burgess said: 'Gunnar was a fool to come back. As it is, the coup is complete, the island has fallen to Yi-Fang's men,

265

and that's all there is to it. All I did was to keep him informed.' He glared at her with red, accusing eyes. 'You always pretended to love these island people, that old idiot of a headman and the others! Why change now just when they have got their independence?' He coughed as the spirit caught at his throat. 'My God, I wish I had a pound for every British Colony which has got its independence by drawing a bit of blood! I didn't hear any American protests about those!'

'But these are people! We know them all, and you know as well as I do that Tao-Cho is no party to all this! He is merely the reason *given* by Yi-Fang——'

She broke off with a cry as Burgess seized her wrist. 'You stow that sort of talk! I want to get clear of here with a good skin!'

She pulled her hand away and stared at him with angry contempt. 'So it's true! You've been helping the Communists just as Mark Gunnar suspected!'

Burgess gave a sloping grin. 'Your Mister Gunnar knew no such thing! He thought an attack was coming from the outside, his sort always think like that. "Remember Pearl Harbour" and all that guff! But these people are too clever for the Gunnars of this world. Right under their noses I did it, *I* did it, understand?'

'I do now.' Her voice had gone very quiet, so that Pirelli wriggled closer to hear it. 'When I thought you were sleeping off one of your drinking bouts you were piloting one of Yi-Fang's landing craft. You were running stores and ammunition for this uprising. I suppose that is what was happening when Lieutenant Inglis was killed?'

Burgess held up his hands. 'I had nothing to do with it. How was I to know that the young fool would land there and then? He was killed by the men guarding the arms cache. Yi-Fang's men shot a couple of prisoners from the camp and dressed them in Red uniforms just to put Gunnar off the scent. *Imagine!* Old Jago believed every word Yi-Fang said to him. His protégé, his dear little idol, an all-American product!' He laughed with insane delight, so that his daughter shrank away from him.

'And all the other incidents?' Her voice was tight and despairing.

Burgess shrugged. 'Oh, some of Yi-Fang's boys. They thought Gunnar could be scared off, just like that maniac Bella who was killed.'

266

Pirelli wiped his streaming face and looked round the cable locker as if to reassure himself he was awake. One fantastic revelation after another. Bella dead? *Hibiscus* back and facing a rebellion? What the hell was going to happen to *him*?

He heard Burgess say in a more controlled tone, 'I'm going to get the rest of my money, so you stay here and keep out of sight.' He looked down at her with a strange light in his eyes. 'Otherwise you might get something you've not bargained for!'

Another footfall sounded on the ladder, and Tsung, the big deckhand, stood framed in the sunlight. The girl ran towards him. 'You must help me! Take me ashore!' Her voice broke at last. 'Please! I will explain later!'

The big Chinese looked at her in the same strange way as her father. But it was Burgess he addressed. 'I am going now. I leave a guard.' He smiled faintly. 'Just in case anyone gets difficult.'

Burgess nodded. 'I see. If you think it's necessary.'

He sounded almost humble, and the girl cried: 'What are you saying? What is Tsung to do with this?'

The big Chinese regarded her emptily, then began to climb the ladder. Then he called down: 'Not Tsung any more. My name is Bolod!'

＊　　　＊　　　＊

Like a blind man using his stick, the *Hibiscus* crept forward at a dead slow speed towards what appeared to be an impenetrable wall of fallen cliffs. Only an unbroken flurry of white surf betrayed the narrow entrance of the channel, and it was hard to believe that the chart was not lying about its width.

Maddox ran from one side of the wheelhouse to the other, leaning first over one wing and then the other. He felt cold, yet the sweat poured down his body, soaking his shirt and making him shiver uncontrollably. 'Eight fathoms, sir.' The voice broke in on his aching mind, so that he had to wrench his eyes from the swaying shoreline and concentrate on the ship's cautious approach. Paice was at the wheel, lifejacketed and with a heavy pistol at his belt. Like everything and everyone else he was accepting the new role, playing the part for which each man was trained, yet which so rarely overshadowed everyday routine. In the hours it had taken Maddox to con the ship close inshore amongst the treacherous and deceptive islets, the ship had transformed itself into a compact fighting unit. Helmeted gunners crouched beside the forty-millimetre and the six slender twenty-millimetres, whilst from beside the grey shield of the little three-inch on the fo'c'sle Maddox could see Chief Tasker's bony frame unnaturally distorted by his anti-flash gear and hung about with equipment like a deepsea diver.

'Seven fathoms, sir.'

A low black shadow drifted from the land and glittered momentarily in the sun's path, and Maddox jumped as he heard Regan's voice on the speaker and saw the immediate response of two of the slender twenty-millimetres as they sniffed towards the unknown object like eager terriers.

A lookout reported with relief, 'It's a barge of sorts, Lieutenant!' He steadied his powerful glasses against the glare. 'One of the old L.C.I.s the Chinks were usin'.'

Cautiously the ship idled nearer. The landing craft had probably been blown 'from its moorings in the storm, Maddox decided. There was no sign of life aboard, and its narrow hull was heavy with shipped water.

'Stop engines!'

The *Hibiscus* nudged closer, and Kroner said, 'What's the idea, Bob?'

Maddox wiped his face and leaned over the bridge wing, the sun rasping his neck and shoulders. 'It might come in handy.' He glanced back into the wheelhouse as if to see the chart table. 'I'm worried about the depth. If we could lighten the ship and get rid of some unnecessary gear.' He faltered, uncertain of himself, and at the same time relieved that he had shared the fear which was uppermost in his mind. 'The depth-charges, for instance?' He signalled with his arm and saw a gleaming grappling hook streak across and grip into the L.C.I.s' gunwale.

'It would be better to ditch 'em altogether.' Kroner seemed unable to face the prospect of another delay, even if it meant putting off his own death.

Regan appeared at the rail, his eyes slitted as he stated up at the bridge. 'Are you souvenir hunting?'

Maddox shouted: 'Send a boarding party! I'm going to unload the D.C.s.'

Regan seemed to appreciate the idea, sketchy though it was, and was soon heard bellowing orders as the listing boat grated alongside.

Maddox watched the seamen crawling over its narrow side-deck and said: 'Check our drift, Don. I don't want to pile up just yet.' He lifted his glasses and peered at the shadowed cliffs. A bleak, menacing place. It was quite obviously deserted, yet the fact that he had chosen the correct method of approach gave him no satisfaction. Once through the channel they would be laid bare soon enough.

Thank God the ship was still equipped with the old-style canister depth-charges. Anything more complicated would have taken more time, would have cut away their tiny margin of safety.

The charges rattled and banged as they were rolled along the upper deck, and Chief Tasker goaded another party to rig the lowering gear directly above the landing craft.

Kroner added after a while, 'At least there'll be no danger of getting blown up by our own charges!'

Maddox grunted. It was true. One mortar bomb on the fantail and that would have been the end of it.

He swayed and ran his fingers across his unruly hair. He could never have imagined himself dealing with such a situation, but he knew better than to ponder over his potential too much.

The shore looked much nearer, and with some alarm he realised that the current's possessive drag was more powerful than he had imagined. The chart's instructions were cold and laconic. Once inside the narrow channel the tide would become a race, a veritable sluice which would carry the ship along with it like lumber in a chute. At the narrowest part there would be barely twenty feet on either side of the hull, and any small projection would gut the ship like a herring.

'All unloaded, sir!'

'Right. Tell the engine room what we're doing, and that I want immediate response to the telegraphs!' I should tell Malinski myself, Maddox thought anxiously. Gunnar would have done so. But he would recognise the fear in my voice, would lose what little faith remains. Harshly he said, 'Drop the L.C.'s anchor and cast off.'

'Cast off, sir!' The landing craft wallowed clear and then came up short on its cable. A boat full of unwanted death, a milestone of their failure.

'All engines ahead one-third, steer two eight zero!' The ship trembled and began to gather way. Maddox said quietly,

269

almost in the helmsman's ear, 'In a moment I shall want you to take over, Paice.' He saw the man's finger stiffen on the polished wheel. 'Just hold her in the centre of the channel no matter what else happens. There'll be no time for orders, you'll be on your own, okay?'

Paice nodded without taking his eyes from the gyro. 'Right, sir.'

'I'll use the engines as much as I can if we get into difficulties, but if that happens,' Maddox shrugged, 'we'll not have much room to play with.'

Maddox forced himself to remain still, to refrain from running to the bridge wing as the ship crawled towards the frothing, eager surf. *I was trained for this. The ship was created, planned and built for just such an emergency.* He ground his jaws together. *Or were either of them really meant for such a foolhardy enterprise?*

Steady now. 'Come right, Paice. Steer for that pinnacle above the bluff. That is a good aiming mark for the first approach.'

They were committed. Even if his nerve failed completely, it was unlikely that he could swing the ship clear in time. Maddox dragged his eyes from the creaming water alongside and felt the ship lurch as it crossed into the first savage eddy of the racing current.

'Six fathoms, sir.'

Maddox gnawed at his lip. 'Tell the engine room I want revs for twenty knots!' It was the only way. Like the typhoon's cruel lesson all over again. The fierce current under their tail would soon outpace them without more power.

'It's like shootin' the friggin' rapids, sir!' Paice steadied his perch on the grating and leaned forward against the wheel. 'D'you think you can keep clear?'

'Watch your head! And keep your goddamn comments to yourself!'

Maddox swung his glasses on to the closing cliffs and cursed violently. Paice had almost implied that no one but Gunnar could do it. He looked briefly at Paice's stern face and felt ashamed. 'Sorry, Paice. I guess I'm getting edgy.'

The helmsman grinned. 'You an' me both, sir!'

The engine revolutions mounted, and the slicing stem bit deeply and finally into the narrow strip of confused and surging water. The walls of the canyon-like channel swept past and over them, so that Maddox saw brief and unreal snap-

270

shots of perched gulls, clumps of gorse, and once a long-legged sheep which gazed down at the churning ship with something like reproach.

'Two fathoms, sir!' The talker's voice sounded brittle.

Maddox caught his breath. Jesus! A false move now and the bottom would be left on a rock tooth like the inside of a bucket! 'Steady now!' Over his shoulder, 'Depth in feet from now on!'

Kroner called, 'Christ, look at those rocks!'

'*You* look.' It was surprising how calm he had become now that destruction of one sort or another seemed inevitable.

There was a sideways lurch and the stem began to swing to port. Maddox staggered and almost screamed, 'Rudder hard right!' The ship groaned like a live thing. 'Meet her! Watch that cross-current!' He had seen the tell-tale swirl of black water at the foot of a nearby cliff. He swung towards the voice-pipes. 'Tell damage control to report anything immediately it happens!'

Regan had climbed to the wheelhouse, his helmet hanging in his hand like a cooking pot. 'Like a *miracle*, for instance?' He bared his teeth. 'Going like a steam hammer, isn't she?' He shook his head admiringly. 'That shipyard deserves a goddamn medal!'

'So'll you, once we hit the mortars again!' Maddox glared at him and then forgot his old dislikes as a man yelled, 'Breakers ahead!'

Breakers? Impossible! But even as his glasses steadied he saw the long bar of writhing white foam barely fifty yards ahead. Too late now. 'Hold your course, helmsman!'

With the dropping tide and natural increased power of the sluicing water, some hidden sandbar, or, worse, a formation of fallen rock, lay directly in their path.

Regan wrapped his arms around a stanchion and called: 'Better slow her, Bob! We'll strike for sure!'

Maddox peered at him, shocked by the man's obvious fear. 'Not so frigging easy, is it?' Almost blindly he turned to the talker. 'Well, give me a reading, for Christ's sake!'

The man sounded completely cowed. 'There's nothin' under our keel, sir! Accordin' to the dial we're aground!'

The probing, thrusting stem struck the barrier of packed sand and sent the ship staggering wildly across the channel. For one terrible moment Maddox imagined they would catch against the cliff and turn turtle, but the ship kept going. Some-

271

how, in a determined, fanatical way she thundered over the bar and reeled drunkenly upright, so that every rivet in her frames must have shaken loose.

Then there was a dull, metallic clang which echoed and hummed down the hull, and immediately Paice shouted: 'Swinging to port! Jesus, I can't hold her!'

Ahead lay the flat, unruffled water of the anchorage, another minute and they would have been through.

Maddox almost fell as the ship brushed another obstruction. 'Back the starboard engine!' The deck was tilting and he saw Kroner hanging on to a signalman as if in a drunken dance. Everywhere men cursed and yelled in fear as the ship staggered forward in a crazy, crablike advance.

A telephone buzzed, and as if in a dream Maddox heard Malinski shout: 'We seem to have lost the port screw! Go slow ahead on the other one and use full rudder!' A pause. 'I don't know what the hell you're doing, but half of us are concussed in here, you mad bastard!'

Paice croaked, 'Here she comes, sir.'

The stem flooded with sunlight, and limping like a wounded duck the *Hibiscus* followed the white-flecked flood into the calm of the anchorage.

Maddox wiped his forehead with his wrist and turned to speak to Regan, but he had already left to join his guns. Somehow Maddox had pushed the ship through the impossible. What happened because of their lost propeller and any underwater damage caused by the headlong dash through the channel was no longer Regan's worry. From here on in it was a matter of gunnery.

Maddox groped for his sunglasses as the glare swept to meet them. 'Right full rudder!' He watched the bows pull reluctantly towards the shore. 'Stand by to engage!'

* * *

Pip Maddox lay full length on the concrete roof of the guard-house and cuddled the unfamiliar stock of the carbine against his cheek. Very soon the roof would become a hotplate when the sun had reached its full height above the hills, but right now, as the marine sergeant had already explained, it was a good position. Once Rickover had placed each man of the scanty force in his selected site he had hurried on to supervise another part of the defences, and now as the gulls wheeled

272

angrily above, the young ensign felt desperately alone. Even by raising himself on his elbow he could see nothing of the others. He settled down once more to watch the small, indistinct figures which ran, almost aimlessly, in a loping, diagonal approach across the bottom of the coast road where it vanished around the headland. Still no shots had been fired, and he felt the edge of panic as he watched each busy shape as it moved to some ordered position for attack. It was as if he was facing the whole, anonymous enemy alone. It was all so different, so cold-blooded and final.

He remembered the academy, the music, and the gay, detached approach to the bottom rung of the navy ladder. Nothing, but nothing in his wildest dreams had ever suggested this sort of stark end to his accepted career. He pondered on the change he had seen in his brother, and tried not to think bitterly of the way Bob had taken away his trust. Bob had always been there. Had always been an untapped source of strength and security. But now, he was probably steaming away into the impossible peace of distance. In his heart Pip did not want to blame him, but as each minute dragged by he found it harder to understand.

He jumped, startled as a bugle blared discordantly in the town below. The rifle fire followed immediately, slow at first in its intensity, and then like a storm it gathered power, terrible because of its impartiality. He pulled the butt into his shoulder and squinted through the sights until his eyes watered. It was not like the movies. There, you always knew which bullet was meant for whom. The others acted merely as a warlike background to the main scene. Here it was quite different. The sullen crackle of shots blended together, and only the vague patter of lead against the stout walls told him that he was part of the target. He heard Gunnar shout, 'Here they come!'

Then, as if in a dream, he saw the running figures converging on the road. They flowed out of the pre-arranged muster points, from buildings, from alleyways, and out of the bushes at the roadsides. Then they merged together, a shambling, crouching mob. Some fired automatic weapons from the hip, others pointed aimlessly in the air like Indians in a Western, and all the time the bugle kept up its unnerving, jarring screech, urging them forward, whipping them into a charge.

A whistle blew from the gateway and Pip squeezed the trigger. Around and below him the others matched their sparse firepower against the yelling, screaming mob of run-

273

ning figures, and here and there a man fell. But it seemed to make no difference at all. Pip found that he was cursing and sobbing as he fumbled with another magazine, his mouth spilling out obscenities he hardly understood as he fired again and again until the gun grew hot in his grasp.

Now he could pick out individual faces, see the crazed, screaming mouths of the men who had reached the lower slant of the ramparts. He wriggled nearer the edge and pointed the carbine down on to the heads of those who were worming their way along the wall towards the gate. He saw a man fall, and knew he had killed him. He saw a short, stocky figure, hung about with gleaming ammunition belts, point upwards and yell at the men nearest to the wall. The concrete flew in chips by his face, and he felt the sting of grit on his cheek as he held his breath and fired again. The screaming leader pirouetted and dropped thrashing in the dust, his bright belts following him like snakes. Pip drew in his head as another long burst of machine-gun fire sawed across the edge of the roof and spattered him with powdered concrete.

There was a hollow boom, and he thought he felt the foundations shake as a shock wave stirred the smoke and dust into a miniature tornado above his head. It was followed by a splintering sound and a spine-chilling roar of triumph mingled with screams and the renewed sound of firing.

Pip swallowed the bile in his throat and staggered to his feet. As he peered down into the courtyard he saw with sick horror that the gate had been blasted apart by a grenade and already the gap was filled with brown-clad, struggling figures and the gleam of steel.

Two sailors lay like bundles of rags by the entrance, and the remaining loyal soldier seemed to have been cut in half by the blast. He could see the captain, hatless, a pistol in one hand, beckoning the others to fall back, the gun sparking in his fist even as he shouted above the din.

The seaman who had already been wounded started to run, but was knocked sideways by an invisible hand before he had covered a yard. Two Chinese ran towards him, and Pip retched as he saw the sailor roll over on his back, drawing up his knees in a hopeless attempt to protect his bowels from the quick, flashing bayonets.

Then the Chinese had fallen beside their victim, and the courtyard was momentarily silent.

In the brief stillness Gunnar shouted, 'Fall back!'

274

A sporadic burst of fire cut down some more men by the gate, and Pip saw Rickover and another sailor on the inner wall covering the pathetic retreat. With sudden panic he realised that within seconds he might be cut off from the others, and gathering up his remaining ammunition he ran to the other side of the roof and leapt for the wall. Gasping for breath he ran along the top, his body stark against the bright sky. Bullets whimpered past him, and one seemed to brush against his shirt as he flung himself the last few feet where Rickover unceremoniously grabbed his arm and heaved him over the parapet.

They were all together again. Dashing the sweat from his eyes he peered sideways at the others. The big Texan, O'Brien, covered in dust and smeared with blood, crouched beside the other two seamen, his rifle already barking sharply over the parapet. Chief Anders, compact and fierce-eyed, completely engrossed with a case of grenades, while the doctor, Connell, knelt against the wall, like a man bereft of sight and hearing, his eyes closed to the savage preparations around him.

Sergeant Rickover was smoking a cigar, its smoke mixing with that of his carbine as he peered beneath the rim of his helmet and selected each target with care and precision. Stretched in the dust beside him, Colonel Jago lay like a corpse, only his slow, painful breathing making a sign of movement.

Pip realised that although the Chinese were still shooting, few shots were reaching the parapet. He heard Gunnar say sharply: 'Cease firing! No point in wasting it!'

Pip stared up at the flag and saw it whipping unnaturally in the still air. The Chinese were shooting at it to pass the time while their reinforcements filled in the gaps left by the retreating defenders. Then he looked for the first time at the captain. Unconsciously he realised that it was Gunnar's presence which had stayed with him throughout the whole attack, which had somehow held and sustained him, although he had hardly heard him speak more than a few words. His shirt was half torn from his back, and there was blood on his hands as he played nervously with the big automatic in his belt. There was something compelling and frightening about him, something which Pip had never seen before in any man. He stood in the centre of this chaos and despair, his face pale in the sunlight, his eyes screwed up against the glare as he looked towards the courtyard, a slim, defiant figure, showing neither fear nor pity.

275

He jumped as Jago's voice croaked petulantly from the rear. 'Are they still coming at us?'

A sailor said wearily: 'Soon now. The bastards are just gettin' a second wind!'

Jago slipped back into his state of semi-coma. 'If only I had a hundred marines!'

Rickover glared down at him, his red-rimmed eyes dark with worry and anger. 'Why don't you cut a goddamn disc of that, Colonel? I reckon it'd sell right well back in boot camp!' His teeth gleamed through the grime on his face as Jago cursed him weakly before falling back into silence.

Gunnar moved across and stood between the marine and the young ensign. 'We can't hold them off much longer.' There was no despair in his quiet voice. Nothing. 'They can keep this up as long as they like until they bring up the mortars.' He shaded his eyes as he looked around at the bullet-scarred walls. 'This place was more for show than actual usefulness.'

Rickover nodded. 'When they built it they never imagined that the army would be *outside*!'

Pip Maddox took off his cap and handed it to Gunnar. 'Would you like this, sir?'

Gunnar ran his hand across his hair as if noticing he was bareheaded for the first time. 'Sure, thanks.' He pulled it on, and Maddox saw his eyes relax slightly from squinting against the harsh sunlight. 'I guess I should still look like the captain, eh?'

'How many d'you reckon there are down there, Sergeant?' Gunnar's voice was sharp and detached again.

Rickover shrugged. 'Maybe two hundred. They've left the rest of their group up at the camp. They'll not leave their precious airstrip!'

Gunnar closed his eyes. 'They'll not be getting help by air. Not just yet. It's too obvious and doesn't fit in with their pretence of a natural rebellion.' He shook his head. 'My guess is that they'll get some more "freedom fighters" by sea.' He spoke with offhand bitterness which made the others stare at him. 'It's all to their pattern. You can just imagine how it will seem to the rest of the world. The poor peasants revolting against the imperialist yoke, the U.S. using the big stick to uphold a tottering regime.' His voice hardened. 'Oh yes, I've seen it all before right enough!'

Rickover propped himself on one elbow. 'Surely you don't think our people'd leave it like that?'

Gunnar shrugged. 'What does it matter to the Reds? Either way they've got us bogged down. If we leave Payenhau to the new government it'll be handing it to the Reds on a plate for any purpose they require. If we smash it to bits with an air strike no one will ever know or believe that the Reds weren't telling the truth.' He pounded his fists slowly against the hot concrete. 'There was only one way. To *hold* it, to stop it right here!'

Rickover said quietly, 'I guess you were the only one who realised that, sir.'

Gunnar gave a small smile. 'When you've put your hand in a fire once, you don't do it again in a hurry!'

Pip Maddox ducked as a stray bullet whined off the wall. 'But they must believe we're going to let them take over the island? They'd not leave their men to be mopped up from the air?'

Gunnar eyed him coldly. 'They will if they think it necessary. A few hundred guerrillas are a drop in the bucket compared with the success they've already achieved. They'll tie down another big force, drag our name through the mud like Viet Nam, make us dig deeper into our resources while they're sitting pretty and planning another offensive somewhere else!'

'But the *Hibiscus*, sir?' Pip was desperate. 'She'll bring help?'

'It'll be too late for us, I'm afraid. Too late for a clean finish.' Gunnar stood up and moved towards the doctor. He could no longer face the marine's faith and the ensign's pathetic beliefs in right and justice.

'Are you okay, Doc?' He shook the man's arm and saw a brief spasm of recognition cross Connell's tortured face. 'We'll be needing you again soon.'

Connell pulled his arm away. 'See what you've done? Are you proud now?' He rocked back and forth on his knees like a priest. 'You'll kill us all before you're done.'

Gunnar dropped his hand and dragged himself wearily towards the wounded colonel. Connell was right. In a few more hours or even minutes it would be over. They were no longer a force, representatives of power and stability. They were not even Americans. They were just men. *Mere men*, as the rear-admiral had so rightly observed. Cornered, beaten, yet hanging on because there was no other way.

Jago blinked his eyes and stared at him. 'Have any of my boys shown up yet, Gunnar?'

'Not yet.' Gunnar watched the will to live seeping away from

277

this hard, dedicated man. He almost envied Jago's empty belief and trust in the men who had betrayed him. 'I'm going
to move you soon. Back inside the tower.' The little tower
where he had watched Jago's quick-fired eagerness and confidence so long ago. 'If we had an M.G. it might be better,
but we can't hold them with rifles.'

Jago sighed. 'Did the commandant run for it too?'

Gunnar remembered the mad dash through the citadel's
empty corridors in a frantic search for weapons. He had found
the giant bulk of the commandant in his quarters overlooking
the anchorage. In the quick, nightmare picture he had
appeared like a newly caught and gutted whale. A heavy sabre
lay close by, and Gunnar found time to wonder if the girl he
had tormented for so long had taken her revenge. 'No, he
didn't run, Colonel. He died.'

Jago bit his lip. 'I guess I got the wrong idea about him.
Like everything else!'

A sailor shouted hoarsely, 'Here they come!'

Then they were all up and firing again. Blindly, wildly, with
the quiet desperation of cornered animals. Another seaman
fell, and after a brief pause Connell crawled to his side, but
when Gunnar looked to see if he was treating the great wound
in his shoulder he saw with sick horror that Connell was on
his knees, running a rosary slowly through his bloodied fingers.

Chief Anders was the next to go. An unseen Chinese had
somehow climbed up a wall support from the side of the courtyard while his comrades kept up a continuous fire along the
actual rampart. Anders saw him at the last minute as he clung
to the top of the wall and aimed his automatic at Gunnar's
back. Anders leapt at him, and before anyone could reach
him he had rolled over the top of the wall, still locked with
the other man in a final embrace.

Gunnar pulled the pins from two grenades and pitched
them over the wall, baring his teeth as the ground shook to
the mingled detonations. Soon now.

The air suddenly seemed to come alive with a different
sound, and for one instant Gunnar imagined that the enemy
had at last managed to get round behind with some new, unexpected weapons. His ears cringed from the fierce rattle of
cannonfire, the crash and whine of exploding shells and the
sudden screams from the courtyard below.

A seaman stood up, his arms in the air like a man at a ball
game. 'Jesus! It's the *ship*, sir! The goddamn *Hibiscus*!'

Then they were all at the wall, staring through the blue smoke towards the shallow, limping shape which appeared to be pushing itself through the fringe of fallen rock at the side of the anchorage, as if cutting across the land itself.

Every gun was firing, and Gunnar watched in silence as the vicious cannon-fire cut the attackers down from behind, followed them along the road, blasting them to bloody fragments as they scampered to escape their probing vengeance. The grey three-inch gun was high angled away from the citadel, and Gunnar knew that it was seeking a target further inshore, probably the mortars.

But he could no longer see clearly, and even the ship's shape seemed to merge with the sea itself. The ship had returned. To the events on the island it would make little difference.

But to him it meant everything.

17

Final Gesture

The *Osprey*'s cable locker had become like a furnace, so that Pirelli could not even doze to break the tension of waiting, and the sweat poured from his body in a continuous flood, as if he were standing in a shower.

He knew that the girl was still in the cabin adjoining his hiding place, yet because the hatch had been slammed shut he could no longer see what she was doing, and only occasionally had he heard her make any movement. His watch had stopped, and he had little idea of how long he had been listening and waiting. He had heard distant shots and some other vague explosions, but the gurgle of water round the boat's stem had deadened all but indistinct echoes.

Pirelli stiffened as he heard a sudden gust of laughter followed by the tinkle of breaking glass. More laughter, and this time it was accompanied by thuds along the upper deck and one shout of pain. The guards left on the boat were obviously enjoying themselves, he thought grimly.

He almost fell from his perch as the hatch banged open with

a violent crash and the cabin flooded with bright sunlight. There were two, men. He saw their legs first, brown skinned, the feet encased in stout leather sandals. They were both wearing short quilted coats in spite of the heat, and each of them carried a heavy automatic pistol at the waist, and one had a burp-gun tucked beneath his arm like a toy.

The two Chinese were obviously drunk, and stood for several seconds blinking vaguely in the semi-darkness, their eyes like black slits in their heavy, square faces. Surprisingly, they both sat down side by side on the narrow bunk and stared at the girl with flat, expressionless faces, as if she had just fallen from the sky.

Pirelli shifted slightly so that he could see her. She was standing quite still against the far side, her hands pressed on the curved wooden hull at her back, her lips parted in fear as she watched the two intruders. Pirelli could see that her neck and throat were shining with perspiration, and her hair was damp against her tanned skin like a veil. Pirelli found that his throat had gone dry as if coated with dust, and try as he might he could not control the rapid pounding of his heart, so that it seemed to fill the small place with sound. The bigger of the two Chinese was a slab-shouldered, brutish-looking man with a heavy jaw and the thick, roughened hands of a peasant. Pirelli could see the lust growing in his dark eyes, could watch it overcoming the dulled pleasure of the drink which they must have found somewhere on the upper deck. He wondered what had happened to the boat's wizened engineer, and decided that the cry of pain he had heard was probably the last sound he would ever make on this earth.

With a shock he heard the girl speaking. She kept her voice low and steady, as if she was using it with real effort. 'What are you doing here? You must go now!'

The second Chinese looked enquiringly at his companion, who said haltingly: 'You finish. All Yankee dead!' He pointed a thick finger at her and bared his yellow teeth in a wide grin. 'Boom! Boom!' He then translated his comments to his friend, who rocked with laughter until he broke off in a fit of violent coughing.

Pirelli mopped his face. Dead? The man was lying. Why was there still shooting? It was possible, however, that it would soon be over, and then what would he do? The thought of being a prisoner made him feel suddenly sick. He had heard often enough what Communist guerrillas did with their rare American victims.

The big man stood up and carefully laid his gun on the bunk. Very deliberately he unstrapped his belt and put that beside it. All the time he kept his eyes fastened on the girl, while his companion settled down with obvious enjoyment. Here it comes, Pirelli thought desperately, and there's nothing she can do about it.

With a quick movement the girl pushed herself from the side and ran for the ladder. Pirelli's vision was momentarily blacked out as her slim body blotted out the sunlight. Then she was down, pulled from the ladder with the helplessness of a child. She opened her mouth to scream but the big soldier struck her casually across the face so that her head jerked sideways, and she was momentarily stunned as he threw her on to the bunk and ripped her shirt from her shoulders. Straddling her body he pinned her hands to her sides as he peeled the shirt from her and threw it to his companion, who was stooping over to watch more closely.

Pirelli tried to drag his eyes away, but the sight of her naked body shining with sweat as she struggled beneath the man's weight held him like a nightmare. The Chinese said something to his friend and then he began to tug at the girl's belt with the inflamed madness of a wild beast.

There was a heavy thud, and with a frenzied bellow Burgess dropped into the cabin with the force of a sudden storm. His maniacal rage seemed to fill the cabin and swamp the stricken occupants with its fury. Splintered furniture scattered in his path, and taking the nearest Chinese by the throat he threw him full length across the cabin so that his head crashed against the timbers with the sound of a breaking wicker basket. The other man recovered his shocked surprise and leapt from the girl's prostrate body and plunged towards his piled weapons. Burgess wrapped his arms about his waist and together they rolled across the deck, grunting and snarling like panthers fighting over a prey. Lea Burgess pulled herself upright, her half-naked body showing the bright bruises left by the man's powerful hands, her eyes wide with terror as she staggered away from the two grappling figures at her feet.

Pirelli saw the first Chinese dragging himself into his small field of vision, his teeth bared in agony but his eyes unblinking as he moved crabwise across the deck, a heavy pistol clutched in his hand. The girl screamed, a sharp, desperate cry which seemed to unlock the last barrier in Pirelli's reeling mind, and with a frantic kick he pushed open the door to the chain locker and blundered into the open.

Several things seemed to happen simultaneously. The man on the floor at Pirelli's feet lifted his pistol and fired perhaps a split second before the heavy rifle butt crashed down at the base of his skull, and then Pirelli found himself facing the other Chinese, the man's great heaving chest within inches of the levelled barrel. From the corner of his eye Pirelli saw Burgess trying to drag himself clear, his chest glittering with blood where he had been caught by that one final shot.

Pirelli watched the other man's face, lulled momentarily by the completion of the surprise made by his entrance. The girl had her hand across her mouth as if mesmerised. Burgess lay propped against the side, his eyes dulled with pain but nevertheless fixed on Pirelli as if he no longer understood what was happening. Pirelli stood quite motionless, his wild beard and sweat-tangled hair matching his foul clothing and the appearance of complete degradation left by his voluntary imprisonment.

He felt the power moving in his cramped limbs like neat whisky, and almost playfully he allowed the rifle to waver away from the other man's panting body. The Chinese rocked on the balls of his feet and then plunged forward, his hands ready to close around the wavering rifle. With no more than the necessary effort required, Pirelli took half a pace to the right and swung the barrel upwards out of reach, at the same time allowing the butt to complete its half-circle and catch the charging man barely a hand's breadth above the groin. He heard the gasp of agony and watched with cruel satisfaction as the rushing figure stumbled and doubled over beside him. Before he reached the deck the rifle butt rose and fell once more, neatly behind the man's ear. The weapon moved only a few inches, yet behind it was all the anger and hatred which Pirelli had nursed and carried since the death of his only real friend, Grout.

He stepped back. 'No point in wastin' ammo.' His voice seemed loud after the fury of the battle. 'Now let's see what we kin do about you!' He brushed away the girl's dazed questions as he bent beside the bleeding Englishman. 'I was hopin' to get a free trip to Taiwan, see? I guess these bastards have fouled it up somewhat!'

Burgess said thickly: 'You're the deserter. You'll have to go back to your ship now.' He stiffened like a board as Pirelli's probing fingers moved inside his shirt.

Pirelli grunted, 'A right mess!' He fashioned a bandage from a piece of sheet off the bunk, his mind as busy as his fingers. *Hibiscus* was back again, it was not a guess or a rumour any more. He worked busily and methodically, his ears open to Burgess's slow and painful words to his daughter. He was apologising, pleading, and there were tears on the girl's face as she listened. He'll not live long, Pirelli thought bleakly. The bullet is deep inside his chest.

Burgess said through his teeth: 'They promised me gold, plenty of it, if I did what they said. But when the ship came back they thought I had done another deal, had double-crossed them——' He broke off in a fit of coughing. 'Just another failure! Just one more bloody failure!'

She touched his arm. 'Oh, Father, how could you have done it?' But there was no anger in her voice. Just despair, Pirelli thought.

The big Chinese groaned and moved his head very slightly. Pirelli stood up and seized him by the collar of his quilted jacket. The man was heavy, but Pirelli was a product of many years at sea, a hardened fighter who rarely thought of actual physical strain except in terms of combat. He dragged the man up the ladder and laid him beside the hatch. He paused on the ladder as he heard the distant clatter of heavy cannon-fire. *Hibiscus* was definitely back well enough! He bared his uneven teeth in a grin and ran lightly down the steps for the second man. He was an easier load, and without releasing his hold Pirelli pulled him to the gunwale and dropped him over the side. The other one was heavier, and hit the water with such force that a flock of gulls rose angrily from the deserted beach and circled around the *Osprey* in disordered confusion.

Pirelli wiped his hands on his legs and peered down at the two drifting bodies. He turned as he heard the girl's feet on the deck beside him. She had made some attempt to cover herself with the tattered shirt, but her face looked dulled with shock, and her shoulders shook as if she had just been beaten.

Pirelli eyed her thoughtfully. 'Got rid of them jokers. Next thing is to get th' hell out of here!' He gestured at the wheelhouse. 'Go an' see if there's any gas in the tanks.'

She stared at him dully, her face pale and empty of hope. 'What are you going to do?'

Pirelli pursed his lips and tasted their dryness. He had not

283

really looked very far into the future, but first things first. 'Get goin',' he remarked at length. 'The shore seems empty, but we'd never make it through their lines.' He almost laughed aloud. Through their lines! It sounded like one of Alan Ladd's old movies. 'The *Hibiscus* will be bottled up if she's in the bay, but she'll not be hangin' about, not any more.' He rubbed his bristled face. 'The doctor will help your old man, but——' He shook his head. 'I don't think he'll make it much longer.'

She turned away and said in a small voice: 'He'll think I've betrayed him. He'll think I lied to him——' Her head dropped and he heard her sobbing quietly.

Pirelli guessed she was referring to the captain, and said harshly: 'Don't you worry about *him*. He's fully occupied right now, I shouldn't wonder.' With sudden force he gripped her arm. 'It's you an' me now.' He peered into her face. 'I'm making a passage straight to the pen when I get back, but I don't somehow think this is the right time to leave the navy! Even the cage is better than what these bastards'd do to me!' He shook her roughly. 'Get on the wheel and start up. I'm going to slip the cable.' She made as if to go towards the small hatch above the engine room. 'Get to the *wheel*, you've had enough shocks for one day!' Pirelli watched her go and sighed. He had seen the dark streaks of blood which led to the hatch. The engineer had been butchered when the two guards had found the liquor. He licked his lips, better get it over with.

Gritting his teeth and fighting back the nausea he staggered from the engine room with the small bundle which had been thrown down on to the big diesel. The little man hardly made a ripple as he was dropped overboard, but floated with arms outstretched as if taking a quiet bathe.

Pirelli swung the big flywheel and with a shudder the diesel fired and began to rumble resentfully until he cut in the other cylinders and staggered back again to the sun-bathed deck. He gave a thumbs-up to the girl and ran forward to the small hand-capstan. Then, even as the anchor showed its dripping flukes above the surface, he heard the roar as the girl opened the throttle. She was still holding on it seemed. Handling the wheel would keep her mind busy for a bit. He reached the wheelhouse and took the spokes from her hands and spun them hard down. He watched the shore swinging across the bows, felt a slight breeze on his face and allowed himself a hollow belch.

284

She said: 'The tanks are all but empty. My father must have forgotten to take on fuel.'

Pirelli scowled. 'Maybe the Chinks decided to drain 'em just in case of a double-cross on his part!' He saw the pain in her eyes and added, 'It's no fault of yours.' He unslung the rifle and squinted at the shoreline. 'Keep close in. I don't want to be spotted just yet.'

He thought of Burgess in the cabin below. It was wrong for a man to die alone without knowing what was happening. He said gruffly: 'Take the wheel for a bit. I'm goin' to get the skipper.' He saw the girl's eyes beginning to fill again. 'Is there anythin' to drink?' She pointed to the side-locker and he scooped out a pair of full bottles. He held them up to the sunlight and said, 'It doesn't stop anythin', but it makes it easier to bear!'

Pirelli eased the big Englishman down on to the deck at the foot of the wheelhouse and readjusted the sodden bandage. He held out the bottle and was surprised to see a look of dumb gratitude on the man's pain-racked features.

'Thanks. And thank you for saving Lea from those——' He coughed and twisted his mouth with agony. 'I didn't really know——' Each word was painful to hear.

Pirelli felt lightheaded and wild, elated to a point of renewed madness. The boat moved ponderously along its course, and he was in charge of it. For the first time in his life he was needed. He tried to sneer at his own thoughts, to taunt himself for his stupidity at throwing away his chance of freedom for something he did not even understand. But he had been too long with his old way of life, too set in his ways to change after all.

Somewhere beyond the deceptive calm of the coastline there was his ship. If he reached her he would have to think again, but right now it was all that mattered.

* * *

Chief Tasker jog-trotted through the sagging gates to the citadel, his helmet bouncing on his narrow head, an M-14 with fixed bayonet angled across his lean body at the correct angle. He saw Gunnar leaning against the guard hut and skidded to a halt. 'The road's clear, sir.' His deepset eyes flickered across the captain's strained features and moved quickly around the courtyard. It was like a scene from hell. Some forty Chinese lay scattered and broken in the bloodied dust, and the surrounding walls were pitted with grenade fragments and scarred with bullets. Here and there some human remains smeared the pale concrete like some ghastly impressionist painting.

Gunnar shaded his eyes and stared towards the grey cube of the *Hibiscus*'s bridge and the glittering crucifix of her topmast. 'Is the ship secured?'

Tasker lowered his rifle. 'Sure is. It was lucky that wreck shifted off the sandbar. The exec managed to secure to it with not too much effort.'

Gunnar nodded, the sense of Maddox's decision seeping through his shocked mind. 'She'll be able to give covering fire from there.'

Tasker looked hard at his captain. 'You've sure had one helluva battle up here, sir. You've done right well.' He looked up as Sergeant Rickover clumped through the dust and rubble. 'Where's my drunken buddy, sir?' His thin mouth tightened as he saw the look in Gunnar's eyes. 'I see, sir.'

Gunnar pointed to the foot of the inner wall. 'Chief Anders is there. See that he's picked up before we leave.'

Tasker's face showed a rare sign of inner emotion. 'I've known Walt Anders for twelve years, sir. It don't seem possible——' He tightened his jaw and said harshly, 'I'll call up some of my landing party to clear this lot.' He gestured with his bayonet. 'I've got an M-60 mounted halfway down the hill. It'll sweep away any of the bastards who are still around!'

Half a dozen helmeted sailors crowded through the gates, and Tasker added: 'I reckon you're about all in, Captain. You go back to the ship an' I'll hold on here.' He gave a sad smile as Ensign Maddox limped into view, an empty rifle in his hand. 'Jesus, Mister Maddox, your brother'll be glad to see you in one piece!'

The ensign tried to smile back. 'God, look at all these bodies!'

Tasker said unfeelingly: 'There's more than a few of 'em on the hillside. They weren't expectin' the old *Hibiscus* to catch 'em on the jump!'

Pip Maddox swayed and Tasker seized his arm. 'Bear up! The boys are watchin' you, sir!' He gave the young officer's arm a squeeze. 'Hell, sir, the goddamn flag is still up, ain't it? What more d'you want?'

Rickover watched gravely as the first stretcher came down

the slope. 'What d'you aim to do, sir?' He saw his words acting across Gunnar's lined face. 'The Chinks will have a go as soon as it's dark. They'll bring up the mortars and smash your ship to bits!'

Gunnar tried to think. Close your eyes and you could imagine that everything was as before. The hot, unwinking sun across your face, the tang of salt. There was no more firing, and somewhere far off there was a goat crying to be milked.

He shook himself. 'I can't do any more, Sergeant. Without men we can't hold the citadel, and even with luck on our side it may not be possible to get clear of the channel.'

'We're pulling out then?' Rickover's voice was casual but he could see the effect of his words. He could have called it retreat from the answering bitterness in Gunnar's words.

'Yes, pulling out.' His voice quivered with the cold anger inside him. 'I've lost a fifth of the crew I came with. Good, ordinary, uncomplicated men who did as I told them because that's what they joined for.' He looked down at the carnage as if to torture himself further. 'And this is what they got. What *I* gave them!'

O'Brien, unwounded and unmarked to the last, marched across the courtyard, three rifles hanging across his shoulder. He stopped and said evenly, 'That's the lot, sir!'

Gunnar nodded. 'You did well, O'Brien. You all did.'

The big Texan grinned uncomfortably. 'I reckon we'll all get medals for this.' He closed his dust-rimmed eyes. 'I kin just hear it. "Anchors Aweigh" bein' played by the leatherneck band, an' the admiral beamin' all over his pan and sayin', "Here's yer medal, O'Brien, fer bustin' up my friggin' ship!"'

He went off chuckling to himself, his boots kicking the dust across the faces of the dead Chinese.

Rickover watched the torn emotions on Gunnar's features. 'You see, sir? There's nothing "*ordinary*" about men like that!'

Gunnar shrugged. 'Well, we might as well follow the others.' It was final. The finish.

Someone had recovered the whaleboat, and in silence he allowed himself to be ferried across to the waiting ship. Men lounged by the uncovered guns, and cigarette smoke mingled with that which still hovered above the hot muzzles. Empty cartridge cases lay scattered likes fools' gold across the blistered decks, and he saw the black stains below the bridge, the tell-tale punctures of the mortar bombs.

287

Maddox met him at the rail. He was different in some way, but Gunnar no longer trusted himself to assess anything clearly. The exec saluted and Gunnar saw the long red scar on his thick forearm.

'I'm keeping the men at battle stations, Captain, but I'm trying to rustle up some food for them.' Impulsively he reached out and seized Gunnar's hands in his own. 'I'm sorry, Captain, I'm sorry about everything!'

Gunnar looked past him, seeing vaguely that all the men were looking at him, their stained and tired faces curious and without hostility. Gunnar heard himself say: 'Thank you for coming back. You did a good job.'

Maddox forced a grin. 'I'm not sure you'll agree when you hear that I've lost the port prop, sir.' He helped Gunnar across the rail, hovering around him, watching his every move. 'I guess I'll learn ship handling the hard way!'

Gunnar turned and looked back at the quiet hills and the distant wall of the citadel. The discarded bodies, ugly and without dignity, the burned-out jeep by the gates. And above it all the gay patch of colour from Old Glory. He recalled Tasker's flat comment, 'The goddamn flag is still up, ain't it?'

Regan and Kroner had appeared beside Maddox, and they too seemed like strangers. Regan said: 'Welcome back, sir. Sorry we were too late for the big party.'

Gunnar could not face them. Their concern, their pity for what he had done was tearing him apart. They could have thrown his gesture back in his face, and stood aside from the man who would finally pay for his reckless and misguided beliefs.

Maddox said thickly: 'Where's Connell? I've got a couple of wounded down aft for him to look at.'

With sudden shock Gunnar realised that the doctor had not returned.

Rickover said quietly: 'He ran off, sir. I'm afraid he was too quick for me.'

The other officers exchanged uneasy glances, and Kroner asked in an awed tone, 'What, deserted?'

Rickover shook his head. 'Not deserted, sir. He just came apart. It was too much for him.'

Gunnar's eyes narrowed as he stared across the smooth water towards the black shadows of the west channel. It would not be easy with one screw. It was a pity they couldn't go back the way Maddox had brought the ship, through the narrow, impossible east channel. Even now he could not believe that Maddox had managed it. But it would be impossible with a crawling, side-slipping ship, and by now the enemy had probably hauled up some weapons to seal the tiny channel for good and all.

He wondered what the girl was doing right at this moment, what she was thinking of him, of what had happened.

But time was running away like dry sand, he must hold on for a few more hours. After that . . . He blinked away the film from his eyes and said: 'We were under radio silence, but the admiral will still be expecting his usual broadcast from Jago's transmitter. I think Yi-Fang intended to send the normal clearance to allay suspicion, but now that the radio's been smashed he'll have to try another plan.'

Maddox asked slowly, 'Won't they be looking for *us*, sir?' He waved his hand uncertainly. 'I mean, we were expected in Taiwan.'

Gunnar shrugged, 'The typhoon would have put us off course. I expect a hell of a lot of ships were scattered by that. They'll be slow to check up on just one small unit. No doubt they've got a recce plane somewhere about, following the storm just to make sure.' He was finding the physical effort of thought almost too much. 'No, my guess is that Yi-Fang will hurry up his takeover bid as from now. He knows we can't hold the citadel without help. If he's got half the sense I think he has, he'll be moving up his main force.'

Maddox opened his eyes wide. 'What, more of 'em?'

Regan nodded. 'It follows. They have to do something drastic if they're to make good the first move. Once in absolute control they can scream to the world that they've got their independence and that they're allying themselves to Red China, who just *happen* to have troops hanging around to give a hand!' He looked hard at the captain. 'What do you think we ought to do, sir?'

There was a silence and Gunnar could feel them all looking at him, their tired faces bonded together with their personal suffering and despair.

'We'll run for it.' Gunnar's words were like pieces of ice. 'There's nothing more we can do.' His voice hardened. 'If they don't want our help, they can all go to hell.'

He spoke with such vehemence that Maddox studied him with fresh concern. 'No, sir.'

'What d'you mean, "no"?' Gunnar felt the anger welling up

289

again. An argument now would finish him. 'That's what you wanted in the first place, isn't it?'

Maddox nodded. 'It was. Things have changed.'

'Nothing's different, Bob. I led you all into this, and there are enough dead men to prove I was wrong!'

A lookout's voice halted Maddox's reply. 'There's a crowd of 'em comin' along the beach, Cap'n!'

Gunnar snatched some glasses and levelled them on the long procession of figures as it wended its way along the strip of sand below the coast road. These were not soldiers, nor were they any part of the trained guerrillas which had attacked the citadel.

Gunnar could see the small group at the head of the column, Tao-Cho with a look of concentration on his birdlike features as he drove his staff into the sand before each determined step. There were women and children too, more and more, until they edged the beach like an endless bank of small trees.

'What do you make of it, sir?' Maddox sounded guarded. 'Is it a trick of some sort?'

Gunnar moved to the rail and beckoned to the men in the whaleboat. 'I don't know yet, but I'm going to meet him.'

Maddox peered at him with surprise. 'What, after what's happened? Let *me* go, sir!'

Gunnar smiled. 'No, Bob.' He came to a decision. 'But come with me if you like.'

Regan called: 'I'll cover you, sir. One false move an' I'll mow the lot of 'em down.'

Once more Gunnar found himself on the warm sand, his legs and muscles craving for rest and release. Behind him he could hear the clatter of ammunition as Tasker's machine-gun crew moved their weapon below the pier. This time there was no pretence, no hope of compromise. Gunnar tried to read the feelings in his own mind, but there was nothing, just a cold resignation, a last hold of duty.

Tao-Cho halted, and like a slow tide the long column of villagers and children welled up on either side of him and the elders, silent, watchful, and without defiance.

Tao-Cho lifted his long staff and with obvious effort broke it on the rocks near his sandalled feet. Then in a thin, emotional tone he said, 'I have come, Captain. I wish to make my peace with you.'

In the silence Gunnar could hear Maddox's hard breathing and the lap of water along the beach. He felt neither pride nor a sense of any achievement. Perhaps if it had happened when he had made his first contact with the old headman it might have been different. But then he had known his own misgivings too. Now they faced each other without guile or hope. There was shame, but there was understanding.

Gunnar said coldly, 'Your gesture will make no difference now.'

Tao-Cho's hooded eyes flickered like yellow stones in the sunlight. 'I have brought my people to you for protection. There are many women because their men are away with the fishing boats. But there are some men also, and we will do as you direct. Soon all the other villages will follow my example.'

In spite of his outward control the words had cost Tao-Cho a great deal, and Gunnar said quietly: 'It makes no difference. There is a greater power than yours in control now. Those you chose to trust will have no quarter left for you if you come to me for help.'

Tao-Cho said simply: 'They have already killed many of my people. I know now that their tongues were false.' He made a helpless gesture. 'There is no room for independence it seems.'

Gunnar smiled gravely. 'There never was, Tao-Cho.' He saw the people on the edges of the crowd craning forward to hear his words. Some understood, others translated for those at the rear.

Gunnar added slowly: 'I have done what I can. Instead of help and understanding I received lies and threats. My men have been killed, my cause has been dishonoured.'

Tao-Cho said with something of his old power, 'It was not only my people which disbelieved your words, Captain.'

Gunnar thought of Jago and the far-off chain of command. 'That is true. But you can see my ship, you know what I have left. Why should I ask my men to die for nothing?'

Tao-Cho held out his arms, and Gunnar suddenly saw him as a desperate, frightened old man. 'These children, Captain, would you leave them now?'

Gunnar kicked at the sand, his eyes aching with the dull pain in his head. It was unfair, it was so very unfair to use such means now. 'What are you telling me, Tao-Cho? Do you accept that your island is too important to be ignored by either side?'

'I do understand. And I know too that the man Bolod has soldiers coming even as we speak.'

291

Gunnar stiffened. 'So you knew what Bolod was doing?'

'A little. I waited to test his words.' Tao-Cho looked at Gunnar's cold eyes. 'He was known as Tsung.'

Gunnar turned towards the glittering sea and made himself stare at the friendly water. Tsung, the man he had spoken with, had touched, had even allowed to be with him on the islet to the north of Payenhau. One thought crowded upon another, like brush and dry grass crumbling before a forest fire. And he had sent the girl into his hands. At that fleeting moment he knew he would rather that Lea Burgess were dead than to leave her at Bolod's mercy.

'This ship, what do you know of it?' His voice had a sharp, metallic ring, and he could feel Maddox staring at him. 'Well, speak up, man!'

Tao-Cho seemed to wither before his hard stare. 'I do not know, Captain. But it is coming. Yi-Fang's men are staying by their camp until the extra men arrive. Then they will kill everyone who opposes them.'

Gunnar said harshly, 'And if I take my ship away, my leaders will come and destroy this island, and Yi-Fang, and everything else!' He waved his hand with a short, final thrust. 'They will not survive for long!'

Tao-Cho clasped his hands. 'Please, *please*, Captain!' Somewhere in the crowd a child began to whimper without understanding. 'You cannot leave us to die!'

Gunnar turned and faced Maddox. 'What can I do? I can't ask our men to fight now, after all this!'

Maddox bit his lip. 'I know it's your decision, Captain. But I think you'll find there'll be no argument from the rest of us!'

Gunnar faced the old man. 'Take your people to the citadel. Get every man, and woman as well, and arm them with what weapons you can find on the corpses below the walls. Stay there, and shoot at anyone who comes near. I can't, I *won't* promise you anything.' He faltered. 'But I'll do what I can. Without support, and with you turning against them, the rebels can't achieve much on their own.'

The headman sank on his knees, and Gunnar thought he saw tears in his small, hooded eyes. 'We will not forget, Captain!' The rest of his words were drowned by sudden hand-clapping from the watching villagers at his back.

Not cheering, but polite, determined clapping. It was unnerving, but seemed in some strange way to sum up the great gulf between the two ways of life.

Maddox said breathlessly, 'You sure pulled him down a peg or two!'

Bitterly Gunnar replied: 'I found no pleasure in taking away his pride. But it's too late for dignity now.' He stared desperately at the ship and its small wisp of smoke above the stack, 'It's just about late for everything!'

Once in the open water they could turn and run. No one would accuse him, and in any case the blame was already loaded at his door. Somewhere to the west was a ship, or maybe several ships. There was too much at stake for either side to back down now. The Reds had been told what they had to achieve. Gunnar had only himself to ask.

Ten minutes later he was back on the open bridge, the p.a. microphone in his hand.

'Now hear this.' He paused, his eyes fixed on the helmeted heads of the gunners below the bridge. Inwardly he prayed that the girl was already dead, released from the suffering and pain from which there was no escape. He cleared his throat. 'This is the captain speaking. You have seen and heard what is happening. There are people here who need our help, and it is our duty to give them our aid.' He faltered, hating the words which felt barren on his lips. 'I do not know what is waiting for us, but whatever it is we are in a bad condition for a real fight. I can no longer *tell* you to give your lives for nothing, I can only ask . . .' His words died away as a burst of cheering ran along the maindeck.

Maddox grinned up at him, his hands clasped together like a boxer's. 'That a good enough answer, Captain!'

Gunnar turned his face away and walked stiffly to the voice-pipe. 'Report to me when the engine room is ready to proceed!'

There was a hoarse shout from the deck as supported by a protesting Sergeant Rickover, Jago hopped to the rail, his helmet back on his head, his teeth bared with effort. Looking up at the bridge he shouted, 'If you think I'm going to leave the citadel in charge of a lot of goddamn heathens you've got the wrong boy, Captain!'

The grinning sailors lowered the two marines into the whaleboat and continued cheering as Jago was pulled ashore. Several Chinese ran to help him, but with angry determination Jago pushed them away, and using one of the boat oars like a stave began to stagger up the beach.

Regan shook his head. 'Jesus, what a scene!'

Kroner looked up at the bowed silhouette by the screen and said quietly: 'I think Jago understands at last. It's the least he can do now!'

18

Pirelli

Pirelli swore aloud as a sharp stone jabbed into his elbow, but he continued to push himself along the ground with his head just protruding above the short gorse. It had taken him several minutes to realise that he was on one of the smaller islets of Payenhau, but driven by heat and desperation he had given up caring. He was lying on the flat top of a small hill, and somewhere behind and below his position lay the *Osprey*. From a sign of hope and escape she had changed into a useless mass of timber when the engine had gurgled and died for the last time. He had savagely thrown the anchor into the shallow water and lowered himself on to the smooth sandy beach, half expecting a bullet to smash him into the ground with each cautious step.

He had left the girl on the boat, her father's head pillowed in her lap, and he now wondered what he would tell them when he returned. He wondered also why he was being so cautious, the islet, like everything else, was deserted and barren, and in any case what did it matter any more? They could either die of thirst or be taken prisoner at some stage when the rebels had finished their work elsewhere.

He thought of Burgess and the strange, inner determination which was making him cling to life like a drowning man. Pirelli had given him the whisky to ease his last moments, but instead the drink seemed to have sustained, even restored him in some way. He spoke half to himself, long rambling remarks about his past life, about ships and places that meant nothing to Pirelli but which made the girl bow her head and smooth the dying man's hair from his fierce, angry eyes with something like love. She was calmer, more composed, Pirelli thought, but it was unlikely it would last when he got back to tell them he had been unlucky in his search. He was not even sure what he was looking for. An abandoned fishing boat, some food and shelter? He could not be sure. He just had to get away, to do something, *anything*.

He stiffened as a gentle splutter of engines moved into his confused thoughts, and he wriggled towards the edge of the hill, which ran down into a narrow wedge of beach in a long slope of broken, gravel-like stones. Pushing the rifle in front of him and ignoring the sharp stones under his legs he eased his way to the very edge, until he was only half covered by a patch of stubborn gorse. For a moment he thought of running back the way he had come. If a boat was coming it could only mean more danger. It might fall upon the helpless fishing boat, and that would be that. But every limb and muscle ached with fatigue, and in the steady glare from the sun he felt dull and sick.

With a start he realised that the left side of the fallen rock wall had changed shape, had hardened into a firm vertical line as a small, dirty landing craft thrust its blunt bows into view and headed for the beach. Pirelli blinked away the sweat and gripped the rifle with nervous determination. He realised that his reactions were already slower, and this knowledge made him hold his breath as the boat grew larger and grated noisily against the shingle. It was making hard work of it, and Pirelli realised that it was heavily loaded, although he could not see more than four heads above the hull's flat sides.

In a flurry of foam the twin screws pushed the bows on to the beach, and with a final roar died into silence. The ramp fell like a drawbridge, and Pirelli gasped with amazement as he saw the boat's contents. Even in the heat haze which persistently hovered above the water he could recognise the bulky, uncompromising shapes of navy depth-charges. He could also see the big yellow numbers painted on the nearest ones, the *Hibiscus*'s numbers!

Two Chinese in quilted jackets wandered down the ramp and relieved themselves in the swirling water, their backs towards him, and another lounged against the charges, a rifle across his shoulder as he shouted down to them.

Pirelli lowered his head and tried to think more clearly. *Hibiscus* had probably dumped her charges for safety's sake, and now these Chinese were about to make use of the little L.C.I. for their own purposes. As if to confirm this he heard a grating bang, and looked up to see the first depth-charge being rolled down the ramp to land heavily in the shallow water.

Pirelli squinted along his sights and toyed with the idea of shooting the nearest man in the back. The second charge rumbled down into the sand and lodged firmly against the first. Pirelli relaxed his finger on the trigger. It was no good. At this range he might only get one, two at the most. The others were still safe aboard the boat, and he had already noted the unsheathed Browning mounted beside the steering positing. No, he would have to think of something, and fast. The L.C.I. was not much of a craft, but it floated, and it was mobile. After the storm, it was probably one of the few left serviceable in the whole island. With it he could easily reach the *Hibiscus* before she sailed. After that he would take his chances again. But at least he would be with his own kind.

He almost screamed as a hand touched his arm, and as he swung the rifle he choked: 'Jesus! I coulda killed you!'

The girl lay quite still, her face only inches from his own. Then she looked past him at the boat and the struggling soldiers who had almost succeeded in levering the second charge clear. 'I had to come.' Her voice was steady, but Pirelli could see the agony in her dark eyes. 'My father is getting worse. I think we should stay together.' She stared at the L.C.I. 'What are they doing here?'

Pirelli controlled the tingling nerves in his body with an effort. 'They're dumpin' the charges. Too much weight, I guess, for what they have in mind.'

Her mouth trembled. 'I wish we could kill some of them!'

Pirelli ignored the venom in her tone and said sharply, 'How do you feel?' He saw the anger change to uncertainty in her eyes and added hastily: 'I've a plan. It might not work, but I need your help.'

She gripped his wrist, her hand firm and hot. 'Anything. Just tell me what to do.'

Now that he had committed himself Pirelli was apprehensive, yet filled with a kind of eagerness which he had never known before. He was making more decisions, holding their lives in his hands. He rubbed his chin and said doubtfully: 'I want those jokers distracted. They'd no doubt shoot anyone that appeared on 'em sudden like, but you,' he stared hard at her face, 'you might just do it.'

There was a shout and another figure appeared by the ramp. He heard the girl gasp: 'That's Major Yi-Fang! This must be important!'

Pirelli grinned coldly. 'We'll see!' He pointed to the sea

beyond the right side of the beach. 'Could you swim from there? I mean, can you get into the water without them seein' you?'

She nodded gravely, her face suddenly calm and determined. 'I will do it.'

Pirelli felt suddenly anxious and uncertain. 'It might not work. They might kill you before I get a chance to——'

She gave a small smile, her eyes searching his face with something like tenderness. 'You are a strange man. You are worried about *me* when you are in so much danger. I think you are not so hard as you pretend!'

He grinned. 'I surprise myself sometimes!'

She squeezed his arm. 'I will go now.' She moved into the gorse and disappeared, so that it was hard to imagine she had been with him.

A spasm of fresh nerves made Pirelli reach feverishly through his pockets for fresh magazines, and then with painstaking care he brushed the sand from the rifle sights and made one last check of the firing mechanism. There was no time for the slightest error. Even now he could not be sure how he had persuaded the girl to risk her life with such a mad scheme. He was not even sure he had intended such an idea. It was almost as if *she* had decided, had been determined to sell her life to give him a chance to save her father.

He tried again to settle himself more comfortably in the sunbaked stones, and watched as the Chinese rolled another charge from the ramp.

Pirelli caught his breath as from the corner of his eye he saw a quick flash of spray a few yards from the beach to the extreme right. His shoulders and fingers ached with concentration as he kept his eyes riveted on the labouring Chinese, and felt relief as first one then the other of the two on the beach halted, caught off guard, and then gaped along the sand as the girl reached the steep shelf of the beach and began to wade ashore. Pirelli heard them shout, and allowed his narrowed eyes to stray briefly before he wrenched them away and back to the men by the boat. She was naked, her hair plastered against her shining limbs, her supple body glittering with droplets of salt as she waded slowly but steadily on to the hot sand. There she paused, not looking at the soldiers, then with slow deliberation she lifted her hands behind her head and equally calmly began to shake out her hair from her shoulders.

The two soldiers shouted, and with arms outstretched began

to shamble towards her. The one with the rifle had already come down the ramp and was yelling encouragement, his teeth white, everything but the naked girl entirely forgotten.

Pirelli felt his hands tremble as he moved the rifle a bare half-inch and squinted at the officer inside the open hull. He alone seemed in control of himself. Pirelli knew enough about officers to understand what this distraction would do to the man's immediate plans, and saw Yi-Fang stride angrily to the head of the ramp, his pistol already out of its shining holster. Yi-Fang would know the girl, he would realise what had happened even if he did not already know the fishing boat had escaped from his guards.

Pirelli blinked away a film of sweat, ignoring the soldiers' hoarse shouts, shutting out the realisation that there were only seconds before they reached the helpless girl. The narrow point of the foresight hovered and steadied on Yi-Fang's contorted features and then dropped to a point below his stomach. There was no point in taking chances. Gently, lovingly, his finger squeezed, and his shoulder hardened behind the small impact of the gun's recoil.

Yi-Fang must have moved at the very instant of firing, yet even as the smoke fanned back across Pirelli's face he threw up his hands and swung sideways, his left leg buckling under him as if it had been hewn away by an axe. The armed sentry seemed petrified, and for his last few moments could only gape at his writhing officer. Pirelli's second shot went home. This time the target had not moved, and without a sound the man fell back across the waiting depth-charges.

The running Chinese had skidded to a stop, their deep footmarks barely two yards from those of the girl, who stood like a statue, her arms still in mid-air.

The two wretched men looked back at the silent boat, and then peered helplessly towards the sea. They were caught in the open, without their weapons, and there was nothing left of their earlier strength and open lust. Yet Pirelli felt neither compassion nor pity. Only the sense of urgency remained, yet he waited until the girl had turned her face away and then he fired one short, vicious burst. The sand leapt at their feet, and beyond them the water threw up a small pattern of dancing white feathers. It was over. The two Chinese lay side by side, their dark shapes waiting for the gently lapping tide.

Pirelli stood up and with a further glance at the boat vaulted over the edge and slithered down the steep slope, his mind clearing with the pain of his sudden descent as he realised that he had succeeded.

After glancing briefly at the sentry's glazed eyes he turned and looked down at Hi-Fang. The major was lying propped against the side, his face screwed up into a tight knot of agony as he clasped his hands across his shattered knee. Deftly he kicked the man's pistol into the water and walked slowly around the charges which still remained aboard. There were seven all told, but it was too late to do anything about them.

There were no other Chinese aboard, and with a further glance at the wounded officer to ensure that he was really helpless, Pirelli walked back to the open beach. The girl was exactly as he had last seen her, and with sudden shock Pirelli realised just what her actions had cost her. Quickly he picked up a quilted tunic from the ramp and ran towards her. She did not even try to hide herself from his eyes, but stood staring at the two dead men by her feet, and Pirelli could see the quivering on her skin as if she were standing in an Arctic wind instead of hot sunlight.

Gruffly he said: 'Put this on. There's no time to find your clothes.'

Obediently she allowed him to drape the jacket around her, then she said, 'I'm all right now.'

Pirelli stared at her. Whatever it was costing her, she was in control of herself, he thought.

As they appeared on the ramp Yi-Fang bared his teeth and said between gasps of pain: 'You are fools! You cannot escape!' Then he fell silent as the rifle muzzle lifted to within an inch of his face.

Pirelli said calmly, 'Just keep goin' like that an' you'll get yours!'

Yi-Fang looked at the girl, his glazed eyes focussing with difficulty on her tanned legs which still gleamed from her swim. 'It is over for you. Your captain is going——' He groaned as a new spasm of pain lanced through him. 'But he will soon be dead with the others!'

Pirelli said harshly: 'You just go aft, miss. I'll take care of this bastard!' The rifle wavered in his grasp and he knew that the lust to keep on killing was stronger than ever.

Yi-Fang added slowly: 'Our leader knows what he is doing. Even now a ship is drawing near to finish your captain and his damaged *Hibiscus*!' His words were like insults, spat out with all his remaining hatred. 'Then you and your kind will be done for! But slowly, until you are made to pray for death!'

Pirelli began to winch up the ramp. So *Hibiscus* was damaged. And she was sailing to intercept some other ship. Yi-Fang had no cause to lie, not now.

He heard the girl say, 'We must hurry!'

Pirelli ran aft and paused beside the controls. 'What about this maniac? Shall I drop him overboard?'

She shook her head. 'I want him to *see* what he has done!'

Pirelli sighed with relief as both engines whined into life. Easily he backed the boat into deep water, and with his eyes squinting against the glare he gunned the motors to full power and sent it pounding away from the beach where the two figures still lay as they had dropped. It took another precious twenty minutes to encircle the islet and manœuvre alongside the anchored *Osprey*.

He settled Burgess as comfortably as he could beside the depth-charges in a position where he could not see the wounded officer, and then roughly grasped the girl's arm and said, 'It's no use, we'll have to ditch her!' He saw the anguish on her face. 'The Chinks may have some fuel. They'd soon catch us in her!'

Using the L.C.I. as a bulldozer, he nudged the big fishing boat into deeper water, and then with the engines turning very slowly he ran back aboard the deserted deck, past the bloodstains now black and dried in the sun, and down into the silent engine room. It was a matter of minutes to open the sea-cocks, and by the time he had returned to the other craft the *Osprey* was already listing and beginning to settle down.

Burgess called out: 'What's happening? What have you done to my boat?'

Pirelli's eyes fastened on the girl's face. She was crying silently, but her voice was steady as she called: 'It's all right, Father! We'll come back for her later!'

Pirelli gunned the engines so that Burgess should not hear the savage inrush of water, the sickening clatter of falling gear as the *Osprey* began to roll over on to her side. The boat I was going to Taiwan in, he thought vaguely. He rubbed his sore face with dulled amazement, but his brain still refused to accept what he had done.

She said quietly: 'Thank you. The *Osprey* meant all the world to him.'

Pirelli nodded. 'I kin understand that.'

300

She added after a few moments, 'What did Yi-Fang mean about the other ship?'

He shrugged, his eyes watching a nearby clump of fanged rocks. 'I guess it was only natural for the Reds to bring up more support. No goddamn risin' would be any good without that.' He nodded as the thought came to him. '*Hibiscus* is all there is. The cap'n'll have to take a crack at 'em.' He added grimly: 'Don't worry. Old Gunnar is a cool bastard.'

She stared up into his craggy face. 'Is that what you think?'

Pirelli grinned. 'He may be a nice enough guy for *you*, but he's been a right tough cookie as a skipper!'

Burgess called, 'Are we there yet?' Then in a different voice: 'Tell the quartermaster I want the first lieutenant immediately! I'm going ashore to see the admiral about the regatta. Yes, that's what I'll do.' He laughed a deep, hollow sound. 'We'll show 'em who's cock of the fleet!'

The girl said, 'My God, he's rambling again!'

'Leave him. It's better this way.' Pirelli jumped as a distant squawk echoed around the hills and sent the gulls skyward again. 'Jesus, that's *Hibiscus*! I'd know her old hooter anywhere!'

There was gun-fire, followed by the distorted sounds of falling rock. Flatly he added: 'She's sailed. We've missed her!' He stared back at the boat's frothing wake. 'Christ, after all this!'

They rounded the last islet, and before them lay the empty anchorage. Then he felt the girl at his side. 'Look at the citadel! The flag!'

Pirelli whistled softly. 'There are some of 'em left then. No wonder your cap'n is goin' to have a go at the other ship!' He steered towards the sagging pier, his eyes taking in the crumpled bodies, the black craters of shell- and mortar-fire.

A few rifle shots sounded occasionally and he said at length, 'Snipers, I guess.'

The boat banged into the piles and brought down a tangle of broken planks, but Pirelli cut the engines and swung the Browning on its mount to cover the road. He heard her cry, 'I can see the sergeant on the wall!' And a minute later, 'He's coming!'

Sure enough, the big marine was loping down the road, his head bowed as he weaved from side to side, a carbine held before him like a spear. Rickover threw himself the last few feet and lay face down on the pier. 'Well, I'll be!' He grinned

301

at the girl. 'Back with us I see!'

Pirelli grated, 'Give me a hand!' Then he leapt for the Browning his eyes flashing. 'Jesus, what was that?' He had seen a brief movement near the beach.

Rickover pushed the barrel down. 'Forget it. It's Connell, your doctor.' His eyes were empty as he watched the stooping, haphazard movements of the distant figure. 'He's administering rites or something to all the dead back there.' He sighed. 'I can't get to him, it's completely zeroed in by snipers. But they don't shoot at madmen.' He added bitterly, 'It's about all they don't shoot!' Then he retrieved something of his old competence. 'Well, come on with me. I've got half the island population up there, and a few soldiers who've found their way to us.' He grinned. 'Like Noah's goddamned ark it is!'

Burgess called out, 'Where is the *Hibiscus*?'

Rickover shrugged. 'Shot her way out just now after knocking off a coupla mortar teams on the headland! You shoulda seen her!' In a more serious tone: 'The captain's off to intercept some Red ship or other. All we can do is sit tight and pray for the cavalry to arrive before the Injuns!'

Burgess called weakly: 'Pirelli, come here! Come *here*!'

There was such a rasp in his voice that Pirelli imagined he was wandering again. He gestured forward. 'Yi-Fang's down there, Sergeant. Take him up to the fort. I'll bring the ole commander here.'

Rickover gave a silent whistle. 'Yi-Fang! Jesus H. Christ, my colonel'll sure be glad to see *him*!' He yanked the groaning officer to his feet and threw him across his broad shoulders. 'Right, come as soon as you can. It's a bit dangerous around here!'

Pirelli spat, 'It ain't exactly bin a picnic for *us*!'

The marine laughed and took a quick look across the roadway towards the low bank of hills. 'Well, here goes!' He called to the girl, 'Just keep on my right and you'll be okay!'

She hung back. 'I'll come with my father.'

Rickover shifted his unwilling load, then broke into a shambling run, each step bringing a cry of agony from the helpless Yi-Fang.

Pirelli dropped beside Burgess and said quietly, 'Is it bad, skipper?'

Burgess shook his head. 'Must speak to Lea. Must. Urgent!'

So he's giving in at last, Pirelli thought. 'Here, miss!' She climbed down beside them, and Pirelli tried not to stare at her face as she knelt down on the rough decking.

Burgess opened his eyes as if to devour every part of her. 'You're a good girl. I can never forgive myself for what I said to you, for what I did. There is still time to make amends, perhaps, with luck.' He coughed harshly. 'I wanted to keep you clear of all this——'

Pirelli bit his lip. Burgess had not seen his daughter naked and alone on that beach like a tethered goat for a man-eater. He stiffened as Burgess added: 'Please go with Pirelli. I want to stay here!'

'I'll not leave you, Father. Not now.' There was no tremor, just a faint hoarseness in her voice which made Pirelli want to take her away.

Burgess struggled up into a sitting position. 'Go now!' With a touch of anger, 'That's an order!'

There was a clatter of falling stones and Rickover peered down at them. 'For God's sake, are you still chirruping down there?' He sounded anxious. Pirelli helped her up on to the fallen piles and watched Rickover's hand fasten on her wrist.

Once more he bent over Burgess and then stiffened as the dying man began to speak directly into his ear.

Rickover unslung his carbine and peered round the broken woodwork, his eyes moving very slowly across the silent hills. 'It's too open here. We should get going!'

She was about to reply when the L.C.I.'s engines roared into sudden and violent life, so that the pier all but collapsed in the savage backwash from the racing propellers.

'What th' hell!' Rickover dragged her clear as Pirelli's face appeared beside the controls.

Pirelli cupped his hands. 'I've gotta go with him! He'd never make it on his own!'

Rickover yelled, 'Come back, you goddamn fool!' He tugged the girl behind him as a single shot whimpered overhead. 'The mad, crazy bastard!'

The girl struggled to reach the pier but Rickover held her pressed inside his arm. 'It's no use,' he said heavily, 'they're clear.'

The boat swung in a tight arc and began to gather speed. Once Pirelli looked back and cursed himself. He could see the tall marine with the girl in her soldier's jacket close at his side. He had wanted to say a lot of things, to try to explain, but it was too late now.

He felt Burgess's fingers tugging at his leg and looked down

303

with a sad grin. 'Come on then, ole fire-eater! Let me prop you at the wheel while I get the Browning rigged up.'

The L.C.I. entered the main channel, so close to the high rock walls that it was almost invulnerable.

Pirelli propped the dead Chinese soldier beside Burgess and slapped a cap on his lolling skull. 'Might throw them a bit!' He reached for his whisky bottle. 'Well, come on, skipper! What about one last snort?' He drank long and deeply, his eyes watering as he held back his head and allowed the spirit to soak down his chin.

Burgess sat slumped behind the wheel, his eyes fixed on some invisible point over the bows, his face set in a mask of fanatical determination.

Pirelli peered astern, but the side of the cliff had blotted out the pier and the anchorage. He felt suddenly lost and afraid, but as the neat spirit ground harshly across his empty stomach he threw back his head and laughed again and again.

Long after the boat's wash had smoothed from the channel's twisting surface, his laugh hung behind like an epitaph.

19

'It will be an Honour'

'Stop engine!' Gunnar stepped from the forward grating and allowed the heavy glasses to fall against his chest. The slow westerly breeze had almost dropped away, so that the ship glided with her own momentum on an unbroken sea, the surface of which shone like undulating green glass. The wraith of stack smoke hovered around the signal halyards, and throughout the whole ship there seemed to be an unnatural silence.

Across the slowly swaying stern Gunnar could see the brown smear of Payenhau, a casual brush stroke against the two prominent colours of sea and sky, made more indistinct by the hovering mist which broke the fineness of the horizon lines like fallen cloud.

Gunnar found time to marvel at the way his ship had managed to get this far on half power, with the quartermaster fighting screw and rudder every foot of the way. He realised dazedly that he had hardly moved more than a step or so in either direction since *Hibiscus* had made that last push through the channel, had deluged the waiting mortars with such a savage curtain of fire that within minutes they had been blasted to fragments. At one point the ship's maddened gunners had brought down a whole section of cliff, complete with a machine gun and some half a dozen Chinese guerrillas.

The first tense moments were past, lost with all the other terrible memories until some future time. The milky sea seemed at peace, with only their small vessel to mar its unbroken waste and disturb its vigilance. Was it the same sea? The typhoon's fury, the aftermath of destruction and misery, where were they?

He wiped his face as Maddox stepped on to the bridge, his face grim and heavy. 'They're ready, Captain.'

They were all waiting again. Even the ship seemed to be cocking her ears as he stepped down on to the ladder and climbed slowly to the gently swaying maindeck. The men at the guns watched him pass. Some nodded companionably, like greeting a casual friend, others studied his face as if to read their own fate.

On the small fantail the bodies were lined neatly along the lowered rail. In the cramped space the shock of seeing them made Gunnar falter, there seemed to be so many of them. Pathetic and without familiarity, dressed in quickly sewn canvas, they were already part of something lost. Two seamen held the only remaining spare flag across the centre of the line like a canopy, their grimy faces like masks as they stared at each other without recognition. Other men crowded around in an untidy semicircle, heads craned, hair ruffling in the small breeze. Here and there a hand moved, or a man touched his own face with uncertainty and tightly held grief.

He saw Malinski, white-faced and strained from his constant battle with the engines, standing close beside his giant chief, Duggan. There were firemen and seamen, an aproned cook and Slattery, the steward. Ensign Maddox, stiff-backed beside Kroner, his young face lined with determination, but his eyes bright with the hidden lie.

Maddox handed Gunnar the scribbled list and removed his cap. Gunnar looked slowly down the list of names, and as he did so the dull, inert shapes seemed to come alive again for those few passing seconds.

Chief Anders. Bella, seaman yeoman. Carkosi, radioman.

Norris, quartermaster. Dabruzzi, seaman. Chavasse, seaman, Jackson, signalman. Laker, sonarman. Shafer, machinist's mate. Carmody, fireman. He found that he was reading their names aloud, speaking to them. There were so many. Too many. And this was not even the end. The rest of them might not even get time for a burial.

He opened the well-thumbed Book and began to read. From the corner of his eye he saw Chief Tasker bend down and brush a piece of loose thread from his friend's shroud and then return to his position of rigid attention.

Gunnar's words hung in the air: 'We commend unto Thy hands of mercy most Merciful Father, the souls of these our brothers departed . . .' How much more could he stand? He gritted his teeth as the first splash came alongside. One by one, and he felt the sting of salt against his cheek as the last man went overboard.

He looked over the Book, searching his men's faces. There should have been more for them, so much more. But there was only his own voice. Somewhere in the press of figures he heard someone sobbing quietly, without shame, and another had his arm around a friend's shoulder.

Gunnar thought back to what he had just read, the words' real meaning only just reaching him. 'The days of man are but as grass; for he flourisheth as a flower of the field. For as soon as the wind goeth over it, it is gone: and the place thereof shall know it no more.'

He looked up, his eyes dull and empty. The deck was bare again, and the two seamen were folding the flag in silence.

Chief Tasker faced him. 'Thank you, sir. He'd have liked that.' Then without waiting for the dismissal he turned on his heel and strode away.

Maddox saluted. 'Fall out, sir?'

Gunnar nodded. He wanted to add something. He could not make it right, but it would break the dreadful silence.

He returned the salute. 'Very well, Mister Maddox. Carry on.' He pushed blindly through the watching men and made his way back to the bridge, where Regan waited beside the compass, his cap beneath his arm.

'Tell the engine room to continue with revs for seven knots, Mister Regan.'

The telegraphs answered below his feet, the screw began to thrash at the lapping water. He had a brief but stark picture of the canvas-shrouded figures as they glided deeper and deeper into permanent darkness. The little ship began to move forward again with nearly two thousand fathoms beneath her slender keel. It was a long journey to the bottom, Gunnar thought.

He swung his glasses slowly across the hazy horizon, blotting out the faces and memories behind him.

Regan said flatly: 'We can't rely on the radar, sir. It took quite a few slugs as we came through the gap.'

Gunnar nodded. It hardly seemed to matter now.

'Would you like me to take the con, sir?' This time it was the exec's voice, concerned and husky.

'Thank you, Bob, no.' If Maddox had been angry or defiant it might have been better.

Maddox leaned on the screen, his eyes closed against the sun. 'While you were reading, sir, I was thinking.'

Gunnar tightened his jaw. Don't say any more, for God's sake. Don't you know how close I came to breaking back there?

Maddox said: 'I kept thinking of a musical I went to see when I was just a kid. It was *Oklahoma*, and I remember how I balled when they sang "Poor Jud is dead——".' He glanced at Gunnar's grave face. 'Is that stupid?'

Gunnar said quickly, 'What are you going to do if you get out of this?' He had to force Maddox out of it. He could not stand much more of his compassion.

'Me?' Maddox scratched his chest. 'I guess that as soon as we hit the dock I'll send a wire. Not just a goddamn letter.' He tapped his breast pocket. 'No sir, a real urgent wire.' He grinned in spite of his obvious tenseness. 'Why should Pip get married before me, eh?'

Gunnar nodded and turned towards Regan. 'Tell the lookouts to keep their eyes skinned. Any ship will be hard to spot in this haze!'

Maddox said: 'Do you really expect trouble out here, sir? I mean, they're cutting it rather fine.'

Gunnar shrugged. 'It's only been a matter of hours, even if it seems a lifetime. They'll be here all right, and whether they expect us or not, they'll be all out for a quick victory!'

Maddox eyed the captain's profile with growing anxiety. Every second of strain and danger had left its mark on Gunnar's pale features. He saw too the way Gunnar moved his hands with quick, nervous movements, as if he were only half aware what he was doing.

It's the girl, Maddox thought. He keeps thinking of her instead of himself. On one hand there's the ship, a broken, limping wreck which at any moment he will be expected to take right down the enemy's teeth with neither hesitation nor question. On the other there's Lea Burgess. If she was dead Gunnar might be satisfied. But to have her and then lose her to a fate he could only guess at was tearing him apart.

There was an excited shout behind the bridge, and for one instant Maddox imagined that a ship had indeed been sighted. But Kroner galloped on to the gratings, his film star's face alight with surprise. 'Sir! I've got radio touch with the island!' He stood aside as two of his men gently lowered a chipped khaki radio set on to the deck at his feet. 'It's the one we were using during the survey. It's one of Colonel Jago's close-link sets of the type used the day Inglis was caught in the ambush.'

Kroner knelt beside the battered case, his hands moving carefully across the controls. 'It's stretching it a bit, but I'll have a go.' They all stood and watched as Kroner tried each dial in turn. 'Hello, Dodger, hello, Dodger, do you read me?' Kroner sensed the tension at his back. 'I'm doing my best, but it's asking a lot of this set.' He tried again: 'This is Spartan, come in, Dodger. Hello, Dodger, do you read me?'

Then it came, faint and uneven, the voice distorted like a man calling through a waterfall. 'This is Dodger. Come in, Spartan——' There was a loud interruption and they all stared at the set as if it were some sort of talisman.

The voice was Rickover's, there was no doubt about that.

The set squawked again, 'We are holding the citadel.' A pause and more rushing sounds. 'We can see you from the tower, but only just. Very bad visibility.'

Regan said in a surprised voice: 'See us? How in hell can they?'

Gunnar waved him down. The little tower was high above the citadel, which was itself at the top of the island's main range of hills. Yes, they could quite likely see the little ship afloat in the haze even if objects closer inshore were invisible.

He listened intently as Kroner spoke back across the glittering water. It was not much help, but it was a small link. It seemed to make all the difference to know that someone, somewhere, knew what was happening, and cared.

In a tight voice he said, 'Ask him how many are safe in the citadel.'

Kroner blinked up from his toy. 'Yes, sir.' He repeated Gunnar's enquiry almost word for word, and then gave a yelp of indignation as Maddox shoved him aside and seized the handset. 'This is Spartan. Is the girl, Lea Burgess, alive?' His words seemed to crash into the silent bridge like grenades, but Maddox did not look at the others.

Rickover sounded as if he was laughing. 'Alive an' well. She's right here beside me, she sends her——' There was a rush of static and Maddox handed back the set to Kroner. 'Sorry, Don. But you take a helluva long time to get to the point!'

'I don't see——' Kroner caught Maddox's eye and grinned sheepishly. 'Oh, I *see*!'

Maddox felt Gunnar grip his shoulder, but when he turned the captain had walked to the front of the bridge, his face hidden from all of them. There, thought Maddox breathlessly. Just hold on to that one bit of good news, you poor bastard!

The set whistled and banged, and then Rickover said urgently: 'In two minutes you will have crossed into a dead patch. The hills will kill what little reach we have.' Another pause, and they were all looking at the scarred speaker. All except Gunnar, who still stood with his face to the sea.

'This is Dodger. Now hear this. There is smoke to the northwest of you. At a guess I would put it at fifteen miles.' His tone was urgent. 'Yes, it is smoke.' The voice was fading, curtained away with a final roar of static: 'Good luck. Good luck. Good luck.' Then the speaker went completely dead.

Gunnar turned slowly and leaned on his elbows against the screen. He looked at their faces and suddenly smiled. 'Well, at least we don't have to rely on the radar now!'

Regan said sharply: 'The enemy'll be up to us very shortly, sir. What's the plan?' He spread hands. 'We've not got a lot to offer!'

Gunnar nodded. It seemed to sum up their entire position. One screw, and such scanty gunpower that it was almost out of the question to consider a head-on clash.

'A bit of bluff, and a bit more guts,' Gunnar said at length. How trite the words sounded, yet he was conscious of a feeling of unbelievable peace within him. The little contact with Rickover had seemed to sweep away the uncertainty and the bitter despair. Whatever happened, they were no longer alone. Perhaps they never had been. But *she* was safe, that compensated for so much. Bolod was not important now. If he died, there would always be others like him.

309

'Send the men to battle stations.' He listened to the harsh clamour of alarm bells. 'And hoist that other ensign. It'll show we mean business.' It'll also serve as a shroud for us, the inner voice added.

Regan turned to leave. 'I guess it'll be up to my little three-inch, sir?'

Gunnar eyed him with sudden affection. Whatever his other shortcomings, Regan was completely reliable in this sort of situation. Perhaps because he was unimaginative. Perhaps because he knew it was pointless to be any other way now.

Gunnar said, 'I'll get you as close as I can.'

A bridge lookout yelled shrilly: 'Smoke, sir! Dead ahead!'

Every glass was trained, each man held his breath as he sought to pierce the heavy, unmoving haze.

Maddox said quietly, 'I'll get aft then, sir.'

'Yes, you do that.' If he was killed Maddox would be clear and ready to take over. Then it would be Regan's turn. Dead men's shoes. He turned involuntarily and held out his hand. 'Thanks, Bob. And take care.'

Maddox gripped his hand. 'I guess we're all wishing we were ten thousand miles away.' He paused, his eyes moving with sudden anxiety to his brother who stood by the after screen. 'But if we have to be here, there's no one I'd rather have balling me out!'

He moved away and paused by his brother. 'Look after yourself, kid, and we'll make it a double wedding.'

Pip Maddox tried to smile, but his face froze as the talker repeated: 'Ship at twelve thousand yards. Destroyer, sir.'

Gunnar felt the chill at his throat. 'Clear the bridge!' The wheelhouse would offer some protection for a while. 'Increase to twelve knots!' He ground his teeth as the ship's remaining engine valiantly tried to reply. More speed than that and the ship might become unmanageable. He paused on the port wing and looked up at the two big flags. For a moment longer he wondered if he would ever see them lowered. Then he slammed the steel door and said, 'Tell the gunnery control to hold on until I give the order.'

There would not be long to wait now.

*　　　*　　　*

The wheelhouse seemed airless and darker than usual, although the bright sunlight made fine-edged gold bars through

310

the narrow observation slits and gleamed across the set faces of the bridge team.

Kroner said: 'You were right, sir. She's an ex-Russian "Gordy" class, nearly two thousand tons, and thirty-six knots.' He seemed to drag out the last piece of information as if he could not accept such crushing superiority.

Gunnar steadied his glasses and watched the other ship's high, unbroken bow-wave as it cleaved through the low surface mist and turned slightly away from him. She was big all right. Even with the poor visibility he could see the powerful five-point-one mountings, all four of them, and the low breaks in her superstructure where her torpedo tubes were housed and ready. A low plume of smoke floated from her raked stack like a banner, and he could see the glitter of glass on her high upper bridge as she turned imperceptibly to cross *Hibiscus*'s slow line of approach.

It *would* be a destroyer. He guessed that below that craggy silhouette there were troops as well, crammed like sardines with the usual Chinese disregard for comfort and efficiency, but under the present circumstances a very real menace.

'Right standard rudder.' He heard the wheel squeak behind him, and watched the narrow wedge of the bows begin to swing. 'Steady as you go, meet her.'

His body felt limp and weightless, and he found that his breathing had become short, even painful. It was as if he knew he was beaten before he had started. Another gesture, another set of patterns.

'Steady on zero four five, sir.'

'Very well.' Gunnar wiped the back of his neck and watched the other ship growing out of the clear water like a nightmare mirage. He must not think of defeat, yet it seemed vital to consider what had to be done after the *Hibiscus* was destroyed. The thoughts and ideas crowded through his aching mind in disordered confusion. Perhaps a landing party might be sent to help defend the citadel, or the dying ship herself might be sunk in the channel to prevent a quick entry by the destroyer.

A voice said flatly, 'Gunnery control reports ready to engage, sir.'

Gunnar steadied himself with an effort. If Regan could visualise this grey mass of steel as a target and not as a messenger of death, then it was up to him to act accordingly.

Kroner shouted, 'They've opened fire!'

311

But Gunnar had already seen the two foremost guns wink briefly, their twin detonations almost lost in the harsh glare. With the sound of tearing silk the shells ripped overhead and plummeted into the open sea in two tall waterspouts.

Surprisingly, the effect on Gunnar's nerves was instantaneous. Calmly he ordered: 'Come right to zero eight zero. Open fire!'

Almost before the wheel had gone down the three-inch cracked like a steel whip, the sudden crash making their ears sing as the slender barrel lurched back on its springs and a long tongue of flame leapt towards the enemy.

'Short!' The talker held his hands across his earphones, afraid of hearing anything but the voice at the other end.

Gunnar watched the *Hibiscus's* first offering with sadness. A thin wafer of spray directly in line with the destroy's bridge. He heard the clang of the breech, the clatter of an ammunition hoist, and almost immediately, 'Shoot!'

The bridge lurched again, and with disbelief he saw the destroyer swing away on a diverging course.

Ensign Maddox shouted, 'She's pulling off, sir!'

Gunnar bit his lip. 'She's carrying mines. Those sort always do. She's not ready to be blown sky-high by her own cargo.'

He saw the enemy's guns give their lethal flashes and waited, counting the seconds. Again the awful screech followed by the double crump, crump and the tall columns of water. How beautiful they looked, graceful and glittering in the sunlight. The columns seemed reluctant to fall, like jewelled curtains, yet Gunnar could sense that they were much closer than before. The Chinese captain was taking no chances with the *Hibiscus's* pea-shooter. He would haul off out of range and pound her into scrap with his big guns at leisure.

'Give me a course for the west channel!' He heard Kroner fumbling at the chart table.

It was impossible for the destroyer to land its troops anywhere quickly but beyond the west channel, *Hibiscus's* own survey had proved that. The Chinese commander would naturally expect the limping *Hibiscus* to keep clear, to give him room to do just that, for her own safety's sake.

Gunnar tightened his jaw. If this was the only way to shorten the range, this was how it would be.

'Tell Malinski I want to up the speed. Keep giving me revs until I order otherwise!' To the silent helmsman he added, 'Hold her, Paice, and tell me immediately she starts to swing!'

312

'Range five thousand yards!'

Maddened by the *Hibiscus*'s alteration of course, the destroyer turned again, this time to run parallel. This manœuvre enabled her after guns to bear, and within seconds the shells were falling almost alongside. Gunnar felt the hull tremble with each body blow, heard the thunder of the guns as they dwarfed and swamped the *Hibiscus*'s solitary reply.

'Left standard rudder! Meet her!'

He heard Paice swear and saw him swing the wheel with sudden anxiety as the compass began to tick past the line. 'Comin' left too fast, sir!'

Gunnar tore his eyes from the spray-shrouded destroyer. 'Reduce to seven knots! Rudder hard right!'

It was as if the ship was trying to save herself and was no longer content with man's efforts alone. As her narrow bows disobeyed the labouring rudder, two waterspouts rose directly on her starboard bow. There was one heart-stopping bellow of sound as the shells exploded on the surface within yards of her hull, so that the ship quivered as if struck a direct blow.

Christ, Gunnar thought, if she'd been on course she'd have taken both shells smack on the forecastle!

He snapped: 'Drop the smoke floats, and tell Malinski to make smoke too. I want the best goddamned screen this ship has ever had!'

A handset buzzed and then Kroner reported tightly: 'Two gunners wounded, sir! Request replacements from the twenty-millimetre crews!'

'Do that!' The light automatic weapons were useless in this particular fight. And at any moment the three-inch might go. He dashed the sweat from his eyes. 'Come right to zero nine zero!'

From his position by the chart table Ensign Maddox felt like a mesmerised spectator. Gunnar and Regan were holding the show on their own, while lost in his maze of racing machinery Malinski was doing his best to bring the *Hibiscus* into the jaws of the other ship. Every time the gun fired or an enemy shell exploded nearby, Pip Maddox felt as if the very life was being squeezed out of him. His eyes felt swollen and too big for his head, and he knew that his face was shining with sweat, sweat as cold as ice-rime, although the wheelhouse was like a potter's oven.

He tried not to think of the quick, moving burial, nor of what would happen to him in the next few moments of his life. He looked instead at Gunnar, as if to see him more clearly, to gain some support and strength from his example. Perhaps if you met Gunnar in a shore establishment, or in a corridor of some staff office, you might not notice him. Just one more officer, just another small link in the navy's chain of control. Yet here he was alone, an individual captain like so many of his predecessors. Pip tried to remember the names which had been drummed into him at the academy, men and ships which had on those rare and gallant occasions cut loose from the fleet and the command of great admirals and had fought their battles alone, like private jousts, without fear and without hope.

Pip noticed that the captain was still wearing the cap he had given him in the citadel, when that too had seemed hopeless and ended. The thought and the sight of Gunnar's impassive face gave him a small spark of determination, and he clung to it like a drowning man.

Kroner held his hand across a telephone. 'It's the exec, sir! He says that there are landing craft in the channel, two, maybe three of them.' He waited as Gunnar wrestled with this new implication.

Gunnar said, 'Probably coming for the troops aboard the destroyer——' He ducked his head as a violent explosion thundered against the rear of the bridge and filled the wheelhouse with black smoke.

Voice-pipes shouted and several telephones began to buzz simultaneously. Gunnar grinned. 'Very near, but not a hit!' He opened a shutter and peered aft. The floats were already bobbing astern, the stack too was adding to the screen, and it had been from there that the smoke had come to fill the wheelhouse. A freak explosion alongside had sucked it down and blotted out the forepart of the ship in a dense, choking cloud.

'In a minute I'm going to turn back into the screen, then I'll move around his stern and have a go for those mines. I can't beat him to the channel now.' Gunnar masked the disappointment in his voice. The smokescreen gave everybody a sense of safety, yet he knew that the destroyer's captain was so confident that he was more interested in getting rid of his human cargo than facing a straight combat.

Aft on the fantail Maddox rubbed his hands as the last float splashed astern. He grinned at Tasker and said, 'It all helps, Chief!' He felt the deck cant very slightly. The *Hibiscus*

314

was wallowing round into her own screen.

A seaman yelled: 'How are we doin', Mister Maddox? Are we pullin' out yet?'

Maddox shrugged and wiped his grimy features. 'Just getting a second wind.'

The sunlight closed over the ship as she steamed slowly back along the side of the smoke, her stack adding to the same impenetrable bank. Maddox opened his mouth to call to his waiting men, when it happened.

With the scream of a maniac wind the shells dropped in one tight group. Whether the Chinese had used guesswork or radar no one knew, but even as two shells thundered alongside, a third struck the deck below the starboard side of the bridge, and a fourth cleaved across the maindeck without exploding.

The man standing next to Maddox was plucked from his feet and flung over the side like a piece of torn canvas. He felt Tasker pulling him to his feet, heard his voice as if from afar off shouting, 'The bridge, sir!'

Everywhere men were running and yelling amid a tangle of firehoses and twisted metal. The deck beside the bridge was pouring smoke and flame, and the hull itself looked as if it had been clawed by some giant steel hand.

Maddox thrust his handkerchief over his mouth and staggered blindly up the bridge ladder, his shoes skidding as he almost fell across the tangled remains of something which had once been human. The wheelhouse door was jammed and he had to throw his full weight to free it. Inside it was a fog, a place where nothing seemed either familiar or real.

A figure blundered from the smoke, his skin gleaming like silk in a single shaft of sunlight which appeared to be shining upwards through the far side of the bridge.

Maddox grasped his brother's arm and pulled him towards him. Pip's shirt had been blasted from his body, and even his watch and identity tag had vanished. Pip retched and clung to his brother, his lungs wheezing in real pain as he drew in the air from the open doorway.

Tasker reached the wheel and stared down at Paice's crumpled body. The side of his head had gone, there was nothing that could be done for him.

Maddox slowly regained control of himself, and then as the smoke funnelled away through the door he saw the true extent of the damage. The side nearest the explosion was riddled with holes and one large split which pushed the metal inwards like paper. The talker had been almost cut in half and lay with his shattered headphones still clamped on his gleaming skull like a being from another world.

Tasker shouted: 'Here, sir! Over here!'

He ran to Gunnar's side and helped Tasker to lift him into a sitting position beside the bent and ruptured voice-pipes. Tasker said thickly, 'I'll take the wheel!'

Gunnar opened his eyes and stared at Maddox's grim face without recognition, but then, as the first shock wore off, he grimaced and doubled over in agony. 'My side! Christ, Bob, something hit me there!'

Maddox held Gunnar's probing fingers away and carefully tore aside a strip of bloodied shirt. He kept his head lowered to hide his face from the captain, and then in a firm voice said, 'I'll try and make you comfortable.'

He saw Pip's white face and heard Gunnar say between his clenched teeth, 'I'm glad you're okay, Pip.' Then full realisation seemed to flow back into him, and his eyes which had been dulled with pain blazed with sudden urgency and anger. 'Get me up!' He struggled even as Maddox tied the dressing around his waist. 'Get me *up*, damn you!'

Maddox looked at his brother, but the boy was only half aware what was happening. Gunnar was wounded, how badly he could only guess, but it might kill him without proper care. He thought fleetingly of Connell's calm face and his smooth, cynical words. Damn Connell! Damn the whole goddamn mess!

He felt Gunnar's fingers on his arm and heard him say: 'Bring her about, Bob. I'm going in after that destroyer!'

Slowly, painfully, the *Hibiscus* turned through ninety degrees and re-entered the smoke. On her fo'c'sle the gunners waited behind the shield, a shell in the breech and others ready to load. The jackstaff glittered in the sunlight, next the anchor cable and then with a final thrust the ship was through and out of the smoke.

Gunnar clung to a stanchion and tried to level his glasses. The destroyer was still there, a couple of points off the starboard bow, her hull beam on. There was only a small bow-wave under her raked stem, and Gunnar could see the small shapes of other craft creeping out from Payenhau's brown mass to receive their reinforcements. He could feel the pain above his hip like a vice which seemed to be tightening across

316

his whole body, the agony blunting his senses and making a mist across his eye.

'Report damage, Bob!' He forced the words from between his teeth. Then as the exec moved reluctantly towards the rear of the bridge Gunnar said, 'You come here, Pip.' He saw the desperate, helpless look in the ensign's eyes as he slipped his arm around his shoulder and used him like a prop as he watched the other ship.

The gun opened fire, but the sound was muted as it pointed directly over the bows.

Gunnar clung to the boy's shoulder, feeling the smooth skin under his hand and remembering the girl who was waiting in Payenhau.

How well the Chinese captain handled his ship, he thought. There was no longer any point even in running away. Just one of those torpedoes would be enough for the poor *Hibiscus*!

Maddox called, 'Four more killed, sir, and all the starboard battery out of action!' He paused, unwilling to add to Gunnar's anguish. 'Don Kroner's dead too, sir.' Maddox swallowed and tried not to think of the gaping, terrified eyes above that frightful wound. Could it really have been the debonair, clean-featured Kroner? He forced himself to continue: 'Engine room report hull damage in three frames, sir. But the pumps are holding the intake so far.'

Gunnar did not answer. Instead he turned to the ensign. 'Let me see the ship!' He struggled to the open door and peered along the full length of his listing command, each foot of the inspection making his heart bleed. He saw the great splinter holes and twisted tubs, the flame-scorched paintwork around the dead and crumpled gunners.

Two waterspouts alongside blinded him, and as he reeled back he tasted cordite amongst the falling spray. He felt the familiar hot breath against his neck and cringed as another shell found its mark. He watched the mainmast stagger and then plunge over the side, and heard the crash of falling machinery. Through the mist across his eyes he saw a man's hand lying on the grey steel like a discarded glove, and above the crackle of exploding machine-gun ammunition he heard someone screaming, the sound scraping at his ears until he found that he was willing the unknown man to die.

Maddox broke into his dazed thoughts. 'Starboard engine's stopped, sir!'

Gunnar thrust his way from the startled ensign and

317

wrenched a telephone from its hook. 'Captain here! Report damage!'

Malinski sounded spent. 'We're done for, Captain. I'm sorry, but that last one has put the shaft right out of line! Even if we had the time it would be a dockyard job!'

Gunnar nodded blindly. 'Yes, I see. Well, you'd better bring your people up top.'

'What's happening, sir?' Malinski seemed very far away.

'The destroyer is turning towards us. They seem to think we are stopping their unloading after all, so they're coming to finish the job.'

He dropped the handset and heard Maddox ask, 'Will you strike, sir?'

Gunnar smiled and glanced up at the remaining flag. 'I think not. What would be the point anyway?'

He leaned on the boy's shoulder and levelled the glasses once more. In the powerful lenses he could see the high stem, the black gun muzzles and the bridge beyond. With surprise he saw that there was a scar across her raked hull and realised that at least one of the *Hibiscus*'s small shells had gone home.

It was over. *Hibiscus* could neither move nor manœuvre, and he could feel her deck dragging heavily in each small swell. Another shell exploded near the bows, and Gunnar's heart sank even more as the little gun fell silent.

He turned away as Tasker dropped his handset and reported: 'That's it, sir. Gun's out of action,' he faltered, 'an' I'm afraid the gunnery officer is dead!'

Gunnar pressed his head against the warm steel. Poor Regan. He gritted his teeth in his misery. Poor *Hibiscus*.

There was a far-off rattle of machine-gun fire and he dragged his eyes unwillingly towards the sea once again. The destroyer was slewing round, her stem biting hard into the water as she heeled over in her racing turn. All of her fifty thousand horsepower seemed to be tugging at her superstructure, so that her guns fell silent as she swung off course and away from the *Hibiscus*.

Maddox ran out on to the open wing his glasses already following the change of tactics. Perhaps the torpedoes would come now? He thought of Mary, of his brother, and Lea Burgess, the memories and faces crowding his mind even as the destroyer turned on a course parallel to the listing submarine chaser and headed again towards the waiting landing craft. Something was wrong, but what?

He heard Tasker yell, 'One of the L.C.s is poopin' off at them!' He sounded as if he no longer believed what he saw.

Gunnar watched the strange drama like a man who follows a silent film for the first time. He could see the tiny, puny pin-points of fire from the landing craft's machine gun, and the frantic efforts of the destroyer's gunners to depress their wea-pons to reply. But the racing ship was already too close, and when one of her guns did fire the shell struck the water astern of the little box-like craft and ricocheted across the surface like a whirling comet.

Maddox was screaming at the top of his voice: '*Jesus!* It's Burgess!'

Other men crowded the listing wheelhouse, pointing and shouting like madmen. One yelled, 'An' there's ole Pirelli!' And another: 'Holy cow! He's committin' suicide just like us!'

Gunnar heard the words without bitterness. It was all true. Burgess had turned the destroyer's charge with the precision and coolness of a matador with a maddened bull. How he had got hold of the craft and where he had come from did not seem to matter. He had come to help, and although his gesture would be as fruitless as that of his own ship, Gunnar found that he was shaking with silent emotion.

The destroyer tore in for the kill, and through his glasses Gunnar saw Burgess sitting bolt upright beside Pirelli, who appeared to be pounding the machine gun with a bottle.

Gunnar dropped his eyes as the destroyer's tall stem rose above the slow-moving craft and then seemed to fall on it like a giant axe. He could hear the splintering of woodwork and the scream of its thin plating.

Then Maddox yelled, 'Hey, that's the L.C.I. I found before I——'

He never finished the sentence. As Gunnar looked again and saw the victorious destroyer slicing through a few pieces of bobbing flotsam, the seven depth-charges from the sunken landing craft exploded as one.

Directly amidships, and at a minimum depth setting, the explosion could be compared with that of a mammoth bomb.

Gunnar fell back as the searing shock-wave thundered across the mile and a half of smooth water, and flinched again as a second detonation filled the sky with a thousand flying fragments. The explosions went on and on until the handful of unwounded men on the *Hibiscus*'s battered decks felt cowed and dazed, beaten down with each successive blast.

319

When Gunnar looked again there was nothing between him and Payenhau. Only a widening patch of oil and a few specks of floating driftwood remained to mark the finality of Burgess's last deed.

Gunnar did not know how long he stood staring at the oil slick, nor what anyone else said. It was as if from a drugged sleep that he heard a man report: 'Ship, sir! Bearing one four five!'

Then a few seconds later, as the diamond-bright light stabbed across the water, 'It's the British destroyer *Bosworth*, sir!'

Maddox reeled against the wheel and mopped his face. 'I never thought I'd be pleased to see *him* again!'

The *Hibiscus*'s last remaining signalman read the flickering light. 'Have doctor aboard and will come alongside to render all assistance.'

Maddox said quickly, 'Tell him we'd be glad of his help!'

He moved to Gunnar's side and helped his brother to support him as the light began to reply from the other ship.

The signalman read, 'It will be an honour!'

Maddox was grinning like a schoolboy. 'I guess this'll mean another trip to the yard and another refit before we pay off?'

Gunnar looked round at the silent, smoking ship and pressed his hand against the pain in his side. It was like sharing *her* pain, he thought.

'I'll be sorry to lose the *Hibiscus*,' he said at length, and this time he knew that he meant it.